The Sergeant

Christa Tomlinson

Torlina Publishing

The Sergeant
Copyright © March 2014 Christa Tomlinson

ISBN: 978-0-9960370-0-6
Editor: Kris Kendall
Cover Design: Melody Simmons of eBookindiecovers
Formatting: Polgarus Studio
Published in the United States of America

Published by
Torlina Publishing
PO Box 40841
Houston, TX

ACKNOWLEDGMENTS

There are lots of people I want to thank, starting with everyone who favorited, followed, and reviewed SC&L. Thank you so much. All of your interactions gave me the confidence I needed to start writing again.

Special thank you to several reviewers I totally bonded with: SJA, HDN, LP, JT, BDB, MS & BP. Your encouragement and Twitter snarking taught me a valuable lesson, people dig my smut.

Thanks to the lovely beta brains of Amanda, Amanda, and Bullet. There's nothing better to a writer than a fresh set of eyes and an honest opinion.

Shout out to my team, The Bosses. Because they're my family. And because I have a vague memory I said I would thank them here.

Thanks to my niece, Tan. She helped me pick out names and patiently listened to me yammer on about Logan and Clay for months.

And finally to my two pups, Mindy and Chunky. Sorry I didn't take you to the park as much while I was writing this, and thanks for letting me rub your bellies whenever I needed a distraction.

Thank you,
Christa

1

Sergeant Logan Pierce walked back into the police station with his team. Everybody was laughing and relaxed as was usually the case after a successful callout. Their SWAT team was the best on the Houston Police Department and one of the best in the country. Logan's gaze was drawn to one of his scouts, Corporal Clay Foster. He liked to keep an eye on his boys, his scouts in particular. They had one of the more dangerous jobs, moving first into critical situations to scope them out for the rest of the squad. He wanted to make sure they were handling the stress of their position. But that wasn't the only reason he watched Clay.

His scout smiled as he described the look on the gunman's face when he'd realized he was surrounded by SWAT. The entry team blocked his way out the front. He hadn't been aware of Clay and his other scout, Corporal Quan Pham, at his back. His face was so full of amazement when he spun around and saw them that Clay's order to get on the ground had been tinged with laughter.

Clay ran his fingers through his hair, the short black curls slightly flattened from his helmet. Logan looked away. He didn't want anyone to catch the expression on his face as he imagined running his own fingers through that silky hair. He'd desired Clay for a long time, but lately it had grown to the point that it was on his mind whenever they weren't working.

Clay was definitely attractive with those dark curls. His face was clean shaven and lightly tanned. Long, dark lashes framed blue eyes that were so bright he had to control his reaction the first time he'd looked into them. And Clay's mouth made him think of all sorts of things that were inappropriate for the work place, especially the sweet curve of his bottom lip. The strong line of his jaw and the hard body that he carried with such confidence kept him from being pretty. And he was tall, only a few inches below Logan's own height of six foot three. He filled out the dark SWAT uniform very well. Corporal Clay Foster was a mix of beauty, strength, and brave intelligence that had intrigued him for years.

The group split up as they reached the locker room areas. The two women on the team went one way, the rest of them another. Lockers banged and gear bags dropped to the floor as they got ready for showers. Houston was hot and muggy, even in early spring. Carrying fifty pounds of gear wasn't conducive to staying cool and dry in the heat. There weren't enough showers for everyone to use all at once. So, as he always did, Logan let his team go first. He sat on the bench in front of his locker, giving kudos or advice to his men and going over the night with them while he waited.

When a shower finally opened and no one was in line before him, Logan grabbed his soap, shampoo, and a towel and stepped into the stall. Yanking the curtain back, he turned on the water full blast. Logan stood underneath the hot stream, letting the water ease the final bit of tension from his muscles. He never completely relaxed after a callout until this moment, when his whole team was back safe and he was alone in the peace of a hot shower. After taking a few moments to enjoy the feel of the water, he washed up quickly. He was eager to get something to eat and get home.

When Logan came out of the shower bay, he saw the locker room was empty but for one person. Clay sat on a bench, fully dressed in jeans and a t-shirt, engrossed in his phone.

"Clay, what are you still doing here?"

The other man looked up. "I wasn't up to going out with the rest of the bunch. Kinda wanted some quiet. But I'm hungry so I'm trying to figure out where I want to eat before I leave."

Logan realized this could be his chance to be alone with Clay for a little while. "You can come with me if you want. I'm headed over to Lucy's. It's quiet and the food is good."

Clay smiled. "That sounds perfect. Thanks for the invite, Sarge."

Logan tried not to get excited. They were just going out for a meal. But he couldn't deny that he was happy to have Clay to himself.

2

As he'd predicted, Lucy's was quiet. The place was a small family-owned restaurant off the beaten path of most downtown foot traffic. It did a steady business, but was mostly frequented by people who, like him, were looking for a quiet place to relax as they ate. The comfortable seating, low lighting, and homey décor all helped build that atmosphere. He handed his menu to the server after placing his order and spoke to the man across the table from him.

"So what's up, Clay? Everything alright?"

Clay looked at him over his glass of water. "You didn't ask me along just so you could analyze me, did you, Serge? Because I'm alright."

Logan's lips twitched but he didn't smile. "No, I'm not trying to analyze you. Just opening that door if you need it."

Clay set his glass down and leaned back in his chair. "Nah, I'm good. But thanks."

Logan nodded and let the subject drop. They spent the next few minutes going over some of their recent operations, breaking them down and discussing anything they could have done differently. They reviewed often, with everyone sharing their input. Logan was their team leader, but everyone's opinion was valued. That's how their team worked and it was how they continued to get better.

The server came back and put their plates down in front of them. Logan glanced at his food in appreciation. He'd ordered a thick steak, new potatoes, wild rice, green beans, and dinner rolls. He caught Clay staring at him as he picked up his knife and fork.

"You're really going to eat all that?"

Logan grinned. "What can I say? I'm a big boy."

Clay ran his eyes over the width of his chest and arms. He looked back up at him. "Yeah. You are."

Logan froze for a moment. That sounded like Clay was flirting with him. He wasn't sure how to respond. For one, although he suspected Clay was bi-sexual, he wasn't positively sure. Second, they worked together. Third, he was Clay's superior. There could be serious repercussions if he took Clay's comment as a flirtatious remark and it wasn't. Since they had a whole meal to get through, he decided to let it pass. He gestured at Clay's plate. "I see you're eating light."

Clay laughed and cut up a piece of his grilled chicken. "We've got a PT test coming up. It's not as easy for me to stay in shape as some of you," he said with a pointed glance at Logan. "Besides, one bite of all those carbs and I'm headed down to the cage, trying to get a flak vest in the next size up."

Logan shook his head in amusement. It was true that he was big and muscular. He'd been stocky his whole life and started putting on muscle in high school to play football. Clay was well muscled too, just in the long, lithe way of a swimmer. The conversation slowed as they ate. Once they were done, they settled back with satisfied sighs.

Clay rubbed his stomach. "Man, you were right, Sarge. That was good."

Logan took a last drink of his water. "Glad you enjoyed it. You're welcome to come here with me anytime."

Clay smiled slightly. "Strange you never had the team here. Or that we've never eaten alone before."

Logan arched a brow. "Really?"

"Yeah."

Logan looked directly at Clay for a moment before he answered. "Maybe I was saving it for the right time."

Clay's eyes widened slightly and he looked like he was about to say something. But just then, the server came up to ask if they needed anything else. She dropped their check when both men turned down dessert. Logan reached for it. "I've got it."

"Thanks. You sure know how to take care of your team," Clay joked.

Logan didn't say anything to that. If only Clay knew how much he really wanted to take care of him.

Outside, they headed to their cars. They both drove dark, unmarked Dodge Chargers issued by the Houston Police Department. Logan closed his eyes as the cool night breeze blew Clay's scent back to him. He inhaled deeply, stifling a groan as he took that wonderful scent down into his lungs.

Clay always smelled so good. Logan wanted to grab him and rub his face against Clay's skin and just breathe until he couldn't smell anything else. But at the rate things were going, that was never going to happen.

Clay turned to him, thanking him for dinner once more. Logan accepted his thanks, and then hesitated. Clay waited, looking at him with an expectant expression. Logan wanted to approach him, to let him know he was interested but he just didn't know if that was wise. With an inward curse, he let the moment pass—again. "Good night, Clay."

A frown creased Clay's brow before he said good night too and went to his car. Logan opened his car door and got in. He started the ignition, determined to ignore the disappointment in his chest.

3

The sound of gym shoes squeaking on mats and boxing gloves connecting with bodies was loud, echoing in the large space. His team wasn't on rotation this week, but they were still in house getting in some training. Today they were boxing. They had guns, but you never knew when you'd be in physical combat with a suspect. Knowing how to fight had saved their asses more than once.

Clay was on the blue mats with Senior Corporal Jody Stillman, one of the two women on their team. He was teasing and taunting her, trying to make her lose her cool. Logan knew that wasn't going to happen. Jody had the most stoic personality of all of them and she stayed calm in every situation. That trait served her well as a sniper. She didn't get flustered, she didn't hesitate, and she didn't miss. Jody caught Clay with a hard jab to the ribs and he stopped playing around. Logan watched their technique for awhile, making sure they kept their guards up and didn't telegraph punches. But, eventually, his attention and his eyes wandered.

They weren't required to stay in dress code when they weren't on rotation. As a result, they all wore a mix of HPD sweats, tees, and their own clothes. Clay had on nothing but a pair of baggy blue gym shorts and sneakers. His torso was bare and Logan greedily ate up the sight of his sweat slick skin. The Navy anchor tattoo on Clay's chest was familiar, he'd seen Clay without his shirt plenty of times, but Logan's gaze still lingered there for a moment. Clay spun out of Jody's reach but she stayed with him. So did Logan. He kept watching, his eyes moving down to take in how low Clay's shorts hung on his hips, revealing the dip in his lower back. Logan imagined running his tongue along that spot, licking up the sweat beaded there.

Clay danced away from Jody so he was facing Logan again. Logan's eyes were immediately drawn to his stomach and the soft line of dark hair that trailed down from his navel, disappearing into his shorts. Logan wanted to run his fingers down that path and along the curve of his hipbones. He knew that skin would be sensitive and he wanted to see Clay shiver at his touch. His imaginings were stopped from going any further when a throat cleared their throat next to him.

"You look pretty intense, Sarge. Taking mental notes?"

Logan started and looked to his left. His senior assistant, Senior Corporal Carlos Ortega, was sitting in the folding chair next to him. His friendship with Carlos went back to before they'd joined the force and Carlos was one of the few in the department who knew he was gay. He answered his question with calm nonchalance.

"Just watching."

Carlos snorted. "I bet."

Logan ignored that.

"I hear you took Clay out to dinner last night."

Logan rolled his eyes. "I didn't take him out to dinner. We just went to get something to eat."

"And you weren't wishing it was something more?" Carlos looked at him with his dark steady gaze. "I doubt that, especially with the way you're probably about to pitch a tent just sitting here, staring at him."

Logan scrubbed his hand over his forehead. "Fuck, man. I don't know what's wrong with me. Lately, I can't stop thinking about him."

"Maybe because you haven't dated anybody in over six months.Why don't you go for it? If you don't, eventually you'll be checking out his ass when you're supposed to be watching his back. Have fun explaining your wood then."

Logan cut his eyes at Carlos. His friend was right, he hadn't been with a guy for some time. But this wasn't the time to discuss it."Shut up about his ass, Los." He noticed Clay and Jody were done. "And be quiet before someone hears you."

Clay stepped off the mat and came over to them. "Sarge, I don't think it's right I have to fight a girl. They are the weaker sex after all." He threw a taunting smile over his shoulder at Jody.

"Do I need to remind you about Operation Chimney Sweep," Logan asked.

Chimney Sweep was an operation where they served a warrant on a female suspect dealing X and meth out of a ridiculously innocent looking house with a huge red chimney.

Turned out the woman was an MMA fighter when she wasn't dealing drugs. She played docile until Senior Corporal Mike Dorsey was close to her and had put his gun away to cuff her. Then she went ape shit, punching and kicking with a fury that brought him down. Logan hadn't wanted anyone to take a shot with her so close to Mike, so they ended up using the taser to subdue her.

Jody snorted and came up next to Clay. "Keep talking shit and maybe I'll break your nose like that crazy woman did to Mike."

Clay held his hands up in front of his face. "You're so mean, Jody."

She laughed and headed off to the locker rooms. Clay stayed behind. He took his head gear and gloves off. "We look good out there, Serge?"

"You did." At Carlos's snort, Logan cleared his throat and corrected himself. "You both did."

Clay grinned. "Thanks. Jody's got a mean right jab. Caught me right in my fucking ribs." He raised his arm to peer down at his side. "Probably gonna bruise and be sore as hell."

Logan stared at that smooth skin. He wanted to reach out and run his fingers along it, soothing any hurt that Clay might feel. But he couldn't. For many reasons, he couldn't. He dragged his gaze away.

"You know better than to tease her like that."

Clay laughed. "Yeah but it's so much fun." He plopped down in the seat next to Logan to watch the next members of the team take their turns on the mat. "So what are you guys over here talking about over here?"

Carlos looked at him with a shit eating grin on his face. "Camping. Sarge is worried about where he's gonna pitch his tent."

Clay glanced over at him. "You're going camping, Serge? Where at? I know some good places."

Logan gave Carlos a dirty look before he answered Clay. "I'm not going anywhere. But Corporal Ortega here is about to go take his turn on the mats. Right, Los?"

Carlos got up and cracked his neck. "Whatever you say, boss."

Clay watched the big man gear up. He got a vibe like he'd just interrupted a conversation about something other than camping. He was curious, but he didn't ask. "Why aren't you taking him on? He needs to pick on someone his own size." Carlos was big and muscular like Logan. It was why they were the breachers on their team, both strong enough to swing the heavy battering rams with enough force to bust open nearly any door. And with his shaved head and dark, watchful eyes, Carlos was pretty intimidating. Logan was intimidating as well, but in a different way. His military bearing, strong jaw, and sharp hazel eyes let you know that he was in charge. Even his hair obeyed him, the dark blonde strands rarely straying from their proper place. Clay ran a hand over his own hair, which as usual was a mess of curls all over his head. He was sort of tempted to touch Logan's hair to see if he used hairspray to keep the side part so neat, but he didn't quite have the nerve.

Logan laughed. "Mike is doing just fine."

Clay snorted. "Guess he learned from that broken nose."

They sat and watched the sparring, comfortably making observations until everyone was done. Clay liked that he could be so easy going with his sergeant. He'd been under the command of some real dicks during his time in the military and police force.

The last pair stepped off the mats and Logan stood up, ending their conversation. "You're all dismissed. Clean up and get out of here. Make sure you get plenty of rest. Endurance training in the morning."

Clay groaned along with everyone else. No one liked the long runs with all their gear on, but they were a necessary evil. Carrying all that equipment, armor, and weapons wasn't easy, especially in the Houston heat, but they had to keep their bodies conditioned for it. Clay got up and followed the guys back to the locker room to shower and change.

Logan headed out of the station after making sure everyone on the team was gone. At least he thought everyone was gone until he saw Clay standing at the door, staring outside.

"What are you doing?" Logan stepped up beside him.

"It's raining."

Logan looked out the glass doors. "I see that." He laughed. "You jogged to work today, didn't you?" Clay jogged nearly every day they weren't on call and he didn't have to haul all his gear. "C'mon, I'll take you home."

Once they were in the car, Logan didn't have to ask for directions. He knew where each one of his team members lived. They headed up Dallas Avenue to Clay's loft apartment. He pulled into a space and put the car in park. But Clay didn't immediately say thank you and leave. He turned to Logan with an impish smile on his face.

"Be honest, Sarge. Do you like the endurance runs?"

"No, I hate them." He looked at Clay with a sideways smile. "Sometimes I'm tempted to take them off the training rotation."

Clay laughed. "That makes me feel better. You never complain about them, but now I know your secret. You're just as human as the rest of us." He gave him a conspiratorial wink. "But don't worry, I won't tell the others."

****

Twenty minutes later, they were still in the car. Logan had long since turned off the engine and the rain had slowed to soft drops falling against the windshield. They'd talked about everything from work to baseball to their respective careers in the military. Logan served in the Marines and did two tours in Iraq while Clay had been all over the place in the Navy. Now they were both quiet, their heads lolling against the headrest.

Clay's eyes drifted closed. Logan knew he should tell him to go inside and get to bed. But it was such a rare, private moment between them that he didn't want it to end. Instead, he took advantage of the opportunity to study Clay. As always, the sight of that curly black hair made him smile. The length of his hair was within regulation, barely. He knew part of the reason Clay kept it that long was to thumb his nose at their captain. Captain Hayden was constantly talking about the image of HPD and SWAT. He didn't approve of Clay, with his longish hair and playful personality, at all. But Logan loved Clay's hair and hoped he'd never cut it. His eyes drifted down to the other man's mouth, that full bottom lip even poutier than usual as he relaxed. Logan thought about kissing him, wondering what Clay would do if he sucked that lip into his mouth. In his head, Clay would respond to him, kissing him back eagerly.

He looked back up and saw that Clay's eyes were open, watching him. They held eye contact for a long moment. The air in the car turned electric, tension crackling between them. Logan's heart pounded. This moment couldn't be ignored. He could apologize and send Clay inside. Or he could do what he'd wanted to do for so damn long. The decision was easy. He leaned forward and pressed his lips to Clay's. They were warm and soft, just as he'd imagined they'd be. Logan pulled back, waiting to see Clay's reaction. When he didn't say anything, Logan kissed him again. This time, Clay returned the kiss with a light touch of his lips.

Logan took that as encouragement and brought their lips together for several more kisses. Logan was surprised this was happening. His heart raced as they kissed in the warm, dark car. He kept things relaxed and easy, letting Clay know they could stop whenever he wanted. He ran his tongue across the seam of Clay's closed lips, wanting him to open up so he could get a real taste of him. Clay's eyes drifted closed again and he parted his lips, allowing Logan to sweep inside. He stroked his tongue slowly against Clay's before exploring the warm sweetness of his mouth. Clay's tongue darted out once to touch his. He was hesitant, almost shy. Logan's body tightened, his shaft hardening as he gently coaxed him to play more. He curled his tongue against Clay's and soon Clay was following his lead, licking into Logan's mouth in slow, deep kisses.

Neither of them spoke. It was silent except for the sound of the rain and their quiet breathing as their lips clung and released again and again. Logan fought to keep the kiss soft and slow, pushing back his urge to control Clay's mouth and touch his firm body wherever he could reach. Then Clay whispered a breathy little moan as he relaxed further into the contact. The sound touched off something deep inside Logan, made him want more. He brought his hand up, sliding into those silky curls and cupping the back of Clay's head, holding him in place to deepen the kiss. He thrust his tongue inside to tangle with Clay's, swirling against it in a hot, slick slide. Logan groaned as he kissed him faster, harder. Clay was right there with him, kissing him back with just as much intensity.

Logan slid his fingers down until he held him by the back of the neck, pulling Clay up against him until their chests touched. Clay gasped and pressed even closer to him. Logan smoothed his other hand down Clay's back, feeling the solid warmth of him through his t-shirt. But Logan didn't dare touch him anywhere else. Not there in the car and not without discussing things with him first. He pulled back slightly, looking at Clay to see if he was showing any reluctance. What he saw were eyes wide, sparkling with desire and lips swollen from his kisses. There was no sign of hesitation on his face.

Logan dove right back in, sucking at that full bottom lip that had been teasing him for years. Clay's hands came up to his chest and Logan thought, *Yes. Touch me.* But then he realized Clay was pushing him away.

Logan released him and watched in confusion as Clay grabbed his bag from the car floor and snapped, "Goddamnit!" He slammed out of the car and stalked off towards his building.

Logan sat there in disbelief before he banged his head against the steering wheel. What the *fuck?* He hunched over the wheel for a moment, trying to figure out what just happened while willing his hard-on to go down. Eventually, his body calmed but he was still clueless about Clay's abrupt exit. He knew he wasn't going to figure it out sitting there in the dark by himself, so he started the car and drove home.

4

Logan pulled into the garage of his two-story, brick faced home. It was a little more than he needed, but his parents gave it to him when he returned from overseas. They said he was doing them a favor since they traveled all over the country in their retirement and didn't want to worry about maintaining the home. He tried to buy it from them, but they turned him down. Instead, they asked him to take over visiting his grandfather in the Texas Hill Country. That was no chore. Logan loved his grandfather and enjoyed visiting him as often as possible. It was his grandfather, a former Marine himself, who influenced his decision to join the Corps. His grandfather was also the first person Logan came out to just before he'd enlisted. He had accepted Logan and told him there was nothing wrong with being gay. But as a young enlisted he should keep it quiet. All these years later he was still following that advice. Sometimes it made sense to him, the police department culture wasn't always welcoming to gay men. But sometimes he was ashamed of himself for not being upfront about who he really was.

He got out of the car and went in through the kitchen. It was a large room with windows that let in plenty of light during the day. The whole house was really too big for one person. He looked forward to sharing it with someone someday. Tossing his keys on the butcher block island, Logan went through the mail he'd brought in with him. Nothing was important enough to hold his attention. He headed upstairs to his bedroom.

The many kisses with Clay were still on his mind. He couldn't help but worry he'd made a huge mistake. He was Clay's superior and he'd made a sexual advance on him. Fuck! That hadn't been smart on his part. But he'd wanted Clay for so long. And in the warm cocoon of the dark car, he'd let his guard down, forgetting all the reasons that he shouldn't pursue his fellow officer.

Logan carefully unpacked his bag and secured his weapons. He undressed then flopped onto the king sized bed. He couldn't stop thinking over their moments in the car. Seriously, what the fuck? Where had he gone wrong? Clay had seemed to be into him, responding just as sweetly as he'd always imagined. Logan had either gotten too heavy with the way he'd deepened the kiss, or Clay realized it wasn't a good idea to make out with his superior. His *male* superior.

Logan blew out a frustrated breath. He wanted Clay so bad that whenever he was near, his fingers ached with the urge to grab him and pull that slender body up against his own. However, he wanted Clay for more than just one or two nights in bed, which meant that if he did win him for his own, eventually he would have to come clean about his …

preferences. If Clay wasn't into that and it scared him off, Logan would be left with the knowledge that he'd run off the one man he wanted to build a relationship with. Clay already bolted after their kiss tonight, which didn't bode well for the possibility of future sexual activities. Logan would have to walk a fine line between what he should do and what he wanted to do if he pursued Clay.

As Logan thought about their kiss, his erection came surging back. Clay's mouth had been so warm, his tongue soft. Logan wanted to kiss him again. He wished he still was. Logan's eyes closed and his hand drifted down his belly to grab his cock through his boxers as he thought about what else could have happened in the car.

In his head, he heard Clay whisper how much he liked Logan's mouth as he gave that sexy little moan again. Logan would have whispered back, "Let's see what else you like," before kissing his way up Clay's jaw line to his ear. He'd nibble the rounded shell of his ear before sucking the tender lobe into his mouth and biting down sharply. Clay would gasp at the pleasure-pain, his body arching towards Logan's as he sought more of the same.

Logan's imaginings had grown into a full-blown vision behind his closed eyelids and his cock head was already slick. There was no way he would be able to fall asleep without giving himself some relief. He pushed his boxers down his thighs and fisted his naked cock as his fantasy played out.

"Did you like that, baby?"

"Yes. Do it again," Clay moaned.

Logan shook his head as he moved down to lick at the rapid pulse beating in Clay's neck. "That's not the way this works. You don't get to issue demands." He bit down on the spot and sucked the warm skin into his mouth before releasing it. "Understand?"

When Clay nodded, Logan grabbed one of his hands and brought it to his chest. "Touch me." Clay complied, stroking his hand over the muscles of Logan's chest before moving up to massage his shoulder. Then his hand swept back down Logan's torso, hesitating when it met the hem of his shirt. Logan smiled when Clay looked at him as though asking permission. He liked that. "What, baby? Tell me what you want."

Clay bit his lip before whispering, "I want to touch your skin. I want … I want to touch your cock."

Logan slid his hand up Clay's throat and pulled him close enough for their lips to touch. "Then go ahead," he whispered back. Logan pressed his lips to Clay's just as the other man's fingers lightly rubbed against his stomach. They hesitated, dancing across the skin before moving down and opening Logan's jeans. Clay trailed his fingers up Logan's cock and he groaned. Logan was hard and aching, trapped behind his boxers. When he felt Clay tugging at the material, he lifted his hips slightly so he could drag his underwear down enough to free him. Clay's hand wrapped around his shaft and Logan rewarded him by sucking that earlobe back into his mouth, biting down just a bit harder than he had before. Both men moaned. Logan moved back to Clay's mouth, kissing him deeply, their tongues rubbing against each other as Clay stroked his fist up and down Logan's cock.

Logan broke their kiss to speak against Clay's lips. "Faster. Make me come." Logan thrust his hips up as Clay tightened his *grip and sped up his pace. The precum pearling on Logan's cock aided his slide through Clay's fist. Logan grabbed Clay by the back of the neck again to pull him into a rough kiss, their lips smashing together as he felt his orgasm building low in his stomach, his balls tight and ready to erupt. This time, Clay broke their kiss as he leaned up to whisper in his ear, "Logan, I want you to fuck me." Then he rubbed his thumb across the slit on the head of Logan's cock before squeezing him tight. Logan threw his head back against the headrest, groaning long and deep in his throat as his orgasm came barreling up his shaft …*

On the bed, Logan's hips rose over and over as he fucked into his fist, his hot cum shooting out of his cock to cover his fingers and stomach. "Fuck!" He stroked himself a few more times until all the tension drained from his body. He lay there on the bed, gasping for breath. His decision was made. That small taste wouldn't let him go back to desiring Clay from afar. He reached down and grabbed the shirt he'd dropped earlier to wipe himself off. He had to have Clay.

5

The next day, Logan strode into the station full of purpose. He knew he'd have to talk to Clay about what happened between them. It was important from a professional standpoint, but he also wanted to let Clay know how he felt. Logan waited for Clay, looking around the plain white walls of the small room. Everything in it was functional, from the desk to the file cabinets to the barely comfortable chairs. It was hardly the place to talk romance but at least it was private. Twenty minutes later, he saw Clay walk past his open door. He called him in before he was out of range. "Clay, could you come in here, please?"

He came into the office warily and stood at attention. "Yes, Sergeant?"

Logan rolled his eyes and stepped around him to close the door. "At ease. You know I didn't call you in here for something work related."

Clay relaxed from his stance but he still looked tense.

Logan got right to the point. "Why did you run away last night?"

Clay scoffed. "I didn't run away."

"Fine, stalked off in a manly rage, whatever. Why did you leave?"

"Because you kissed me."

"I did. And it seemed like you liked it." Clay didn't say anything. "Alright. Answer me this. If I wasn't your team leader, would you have liked it?"

Clay looked at him suspiciously. "Is this a trick?"

"What?"

"Are you trying to get me to say that I'm gay or something?"

"No! No, this isn't like that at all." Logan sighed. "Clay, listen to me. I'm gay. And I kissed you because I wanted to, not for any other reason. I've been attracted to you for a long time, and I think you've been attracted to me as well. Am I wrong in thinking that you're gay too? Or bi-sexual?" Clay shook his head so Logan continued on. "Now that it's out in the open, I hoped we might explore what's between us." He sighed again as Clay just stood there, looking dumbfounded. "I know I've gone about this in the clumsiest way possible. I didn't intend that. It was just, last night with us alone in the car, it seemed very … intimate. I lost my head for a moment and kissed you."

Clay met his eyes. "Oh."

Logan had to smile. Clay always had a smart comeback for everything, but he seemed incapable of speaking at all at that moment. "So back to my original question. Why did you leave so abruptly last night?"

Clay shrugged. "It just seemed like the right thing to do."

Logan walked closer to him. "Why?"

Clay didn't know what to say. When Logan kissed him the night before, he'd been surprised as hell. And now there he was. Standing so close in front of him. Those normally sharp hazel eyes watching Clay with warm interest.

"Clay, did you like my kiss?"

Clay nodded slightly, unable to look away from that gaze.

"And do you think you'd like it if I kissed you again?"

Clay swallowed hard. That low, seductive voice. He'd never heard Sergeant Pierce sound that way, not that he'd had any cause to. But Clay liked the sound of it. It made his belly swoop with desire. "Yeah, but…" He trailed off, not quite sure how to say what he was feeling.

Logan moved closer to him, so close that their chests brushed together as they breathed. "But what, Clay?"

"But you're my sergeant. And I don't want to mess up our team if things don't work out between us."

Logan smiled. "We've only had one kiss and you've already got us breaking up."

"You know what I mean."

Logan sobered. "I do. I can't promise things will work out between us but I do know that I'd hate for us to not even try. Neither of us are out and I know that we'd both respect that decision. And I know that you, that both of us, are too professional and love this job too much to let anything between us interfere with the team. Am I right?"

Clay shrugged, not wanting to commit to anything right then.

Logan touched his jaw lightly. "Think about it. We'll hang out as usual while you decide if you want to give us a try. Is that alright?"

Clay only nodded. It seemed he was still too surprised by everything to use his words.

"Alright, I'll see you in the strategy room later."

Clay went to leave the office but stopped when Logan spoke again.

"And Clay?"

He turned back to see Logan looking at him with a teasing gleam in his eyes.

"Just know that while you're thinking about that, I'll be thinking about kissing you again."

6

Clay drove home after their shift. He was still blown away by what had happened between him and Sergeant Pierce the night before and that morning. Out of all the men he'd ever been attracted to, both in the military and on the force, the one he'd least expected to make a move was Logan Pierce. He'd dated plenty of guys, but never a fellow cop.

He'd known, or at least suspected, that his sergeant was attracted to him. When they first met three years ago, a pulse of heat had sizzled between them. And over the years, he'd caught Logan's eyes on him a few times. He didn't mind. He'd been just as busy sneaking glances himself. Logan was tall and muscular, his dark blond hair cut and parted on the side in a typical policeman's hairstyle. His jaw was square, his mouth firm. And his eyes were a striking hazel, always sharp and direct. His military training gave Sergeant Pierce a commanding presence that was always with him, whether he was in their SWAT uniform or not. Sarge was definitely worth looking at. But as Logan said, neither of them was out at work, so he figured nothing would ever come of it. *Until last night.*

Last night, when he'd opened his eyes and seen Logan watching him with such heat in his expression, he'd been surprised. He'd held still, his heart pounding, waiting to see what he would do. When Logan kissed him, he discovered that firm mouth could be soft. Logan had kissed him softly at first, almost hesitantly, like he was afraid Clay would bolt. That turned out to be a smart move since he *did* take off. He hadn't wanted to. He'd wanted to stay in that car with Logan and keep kissing until the windows fogged over. But the realization that making out with *his sergeant* was probably an incredibly stupid career move hit him and he'd left the car.

He'd been apprehensive when he was called into Logan's office. Thoughts of reprimands and being ostracized ran through his head. Shit like that happened – he had some experience with it himself. But that hadn't been the case. Sergeant Pierce laid all his cards on the table, openly admitting his attraction for Clay. Now Clay was actually considering dating him. He wasn't sure if that proved how fucking crazy he was or how much trust he had in Sarge. A relationship between them had the potential to blow up in their faces, causing all sorts of destruction. He'd have to really trust Logan if he went through with it. Attraction was all well and good, but it wasn't worth losing a job he loved. So before things took another step, he'd have to decide. Did he trust they could have a relationship without damaging their careers and their reputation?

7

"Thanks for bringing your team up, Sergeant. We definitely need the help."

They were in Arlington, TX completing a training session for the Arlington Police. Their team occasionally traveled to other law enforcement agencies to help both new and established SWAT teams increase their skills. Arlington was a small city, sandwiched between Fort Worth and Dallas. But it had its share of violent crime and couldn't always rely on its two big brothers to help them out.

"You've got a good squad." The heavy-set, slightly balding captain nodded towards where Clay was working two of the Arlington men. "That one is a good teacher. Lots of patience."

Logan looked over at Clay. He appeared calm and patient as he had them go through a drill on the typical single file SWAT entry into an area for the fourth time. "Thanks. I handpicked them all myself. We work well together and we get along. No one is allowed on this team who isn't a good fit for the rest of us. That's one of the main reasons we operate so smoothly."

"Well, whatever mojo you guys got, it's working. This is the best I've seen my boys look. You'll have to let us take y'all out for a drink tonight as thanks."

Logan nodded. "Sounds good."

****

The bar they were in was a typical Texas bar. Dark hardwood floors were decorated with scuff marks while the darkly paneled walls were decorated with the Texas flag, bleached long horn skulls, and dried bunches of Blue Bonnets. Clay didn't mind being there. He used to have a problem with drinking and for a long while, he couldn't be around it while he worked on his addiction. But he'd since gotten over being uncomfortable around alcohol and no longer craved it like he used to. He looked up from where he sat with Q and saw Logan watching him. Heat curled through his belly and he looked away.

Three weeks had passed since their talk in his office. He hadn't given Logan the answer he knew he was waiting for. Yet. Each day, he wanted to give in just a little bit more. They were as professional as always at work. But whenever they went out, always with a few other members of the team, he would catch Logan watching him. Or they would have a few moments alone to talk. He knew Logan was thinking about kissing him again. He knew it because he was thinking about it too. He thought about it a lot. Especially the other night when Logan drove him home again.

It had rained, but very lightly. Still, Clay hung out by the door, declining offers of a ride until Logan came out. When Logan asked if he wanted a ride home, he said yes almost embarrassingly fast. Logan hadn't said anything. He'd just smiled slightly and drove him home. When they'd reached his apartment, he half wanted Logan to move across the seat and kiss him again. But he still wasn't sure that it was a good idea for them to get involved. Logan read his hesitation and lightly tapped a finger against Clay's lips, telling him, "Take your time. There's no rush." Clay left the car much calmer than the last time Logan had given him a ride home.

Logan came over to him and Q. He nodded at the glass in his hand. "What number is this?"

Clay laughed and held up four fingers. He'd given up beer and alcohol, but now he guzzled root beer whenever he was out with friends. It was a running joke among their team to keep track of how many glasses of root beer he drank in a night. It was all good natured, none of them would ever try to pressure him into falling off the wagon. They stood there talking for awhile, mostly running down that day's training session. Q eventually drifted away and they were alone.

"You did good today. Their captain even pointed out how well you were doing as a teacher."

Clay smiled. "When we get back, I'll be sure to tell Mitchell I'm about to take his job." Sergeant Reed Mitchell was their top SWAT training instructor.

Logan laughed. "Don't think just because he's in the classroom instead of the field that he can't put you down."

Clay laughed too. Reed believed in teaching by example. Which meant if he had a move or technique he wanted to teach, he didn't just tell you, he put it *on* you. All of them had been taken down hard by the tough instructor.

Their laughter died down after a moment. It was replaced by that tension that often cropped up between them now. Clay looked down, away from Logan's direct gaze.

"Do you think we'll still be comfortable like this if we …" He didn't finish his sentence but he looked back up at Logan, knowing he'd understand what he meant.

Logan answered Clay's question honestly. "I think we might be a little tense at first. But we've been co-workers and friends for a long time, Clay. We'd settle down, settle into it with ease. And, like I said before, we both care about this job too much to let anything interfere with it."

He watched as Clay nodded slowly. He could see that he was close to saying yes, close to becoming his lover. Still, Logan didn't push. He knew he was playing a dangerous game in pursuing a subordinate, someone on his team no less. But his desire and need for Clay was so strong that he was willing to take that risk. He knew they could keep things professional. He swallowed the last of his beer then turned to leave.

"I'm going to take off." He always left a little early in case the boys wanted to loosen up more than they would if he were there. He trusted them to keep it sane and get enough rest to stay sharp. He left Clay with one last thought. "I'll be up for awhile. And you know my phone is always on."

****

Clay sat up in his hotel bed. He left soon after Logan but he wasn't at all close to falling asleep. He kept thinking about things with Logan. He was definitely attracted to the big man who led their team with such cool and calm efficiency. And now Logan was pursuing him. He had to admit that if it wasn't for their job, he would have already given in. That spark of attraction that he'd pushed aside for three years because of their positions was now a sensual heat that danced along his skin whenever their eyes met. He wanted to explore the attraction between them and see where it went. And he wanted to get to know Logan outside of work. Find out if he was always so calm and serious.

At least two people on their team were already aware of their changing relationship. He'd overheard Logan and Carlos talking about him one night. Carlos made an exasperated noise and said, "Just put a collar on him already." Clay laughed as he walked away. What did Los think he was, a puppy? But if Carlos knew, that meant his girlfriend, Tiffany Jackson, also knew. She was the explosives specialist on their team. Tiffany and Carlos were close, closer than most couples, and he was pretty sure they didn't keep any secrets from each other.

He looked down at the phone he'd been holding for the past ten minutes. He had a message to Logan up on the screen, but he'd been debating about sending it for so long that it kept going dark. He slid his thumb across the screen once more to wake it up. He looked at the message and wondered if he should send it. *About to watch a movie. Come over if you want.*

Room 314. Then a thought occurred to him. He trusted Logan with his life, so why couldn't he trust him to be professional in this? He cursed under his breath. "Fuck it." He hit send.

****

Logan flipped through the channels without any real interest. He heard his phone buzz and sighed. Carlos had already texted him twice. He almost wished he'd never told his friend the way he felt about Clay. Now that he was aware of it, and knew Logan finally made a move, he wouldn't leave him alone about it. He was either offering advice or teasing him. Logan didn't really want to hear it, but with Carlos, once he got going, he was like a fucking dog after a meaty bone.

As much as he wished Clay was already his, he was willing to go slow, letting things progress as they would. He knew it was a big decision for both of them to make. So he just hung out with Clay like always. Except things were different. There was a delicious sexual tension that popped up between them. He loved it, relished it, but it was driving him crazy. He could tell from Clay's body language whenever they were alone that Clay wanted to kiss him again. And Clay had opened up to him even more than before, sharing parts of his history that Logan hadn't known. For instance, Clay never talked much about his family, but he told Logan his parents were well-off and lived in The Lakes, and he had a brother who died when he was in high school.

Clay was obviously warming towards him and it was hard not to rush them into the next step. His natural instincts and aggression told him to take Clay and make him his. Every time Clay sent him one of those shy and curious glances, Logan had to mentally restrain himself from snatching him up and taking another taste of his sweet lips. But he was determined not to scare Clay off. So he reminded himself often that if he wanted to win him, he'd have to walk a fine line between what he wanted to do and what he should do. Logan kept calm, not pushing, waiting for Clay to come to him. Carlos told him he was crazy, until he reminded him of how long he had to wait for Tiffany to agree to become his. That shut him up real quick. He laughed just thinking about it.

Logan finally looked down at his phone to see what Carlos had texted him this time. He'd already sent two pieces of advice so it was probably time for some taunting. But the message wasn't from Carlos. It was from Clay, asking him to come over and watch a movie. A slow grin spread across Logan's face as he sat up in bed. This was definitely a good sign.

8

Logan knocked on the door to room 314. Clay opened up after only a few moments.

"Hey." He stepped back to let him in.

"Hey."

"I thought we could hang out by ourselves and watch a movie."

Logan smiled. "That sounds good. What are we watching?"

Clay shrugged. "I haven't picked yet. Figured we could just page through till we found something we both wanted to watch." He held up a package of candy. "But I went and got movie snacks."

Logan took the package from him. "Twizzlers?"

"What, you don't like Twizzlers? That's just un-American."

Logan opened the package and took out a piece of the waxy candy. "I like Twizzlers just fine. I just like chocolate more."

"Oh, well, if we do this again, I'll get chocolate."

Logan smiled. *There was definitely going to be a next time*, he thought.

****

Logan had never considered himself a masochist, but it was obviously time to reevaluate. Because there he sat, late at night, on a bed, with the man he wanted above all others. And he couldn't touch him. All his reasons for being willing to wait were slowly disappearing from his mind. They were so close on the bed he could feel Clay's warmth seeping into his side. He had no idea what had taken place in the last twenty minutes of their movie. He was too busy trying to keep the hard-on that wanted to pop up and make its presence known under control. He currently had a parade of hunched-backed old ladies with droopy tits and wearing giant granny panties marching through his head. He didn't know how much longer that was going to work. Clay shifted and offered him another Twizzler before biting into one himself. Logan figured it wasn't going to work for too much longer. Yet there he sat. Yep. He definitely liked to inflict a little self-pain.

As the credits rolled, Logan swung his legs over the side of the bed and spoke in a rush. "Well, I guess I better get out of here. Thanks for the movie. I'll see you in the morning." Logan knew he sounded a little abrupt, but if he didn't get off that bed soon, he was going to yank Clay underneath him and grind them both into orgasm, promises to wait be damned.

"What if I don't want you to leave yet?"

Logan's head snapped back around to look at Clay. "I'd want to know why you wanted me to stay."

Clay didn't meet his eyes. "Maybe I think I'm ready for you to kiss me again."

Logan eased back onto the bed and grasped Clay's chin, forcing him to look him in the eye. "Maybe you'd better be sure of what you want. Because if I kiss you and get my hands on you tonight, I am *not* letting you go again. Do you understand?"

Logan waited for Clay's answer, his heart thundering, reminding himself over and over to wait for Clay to decide before he kissed him. He watched as Clay sucked that full bottom lip into his mouth. Finally, he nodded.

"Yeah, Logan, I want you to kiss me again."

Logan smiled. "It's about time." He leaned forward and kissed Clay. The first touch of their lips was a soft greeting. Then Logan used his thumb to press down on Clay's chin, opening his mouth for his seeking tongue. Again, Logan kept the kiss slow, only touching Clay where their lips joined and with the hand he still had on his chin, wanting to ease them into it. He gently rubbed his tongue along Clay's, tasting the sweetness that was a mix of Twizzlers and Clay. Clay moaned softly as he exhaled, just like he had before, his body melting towards him. Logan inhaled, feeling like he wanted to take that sound and make it a part of him.

He leaned over Clay, slowly pushing until he was on his back with Logan on one elbow, leaning over him. He repeated his new mantra in his head. *What I want to do is not what I should do*, to remind himself to keep things vanilla. He kissed Clay deeply, their tongues tangling, his teeth nipping at Clay's beautifully curved bottom lip. Logan sucked it into his mouth, savoring the taste before releasing him slowly.

"I like kissing you, Clay. You won't make me wait too long before I get to do it again, will you?"

Clay, with a flush riding high on his cheekbones, shook his head no.

"Good." Logan trailed soft kisses up Clay's jaw line to his ear. He wondered if warm flesh and blood Clay would react like his fantasy Clay. He pulled Clay's earlobe between his lips, lapping his tongue against the soft skin before catching it in his teeth. Flicking his tongue against it one last time, he bit down on the tender flesh. Clay gasped as a shiver went through him. He reached up and grabbed Logan's arm, pulling him closer. Logan smiled to himself. Definitely better than fantasy Clay. He pressed soft kisses down Clay's neck, pausing when he reached his collar bone. He pulled Clay up slightly so he could drag his t-shirt up his torso and completely off, throwing it to the side of the bed. His own shirt went the same way. Logan pressed their chests together, both men groaning at their first touch of bare skin against bare skin. They kissed again, their hands now roaming and touching everywhere.

Clay broke away. "I don't want to sound like we're about to play a round of 'just the tip' but I'm not ready for more than kissing and touching. I know it might not seem like it, but I like to take things slow."

Logan chuckled at Clay's way of phrasing things. "That's okay, I understand. Don't worry. I can still make you feel good. Just trust me." Logan stroked his hand over the nylon of Clay's gym shorts, bypassing his groin. He slid his hand under the material, feeling the warm skin and taut muscles of Clay's thighs. He'd only caught a few glimpses of them over the years, but those glimpses were enough for him to be eager to get his hands on that part of him. They were smooth and lightly muscled. It felt good to finally touch him there. Logan squeezed his hand around Clay's leg, digging his thumb into the crease where thigh met pelvis. Logan kissed the dark ink of his anchor tattoo before sweeping his tongue across one of Clay's nipples. He sucked the hard little nub into his mouth, remembering that Clay's nipples were pierced. Logan wished those rings were in so he could tug on them and see just how much Clay could take. He'd have to remember to ask Clay to put them in for him.

Logan lightly dragged his fingertips up and down Clay's thighs at the same time that he bit down hard on Clay's nipple. His beautiful lover cried out, his hips arching up off the bed. Logan groaned and his cock grew incredibly hard at that response. Clay seemed to like a little bit of pain with his pleasure. He kissed his way across Clay's chest to his other nipple, giving it the same attention. Logan licked and kissed and bit down Clay's torso, taking note of Clay's reactions to everything he did. Every shudder, every gasp, every moan.

Logan looked down and saw that Clay was hard, his cock pushing up against the soft material of his shorts. Logan brought his hand out from under Clay's shorts to rub his palm down that hard shaft. Clay's moan brought Logan's eyes back to his lover's face.

"Logan. Please. *Touch me.*"

Logan again stroked him lightly through his shorts. "I am touching you, Clay."

Clay looked up at Logan, his eyes pale in the flickering light of the TV. "Touch *me*. Not ..." He broke off, gasping as Logan squeezed his hand around the hard flesh he held.

"Not what?" he prompted when Clay didn't speak again.

"Not through my shorts," he choked out as Logan continued to rhythmically squeeze his cock.

Logan leaned down to whisper against Clay's lips. "Are you sure that's what you want?" Clay moaned out a yes and Logan tugged the nylon shorts down, watching as Clay's stiff cock bounced free against his stomach. As Logan wrapped his hand around that hot, silky flesh, Clay's hips shot up off the bed, pushing his shaft through Logan's fist. Logan immediately let him go. He felt a shiver go through Clay's slender frame as he held him down with one hand on his hip.

"What are you... why'd you stop?"

Logan gently bit Clay's lip. "I want you to stay still. Understand?" Clay nodded, his eyes wide. Logan smiled to himself. He could sense Clay's surprise at his behavior. He was going to be in for a lot of surprises as their relationship progressed. Logan grasped Clay's cock again and this time when Clay didn't move, Logan started to stroke. He rubbed his palm across the head, spreading the pre-cum through his fingers and using it to aid his pumping. He kissed Clay, thrusting his tongue into that sweet mouth as he started to speed up the pace of his strokes. Clay pulled back from him, gasping, but Logan wrapped his hand around the nape of his neck and pulled him back. "I didn't say you could stop kissing me." Logan meshed their lips back together, refusing to let Clay break the kiss.

Clay's head was spinning and shivers chased up and down his spine. Logan's big hand felt good wrapped so tightly around his erection, stroking him fast and steady, but it was killing him not to be able to move his hips like his body demanded. His stomach muscles were clenched tight as he fought to follow Logan's order. But that kiss! Logan's fierce kisses were robbing him of breath and his ability to concentrate on not moving. As Logan's grip on both his neck and his cock tightened, Clay knew he wouldn't last much longer. He tried to speak, to tell Logan he was about to come, but he couldn't with Logan's tongue thrusting in his mouth. In desperation, he bit Logan to get him to pull away so he could talk, but Logan just bit him back. The sharp nip of Logan's teeth on his tongue sparked another burst of pleasure. Clay lost it and exploded. His hands flew up to Logan's back, his fingers digging into the hard muscles there. His shout was muffled by Logan's lips as his cock pulsed, shooting hot streams of cum all over his stomach and Logan's hand. Clay's whole body trembled as he strained to keep his hips still in the midst of the best hand job he'd ever had. Finally, his orgasm eased up and every one of his muscles relaxed until he lay there limp. He looked up at Logan in dazed surprise as the big man smiled down at him.

"Is that what you wanted?"

Clay groaned out a laugh. "God, yes." He rose up on his knees. "But what about what you want?" He pushed Logan onto his back and pulled his sweats and boxers down to mid-thigh. Clay bit his lip as he looked down at Logan. A light dusting of blond hair covered the thick muscles of his chest, narrowing to a thin trail down his abs. His eyes dropped down to Logan's erection. It was big and thick, the head broad, the vein underneath strong and throbbing. Clay swallowed, his mouth dry. He was already starting to regret his stance on not going further than kissing and touching. He looked back up at Logan and saw he was watching him with his lids partially lowered over those intense hazel eyes. Clay drew his finger up Logan's shaft from root to tip. "Do you want me to return the favor?"

"Fuck, yes," he growled.

Clay slicked his hand in his own cum still on his stomach before fisting Logan's erection. Squeezing tight, he pumped his fist up and down Logan's cock, pleased when moans immediately came from him. After what Logan had just done to him, he was glad he could make him feel good. Clay swung his leg over Logan so he was straddling his thighs, the shorts still around his thighs stretchy enough to allow the movement. He continued stroking as he leaned down and pressed kisses against Logan's throat, licking the skin there before moving down to his chest.

Logan groaned at the feeling of his cock in Clay's strong hand, barely able to believe he had that sexy lithe body atop his own. Deciding he'd probably already surprised Clay enough for the night, he kept his mouth shut. But he couldn't stop his hands from coming up to grasp his ass. His cock throbbed and his balls tightened at the feel of that firm round flesh in his hands. He wanted Clay's mouth again, but before he could ask, Clay's lips were on his, his new lover slowly plunging his tongue into his mouth as he stroked. Logan knew he wasn't going to last long after being hard all night and helping Clay reach his pleasure, so he didn't even try. Logan moaned and let himself go, his orgasm rushing up his shaft in the sweet release he'd been craving for weeks. He held his grip on Clay's ass while Clay pumped him until every last drop was wrung from his body.

****

Logan wrapped his arms around Clay's slender frame and pulled him down tight against him. "Was that alright?"

Clay rolled off him slightly, landing to his side. "Yes. I'm glad I finally made up my mind."

Logan laughed. "Me too. Especially after sitting next to you all night. Thought I was going to go crazy wanting to touch you."

Clay ducked his head and smiled. "I could feel how tense you were."

He lightly grasped Clay's chin, looking into his eyes. "We're going to give this a try." It wasn't a question but Clay still nodded in agreement. Logan couldn't have been happier. Finally, he had the chance to make Clay his.

9

Two days later, they were back in Houston. Clay was in one of the gyms at the station, working out with Q. Well, he was supposed to be working out. He was mostly just sitting there, holding a dumbbell in each hand while he stared into space. Again, Logan was on his mind.

"Hey, man. What are you doing? You trying to think yourself strong?"

Clay looked up at his partner. Quan, or Q as most everybody called him, was a second generation Vietnamese American. He had smooth tan skin and dark eyes. His black hair was styled in a thick crew cut. The ladies were always checking him out, especially when he was in uniform, but he was completely devoted to his wife, Cassie. Clay made a half-hearted curl with the weight and answered his question. "No, just thinking."

"That's obvious. What's up?"

Normally, he would have spilled his guts to Q with no problem. They were close. Putting their lives on the line together so many times had created a deep bond between them. But this wasn't something he was sure he should share. "I'm seeing somebody."

Q looked around then moved closer to him. "Serge?" he asked quietly.

Clay's eyes widened. "Fuck, man, how did you know? Does everybody else?"

"No! At least not as far as I know. But c'mon, man. We're together all the time. I couldn't help but notice he's been coming around you a lot more. And when he does, he looks at you differently than he used to."

Clay set his weights down, not even pretending to work out anymore. "Well, shit. Since you know, what do you think?"

Q sat on the bench next to him. "First off, I was surprised as hell when I figured out Sarge was gay. You know I don't have a problem with it, it just never crossed my mind with him."

Q had long known that Clay was bi-sexual. He was one of the few people on the force that did. Clay wasn't ashamed of it, but he didn't want to deal with any bullshit from macho cops either.

"I'll admit I was a little worried when I thought about it. You know, two people on the team dating. But Carlos and Tiffany manage without a problem. I don't see why you two can't."

"Our situation is a little different. Carlos isn't the team leader and Tiffany isn't a man."

"He's higher ranked than her. But I see what you're saying." Q shrugged. "I guess it just depends on if you think it's worth it."

Clay didn't say anything to that. He'd already jumped into the fire so to speak. He looked at Q. "That's not the only thing I was thinking about. I finally let him come over last night."

Q looked slightly horrified. "Fuck, you're not about to tell me what Sarge looks like naked, are you?"

Clay laughed. "Shut up, man. Do you want to hear this or not?" Q mimed zipping and locking his lips. "Logan…" He paused for a second. He'd called him by his first name before, but now it felt strange. He'd have to get used to that. He plowed on. "Logan was different than usual when we got physical. His personality seemed different."

Q frowned. "What does that mean? He wasn't an asshole, was he?"

Clay shook his head. He couldn't imagine their clean cut leader being anything but respectful. "No, he wasn't an asshole. We wouldn't be sitting here talking about this if he was. He was just, I don't know. I guess intense is the word I want to use."

"Oh, well, that's not surprising. We're all fucking intense. With this job, you have to be. If you liked it and it didn't freak you out, I say go with it."

Q was right. They *were* all intense. Clay thought back to the night before and how Logan had ordered him to keep still while he stroked him off. He'd never come so hard from a hand job in his life. He definitely liked it. He lightly kicked his friend in the leg. "You give such good boyfriend advice, Qlinda. You're the best BFF ever."

Q shot him a hard glare. "Watch it."

****

A few of them were at Rudy's pub, a local hangout popular with the HPD. The place was mostly dominated by SWAT. Clay was drinking root beer and his glass was almost empty. He was about to get another drink, but decided to have some fun first.

He was sitting next to Logan in a big booth with Carlos, Tiffany, and Brady on the other side. Brady was one of the snipers on their team. He wasn't known for picking up on subtle nuances. Basically, just about everything went over his head, but he was a damn good shot.

Clay scooted his foot closer to Logan's under the table and slowly rubbed his bare leg against his. Logan abruptly stopped talking and went still.

Brady looked at Logan confused. "Umm… Sarge, you gonna finish your sentence or what?"

Clay eased off a little and Logan went back to his story. Clay waited a minute then leaned back casually in the booth, dropping his hand down onto the seat. He walked his fingers slowly up Logan's muscular thigh, stopping just shy of his groin. Clay rubbed his fingers lightly back and forth, occasionally grazing over the growing bulge in Logan's shorts. Logan stopped talking again.

This time Brady looked concerned. "Are you alright, boss?"

Clay kept his hand right where it was, massaging Logan's thigh. He looked up at Logan with his eyes wide. "Yeah, Sarge, what's wrong?" He took a drink of his soda, hollowing his cheeks as he sipped through the straw. Logan's Adam's apple bobbed as he swallowed hard.

Carlos and Tiffany burst out laughing and Logan's gaze shot over to glare at them. "Nothing, I'm fine. Just lost my train of thought."

Carlos smirked. "I bet you did." Carlos got up, pulling Tiffany with him. "We're gonna get another round of drinks."

Clay gave Logan's thick thigh one last squeeze and got up too. "I don't trust you two to get the right root beer. I like Barq's not IBC. IBC doesn't have bite. I'll come with you."

They started to walk off but Carlos stopped and looked back at Logan. "Oh, man, Sarge, I didn't mean to be rude. Do you want to come too?"

Logan spoke through gritted teeth. "Not right now."

Carlos laughed and Clay grinned. They both knew why he couldn't get up. He walked off, leaving Logan there with a hard-on that he'd have to get under control before he could leave the booth. Brady stayed behind, pestering him to finish the story.

Clay stood with Carlos and Tiffany at the bar, waiting on their drinks. Tiffany was still laughing.

She pushed her mass of thick dark hair over her shoulder. "I can't believe you did that! Of course, Brady is so clueless he'd never pick up on it, but I bet you're gonna be in trouble tonight. Don't be surprised if you get a—"

Carlos spoke up, cutting her off. "It's good for Sarge to loosen up and be teased every now and then. He's always so damn serious."

Clay watched Carlos bring his hand to the back of Tiffany's neck and give a slight squeeze. He gave her an oddly stern look and she dropped her eyes. *The hell?* Clay didn't know what had just passed between the two of them. Tiffany wasn't normally one to be cowed by anyone. Not even Carlos, who she'd been dating almost as long as she'd been on SWAT. With her rich dark skin, full lips, and fluffy hair, she looked like she was about to take the stage and belt out some smooth blues melody. But he'd never seen her back down from a fight. And she was crazy. She had to be to gleefully handle bombs the way she did. Before he could analyze that any further, he heard Logan's voice behind him.

"Clever. Real fucking clever. I love a good joke. I might have to have you guys run some hills this week to show my appreciation."

Clay didn't touch Logan because of where they were, but he stood close enough to feel the body heat coming off the big man.

"You're exempt, Clay."

Carlos frowned. "How the fuck is he exempt when he started that whole thing?"

Logan shrugged. "I like him more than I like you so he can get away with more."

Carlos just rolled his eyes as the rest of them laughed. They knew Logan wasn't serious. "Where's Brady?"

"He cut out. Had to get home to his wife." He looked at Clay. "Or maybe he was bored because I couldn't get my mind back on track to finish my story."

Clay smirked. "SWAT should be able to concentrate no matter the circumstances."

Logan gave him a dry look. "Somehow, in all the training I've done over the years, I missed the one about staying focused while your lover gets you worked up."

Clay and Tiffany laughed, but Carlos had a thoughtful expression on his face. "You might have just given me an idea, Logan." Tiffany turned to him with her eyes wide. "Don't even think about it." Carlos just smiled and pulled her in close with an arm around her waist. "Sorry, pet. It's already a done deal."

It was Logan's turn to laugh as Tiffany shot him a dirty look. They stood at the bar talking for awhile longer, long enough for Clay to finish his root beer and order another. Before it arrived, Logan touched his arm to get his attention.

"Come home with me tonight?"

A shiver chased across his skin at Logan's invitation. He was really enjoying the time they spent together alone. He nodded in agreement, Logan's cool hazel eyes warming with pleasure as he did. The four of them talked for a few more minutes before Logan suddenly looked at him and said, "You know, I think we're going to get out of here."

Clay arched a brow. "We are?"

Logan gave him a look nearly identical to the one Carlos had given Tiffany earlier. "Yes. We are."

Clay found himself agreeing. "Alright." Logan clapped his hand on the back of Clay's shoulder in a move that was casual enough for any two friends to do, but still allowed them to touch. They said their goodbyes but before they made it out of the bar, Carlos called out to him.

"Clay! Don't you want your damn root beer?"

Clay looked back over his shoulder. "You drink it, fucker!" he shouted back. He and Logan both laughed as they headed out into the night.

10

Logan waited in the driveway for Clay to pull in behind him. Clay got out of the car and locked it. Once he joined him, Logan headed for the front door.

"Aren't we going in through the garage?"

Logan laughed. "You just want to see my cars again." He'd built an addition to his garage for the two muscle cars he'd restored. Clay had been in awe the first time he'd seen them.

Clay smiled sheepishly. "Maybe."

Logan grabbed his hand and tugged him forward. When they were in the house, Logan immediately pulled Clay into his arms for a kiss, walking him over to the stairs. He separated from him long enough to allow Clay to go up the stairs before him. But he kept his hands on his lover, stroking his palms underneath Clay's t-shirt to touch the smooth skin of his stomach. Clay gasped as Logan lightly trailed his fingers down the soft hair that led into his shorts and moved faster down the hallway.

Once they were in his room, he pushed Clay up against the closed door and plunged his tongue into his mouth. Fuck, he wanted to punish Clay so bad for teasing him his fingers were tingling. But he couldn't. Not yet. He was happy that he'd gotten Clay to agree to date him. He didn't want to spring anything else on him just yet. So he settled for kissing him furiously, barely giving his lover a chance to breathe. He clenched his fists against the door on either side of Clay's head to restrain himself from spanking that tight, round butt. He finally pulled back and looked at Clay. His lips were wet and swollen from his kisses. He opened his eyes slowly.

"You're a really good kisser, Logan."

Logan chuckled as he stripped Clay's shirt up over his head. "You think so?"

"Yep."

Logan leaned back in and kissed Clay slowly this time. He stroked his tongue in and out before he sucked at that sweet bottom lip that always seemed to be begging for his attention. He ran his hand down Clay's belly, into his shorts, and grasped Clay's shaft. He was already semi-erect. Logan pulled his lips away from Clay's, watching as desire tightened his features. Logan started to pump and Clay was hard in his hand within seconds. Squeezing once, he rubbed his thumb over the tip, feeling it already slick and hot. Clay's head knocked back against the door.

"And you definitely deserve a blue ribbon for best hand jobs."

Logan pushed Clay's shorts down and Clay toed off his sneakers. "Where would you find a ribbon for that?"

"I don't know," Clay answered, breathing hard. "But I'll make you one myself if you just keep doing that."

Logan slowed his strokes on Clay's cock. "Keep doing this?"

"Yes, but do it faster," Clay ground out between clenched teeth.

He brought his hand down to wrap around Logan's fist, urging him to move faster. But Logan grabbed it and pressed it back against the door. He looked his lover in the eyes. "Baby, you are going to learn not to do that." He quickly stroked Clay several times and as soon as he started gasping, his hips rolling, Logan let him go.

Clay groaned. "Jesus, Logan! You can't keep doing that to me."

Logan smiled but he didn't say anything. He just picked Clay up with one arm around his slender waist and headed over to the foot of the bed.

"Oh, Logan! You're carrying me like a big manly man," Clay mocked in a girly falsetto.

"I could always throw your ass onto the bed."

Clay scoffed. "You wouldn't dare."

Logan stopped and went to change his hold so he could throw him. Clay stopped him before he could do so.

"Okay, I'm sorry! I was just teasing."

Logan laughed and laid Clay down on the bed. God, he was beautiful. His body was long, lean, and lightly muscled. His skin was already tan from all the swimming he liked to do. And fuck, those thighs! So smooth and round. They hadn't gone further than pleasuring each other with their hands and mouths yet, but Logan was already addicted to having them wrapped around him. Clay nudged him with his foot.

"Am I gonna lay here naked all by my lonesome?"

Logan stripped off his own clothes then eased one knee onto the bed. "I was just admiring your pretty thighs."

Clay laughed. "My what?"

Logan ran his hand up Clay's leg, trailing his fingers over the colorful ink of another tattoo. This one featured a sailor themed pin-up girl swinging on an anchor. "You heard me. I've been fantasizing about licking my way up these for a long time."

Clay drew one of his knees up, his blue eyes focused on Logan, passion swirling in their depths. "Well, they're here now."

Logan moved the rest of the way up on the bed. "That they are." He smoothed his hand down Clay's raised leg, pressing slightly to open him up even further. Leaning down, he licked a long wet trail up the inside of Clay's thigh from knee to groin. He heard Clay's breath catch as he swiped his tongue across his tight sac before Logan continued on to the other leg. He sucked the warm skin into his mouth, making Clay jump as he bit him lightly.

"I like that you shave."

Clay laughed softly. "I like that you don't."

Logan laughed too then went back to what he was doing. He paid each thigh lots of attention, kneading the smooth flesh, kissing and sucking his way from thigh to thigh then lapping at Clay's sac with each pass until Clay's legs shifted restlessly on the bed, his hips swiveling. When he moaned Logan's name, Logan licked one long stripe up Clay's hard cock before responding. "Yeah, baby?"

One of Clay's hands came down to rest on the back of Logan's head. "Suck me, please."

Logan shook Clay's hand from his head and surged up his body until they were face to face, groin to groin. "I like the way you say please." He grasped Clay's wrists in his fist and stretched his arms up to the headboard. Logan looked down and the sight of his big hand restraining Clay's smaller wrists sent a surge of possessive pleasure running through him. A picture flashed in his head of those same wrists in a set of leather cuffs and Logan groaned. Soon. He'd have Clay that way soon. When he spoke, his voice was low and rough with desire. "Don't move your hands from this spot and I'll give you what you want." Logan thrust his pelvis against Clay's rubbing their cocks together. Clay moaned and his fingers twitched. Logan squeezed his hand around Clay's wrists in warning. As he looked at his lover, Logan thought he might have seen a flash of excitement in his blue eyes before they closed.

Logan slowly released Clay and braced his hand on the bed. He ground his hips against Clay's again, loving the feel of their hard cocks sliding together. Logan moved back down Clay's body, stopping to lick at his nipples. He spoke against Clay's skin. "Next time we're together like this, I want you to have your nipple rings in." Clay nodded but that wasn't enough for Logan. He bit down on the nipple in his mouth. "I didn't hear you."

"Yes! I will."

Logan gave an appreciative murmur before continuing his path down to Clay's cock. He flattened his tongue and licked across the head of Clay's shaft, tasting the salty pre-cum that had already beaded on the slit. "You taste so good, Clay." He blew a warm breath across where he'd just licked before sucking that hot hard cock into his mouth. Logan bobbed up and down, sucking slowly. He tongued the sensitive underside, watching as Clay's back arched off the bed in pleasure. Logan brought his hand between Clay's legs, cupping and squeezing his balls before lightly running one finger up and down the tender skin just behind them. "Fuck!" Clay cried out.

Logan looked up his lover's body again and saw that even though he was straining and gasping, he hadn't moved his hands from where they'd been placed. Clay was doing so good at following the orders Logan gave as he eased him slowly into being his sub.

Clay felt as if his whole body was on fire as he submitted to the pleasure Logan was giving him. Logan's mouth was so hot and wet as he pulled at him with the most exquisite suction that he could barely stand it. When he lightly dragged his teeth up the underside of his cock, Clay almost reached down to touch his lover but managed to hold himself back at the last second. But he couldn't stop the words that burst from his mouth. "Logan, please. I want to taste you too."

Logan kept sucking but he scooped his hand under Clay's hip, pulling until he caught on and turned onto his side. Then Logan moved his big body around until his cock was lined up with Clay's mouth. He pulled his mouth off Clay long enough to tell him he could move his hands. Clay didn't hesitate. He reached out to hold Logan's shaft steady and sucked him down. His brain fogged over until he was aware of nothing but the feel of Logan hard and strong in his mouth, Logan's tongue sliding across his own cock, and the wet sounds and moans coming from them both. As Logan started to move on him faster, Clay felt the tingling in his balls and the tightening in his belly that signaled he was about to come. Then, without warning, he felt Logan's slick finger probing at his entrance, slowly pushing inside. His hips pumped beyond his control and he tore his mouth from Logan's cock, moaning as his orgasm poured from him and straight into the hot mouth of his lover. Clay was lost in the pleasure coursing through him. When he came down, Logan smacked him sharply on the ass, reminding him that he was neglecting his generous partner.

Clay rose up on his knees and pushed Logan onto his back. Then he leaned down and took him back into his mouth. Logan's hand came down to grasp the back of his head, guiding him.

"That's it, baby. Suck me."

Clay crowded in tight against Logan's body and moaned.

"I like that. Do it again."

Clay moaned again, longer this time. He looked up and saw Logan propped up on one elbow, watching him. Clay was unable to look away from those sharp hazel eyes. Their gazes remained locked and Logan's fingers clenched tightly on his head while his hips started to fuck upwards. Goose bumps chased across Clay's skin as Logan spoke in a low voice.

"Relax. Let me fuck your mouth."

Clay did as Logan asked without thought. Logan's thrusts became more forceful and he kept talking to Clay in that husky voice.

"Take it, baby. You're doing so good. Take it all. You've got me so hard in that hot little mouth."

Clay moaned again. His fingers tingled and his stomach clenched with desire. He was getting insanely turned on by the way Logan was talking to him and holding him in place.

"I'm about to come in your mouth, Clay. You gonna drink it all down for me?"

Clay squirmed, hard again and already at the edge of orgasm.

Logan smiled. "You want to come again don't you, baby?"

Clay nodded swiftly, not caring if he looked desperate.

"Touch yourself."

Clay reached down and grabbed his cock, pumping in time with Logan's thrusts. It wasn't long before Clay's belly clenched and his balls drew up tight against his body. He started to come at the same time he felt Logan's release flooding over his tongue. Clay tried not to choke, his concentration split between his own orgasm and swallowing down Logan's. Through it all, he and Logan maintained eye contact until they both shuddered one last time.

****

Clay released Logan and laid his head on his lover's flat stomach to catch his breath. Logan scooted around to the top of the bed, dragging Clay with him. They kissed and caressed each other lightly as they relaxed. Clay laughed softly and teased the big man holding him. "You've got such a dirty mouth, Logan. I wouldn't have ever thought that from the proper and militant way you're always bossing us around."

Logan tensed. "Does that bother you?"

"No. I like it."

Logan was glad to hear that and he pulled Clay close for a kiss to show it. He only meant for it to be a quick kiss, but Clay's lips parted beneath his and he couldn't resist the invitation. He swept his tongue inside, savoring the taste of himself inside his lover's mouth. His arms went around Clay's slim waist and before long, they were pressed together and kissing deeply. When he finally eased back, they were both breathing hard.

Clay sighed. "I'd better go so I can get home and get some sleep."

Logan's arms tightened on his lover for a brief second before he let him go. He wanted Clay to stay and sleep with him. Instead, Clay went home after each night they spent together. He wasn't going to allow it for much longer, but for now, he let him get up and get dressed. Logan pulled on his boxers and walked him to the door. He gave him a quick kiss.

"Goodnight, Clay."

Clay grinned. "Good night, Sergeant Pierce."

Logan pulled him back, this time giving him a hard kiss. "Watch it, Corporal." Clay relaxed against him, accepting the kiss until Logan released him again. "I'll see you in the morning." Clay nodded and headed down the walk to his car.

Logan watched him back out of his driveway and drive away until he couldn't see his tail lights. Things were going well between them. But he still wanted more.

11

Logan strained, ignoring the sweat that ran into his eyes as he pressed the weights in his hand over his head again and again. He'd passed the number of reps he usually did but he kept going, trying to burn off the sexual frustration that was building in him each day. He laughed ruefully to himself at the thought that he was sexually frustrated when nearly every night he released onto Clay's belly, or in his hand, or fuck, into his sweet mouth.

He was frustrated because he still hadn't told Clay he was a Dom. Which meant that he hadn't restrained Clay the way he wanted to. He hadn't controlled him, withholding his lover's release until *he* was ready for him to come. He hadn't slapped his hand or one of his toys across Clay's ass to punish him for the way Clay often teased him. He wanted to so fucking bad. He just wasn't sure how Clay would react to Logan asking him to be his sub. Yeah, Clay liked when Logan talked dirty to him and Logan had noticed that look in his eyes when he held his arms down. But that alone didn't make him a submissive. And now that Logan had a taste of him, he didn't think he'd be able to take it if Clay wanted no part of his BDSM world and took off.

So here he was, so frustrated he was ready to explode, pumping iron like crazy to try and ease the tension. He stopped when he heard somebody calling him.

"Damn, Serge! You in the zone or what?"

He stopped and saw Tiffany standing in front of him with her phone in her hand. He'd practically forgotten they were working out together. "Sorry. What's up?"

Tiffany held the phone out to him. "It's Carlos."

He wiped the sweat out of his eyes and snorted. "Who else would it be?" he asked, not expecting an answer. "Los. What's going on, man?"

"Nothing. Bored to tears sitting in that courtroom."

Carlos had been called out to San Antonio as a witness in court.

"Any of those cops sniffing around my girl?"

Logan laughed. "You've been gone three days. I don't think that's long enough for anybody on this force to stop fearing the wrath of Big Los. But you know she can take care of herself, right?" He looked at Tiffany, holding back another laugh as she flexed her bicep then kissed the muscle.

"Yeah, but she shouldn't have to. That's my job and I love doing it. And don't tell me you wouldn't feel the same if you were stuck away from Clay."

Logan didn't say anything. The thought of being away from his beautiful lover, or worse yet, someone else putting their hands on what he wanted to claim as his, had his fist clenching tight on the phone.

Carlos's low laugh came across the line at Logan's silence. "Exactly. Anyway, I'll be back tonight and we're going out tomorrow evening. Bring Clay and come have a drink with us."

Logan agreed and handed the phone back to Tiffany. He watched as she blushed at whatever Carlos said and then ended the call.

****

The next night, they were at Itza's, a small place off the beaten track of places HPD favored. The four of them sat at a fairly secluded table in the laid-back bar. Conversation flowed easily as they caught Carlos up on what had gone on in his absence.

Logan took a sip of his soda. He knew it didn't bother Clay when people around him drank, but he liked to show his support. He set his empty glass down and saw Carlos watching him with a questioning expression. Shit, his best friend was too perceptive. He wasn't surprised when Carlos asked Tiffany to go get him another drink, eyeballing her a silent message as he did so. Tiffany smiled at Clay.

"Come with me, Clay. I'm just gonna get a round for everyone and I can't carry four drinks by myself." Clay shrugged and slid out of the booth to follow Tiffany to the bar. Carlos immediately started in on him once the two were gone.

"Why are you so tense? I thought things were going alright with you and Clay?"

Logan rolled his shoulders. "I'm not tense."

Carlos laughed. "Cut the crap, Logan. If I tapped you with a hammer, you'd shatter. What the fuck is up?"

Logan blew out a breath and clenched his fingers around his empty glass. "I haven't told Clay that I'm a Dom yet. We've been pretty vanilla so far."

Carlos's eyes widened. "Holy shit, man. No wonder you're worked up so tight. How in the hell are you holding that back?"

Logan laughed with very little humor. "Believe me, it hasn't been easy."

Carlos shook his head. "Logan, you can't keep that from Clay for much longer. He needs to know and you look like you're about to explode."

Logan didn't respond. Carlos spoke again.

"Besides, don't you want to collar him?"

Logan sucked in a breath at that. It was the one thing he hadn't let himself think of. Clay, with *his* collar around his throat. Fuck, he wanted to see that sign of his ownership around his lover. Just the thought of it, of Clay acknowledging him as his Dom, sent a wave of possessive arousal through him. But he wouldn't get to experience that if he didn't come clean with Clay. That made up his mind right then and there. Carlos must have seen the look of determination cross his face because he laughed.

"That's what I thought."

Tiffany and Clay came back to their table and put their drinks down. Logan looked at Clay. "We're leaving." Clay gestured at the sodas he'd just set down.

"We just got these!"

Logan stood up and let some of his dominance into his voice. "I said we're going. Now."

Clay's eyes widened but he nodded. He immediately backed up so Logan could leave the table. They said a quick round of goodbyes to Carlos and Tiffany then left the bar.

****

They drove to Logan's house in near silence. When they reached his house, he took Clay straight to his bedroom. He walked Clay backwards until he was sitting on the bed, looking up at him.

"There's something I haven't told you." He cupped his palm around Clay's cheek and looked him in the eye. "I like to be in control in my relationships."

Clay's brow creased in confusion. "So you like to top? I think I've proved I'm okay with that."

Logan reached out to wrap his hand around Clay's neck, tilting his head back. "Not just top, baby. I'm a Dominant. If we're going to be together, I need you to be my submissive." A look of dawning comprehension flashed across Clay's face. His hand came up to rest against Logan's chest.

"I didn't say you could touch me." He watched, incredibly pleased, as Clay licked his lips and dropped his hand down to his lap. He tightened his fingers around Clay's throat. "Do you think you can handle that? Giving up your control to me?" Clay swallowed hard, but his eyes were shining with interest and desire.

"Show me."

12

Logan's hand wrapped around his throat made Clay feel vulnerable in a way he'd never experienced before, but he didn't try to move it. His lover had just confessed to being a Dom and the moment he did, so many things clicked in Clay's head that he wasn't as shocked at the revelation as he should have been. Clay *was* surprised at how quickly he'd asked Logan to show him. Yet looking at the triumphant expression on Logan's face, he was glad that he had. Logan drew him up by the hand he still had around his neck and pulled him in until their chests pressed together.

"Before we go any further, I need to know how far you want to go tonight. We haven't had sex yet and I don't want your decision influenced by anything that happens."

Clay looked into those hazel eyes that were watching him so closely. He knew Logan would wait if that's what he wanted. But he didn't want to wait any longer. He spoke with clear honesty. "I want everything, Logan." At his response, his lover lowered his lips to Clay's and kissed him, his tongue stroking against his over and over again. When Logan finally pulled back and dropped his hand from around his throat, Clay was breathless.

"Strip," Logan commanded.

A chill chased across Clay's skin at that deep voice, and he immediately pulled his shirt over his head. As he continued to undress, he couldn't help but think of the other times he'd automatically done what Logan told him, especially when he used that voice. Had he subconsciously been submitting to Logan all along? When Clay was done undressing, Logan spoke again.

"Kneel. Head bowed, hands on your knees, palms up."

Clay complied, dropping slowly down to kneel at Logan's feet. He waited for the burn of humiliation but all he felt was curiosity to see what Logan would do next. As well as a strange feeling that this is where he was supposed to be.

Logan stroked his finger down clay's cheek. His dark haired lover looked so beautiful, naked in a pose of submission. All the tension Logan had from holding back with Clay was gone. Now his blood raced with anticipation for what would happen between them next. "You know what safe words are?" Clay nodded without looking up. "Good. Choose one." Clay was quiet for a moment before he named it. Logan's lips twitched at his choice. Even now, he still managed to be a smart ass. Logan stepped away to get a few things he needed and laid them on the bed, out of Clay's line of vision. He tossed the condom and lube carelessly on the nightstand then circled back around to stand in front of Clay. "Undress me." Clay reached for his belt but then he hesitated. After a moment, he looked up at Logan.

Clay froze for a second, his breath stuck in his throat. Was he really going to do this? Could he really submit to Logan? Did he *want* to submit to Logan? He met Logan's stare. Logan just waited calmly. Clay knew that Logan wouldn't force him. It would have to be his decision. *He* would have to let go and accept Logan's control. Clay released the breath he'd been holding and unbuckled Logan's belt. After that first step, it was suddenly easier. He opened Logan's jeans and pulled them down his muscular legs along with his boxers. He untied his shoes and pulled the shoes, pants, and underwear completely off. Logan helped him by balancing on one foot at a time. Looking up, he saw Logan's erection tenting against the t-shirt he still wore. Clay wanted to touch it but instinctively knew that wasn't allowed. Instead, he asked, "Can I stand up to take off your shirt?" Logan nodded and Clay stood, amazed that he was already turned on at serving Logan like this. He grasped the hem of the t-shirt and raised it up while Logan bent down. Clay dropped the shirt on the floor, admiring Logan's strong body as he waited for his next command.

Logan brought his hand up to grasp Clay's neck again. That beautiful neck that he couldn't wait to put his collar around. The thought that he would actually be able to collar Clay sent a hot wave of arousal and possessiveness streaking through him for the second time that night. He pulled Clay into a rough kiss, coaxing his mouth open and plunging his tongue inside. He sucked on it, drawing a moan from his lover. When he stopped, Clay was breathing just as hard as he was with his eyes closed and head slightly tilted back to accommodate the hand around his throat. Logan's heart thumped just looking at Clay. He just knew Clay would be the perfect submissive for him.

He walked Clay backwards again until he was up against the bed. "Lay down with your arms over your head." While Clay did as he commanded, Logan picked up the items he'd retrieved from his bag earlier. The cuffs he kept in his hand, the other two items he slid under the pillow, still out of Clay's sight. Logan climbed up on the bed and lay down next to Clay, propping himself up on one elbow. "You're going to be restrained tonight." He held up the cuffs for him to see. Clay's eyes widened slightly but he didn't protest.

Logan grasped his arm, rubbing his thumb over the inside of his wrist. He latched the cuff onto his wrist, a soft sound escaping Clay when the metal clicked closed. He shifted on the bed, his tongue running over his lip once Logan applied the other cuff. Logan bit back a groan at that reaction and continued to attach both sets of cuffs to the headboard. Clay tugged slightly on the cuffs and Logan saw that flash of excitement in his eyes. That pleased him. It looked like restraints were going to be a favorite kink for the both of them.

Logan leaned down and whispered, "You're going to be mine, Clay," before lightly kissing him on the lips. Logan moved to Clay's ear, curling his tongue around the sensitive skin with teasing licks. He repeated his actions on Clay's other ear and felt a slight shiver run through him. Logan trailed light sucking kisses down Clay's neck, nipping at the soft skin. He was so happy he wouldn't have to hold back during their first time together that he had to force himself to go slowly. He moved down to Clay's chest.

Clay had his nipple rings in like he'd been told. Logan had been eager to get his mouth on the silver jewelry ever since Clay removed his shirt. He flicked his tongue against one before pulling both nipple and ring into his mouth and sucking hard. Clay moaned and Logan sucked harder before releasing him. He blew on the hardened nub then quickly sucked the other into his mouth, pulling on the ring with his teeth. Clay moaned again, moving restlessly on the bed. Logan slowly brought his teeth together with the nipple between them. His lover went still in anticipation. He held it there for a moment before he bit down, drawing a soft cry from Clay.

Logan let Clay's flesh go with a wet, sucking pop and looked down. Clay's nipples stood up in hard little peaks, glistening wet from his mouth, the silver rings flashing with every deep breath Clay took. Logan could have played with them for hours but there was so much more he wanted to do to Clay. Scooting down the bed, he rubbed his face against Clay's belly, inhaling deeply. "You smell so good, Clay. I always know when you're near me just by your scent."

Clay's hands twitched in their restraints. He wanted to touch Logan so bad. Not being able to was its own form of torture.

Logan's lips brushed over the thin, sensitive skin of his hips before biting down sharply. Clay cried out, his hands involuntarily yanking on the cuffs that chained him to the bed. He tried to calm down but Logan licked across his groin, coming close to, but not quite, touching his cock as he moved down to suck on his inner thigh. Clay drew one knee up, his hips rising to get closer to what he wanted. Logan slapped him on the thigh and Clay gasped out his name.

Logan moved back up Clay's body and bit him on the lip. "Sir."

Clay gave him a questioning look.

"You will refer to me as Sir."

Clay nodded and Logan bit him again. This time, Clay caught on and responded correctly, "Yes, Sir." His eyes were wide and the pupils so dilated with arousal only the smallest ring of blue surrounded them. Logan smiled down at his lover. "Since you interrupted me, I'll have to start over." Logan laughed to himself as Clay closed his eyes and groaned. Logan repeated his teasing journey down Clay's body. This time, he dragged his tongue across Clay's smoothly shaved balls, but still didn't touch his hard shaft. He wanted to push Clay as close to orgasm as he could then hold him there until *he* decided his lover could have his release.

He shifted to lay between Clay's thighs. Pushing his legs apart, Logan flicked his tongue against his entrance. Clay drew in a sharp breath as a tremor ran through him. But that wasn't enough of a response for Logan. He pushed his tongue into

Clay, loving the way the tight muscles gripped his tongue. As he gently thrust his tongue in and out, beginning the stretch for what was to come, he heard Clay pulling at his restraints, hips moving in time with Logan's tongue. Logan allowed it, wanting to see all of Clay's reactions. He brought his hand to Clay's mouth and brushed two fingers over his lips. Clay immediately sucked them in, getting them nice and wet. When Logan went to pull them out, Clay resisted. Logan quickly bit him hard on the thigh.

Clay's mouth opened as he exclaimed, "Fuck!"

Logan laughed and slowly pushed one of his freed fingers into Clay. God, he was so tight. Logan took his time before adding a second finger. He twisted them back and forth, working to stretch Clay even more before crooking them up to search for that sensitive bundle of nerves. He knew he'd found it when Clay's hips jacked up off the bed, his head thrashing back and forth.

"Is that your spot, baby? Does that feel good?"

"Yes … Yes, Sir." Clay moaned.

Logan decided to give his new sub a reward for remembering to address him correctly. He grasped Clay's cock with his free hand and sucked him down. Clay's thrashing increased, moans and curse words falling over each other as Logan continued to suck. He swallowed down as much as he could, tonguing the underside of Clay's cock, lapping the slit to draw forth his pre-cum. When he felt Clay begin to shake, his cock pulsing in his mouth, Logan stopped. He removed his mouth and his fingers from his lover, watching as Clay writhed and begged. Logan dug his thumb into the crease between Clay's thigh and pelvis.

"Settle down. Now." He watched with approval as Clay struggled to bring himself under control. His hands clenched into fists and his stomach sucked in tight with only the occasional moan escaping from his tightly closed lips.

"Open your eyes and look at me." Logan smiled at the dazed and aroused expression in Clay's eyes as he obeyed. "You are not allowed to come until I say you can. Do you understand?"

Clay started to nod but at Logan's warning look, he relaxed his mouth enough to grit out, "Yes, Sir."

Logan reached under the pillow for one of his toys. It was a vibrator he purchased just for Clay and the perfect size to stretch his lover without hurting him. He held it up to Clay's mouth. "Get it wet," he ordered. Clay's tongue came out and licked at the slender vibrator before he took it into his mouth. Logan's cock twitched as he imagined those lips wrapped around him instead. He removed the vibrator from Clay's mouth and teased it against his ass. Logan slowly pushed the vibrator into him, giving him time to adjust before fucking him slowly with it. Clay started to move again, his hips rolling as Logan picked up the pace. A beautiful sheen of sweat broke out on his tan skin, making his tattoo stand out even more than usual. Logan leaned down and sucked at his neck, getting the taste of that sweat on his tongue. Logan pressed the vibrator up and held it steadily against that sensitive place inside him. Then he sucked Clay's shaft back into his mouth at the same time he flicked on the vibrator. Clay screamed.

13

Clay was in so much ecstasy he couldn't even think straight. Logan had him so aroused he had no control over his own body. He trembled and gasped, hips jerking up frantically. The combination of that vibrator tickling against his prostate while Logan slid his wet mouth up and down his cock had his orgasm so close that his vision blurred and his fingers tingled. He didn't think he could hold on much longer and he managed to gasp out a warning. Logan stopped everything and told him, "Not yet." Clay groaned when he felt Logan's hand sliding down his shaft. Suddenly, his impending orgasm seemed to be restrained yet magnified at the same time. He raised his head from the pillow to look down and saw that Logan had put a cock ring on him. Logan turned the vibrator back on. As the pleasure started to tingle through him again, Clay bit his lip, wondering stupidly if it was possible to die from something feeling too good.

Suddenly Logan's lips were on his, demanding that he kiss him or he'd stop again. Clay kissed his Dom – he had no problem calling him that 'cause *fuck yes* he was being dominated – frantically. Logan turned up the speed on the vibrator. Clay whimpered as he continued to kiss Logan, not even sure if he was breathing anymore. Logan finally released his mouth and turned off the toy. Clay dragged in deep breaths. He didn't realize tears were leaking from his closed eyes until he felt Logan's rough tongue licking them from his face. He wanted to beg Logan to take him but all he could manage to do was moan, "Please," over and over.

Logan pulled the vibrator from his ass. Throwing it aside, he fit their hips together, rubbing their cocks against each other slowly. "Tell me what you want, baby," he asked in a low voice.

Clay's eyes remained closed as he managed to gasp out, "I want you inside me."

Logan kept thrusting. "Is that right?"

Clay nodded, his body tight with tension from forehead to toes.

"Then look at me and ask me properly," Logan commanded.

Clay opened his eyes, feeling as though it was the hardest thing he'd ever had to do. He stared up into Logan's hazel eyes, barely able to comprehend that this controlled yet intensely sexual man lurked beneath the stern leader he saw every day. Remembering what Logan had ordered, Clay searched for the right words that would put an end to this sexual torture. "Logan … Sir. I want you inside me. If that's … if that's what pleases you."

Logan smiled down at him, slow and wicked. "Good boy."

Clay felt a funny tingling lift in his stomach. Why did those two simple words make him feel so … so good? He watched, his heart racing, as Logan rocked back on his heels and rolled the condom down his shaft before he slicked himself up with lube.

Clay couldn't tear his eyes away as Logan lowered himself down on top of him. When Logan pushed inside him, Clay gasped. He saw Logan's eyes flare wide. This moment between them felt like it meant something. Clay knew this wasn't just sex between them. He felt as though he were giving a part of himself to Logan. But all of that flew out of his mind as he focused on the sweet stretch and burn of his lover entering him for the first time. Logan moved again. Clay's eyes drifted closed as he tried to relax and allow Logan all the way into his body.

Logan's jaw was clenched tight as he eased into Clay. Feeling that hot channel wrapped around his cock for the first time had him close to losing control. Logan pushed into Clay inch by inch, watching and listening as soft little whimpers slipped from his lover's lips. Finally, he was balls deep in Clay's ass and he groaned, his head hanging loose on his neck. He looked at Clay and saw he had his head thrown back, mouth open as he panted. Logan lowered himself all the way down until they were pressed chest to chest. He whispered roughly in Clay's ear.

"I'm going to own this ass." He started to thrust. "And you'll give it to me whenever I want like a good little sub, won't you, baby?" He brushed his fingers over Clay's straining shaft, still hard and swollen from his cock ring. "This cock is mine too, Clay. You won't touch it unless I say so, whether I'm with you or not. Do you understand?" Logan deepened his strokes, angling up, searching for his lover's sensitive spot. He knew he found it when Clay cried out.

"Yes, Sir! Whenever ... oh god ... whenever you want. I...I understand."

Logan laughed at that gasping response and started to move quickly, pushing deep. "Wrap your legs around me, baby," he directed. "I want to feel those thighs against me." Clay obeyed and they both groaned, the new position tilting Logan even further inside. When Logan felt his orgasm starting to rise, he didn't even try to hold it back. He was too eager to come while inside his lover for the first time. And with the way Clay's chest was heaving, his body sweating and writhing, Logan knew he would explode if he didn't get to come soon too.

Logan rolled his hips, pumping smoothly. Clay's legs were up and wrapped around him. He loved that, loved laying on top of Clay, controlling his body, feeling those silky legs rubbing against his skin. All of it, every scent and sight and sound of their sex, had his release approaching quickly. He sped up his thrusts as he took off Clay's cock ring. Taking Clay's cock, hard and wet with pre-cum, into his hand, Logan began to stroke. "Come for me, Clay," he commanded. Two more strokes of his fist was all it took to send his lover over the edge. Clay strained against his bonds and a soft scream burst from his lips as his cum spilled over Logan's hand, thick and hot. With Clay's tight walls clamping down on his cock and those thighs squeezing his waist, Logan let himself go. He drove into Clay faster, his lower back tingling and his thighs shaking. He pounded into Clay hard enough to make him scream again. And as Clay's ass squeezed even tighter around his shaft, Logan erupted.

"Fuck!" He surged forward one last time, his hips tight against Clay's as his cock pulsed with his release. He leaned down to kiss his submissive, tonguing him fiercely, wanting to be connected to him as much as possible as he came.

****

The moment the cuffs fell free from his wrists, Clay launched himself at Logan, wrapping his arms around his shoulders and hooking his leg over his hip. He pressed his face into Logan's neck as he trembled uncontrollably. Clay had never felt anything so intense in his life. Now that it was over, his brain was all tripped up and he couldn't stop shaking. Instinctively, he'd turned to Logan for comfort. Logan gave him what he needed, pulling him in tightly and stroking his warm hand down his back. Clay lay there, letting Logan ease him down. His breathing finally returned to normal and his body calmed. But when Logan went to get up, Clay protested. Logan kissed his temple.

"Let me take care of you, baby. I'll be right back, I promise."

Clay let him go and just sprawled bonelessly on the bed, absolutely exhausted. Logan came back quickly with a warm, wet towel and a tall glass of ice water. He wiped the sweat from

Clay's face and chest and the cum off his belly before handing him the water. Clay took it gratefully, amazed at how thirsty he was. He drank half of it down before passing it back to Logan to finish off. That whole experience had been intense, both mentally and physically. He wanted to discuss it with Logan, but he was too drained.

Logan lay back and pulled them both under the covers. He tucked Clay's back against his chest and wrapped a leg around him. "You'll stay with me tonight. No more going home after our nights together," he told Clay. Logan smiled as Clay just mumbled in a sleepy voice, "Okay." Logan reached over and turned off the light.

14

Clay walked into the strategy room the next day. He'd gone home that morning to get ready for work, but he still made it in early enough that hardly anyone was there. Logan was there, of course. He was always the first one in. Tiffany sat in the back with her boots propped up on the table in front of her, drinking something out of an insulated cup. Brady and Hector, their other team sniper, sat off by themselves. No doubt they were talking about sniper tactics. And that was it. Clay rolled the orange he carried in between his palms to loosen up the rind as he walked to the front of room where Logan was. "Hey, Sarge."

Logan looked up from the report he was reading. "Morning, Corporal."

Clay's breath caught. Logan's voice sounded normal, as precise as ever. But his eyes were filled with sexual heat as they ran over him. He shuffled the papers in front of him, his voice lowering to a whisper.

"You were such a good boy last night, Clay."

Clay's breathing quickened and his belly made that funny tingling lift again while his fingers clenched on his orange. He didn't know what it was about Logan telling him he was a good boy, but it made him feel good. Like he'd earned the highest of praise. Logan looked down at the papers he held for a moment before looking back at Clay. It looked like they were just talking about work, but the next words that came out of his mouth were anything but work related.

"It'll be tough for me not to let the details of our relationship out now that I've finally had you the way I want you."

Clay heard more people come in the room behind him. Logan's voice lowered further.

"All I can think about is you cuffed to my bed, naked, and begging for my cock."

Clay stood there, captivated by Logan's voice. Desire pooled low in his belly, thickening his shaft. His fingers flexed on the orange he held.

"I guess I'll just have to show a little … restraint."

Clay was about to squeeze the orange in his hand into a mushy pulp. He swallowed hard, trying to think of something to keep his erection down. Hairy backs. Frog sex. Idiots in movies holding their gun sideways. That did it. Clay took a deep breath and relaxed.

Logan gave him a knowing grin. "Did you need anything else," he asked in a normal tone of voice.

Clay shook his head and turned to go sit down. He sat next to Tiffany. She was clearly holding back a grin. "Where's Carlos?" he asked to get his mind off what had just happened.

"He'll be along." She took a slow sip of her steaming drink. "So, Sarge seems extra cocky today. And your face is red as fire after that display up there. Anything I should know about?"

Clay rubbed a hand over his forehead. "Shit, are we that obvious?"

Tiffany smiled. "Nah. Only if you're looking for it."

Clay just shook his head. He yawned and rubbed his slightly sore wrists. Tiffany watched him.

"Rough night?"

"Yeah. Logan can be a bit demanding. Even more so than in training."

Tiffany tilted her head, her eyes direct on his. "Yeah. Carlos too."

It only took him a second to get the message. Apparently, Carlos and Tiffany had a relationship like his and Logan's. He had a bunch of questions he wanted to ask her, but it wasn't the time. Up front, Logan was calling for everyone to get in their seats.

Tiffany dropped her feet down to the floor. "Just a quick word of advice for you, Clay. If you tease Logan like you did the other night, be prepared to find out just how demanding he can be."

15

Logan relaxed in bed with his back against the headboard. He was in an exceptionally good mood. They'd finished up a week of rotation. They'd served several warrants, all safely and smoothly. Now they were on their time off. But none of that was responsible for Logan's good mood. No, what had him so happy was very simple. He had Clay cradled between his thighs, his back against Logan's chest as they talked. He'd explained what he expected from Clay as his submissive. He didn't expect submission outside the bedroom and he didn't go for the more hardcore side of BDSM. Contracts weren't his thing. For him it was more about the control and after care than any strict rules. Clay had lots of questions and Logan answered all of them honestly. Most of them were expected but some made him laugh, like Clay asking if he would ever have to bark like a dog. Logan wasn't sure where he'd gotten that from.

The whole time they talked, Logan couldn't stop touching Clay. He stroked his lover's arms. He caressed the soft skin of his belly. He pressed kisses on his shoulders. And again and again, his hands rose to Clay's neck. His fingers circled his throat, sometimes lightly and sometimes with the slightest bit of pressure. Each time he did it, Clay reacted, whether it was with a slight shiver, or his back pressing tighter against him, or a restless shift of his hips. Clay probably didn't realize what Logan was doing or that his reactions signified Logan was claiming him and that he liked and accepted it. But Logan knew. It took a lot of trust to allow someone to have their hands at your throat. And Clay was not only allowing it but reacting in a way that told Logan everything he needed to know about how his lover felt.

Logan was definitely pleased. He didn't just want to play with Clay. He wanted to claim him as his own, to put his collar on his lover so Clay would know who he belonged to. He'd played with plenty of subs before but none had earned his collar. He'd never felt the urge to claim a sub as his own like he did with Clay. Still, as badly as he wanted it, he knew he would have to exercise a little patience. His lover was new to this and would need some time before Logan claimed him like that. Plus, their relationship was still in its beginnings. So he would wait.

Clay had so many questions for Logan that he felt like a little kid pestering his parents to know why the sky was blue. How long had he been a Dom? How did he even know he was one? Did he ever wear leather chaps? But he couldn't help it. Fucking Sergeant Logan Pierce, clean cut, somber and stern SWAT team leader was into bondage and domination, and apparently had been since returning from Iraq. He would have never suspected. "So how am I supposed to behave in public around you now?"

"The same as always – like a complete smart ass."

Clay laughed.

"In public, we're Sergeant Pierce and Corporal Foster, two members of HPD SWAT. If we ever decide that we want to, we can come out at work, together. But the fact that I'm your Dom and you're my sub…"

Logan's fingers wrapped around his throat again and Clay shivered.

"That will always be private. Well, maybe a select few will know."

"Like Carlos and Tiffany?"

Logan chuckled. "You figured that out already, huh?"

"Kinda. Tiffany clued me in. But I would have figured it out now that I'm in the know."

Logan gave him a squeeze. "Because you're so smart. Actually Carlos introduced me to BDSM. It helped me deal when I came home from Iraq."

"What do you mean," Clay asked.

Logan dropped a kiss on his shoulder. "I'll tell you about that some other time."

Clay let the matter drop. "So who else on the force is into this?" Logan gave him a few names, some of which surprised him, and some that didn't. "Frank, huh? Gotta say I'm not too shocked he's a Dom."

Logan laughed. "Actually, he's a submissive."

Clay turned and looked at Logan over his shoulder. "Seriously?" He hadn't expected someone like Frank to be named as a sub. Frank Larson was an older, hard-nosed cop whom he'd never seen laugh.

Logan nodded, his eyes showing amusement at Clay's dumbfounded expression. "Where a person falls with their dominant or submissive traits doesn't always reflect the way they are in other aspects of their life." Logan nuzzled his neck. "You're a perfect example of that."

That brought up something that had been on his mind from the moment Logan said he was a Dominant. "How did you know that I would be submissive?"

"I didn't at first. I just knew that I wanted you." Logan nipped at his ear then lightly stroked the bite with his tongue. "I wanted you for a long time and once I had the chance to make you mine I hoped that you would submit to me. So I tested you a few times to get your reaction."

Clay's breathing quickened as he remembered Logan telling him to keep his hips still or his hands above his head and a number of other things he'd said. He knew now they'd been orders … and he'd followed every one of them. A small part of him was a little bothered by that.

"You did so well, submitting to me every time we were in bed together."

When Logan's voice deepened and his big hand started to stroke a little harder across his stomach, Clay realized Logan was getting turned on too.

"I planned to give you more time, because I still wasn't sure you'd want to get into the BDSM scene, but I wanted to own you so fucking bad I couldn't wait any more."

Clay stilled. "Own me?"

Logan lifted his mouth from where he'd been kissing Clay's neck. Shit, he hadn't meant to say that. "Yeah. When a Dom decides to take a sub as his own, he collars him. It's a sign of ownership, letting every other Dom know that sub is someone's property. It's also a sign of a deep connection between a Dom and his sub." He stroked his thumb across the pulse beating in Clay's neck. "A sub acknowledges his acceptance of his Master's dominance and a Dom knows the sub belongs only to him." *His to dominate, cherish, and protect*, Logan finished to himself.

Clay turned over in his arms, sprawling across his legs and looking up at him.

"And have you ever collared anyone?"

Logan looked directly back at Clay. "No. Not yet." Clay lowered his lashes, his head bowing slightly. Logan's heart beat harder, his blood running thick and hot. Christ, even that small sign of Clay's submission excited him, made him want to exert his dominance over his lover. And Clay did it naturally, not knowing what it did to Logan. Clay spoke quietly as Logan trailed his fingers along the waistband of his boxers.

"I overhead Carlos once, telling you to just collar me and be done with it." Those clear blue eyes rose back to Logan's. "I didn't know what he meant then." He smiled slightly. "I thought he was comparing me to a dog or something."

Logan brushed his thumb over Clay's lips. "But now you know."

Clay nodded, his tongue coming out to lick at Logan's thumb. "Now I know." Clay was silent a moment before he spoke again. "Sir?"

Logan cock's immediately hardened from hearing that word from Clay. "Yeah, baby?"

"Do you think you could test me again?"

Logan smiled, already reaching for Clay's wrists.

16

They were working a fairly quiet day shift. They'd served a rare daytime warrant early that morning and spent the rest of the day catching up on paperwork and going over tactics. Logan looked through his open door and saw Clay go down the hall into the storage room. He looked around and didn't see anyone near or watching so he got up and went to the storage room.

Clay was reaching over his head to get a pack of computer paper off a shelf. He turned around when Logan closed the door behind him.

Clay looked at him with one eyebrow raised. "What are you doing?"

Logan leaned against the door, knowing his weight would keep anyone from easily opening it. "I haven't touched you all day."

A small smile curled the corners of those full lips. "That's not true. You touched me when you knocked me out of the way of that guy's crazy dog charging at me."

"Let me clarify then. I haven't touched you the way I want to." He crooked his finger at his sub. "So get over here and let me touch you."

Clay's lashes lowered and he slowly made his way over to Logan. He stopped just within Logan's reach. Logan settled his hand at the small of Clay's back and pulled him closer until their bodies met from chest to thigh. He ran his hand up Clay's back, feeling the heat of his body underneath his t-shirt. He wanted to pull the material up so he could get to the supple skin beneath but he knew that was risky. They might have to leave the closet suddenly. So he settled for touching the skin that was already bare to him.

Logan grasped Clay by the back of the neck, stroking a thumb over the velvety skin behind his ear. He leaned down and lightly touched their lips together. Clay pressed closer, kissing him back. Logan groaned and tightened his grip on his sub's neck. He deepened their kiss, stroking his tongue inside Clay's mouth to play and tangle with his. Clay rubbed against his chest until that beautiful little sigh escaped him. At that sound, Logan hauled him up even closer, their hands all over each other, their breaths coming fast as they kissed wildly. He forgot his earlier decision to not disrupt their clothes, yanking Clay's t-shirt out of his pants and roughly kneading the smooth flesh of his back.

It was like he jinxed their private moment together because immediately afterwards, their phones chimed almost simultaneously. There was no doubt it was a call from dispatch. All of their phones had dispatch set to the same ring tone so they'd know immediately when they were getting a call out. Logan cursed. "Fuck." He tucked Clay's shirt back in and dropped his arms from around him.

"We've got forty minutes. Get to the strategy room as soon as you calm down."

Clay nodded, his eyes wide and his cheeks flushed with arousal. Logan cursed again, silently this time. He definitely did not want to leave his sub just then. But they had a job to do. He checked to make sure the hall was clear then left the closet.

****

Their team spread out around the small house. They'd pulled up ten minutes earlier in the Bearcat – the armored truck that transported their team. Support staff already set up a perimeter and their hostage negotiator was reaching out over the loudspeaker. So far, he was being ignored.

It was a tricky operation. They had a guy barricaded inside his ex-girlfriend's house and there were kids inside. Three of them. But they only had eyes on one. There was a scared looking girl in the living room with her mother and the gunman. As always, their top priority was saving the hostages. Logan looked at Clay and Q. He gave them the go ahead to scope out the house and try to get in unobserved, if they could. After a tense wait, he got a quiet voice over the radio.

"We found the other two kids. The fucker tied them up and left them up in the bedroom, terrified."

"Get 'em out of there. We've still got eyes on everyone else. Check back in and let us know if there's anyone else in the house."

"Roger that."

His earpiece went quiet again. Logan looked at his team members, making sure everyone was in place. They had three entry points. The front door, which was blocked by a heavy looking chair, the living room window, and the back door. He signaled for his team to remain still while their negotiator tried to talk the gunman out of the house.

Logan saw Clay and Q run across the lawn in a low crouch, each with a kid under their arm. Two members of the support team ran up and got the kids away safely, allowing his scouts to get back into the game.

Inside, the gunman pointed the gun at the little girl and started shouting. "Stop crying! Stop fucking crying!"

Logan tensed even more. They didn't want to rush it and force a gun fight. But things were escalating beyond a holding pattern.

The gunman turned his gun towards the ceiling and shouted, "I hate you fucking kids!" He pumped off several shots into the ceiling.

Logan gave the order to go. Once he was shooting, it'd be too easy for him to turn the weapon on the woman or kid. They swarmed the house with Logan taking the front. He swung the heavy breacher back and slammed it into the door. The wood splintered and the chair flew forward. Mike was to his left and kicked the rest of the debris out of the way to go in first. They filed inside with Carlos and his group coming in from the back. It was organized chaos to his team, but loud, screaming terror to the hostages and gunman. Thankfully, the woman had enough sense to dive for her kid and drop to the ground.

The gunman had a split second to make the right decision, to drop the gun and put his hands up. He didn't do it. Logan's well-trained team didn't hesitate. Two of them popped off rounds. The gunman's head jerked back, his arms flying out to the side. Blood sprayed and the woman screamed. Almost in slow motion, his body crumpled to the ground. The gun clattered to the floor as he dropped and Logan moved forward to kick it away.

"Clear the house," Logan ordered. There weren't any reports of anyone else in the house but they had to be sure. His team fanned out to check the rest of the place. Logan stayed put as the unis came in to take care of the hostages and the EMTs arrived to see to the gunmen. They didn't rush. It was obvious he didn't need anything but the coroner.

****

They were all back in the Bear. Everyone was safe and accounted for so he could let his guard down. But he still had that adrenaline pumping through his system. He looked at Clay and saw he was feeling the same. Clay looked up and caught his eye. They stared at each other as Clay took a deep breath, releasing it slowly. Heat spread throughout Logan's entire body. That adrenaline was now mixed with the lust from their interrupted tryst earlier. Now all he could think about was continuing where they had left off. Logan knew the exact moment Clay caught what he was thinking. He dropped his eyes, a flush creeping up his neck. Logan looked away, not wanting them to give anything away to the rest of the team. But his eyes kept returning to his lover again and again, watching him sit there quietly. Logan could read his desire and need so easily and he fought to hold back his response.

The rest of their team joked and laughed around them as they came down from their rush, dealing with the aftermath of a death the best they could. But the tension between him and Clay continued to climb until he was wound so fucking tight he had to clench his fists to keep from reaching out and dragging Clay into his lap.

The Bear finally slowed to a halt in front of the station and everyone piled out the back. Logan slapped their driver, Tom, on the shoulder. "Thanks for the ride."

Tom reached back to shake his hand. "Any time. Sorry you guys had to put that guy down."

Logan accepted the handshake. None of them liked killing a suspect. He got out of the truck and followed his team inside. He needed to be alone with Clay. Soon.

17

Gear down and go home. After Action Reviews can wait. Expect me to check in on all of you." He wanted to give his team time to calm. Killing a suspect was never easy for any of them. He looked at Max and Alfonso, the two who'd fired on the suspect. "Guys, you know what to do." Both of them said, "*Yes, Sarge.*" They would have to check their weapons and make an appointment with the department psychiatrist.

Taking off his helmet, he headed into his office. He settled at his desk to get a jump on his own AAR. About twenty minutes had passed when his door opened. He looked up to see Clay was standing in the door way. He set his pen down. "Everyone else?"

Clay came into his office and closed the door behind him. "Gone."

Logan could sense the tension in his sub. Could read it in the way he held himself. He got up slowly. "Lock the door." Clay obeyed him and Logan went to him. "Are you okay?"

Clay darted his tongue over his bottom lip. "I'm okay. I just need…"

He trailed off but Logan knew what he meant. He needed to get that energy out of him. And whether he knew it or not, he needed contact with his Dom. "You did good today. Got those kids out safe."

Clay nodded. "Thank you."

Logan cupped Clay's cheek, sliding his fingers into the silky hair at his temple. He kissed Clay lightly, just barely touching their lips together. But the second he did, Clay opened up for him with a shaky gasp. Logan plunged his tongue into the sweet mouth beneath his, Clay's hands coming up to rest against his shoulders. Logan grasped his wrists and pulled them off him. Clay made a noise of protest but he quieted when Logan bit him sharply on the lip. He pressed Clay's hands to the door above his head. Clay moaned, his hips arching up and pressing against him. Logan loved that response. He loved to see how much his submissive enjoyed being restrained by him. He switched to holding his wrists with one hand so he could have the other free.

Their kiss went on, deep and hot with Clay moaning and panting into his mouth. Logan opened Clay's pants, pushing his hand inside to grasp his erection. Clay cried out, his hips jerking forward while his back pressed hard against the door. Logan stroked him slow and steady, trailing his lips up to his ear. "Is this what you need, baby?"

"Yes. Yes, Sir."

"You need me, don't you?"

Clay nodded, his hair brushing against his cheek as he did. Logan pulled back. "Look at me and tell me that."

Clay met his eyes. "I need you, Sir."

Logan kissed his sub again, pumping him swiftly. Clay was gasping and shaking, his hips curling up to meet Logan's fist again and again.

"Sir, please. I'm close."

Logan knew his sub wasn't practiced at holding back his orgasm on his own just yet. He needed to learn … and Logan enjoyed teaching him. He stopped stroking him and squeezed his fist around his shaft. "Not yet, baby." Clay groaned but didn't object. Logan eased up, brushing his lips against Clay's and caressing the silky wet head of his cock with his thumb in soft circles. Clay's body was still strung tight, but his breathing slowed. Logan smiled, pleased with his control. "Good boy. That's what I want to see."

Clay bit his lip. "Thank you, Sir."

He slowly worked his lover back to the edge again, stroking him tight and fast. In no time, Clay was straining against his hold. "Now, baby. Come for me now." Logan kissed him, sucking his cry into his mouth to keep anyone who might be near from hearing. Clay's hips pumped, his body shuddering as he released in to Logan's hand in hot pulses.

Logan released Clay's wrists. Clay's arms wrapped around his back, holding him tight. Logan returned the embrace, holding his sub until he was calm, his breathing slow and normal. Logan pressed a soft kiss to Clay's neck before stepping away to get some tissue from his desk. When he returned, Clay looked at him as though he were trying to figure something out.

"You make me feel better," he said.

Logan smiled and cleaned them up. "Good. That's what I want to do for you."

"Do I get to make you feel better?"

"You will. As soon as we get back to my place."

18

A few hours later they were at Logan's house. They were dressed to go to the pool in his subdivision, but Logan wasn't going down until he found his sunscreen. Unlike Clay, he was more likely to burn than tan. He heard Clay shout from the bathroom.

"Found it!"

Clay came over with the bottle of SPF 50 in his hand. "Now you won't be all red and peeling." He gestured with the bottle, wordlessly asking if it was okay for him to apply it. Logan nodded and Clay poured some in his hand before quickly rubbing it into Logan's back. Clay continued talking.

"Which is a good thing because I doubt if the team would respect you enough to quit their bitching if you were all twitchy and itchy, trying to get at the burnt and peeling skin under your vest."

Logan laughed as Clay came around to his front. "That's disgusting. You're—"

"A smart ass, albeit an endearing and handsome one?"

Logan raised an eyebrow. "Albeit?"

Clay smiled. "What? I went to school and learned some stuff."

Logan rolled his eyes. Clay was a smart ass. It was a big a part of what had attracted Logan to him in the first place. Logan wasn't known for goofing around and teasing and he admired that in his boyfriend. Logan noticed that Clay had grown quiet as he applied the sunscreen to his front. He didn't seem to be in such a hurry anymore either, taking time to make sure the lotion was smoothed onto every inch of his skin. Clay's hands rubbed slowly across his shoulders, to his chest, and down to his stomach. His fingers teased at the waist band of Logan's swim shorts, his breath coming a little faster. Clay lifted his eyes to Logan's, biting his lip. Logan didn't say anything. He just waited to see what his sub would do.

Clay's throat was suddenly tight, making it a little hard for him to speak. "I'd better get your legs too." Without being told, Clay drifted down to his knees at Logan's feet. As he knelt there with his head bowed, the strangest and most intense feelings washed over him. His hands shook slightly as he worked the sun block into Logan's skin, caressing his legs long past the time necessary to make sure he was covered. But he wanted to keep touching Logan, he needed to. He felt as though he wanted to be as close to Logan as possible, to somehow crawl inside of him until he was a part of the bigger man.

Clay didn't know where the emotion was coming from. One minute he'd been joking as he covered Logan's pale skin in sun block. The next minute it felt less like a favor and more like he was serving his Dom. As he ran his palms over those hard muscles, he started to get turned on, which made sense. Logan was fucking gorgeous and his body made Clay want to just stop and stare. But Clay also started to feel like this is what he should be doing for him, that it was his place to make Logan feel good. And when he'd gone to his knees, just like their first night together, he felt like he was where he belonged. He felt like his only thought should be to please Logan. But fuck! *Why* did he feel like that? How could that be normal for one person to feel towards another? Confused and aroused, Clay looked up at the man standing above him. Clay didn't know why but he expected, no, he trusted, Logan to help him understand what he was feeling.

Logan looked down at Clay and watched as all those emotions crossed that beautiful face. He understood. He could tell that, for the first time, Clay was experiencing much, much more than just the physical side of his submission, and he was confused by it. It was his job as Clay's Dom to help him get through it. Untying his swim shorts, he pushed them down and off. He wrapped his hand around his own cock, already full and hard from having his lover's hands on him. His voice was low and thick with desire as he asked. "Is this what you want?" Clay nodded slowly. But Logan wanted more from Clay. He wanted to draw forth what Clay was feeling to help him acknowledge and accept it. "Why do you want it?"

Clay's lips parted wordlessly in response to Logan's question. What was Logan asking him? "Because I want to taste you."

Logan didn't say anything, he just started stroking himself slowly, his eyes steady on Clay's as he clearly waited for a different answer. Clay's palms tingled, wanting to touch that hard flesh himself. "Because ..." His voice drifted off as he tried to think. But he couldn't! He was so mixed up and a little freaked out and he'd never felt that way before. He just couldn't think. Logan's other hand brushed through his hair.

"Tell me. Don't think. Just tell me."

Clay felt like he always did when he was about to go into a hot situation. His heart pounded with frantic anticipation for what was about to happen. He hovered there, not sure if what he was about to say was the right thing. Clay closed his eyes for a moment before he spoke, feeling like he was dropping into a fire fight, trusting Logan to have his back.

"I want what you want. I want to please you, Sir. Let me..." Clay took a deep breath his chest expanding as he held it. When he exhaled, he accepted his submission like he hadn't before. "Let me please you." Clay caught a look of possession and something else he didn't recognize darkening Logan's hazel eyes before it was quickly gone.

"Good boy. That's what I wanted to hear."

Clay closed his eyes, his head dropping until his chin hit his chest. Those words on top of the way he was already feeling, were too much. He just couldn't take it. But Logan's hand on his chin lifted his face back up.

"Open up, baby," Logan whispered.

Clay obeyed and Logan's hard shaft slid into his mouth. Both of Logan's hands came up to cradle his head, but they didn't push him or even guide him. Logan let him set the pace as he sucked his Dom's cock. Clay took him deep, sliding his mouth down Logan's shaft, inhaling his clean scent as he breathed through his nose. Pulling back, he lapped at the broad head, tonguing the sensitive spot where it met the shaft. He sucked slow, soft kisses along the throbbing vein that ran down the hard flesh until he reached Logan's tight sac. A rough groan told him his Dom liked that so he did it again as he worked his way back up his shaft. When he reached the head, he tightened his lips around it, sucking hard to draw forth his pre-cum, savoring it with a moan when it hit his tongue.

Clay went back to sucking the entire shaft, again experiencing that feeling that it was his place to serve Logan. His belly trembled and he had the crazy thought that he would do this for as long as Logan wanted him to. He saw Logan's stomach clench and felt his cock pulse in his mouth. Clay moaned and braced his palms on those strong thighs as he started to suck faster, his own cock hard and aching for attention. Suddenly, Logan pulled himself out of Clay's mouth and stepped back. Breathing hard, feeling like he'd been denied something he desperately wanted, Clay reached out for him. But Logan stepped back again.

"Go stand in front of the bed."

Clay quickly did as he was told, his skin flushed, his head buzzing, still slightly thrown by what he'd admitted to Logan. He heard rustling and foil being torn then he felt Logan's body heat as he came up behind him. Logan's big hands came around and untied the drawstring of his swim shorts before pushing them down his legs. He stepped out and kicked them to the side. Logan caressed his back softly.

"It's okay," he whispered. Logan's hand closed around his throat, pulling him back against his chest. "Everything you're feeling. It's normal, baby. Don't fight it." Logan grasped his chin and turned his face to his so they could kiss.

As Clay kissed him back, he was relieved to know that he wasn't going fucking crazy. The desire to be a part of Logan and to please him had taken him to the point where he could barely think of anything else. Logan broke their kiss.

"Bend over and put your hands on the bed."

Clay complied immediately, already anticipating having Logan inside him. He had a moment's surprise when Logan began pushing inside him after only minimal preparation instead of taking his time like he usually did. But Clay just relaxed and let him in. If this is how Logan, how his *Dominant*, wanted it, then that's what he would get. The sweet burn as that thick cock slid inside him was stronger without having been stretched first, but he loved it.

A deep rumbling groan came from Logan as his length reached all the way inside Clay. Logan held tight in him, unmoving for long moments. Clay shook as he fought not to move as well. Logan's hand stroked up his back until he reached his shoulders and pressed down. Clay followed the pressure of that hand until he was bent with the side of his face pressed into the mattress, his arms stretched forward, and his ass in the air. Logan kicked against his legs until he opened them, spreading himself wide. Clay's heart was racing. He felt completely owned by the man behind him. He was open and vulnerable to whatever his Dom wanted to do to him and he *liked* it.

Logan squeezed and rubbed his ass while he spoke in that low voice Clay was starting to love. "Don't think about anything but how good it feels to submit to me, Clay." He slid his cock almost all the way out only to slam back in. "You'll know as I'm inside you that you're here for *my* pleasure. Pleasing me is what matters."

Clay moaned at Logan's words and at the feeling of him again slamming into him. Logan sped up his thrusts, never easing back on the strength with which he powered into Clay.

"You'll crave me, Clay."

Clay gripped the comforter in his fists as Logan pounded into him again and again. He was right. It felt incredibly good to just submit and let his Dominant take him as he pleased. Logan started hitting that delicious spot inside him with every thrust, holding his cock in a tight grip. The motion of their bodies sent his shaft sliding back and forth in Logan's fist. Clay's stomach clenched and his balls tightened with his approaching orgasm. "Sir, I'm about to … fuck! I'm about to come."

Logan wrapped his thumb and middle finger tightly around the base of Clay's cock. "Don't. Hold it for me, baby. You can do it."

Clay bit his lip, gripping the comforter even harder as he fought to hold back his orgasm. He was panting, his skin tingled, and the urge to come was almost unbearable with

Logan's hips pumping into him at a furious pace. A part of his brain screamed to just let go but another part told him to wait and do as ordered. His decision was made when Logan spoke.

"You're such a good boy, holding back for your Dom."

Clay moaned. He would do anything to hear that praise from Logan.

"You want to submit to me, Clay, don't you? You like letting me control you?"

Clay nodded his head jerkily. "Yes, Sir." Logan took his hand off Clay's cock and he immediately felt his cum start to rise up his shaft. He pressed his face into the comforter and screamed with the effort to hold it back. He heard Logan talking again when he quieted.

"Say it. Say that you want to submit to me."

Clay shook his head frantically. If he pulled his face from the covers, he would lose it and come, disappointing his Dom, he knew it.

Logan slowed his thrusts. "Say it right now or I'll pull out and jack off all over your back. Then I'll cuff you to this bed to make sure you can't get yourself off then leave you like that all night."

Clay groaned. His cock was so stiff there was no way he could go all night without an orgasm. He dragged his face from the covers, but before he could speak, Logan pulled out of him. Clay cried out, thinking Logan was about to leave him. But Logan only pushed him up further on the bed, turning him onto his back. He followed him onto the bed to slide partway back into him as he waited for his reply.

Clay didn't dare wait any longer to tell Logan what he'd asked to hear. He looked up into Logan's hazel eyes, blazing almost gold in his passion. "I want to submit to you, Sir. I ... I *need* to submit to you." He writhed on the bed uncontrollably as Logan started moving between his legs, pushing hard, reaching deep. "God ... *fuck* ... I'm supposed to. I *have* to," he managed to get out. Logan's big hand gripped his cock once more and started stroking.

"That's right, baby. That's how you should feel."

Logan leaned down and took Clay's mouth in a fierce kiss. Clay was on Logan overload. Logan's thick cock rammed into his ass again and again, his tongue was in his mouth, their sweat slick chests rubbed together, and Logan's hand squeezed and pumped him perfectly. When Logan whispered against his lips for him to come with him, Clay's response was immediate. His cum shot up his cock and erupted all over his stomach, covering Logan's hand as he continued to stroke. Clay moaned into Logan's mouth. His climax felt so good and seemed to keep going and going until he was lightheaded.

When he finally came down, he noticed he'd wrapped his arms and legs around Logan, holding him tight as his Dom came inside him. Clay protested when Logan pulled out to throw away the condom.

"It's okay. I'm right here."

Logan pulled his lover into his arms and Clay tucked his face into his neck. Again, Logan soothed him as he shook with the aftermath. Logan rubbed his back as he whispered in his ear,

"You did good, baby. I'm so proud of you for letting go like that."

Clay nodded against his skin, not speaking. Logan couldn't believe how lucky he was. Clay's submission was so deep and strong. And the way he turned to him to be calmed pleased Logan so much. He wanted to claim Clay as his own right then. He had a feeling he wouldn't wait much longer to place his collar on Clay's beautiful neck. In fact, he was going to be making a call as soon as he had a moment alone. Logan took a deep breath, inhaling Clay's wonderful scent, the intoxicating smell of the sex they'd just had … and sunscreen. Reminded of how this had all gotten started, he looked and saw that Clay was calm. And although he wanted to do things to get him all worked up again, he didn't. He wanted to make sure his submissive was happy both in and out of the bed.

"Do you still want to go to the pool?" After a long moment, Clay nodded. "Okay, then. Get up and get your shorts back on. Let's go, Corporal!"

Clay disentangled their limbs and flopped onto his back. Logan held back a grin at the baleful glare on Clay's face.

"You do all the work and you're still full of energy? What are you, Super Dom or something?"

Logan smiled. "Nah. I'm too manly to run around in little red tights."

19

The rest of the week they'd worked with Narcotics on several buy and busts. And of course the bread and butter of their trade, high-risk warrants. This week they'd rotated from being out in the field to training.

They were in what they called the school house, going over the process of restraining a suspect. This room was set up much like where they worked out their operations. But there were fewer chairs and tables to leave space for demonstrations. SWAT Instructor Sergeant Reed Mitchell was up front. He held out a pair of cuffs and asked for a volunteer. Somebody bitched from the back.

"C'mon, Sergeant Mitchell. Why do we have to go over this? We all know how to restrain an assailant. Besides, half the time it's the unis who cuff 'em anyway."

Logan came into the room at that moment. "Do I hear complaining?"

Everyone in the room straightened up. The complainer answered Logan's question. "No, sir."

Logan swept the room with a hard look. "I didn't think so. We practice everything. It's what makes us the best. And it's what keeps us alive. Everyone is at risk if any of us gets sloppy and lets a suspect wrestle a gun away."

Clay raised his hand to get Mitchell's attention. "I'll be your bad guy." He got up and walked to the front of the room, stopping when he was almost right in front of Logan. A mischievous little devil prodded him to hold his hands out to Logan. "Cuff me," he said with a smirk. He saw Logan swallow hard but he didn't move.

Mitchell came over to him. "Put your hands behind your back, Foster. What's wrong with you?"

He looked at Mitchell. "Perps aren't always just gonna put their hands behind their back for us."

"You're right."

Mitchell went through the motions of getting him cuffed and down on his knees. Once he was kneeling, he looked up at Logan who was still standing in front of him. His question was directed to Mitchell, but he knew Logan would realize it was meant for him.

"So am I a docile and *submissive* criminal? Or am I making you work for it?" Clay saw a flash of heat in his Dom's eyes at his veiled taunt before it was quickly hidden by his normal stern expression.

Reed answered him. "Keep it calm for now. You can go crazy after this."

Clay smiled at Logan. He knew he was playing with fire, but he couldn't help it. He liked to play. And he wanted to push Logan's buttons. He wanted to find out what would happen if he were a little rebellious. Clay figured he'd done enough to get Logan as worked up as he could without becoming obvious to everyone else in the room. Mitchell had him pretend to be someone who didn't want to accept the cuffs so he could demonstrate how to get them on safely both for SWAT and the suspect. He gave his attention fully to Mitchell and went through the exercise. But the entire time, he felt Logan's eyes on him, watching his every move.

****

Logan let Clay into his house. He kept thinking of how Clay had teased him earlier. Naturally, he had to punish his sub for his behavior. And, naturally, he was excited to do it. Before he let Clay know that he was a Dom, he'd held himself back whenever Clay teased him like that time in the bar. But now … Now he didn't have to hold back. His sub would have to accept his punishment like a good boy for teasing his Dom. Anticipation and arousal roughened his voice.

"You shouldn't have teased me like that."

Clay turned around. "*What?*" He drew the word out in exaggerated surprise.

Logan stalked over to him. "Don't even try to play dumb. Asking me to cuff you in front of everyone. You knew what that would do to me." He stopped in front of Clay as he stood there watching Logan with wide eyes. Logan grasped his throat in a firm hold. "Getting on your knees like that in public."

Clay didn't move. He just stared back, a warm flush already tinting his cheekbones. Logan stepped closer to his lover, getting into his space and trapping him against the wall. "For teasing me like that, I have to punish you. You will learn that there are consequences for your actions. Do you understand?" He waited for the dark head to nod before he spoke again.

"Get upstairs into the bedroom." Logan let him go so he could walk upstairs, but he followed close behind Clay. Once they were in his bedroom, he shut the door behind them. Clay was standing next to the bed. Logan crowded against him, trapping him between his body and the mattress.

"Strip. Now."

Clay gestured as though he wanted Logan to back up. When he only narrowed his eyes and didn't move, Clay swallowed hard. He pulled his shirt over his head, his arms brushing against Logan as he did so. He toed off his shoes then stood there with his hands on the waistband of his shorts. He looked at Logan for only a moment before he lowered his eyes and pushed down his shorts and briefs.

"Go stand with your hands braced over your head on that wall." He pointed where he wanted Clay to go, but still didn't step back, forcing Clay to ease his way around him. He heard him suck in a sharp breath as their bodies briefly came into contact.

Logan followed Clay across the room to where he stood as directed. His long body was stretched out, round ass thrust back and exposed, just like Logan wanted. He unbuckled his belt and pulled it from the loops on his jeans.

"Tonight you've earned a spanking with my belt. Ten strokes, baby." A shiver ran down Clay's back. Logan didn't think Clay would need it, but he reminded him anyway.

"Remember, if anything is more than you can take, say your safe word." This was Clay's first punishment and Logan wanted him to know he had a way out and could trust him. Clay nodded in acknowledgement.

Logan cracked his belt sharply across Clay's ass twice in a row. Clay hissed, his back arching slightly. But he didn't move his hands from the wall or ask Logan to stop. Logan lowered the belt and stepped closer to his sub. He rubbed his hand where he just spanked, petting his ass slowly before squeezing the firm flesh. Clay remained quiet. Logan stepped back and gave him another stroke. This time, when he rubbed Clay's ass, he let a finger slip between his cheeks, teasing at his entrance. He noticed Clay's hips move just a bit in reaction. Again he stepped back, snapping the belt forward for two quick strikes. Clay cried out when the belt cracked against his ass for the fifth time.

Clay's cheeks turned a delicious shade of red. Logan dropped the belt for a moment so he could cup that sweet bottom with both hands. He rubbed his palms across the soft skin, feeling it hot to his touch. Clay gasped, his hips jerking back. Logan knew the mix of pleasure and pain from rubbing his palms over the stinging skin was responsible for that reaction. And he was glad to see it. He wanted to push his sub into experiencing just as much pleasure as he did pain from the punishment. Logan sucked a finger into his mouth then eased it inside Clay's tight heat. He thrust slowly while he lowered his head to Clay's neck and ran his tongue up that slightly salty skin. He sucked at Clay's nape, loving the taste of his sweaty skin on his tongue. When Clay started moaning and moving his hips in time to his finger in his ass, Logan added a second. He twisted them, pumping a little faster. A shudder went through his lover as Logan bit down on his neck before finally releasing him. He looked and saw a deep purplish bruise already rising on Clay's skin. Clay gave a protesting cry as Logan pulled his fingers from his ass and stepped back.

"You're halfway there, baby." Picking up the belt, he slapped it across Clay's reddened cheeks. He waited long moments before doing it again. And again he waited, watching Clay's hands ball into fists against the wall, his shoulders rising and falling with each heaving breath. Finally Clay's ass thrust backwards, seeking the belt. Logan heard him moan softly.

"Sir, please …"

Logan spanked him again, the eighth lash harder than all the previous. Clay cried out sharply, his hips pumping and circling at the air in front of him. Logan had to reach into his jeans and adjust himself. He was unbelievably hard from watching his sub take his first punishment, not only without a word of protest but gaining pleasure from it as well. He knew without a doubt that no other man was as perfect for him as Clay. Logan had two lashes left to give, but he felt the need to touch his beautiful submissive first, so he lowered the belt again.

Logan pressed his body up against Clay's. He ran his hand across his soft stomach, feeling the muscles there twitch under his touch. Trailing his hand down to Clay's cock, he found him already hard, pre-cum beading on the tip. Logan took him in hand and pumped slowly. He whispered in his ear. "Look at you. Cock all hard and wet. You like my belt across your ass, don't you?" Clay moaned and nodded. "Tell me you're sorry for teasing me. And beg me to finish your punishment."

Clay's nerves were tingling, making his skin buzz with electric anticipation as he waited each time for the belt to fall. Each time it struck his ass, the initial burning pain morphed into a dark pleasure that had him gritting his teeth, begging Logan to take him or to at least stroke off his hard cock. Clay wouldn't have ever thought he'd be turned on by someone spanking him. But he was so fucking hard and turned on, possibly more than ever before. He knew it was all because of the man behind him, showing him what he needed. What he hadn't even known he'd needed.

"Sir, I'm sorry for teasing you like that tonight." Clay gave his apology freely. He'd earned this by teasing his Dom and felt it was fitting to offer his body to be punished. "Please, please give me the rest of my punishment. I *need* you to punish me." By the end of his sentence, his voice had dropped to a pleading moan, and his hips were moving in anticipation of the belt. Logan gave him another command.

"Stop moving. I want you to stay completely still for your last two lashes."

Clay groaned. He started to drop his head against the wall but caught himself. He wasn't sure if Logan would count that as a movement or not. He braced himself, clenching his stomach and thigh muscles tight. When the ninth lash fell, he bit his lip but remained still. He waited for the tenth lash to come. But Logan was still and quiet behind him. So he waited.

He waited and waited until the building anticipation had his blood rushing in his ears and his heart thundering so hard he felt it in his throat. Finally, when he was about to scream from the tension, the belt cracked across his ass so sharply that his cock jerked in response. He stood there gasping for breath after the strike, still not daring to move until Logan gave him permission. Logan come up behind him and rubbed his sore and stinging butt.

"You did very good taking that part of your punishment."

Clay looked over his shoulder at Logan in surprise. *That part?* Maybe he should have gotten a little more info from Tiffany before he decided to play this game. Logan stepped back.

"Kneel on the floor since you liked being down there so much earlier."

Clay did as he was told, watching as Logan removed his clothes and shoes before going to get what he needed from the nightstand. Clay waited on his knees, palms up like he'd been taught. Logan came to stand in front of him.

"Hands on the floor."

After he complied, Logan circled around behind Clay. He heard the foil packet being torn open and the rubber being smoothed down Logan's cock. He heard the cap to the lube snap open then close again. Logan knelt behind him, and without any further warning, pushed inside him. Clay threw back his head, moaning as Logan clamped a hand on the back of his neck and immediately set a furious speed, pounding into him with brutal force. His ass stung every time Logan slammed against him but he didn't care. The pain was yet another sensation pushing him further into the sharp pleasure already coursing through him.

Clay's fingers flexed again and again as he fought the urge to touch himself. He was so hard, his balls so tight, that he wanted to cry and beg, do anything to get Logan to touch him. He didn't, because somehow he knew that would only lead to his agony being further prolonged. So he just let his Dom take him, listening to the harsh sounds of flesh slapping against flesh. Logan's rough groans and curses and his own gasping breaths blended together. But Logan must have been just as turned on as he was because before Clay knew it, he was giving him another order in a deep growl.

"Fuck! Clay, this ass is so fucking tight! Squeeze it tighter for me, baby. Make me come."

Clay obeyed. He squeezed his inner muscles around the thick shaft invading him. When he did, Logan cursed again, the grip on his neck tightening. Clay's breath caught in his throat. Being controlled and dominated like that felt right. He spread his legs even wider, damn near mewling like a cat he was so into Logan's rough treatment.

Logan was close. He clenched his jaw, fighting to hold on a little longer. Taking Clay like that, thrusting into him hard and staring at his cherry red ass while he fucked him … he liked it more than he could express. With Clay moaning and spreading his legs like a little slut, Logan knew he liked it just as much. He pulled out of Clay and yanked the condom off. Jacking himself off at the same speed he'd just pounded into the tight ass of his submissive, he came. His body jerked and spurted his cum all over Clay's smooth back and ass. With his chest heaving, he rubbed his cum into Clay's skin, wanting to be a part of his lover. Already, he was fucking sick of having a condom between them. They'd be getting rid of those soon. Leaving Clay braced on all fours on the floor, he got up and went to sit on the bed with his back against the headboard.

Clay looked up at him with a tortured expression. Logan knew he must be dying for a release. "Get up and come stand over here," he ordered. He watched as Clay pushed himself shakily to his feet and slowly walked over to the bed. Clay stood there trembling, his fingers twitching, his cock so hard it looked like it hurt as it stretched up to his belly. "Touch yourself." Clay's hand immediately grasped his cock. He moaned as he started to stroke himself, his eyes drifting closed and his head falling back on his shoulders.

Logan was proud of his sub. He hadn't once had to tell Clay not to come and for the first time, he hadn't needed a cock ring or his hand to hold himself back. He was doing it on his own without being told. Clay's skin gleamed with sweat in the low lamp light and Logan just wanted to lick him all over, tasting him on his tongue. "You're so beautiful, Clay," he whispered.

Clay's eyes opened at that and he looked at him. "May I … may I come, please?"

Logan shook his head. Clay bit his lip but he didn't protest, he just closed his eyes again and kept stroking at the same pace, his body tight with tension. Logan told his sub to stop and he did. "Look at me," he demanded. He waited until Clay dropped his hand from around his shaft and looked at him with those bright blue eyes. "Who do you belong to, Clay?"

Clay licked his lips, swallowing hard before he answered. "You."

Logan's eyes narrowed and he asked again. "Who do you belong to?"

Clay bit his bottom lip. "You, Sir. I belong to you." He took a deep breath. "I'm yours. All of me is yours." Logan had never asked him that before, but Clay knew he'd answered correctly this time. Logan got up off the bed and came to stand so close in front of him that his stomach brushed Clay's cock. He couldn't help it. He cried out, his hips shooting forward to seek that contact again. Logan ran a finger up the underside of his cock.

"Poor little sub, you want to come, don't you?"

Clay nodded. His orgasm was so close he was ready to beg if that's what it took.

"You'll have to work for it. But you're not allowed to touch yourself."

Clay bit his lip again as he thought about that. "Can I touch you?"

When Logan nodded, he stepped even closer, bringing their bodies together. Clay threaded his arms through Logan's to grab his broad shoulders. Pumping his hips, he rubbed their cocks together swiftly, grinding hard. It wouldn't take him long. Just as he felt his cock start to pulse with his rising orgasm, he heard Logan's whisper.

"Kiss me."

Clay did, smashing their lips together, sucking on Logan's tongue when it thrust into his mouth. The kiss quickly became frantic as he moved faster, his orgasm teasing at his cock head.

Clay gasped between kisses. "Shit! I'm coming! I can't hold it … please say I can come!"

Logan's arms came around him and pulled him even tighter against his body. "Come for me, baby."

Clay cried out as his orgasm burst forth, spilling onto them both. He felt a shudder run through Logan's big body as Logan kissed him even harder. Clay's brain blanked as he trembled, his cock jerking hard, his hips still pumping as the release he'd been craving for so long washed over him. Finally, he went limp, resting his head on Logan's strong chest, hearing his heartbeat thundering under his ear.

"Logan, you make me feel so good."

Logan gave a quiet laugh. "And you do the same for me."

Clay was surprised when Logan picked him up, barely straining under his weight. Clay wrapped his legs around his waist and tucked his face into Logan's warm neck. Logan walked them over to the bed and Clay let go long enough for them to lie down. But as soon as they were settled on their sides, he was wrapped right back around Logan. He loved lying in Logan's big arms, feeling his warm skin pressed against his, Logan's hand stroking down his back as he hid his face in his neck. He felt safe and protected and able to calm down from the intense feelings Logan always aroused in him when they laid like this. Clay adjusted his position so that Logan could rub cool lotion onto the tender skin of his ass. When he was done Logan pulled him back into his arms and they laid there quietly.

Eventually Logan spoke up. "We need to shower."

Clay protested sleepily. "No. I don't want to wash us off me."

Logan trailed his fingers across the dried cum on Clay's back. He couldn't deny his sub that small pleasure. Truth be told, he liked Clay covered in a mix of their sweat and cum. "Okay, but let me get you some water and turn off the light." Logan smiled as Clay grumbled and slowly let him go. He quickly left to get a glass of water from the kitchen.

He came back and gave it to Clay, watching as he slowly drank with his eyes closed, dark lashes resting against his cheeks. Logan felt a surge of emotion for the man who, although incredibly strong willed, had given himself and submitted to him so freely.

Clay's eyes opened and he smiled as he passed the glass back to him. "You might not make me bark like a dog, but I sure pant like one."

Logan laughed, almost choking on the water he'd just swallowed. He set the empty glass down on the night stand and turned off the lamp. Still laughing, he got back into bed. "One of these days, you're going to have to tell me where this dog fixation comes from."

20

Clay woke up slowly. The first thing he was aware of was Logan's palm stroking softly across his butt. As he felt the soreness there, he remembered the night before. Tiffany hadn't been kidding with her warning about teasing. He looked up to see Logan watching him with concern in his hazel eyes.

"Good morning."

Before Clay could return the greeting Logan leaned down and kissed him slowly. Clay returned the kiss, but just as he was starting to get into it, his body waking up even more, Logan stopped.

"Are you okay?"

Clay nodded. "Yeah, just a little sore."

Logan kept rubbing and gave Clay another quick kiss. "I'll get you some ice before we leave. You took that punishment very well, baby."

Clay's face warmed with a blush. He fought not to hide it in Logan's neck at his praise. "So umm… is what I did – you know to earn that punishment – is that …" Clay trailed off, not sure how to phrase his question.

Logan rubbed Clay's back as he thought about the best way to answer his question. He definitely liked the way his sub teased him, mostly because he knew he'd get to punish him for it afterwards. And Clay had enjoyed his punishment as well, making it even better for them both. But he didn't want Clay thinking he could or should do that whenever he wanted. Clay was already a strong individual. Logan couldn't have him topping from the bottom or their relationship would become chaotic.

"I knew your personality when I chose you. I don't expect you to change now that you're with me, so I won't restrict what you do outside our bedroom." *Well, not completely*, Logan thought. "Just know that you won't be allowed to get away with whatever you want."

When Clay nodded Logan pushed down the covers. "Now turn onto your stomach and let me see." Clay rolled onto his front and lay his head down on his folded arms. His body immediately reacted to seeing his lover naked and stretched out. He tried to get the thought of sliding on top of Clay and taking him just like that out of his mind so he could make sure he hadn't done too much damage. But when he looked and saw the marks he'd left on Clay's ass, he grew even harder.

He'd marked his sub just as he dreamed of doing. The shape of his belt was across Clay's ass in blushing red stripes. The faintest hint of a bruise rose on one taut cheek. Logan knew it had to hurt and he felt bad that Clay had to deal with it. But, it was beautiful to see. He brushed his fingers over the marks. His lips curled in a possessive smile at the result of Clay submitting to his punishment. Having control of Clay filled him with a heady sense of ownership.

Logan bent and brushed his lips lightly across the marks. He pressed a kiss to the bruise and couldn't help but suck the tender skin into his mouth. Clay's hips pressed back against him and Logan heard him moan his name. He loved hearing that. Before he knew it, he was licking across the smooth flesh of his cheeks, his hands coming up to squeeze and spread them so he could dip his tongue into him.

Logan felt a shiver run through his lover, but he also heard him wince in pain. He immediately stopped and got off the bed. Even though he wanted nothing more than to be inside his lover again, he wouldn't take him while he was hurting. Clay turned his head and looked at him.

"Why'd you stop?"

Looking away from those sleepy, sexy eyes and fighting to ignore his hard-on, Logan searched for his pants from the previous night. "We need to get going soon." He looked back at Clay when he heard him moving and saw him push himself up on one elbow to look at the clock on the other side of the bed. As he turned, Logan noticed he'd also left finger shaped bruises on Clay's neck where he gripped him as he pounded into him from behind. Seeing such a proprietary mark had Logan's cock pulsing. He had to clench his fists tight to keep from reaching out and grabbing his sub to pull him underneath him for more of the same. Shit. He wasn't used to feeling nearly out of control like that. He needed to get out of there and take a moment to get himself back together. He pulled on his pants and yanked his shirt over his head.

Clay turned back to him. "We have plenty of time." Logan watched as he sucked his bottom lip, blue eyes dark with arousal. "And I want you."

Logan was torn. He didn't want to deny Clay and hurt his feelings, but he also didn't want to hurt him physically either. Holding on tight to his control, he sat on the edge of the bed and kissed Clay lightly. "Not right now. I was pretty rough on you last night, baby. And we've got a training run to get through today." Logan smoothed his hand down Clay's back, his eyes drawn again to the marks he'd left on his ass. "I don't want you to be too sore."

Clay protested. "I told you I'm fine."

Logan answered with the snap of command in his voice. "I said no." Clay quieted, his eyes lowering to look at the sheet beneath him. "I'm going to get you some ice." Logan brushed his thumb across the marks on Clay's neck. Logan allowed himself to rub the sweet marks on those smooth cheeks one more time. Then he forced himself to go downstairs to get some ice.

****

There were two people waiting in front of Logan's office when he arrived to work. One he was very familiar with, the other he only knew in passing. "Captain Hayden. How can I help you this evening?" Captain Hayden was a dark skinned African American. His concern with his image was clear in how neat he was, from his precisely cut hair, to his carefully trimmed side burns touched with silver, to his stiffly starched uniform. His hands were as presentable as the rest of him, the nails clipped and buffed to a shine. Clay always said he looked like a stuffy prick. Logan was sure Hayden would rather people describe him as distinguished.

"Sergeant Pierce, I brought Ms. Crawford from public relations down to talk to your team. Do you have a moment to speak with us?"

"Of course. We've got a training run tonight but we have awhile yet." He let them into his office. They sat in the chairs in front of his desk while he settled behind it.

"This won't take long. I've brought Ms. Crawford in because I'd like to work on SWAT's image."

Logan held back a smile. Hayden was forever singing that same tune. He gave his attention to Ms. Crawford as she spoke for the first time.

"Sergeant Pierce, you and I both know that the work you do is tough and you're often tasked with bringing in some pretty reprehensible criminals. Unfortunately, some of our citizens don't see that. All they see are the busted in windows and doors and punched out walls that are left when SWAT is done with a scene. Or the panic of the people who sometimes get caught in between you and your targets."

Logan understood where she was coming from. There'd been plenty of times when the neighborhood people yelled at them out in the field, completely disregarding the fact that the men and women they were dragging off were dangerous criminals. "That's all true. So how do you propose we combat the problem?"

Ms. Crawford smiled. "Well, we have lots of ideas we'd like to implement, most of them centered around community involvement. But we thought we'd start off with something fun." She paused and smiled again. "A SWAT calendar."

Logan's brows shot up. "Are you serious?"

She laughed lightly. "I am. It'll be tasteful and fun. That's the whole purpose, to show your department in a friendlier light. Participation will be voluntary, of course."

Captain Hayden spoke up. "Do you have any objections to the idea, Sergeant?"

Logan didn't. He thought the idea was silly, but he didn't necessarily object to it. And since he didn't want to rain on her calendar parade, he didn't voice his opinion. "No objections, Sir. I won't be one of the volunteers, but I'm sure some of the guys will get a kick out of it. Why don't we go out to the pen and present the idea to them right now?" He stood and the others followed suit.

He walked out to the large section of the floor that held the desks for the members of the three HPD SWAT teams. The desks were arranged in neat rows, but the area was still cluttered with filing cabinets, copy machines, extra chairs and the water cooler. They called it the pen because of the metal and glass railing that squared the area off like a pig pen. His team was all there, as well as the majority of the second team. The third team was off rotation that week. "Alright, everyone, listen up." Logan waited until he had everyone's attention. "I'm sure you may have seen her before, but let me introduce you to Ms. Crawford. She works upstairs in public relations for Houston Police. Tonight she's here to talk to you about an upcoming project." He gestured to her that she had the floor. "Ms. Crawford."

"Good evening, everyone. My job here is to make sure that the Houston Police Department looks good. We want to make sure that when people see us, they don't have any negative associations. We want them to think of a force that is there to help them. SWAT is a division that is considered tough, elite, and mysterious. I'd like to put a face to the men and women of SWAT. With that in mind, I've proposed the idea of a calendar to your captain and sergeant and they've approved."

Clay snorted a laugh. "So you mean to literally make us look good. Put us in front of a wind machine for the camera and all that."

Logan watched as Ms. Crawford turned her smile on Clay.

"What's your name, Officer?"

"Corporal Clay Foster."

"Well, we could certainly have a wind machine there if you'd like. Most officers have hair too short for a wind machine to make a difference but I think we could manage to ruffle yours a little. The calendar shoot will be completely voluntary. Are you volunteering Corporal Foster?"

Clay laughed and ran a hand over his hair. "I don't think so, Ms. Crawford."

"Please, call me Alison. And why not? I think you have a great look. You'd be perfect."

Clay leaned back in his chair as he looked over Alison Crawford. She was pretty with hair in a thick cloud of light brown curls that fell to her shoulders and skin that looked like warm caramel. She was petite and wore heels and a dress with a full skirt. But the dress was a powerful shade of red and she carried herself like a woman who was confident and sure in both her brains and her looks. "Sorry, Alison, but I think other folks have a slightly *different* opinion on what a good SWAT officer looks like." He flicked his eyes over to the captain. "And we wouldn't want to ruin this project from jump by putting the wrong guy in there. Would we, Captain Hayden?" Hayden narrowed his eyes at him, looking like he was about to snap, "Get a haircut!" But he didn't say anything. Clay left him alone for once since they had company from upstairs visiting.

"Well, please consider volunteering. All of you consider it. I'll be sending out an email with the dates and details soon. Thank you all for your time."

She smiled once more and left the pen with the captain. Logan gave him an exasperated look before he went back to his office. Clay shrugged at him. He wasn't worried about Captain Hayden. Hayden could suck his—. Clay cut that thought off. He'd rather not go there even as a mental insult. He heard someone whistle and turned around to see Hector grinning at him.

"Uh-oh, Foster. Looked like *Mz.* Crawford wanted you to be the cover model for her calendar. You better watch out or you'll be standing in the front of that wind machine with your shirt ripped open and your gun *cocked.*"

The pen erupted with laughter. Clay laughed too and threw a piece of crumpled up paper at Hector. "Damn, Hector. That was specific. You been sneaking into the romance novel section at the bookstore and looking at the covers or something?"

Hector stuck his nose up. "I'm not ashamed to admit I've looked at a few. It's how I learn what the ladies secretly like."

Clay laughed at his friend and turned back to his work.

****

A couple hours later, they were at the empty shell of a house they used for training. It was located outside the downtown area in a not so nice part of town. Other than the two used for training, the houses left standing were all abandoned. But that was to their advantage. There was no one to complain about their trucks tearing up the grass or the late night gunshots. The industrial buildings surrounding them made more noise than SWAT did.

That night, they were going through the two story house with multiple armed assailants and an unknown number of civilians. Logan went over the scenario with his team. Once he'd given them the details he stepped back to allow them to plan their strategy. He was only observing. He signaled them to get started.

"Q. Clay. You're up."

The two nodded in unison, their game faces on, guns at the ready. They took off, crouched low, sneaking up to the house. The rest of the team fanned out to wait for the go ahead before approaching. At Q's signal, Carlos breached the door and

Tiffany set off a flash bang. Logan laughed to himself. The light had briefly illuminated the smile on Tiffany's face before they headed into the house single-file. Logan walked in behind them to keep track of how they did. But he wasn't worried. He knew his team would ace it.

Fifteen minutes later, the team was all smiles and high-fives. They'd made the run perfectly with no hits to their team. They also came close to setting a course record. Logan got everyone's attention. "Great job tonight. Let's get back to the station." He looked at Clay. It took only a second for his lover to read him and see what he wanted.

Clay turned to Brady. "Hey, man, thanks for the ride over. But I'll ride back with Sarge. Need to talk to him about something."

Brady nodded. "Alright, man. I'll see you later."

Clay walked over to Logan's car and got in. Logan watched to make sure all personnel made it off the grounds before he got in the driver's seat.

"Where to, Serge? Back to the station?"

Logan smiled. "Not yet. We're gonna take a little detour first."

****

Logan sat in Captain Hayden's office. It was much nicer than his. A big window overlooked downtown Houston. Plaques and photos of the captain with local dignitaries made up the stereotypical décor.

"Your team's success rate is phenomenal as always."

Logan offered a quick thank you and left it at that. He wasn't interested in having his ego stroked. His mind started to wander as the captain waxed on about the prestige he brought to Houston SWAT and how many officers felt it would be an honor to train with him.

He thought about that detour he'd taken with Clay on the way back to the station. He'd pulled in between two empty buildings and stopped the car. He turned the ignition off and looked at Clay. "You made it through that run with no problem. Clay had raised his chin in a look of supreme cockiness.

"I didn't just make it through. I was so amazing they'll have to rename that course after me."

Logan had laughed and pulled Clay to him for a kiss, his lover coming into his arms willingly. They'd taken a few minutes to share soft kisses, Logan still wanting to care for his sub after his punishment last night. But they couldn't linger long. They'd driven back to the station holding hands, Logan ever so often stroking Clay's thigh. But he wanted to do more and could tell that Clay wanted to be close to him.

Logan snapped back to the present. He needed to get the meeting over with so he could get Clay back to his house and in his bed. "Let's cut to the chase, Captain. What's this meeting all about?"

Hayden leaned back in his chair and rubbed his palms together. "I think it's time you got some new blood on your team."

"If it ain't broke don't fix it. Besides, we're ten. I like that number."

The captain smiled slightly. "We have some people looking to get onto SWAT. And Officer Mike Dorsey is planning to retire from SWAT soon to take a training position. So you'll have to get at least one new person on your team."

Logan acknowledged that with a nod. "True. Keep me updated on when the department plans to have a round of classes for SWAT school. We could always use some people on the outer perimeter."

"Will do. One more thing. Start thinking about who you would like to promote. It's always good to have high ranked members on the team and you'll lose a well-decorated member once Senior Corporal Dorsey is gone."

Logan immediately thought of Clay. "Corporal Foster would be good."

Hayden's expression froze for a moment. "I don't know if he's the right choice. He still seems like he'd rather buck the system than advance through it."

Logan didn't respond to that. He knew Hayden had a personal dislike for Clay.

"Take some time to think about it and get back with me. Keep up the good work, Sergeant."

Logan acknowledged the dismissal and left the office. He was glad that was over. He wasn't looking forward to having new people on the team. Not because he didn't like welcoming someone new to SWAT, but because he hated to lose a friend and colleague that he'd worked with for years. SWAT as a whole had a high turnover rate. But he worked hard to keep his team stable to minimize that. As a result, they were together longer than most.

Before he'd made it too far down the hall, someone called his name. He turned to see a clean cut blond officer coming towards him with a smile on his face.

"Sergeant Pierce. How are you?"

Logan responded politely. "Well. And you, Officer Bennett?"

The smile grew. "Excellent, actually. It's starting to look like I might be up for an opening on SWAT. I believe your team will have a spot open soon, right?"

Now Logan understood the true purpose of that meeting. Ryan Bennett was one of Hayden's favorites and he would push to get him placed where he wanted him to be.

Ryan lowered his voice. "It could be nice, the two of us working together. Don't you think?"

Logan stiffened. "No. I don't."

Ryan tilted his head to the side, a quizzical smile on his handsome face. "I don't see why not. We're good together in other ways."

Logan looked around to make sure no one was close enough to overhear them. "We won't be together in any way. I'm with someone."

The smile fell from his mouth. "Let me guess. Clay Foster."

"Not that it's any of your business. But yes." Logan's curiosity prompted him to ask. "How did you know?"

Ryan shrugged. "It was simple enough. You talked about him differently than you did the rest of your *perfect* team. And I've seen the way you look at him sometimes." He smiled again. "Does Corporal Foster know he's not the first member of this force you've been with?"

Logan got up close in Ryan's face. "Don't worry about what he knows. He doesn't concern you. *I* don't concern you. If you know what's good for you, you'll keep that in mind and stay away from Clay. Do you understand?" He stared the other man down until he nodded. Then Logan stepped back and continued on his way.

21

Clay was hanging at his friend Ian's place. They were off from both duty and training so he was catching up with his long time buddy. They served in the Navy together and remained close when they were out. He, of course, had moved on to the police force. Ian, on the other hand, had combined his military knowledge and gamer nerdiness to create a line of military themed, first person shooter video games. They weren't as well-known as some others but they were successful and he was doing very well for himself.

Ian was telling the latest story of his trials with women. Clay always ended up laughing in sympathy tinged amusement at these stories. He'd never seen anyone with such bad dating luck.

"So you're telling me that you are surprised that someone you met on a free dating site didn't look like their picture? Shit man, have you ever heard of catfishing? You're lucky it didn't turn out to be a dude."

Ian laughed. "Well, that's enough about me. Let's talk about you. What the hell have you been up to? I had people over the other night for bar-b-que and you didn't even show up."

"I uh… I had a date."

"Really? Who's the lucky chick? Or guy? I can't keep up with you."

"The *guy*," Clay stressed, "Is someone you've met before. Very powerful. A leader. A team leader, if you will."

Ian's eyes went wide and his mouth dropped open. "Are you fucking kidding me? You're screwing around with your sergeant? Sergeant Pierce?" He shook his head. "Hold on. Sergeant Pierce is gay?" He brushed his shaggy dark blond hair back from his face. "This is too much for my mind to take in at one time. What made him come after you?"

"What the fuck is that supposed to mean?" he asked with a frown. He knew he wasn't the stereotypical ripped to shreds gay man. And he was okay with that, for the most part.

"C'mon, man. You know I didn't mean it like that. It's just, you work together. You're on the same fucking team. How is that working out?"

Clay shrugged. "So far it's worked out pretty well, actually. It doesn't affect our jobs. We just have to be sure not to slip up in front of anyone at work."

"I don't think I want to hear about you two making googly eyes at each other."

Clay laughed. He wouldn't say they made googly eyes, but the looks that Logan sent his way always affected him.

"So how is it between you guys?"

"It's good. It's what I need."

Ian gave him a questioning look. Clay was tempted to fess up about their Dom/sub relationship. It would be nice to talk about it but he held back. The whole thing was still so new to him. He wasn't sure if he was ready to share. Besides, unless Ian had some secrets he'd been holding close to his chest, he wouldn't understand where Clay was coming from anyway. He really needed to talk to Tiffany. He made a mental note to meet up with her then made a joke to change the subject with Ian.

"Apparently, I was tired of dealing with chicks and their drama. Now it's my turn to be the drama queen."

Ian laughed and they moved on to talk about his latest game.

****

Late that night, Clay lay in bed, staring mindlessly at the TV. He was wide awake so he was watching baseball highlights. His eyes caught the glow of his phone a second before the text message indicator sounded. It was Logan asking what he was doing. He tapped his thumb across the screen to text back. *Watching TV.* He hesitated a second before he added, *and missing you.* Then he hit send. His stomach flipped when he got Logan's response.

I miss you too, baby.

It was nice to be upfront about how he felt and get the same in return. His phone chirped with another text.

You want help getting to sleep?

Yeah but what are you going to do, text me a lullaby? Clay waited for a response but his phone was quiet. Then it rang. He wasn't surprised to see Logan's name on the screen. He answered and heard Logan's deep voice with its hint of Texas drawl.

"Hey. How was your day off?"

"Good. I caught up with my friend, Ian. He's working on a new game. This one features SWAT so I've been letting him pick my brains. Then I got some stuff done around the house and that's it. How about you?"

"My day was fine. My grandfather is doing well. Crabbing over his team losing as usual."

"Sounds like me."

Logan laughed. "Yeah. You'll have to meet him someday. He'll like you."

Clay was surprised at that and wondered in what capacity Logan would introduce them. Did his grandfather know he was gay? "You think so?"

"Yeah. But that's not happening tonight and you need to get some sleep. Turn the TV off."

Clay protested. "I need it to stare at until I fall asleep."

"I'll help you fall asleep. Turn off the TV, Clay."

The command was obvious even through the phone line. Clay searched around in the covers until he found the remote so he could shut off the TV. "It's off."

"Are you in bed with the lights off?"

Clay told him yeah and Logan asked if he was comfortable in his pajamas. He had a feeling he knew where this was going.

"I'm just in my underwear." His suspicions were proven right with Logan's next words.

"As much as I love those tight little briefs on you, I think I want you to take them off for me."

"Logan, I don't think—"

Logan cut him off. "Do what I say, baby."

Clay tucked the phone into his shoulder and pushed his briefs down. He didn't even know why he bothered to protest. He knew he'd do whatever Logan told him.

"I love your beautiful body, Clay. I wish I could have my hands on you right now. Since I can't, you're going to have to do it for me. Touch your nipples."

Clay trailed his hand down and across his chest until he reached a nipple and started tugging on it.

"Are you wearing your nipple rings?"

Clay breathed out a yes, already starting to get turned on.

"I want those in my mouth. You make the sweetest noise when I pull on them with my teeth."

Clay pulled on the ring and moaned a little bit.

"Hmmm… That's almost the sound but not quite. I've got a surprise for those sexy rings next time I see you."

Clay's breath was starting to come faster as he asked, "What's the surprise?" He could hear the smirking smile in Logan's voice as he answered.

"It wouldn't be a surprise if I told you, now would it?"

Clay shook his head then remembered Logan couldn't see him and said no.

"So you'll just have to wait. Like I'll have to wait to be inside that tight ass of yours again."

Clay moaned, the feeling from tugging hard on his nipples and Logan's words hardening his cock. He wanted to reach down and stroke it but he'd learned not to do that without permission. And he had a feeling that the rule stood even over the phone. "Sir, can I please touch myself?"

Logan's low sexy laugh sent tingles down Clay's spine. "Impatient little sub. Go ahead, baby. Stroke that cock for me."

Clay wrapped his hand around his shaft, gasping when he made contact.

"I can just imagine how hard you are. I bet you'd be even harder if that was *my* hand stroking you faster and faster before I sucked you down."

Clay made a nearly unintelligible sound of agreement as he started stroking himself.

"Don't you wish it was me, Clay?"

Clay squeezed his cock like Logan always did to him. "Yes, Sir."

"Which do you want, my hand or my mouth?"

Clay moaned. *Why did he have to choose?* he thought. "Both." A *tsking* sound came through the phone.

"Greedy, greedy. You're lucky you have a generous Dom. I'd take that cock in my fist and pump you hard while I sucked the head, tasting your sweet pre-cum on my tongue."

Clay groaned, his back arching as his hips started to fuck into his fist. "I need to come."

"Go ahead, baby. Let me hear you."

But Clay held back. "Want you to come with me," he muttered.

Logan was breathing hard as he answered, "I'm right behind you. Now come for me, Clay."

Listening to Logan's harsh breaths in his ear, thinking about him doing the same thing in his bed had Clay's hips pumping faster as he gripped his cock tightly. He drew his knee up and groaned as he started to come, feeling the hot rush of semen pour out of him, over his hand, and onto his stomach. He heard Logan's deep groan and knew his lover was climaxing too.

Clay lay there in the dark with the phone pressed tightly to his ear, listening as Logan told him how much he missed him and that he couldn't wait to see him again. Finally, his heart rate slowed and he started to feel drowsy. "That was way better than a glass of warm milk," he mumbled.

Logan laughed softly. "Sleep well, Clay."

Clay told him goodnight and hung up. He was asleep almost immediately.

Logan ended his call with Clay. They all had trouble getting to sleep at a normal hour when they were off duty. Working late nights often screwed with their sleep schedules. But they all dealt with it. It was just one of the drawbacks of the job. He guessed Clay would be up at that late hour and he'd been right. Logan would do whatever he could to help his sub in any way. That included making sure he got enough rest on his days off.

He wiped his off belly with the boxers he removed earlier. As he settled down to go to sleep, he had a smile on his face. He actually had two surprises for Clay. He'd made a stop earlier and ordered Clay's collar, and for an extra fee, it would be ready very soon. Logan considered the money well spent, because he couldn't wait to *really* claim Clay as his own.

22

Clay relaxed on the couch with a cold root beer. It was their last night of their off-week. The next day, they'd be back on rotation. He'd just taken the last sip of his soda when his phone rang. He was surprised at the rush of pleasure that went through him when he saw it was Logan. They'd grown close very fast. Logan's deep voice came through after he answered the call.

"Hey."

"Hey, Sarge. What are you doing?"

"Driving back. I'm almost home."

"Home as in back in the city? Or home as in nearly at your house?"

"I'm almost back in the city. Why?"

"I was thinking if you weren't too tired, maybe you could come over here to my place."

The line was quiet for a moment before Logan replied. "No, I'm not too tired. I'd love to come over, Clay."

Clay's heart was beating fast. Logan would be in his home for the first time since they'd started their relationship. That made him nervous.

"I'll see you in about thirty minutes, alright?"

"Alright." Clay hung up. He'd been thinking about how he would handle letting Logan be in control in his home. He wasn't sure if he would be comfortable being submissive to Logan there or if he would want to remain the king of his castle, so to speak. It was as good a time as any to find out.

****

Clay got up when Logan texted to say he was in the parking lot. Clay went outside and halfway down the stairs to call out to him. "Do you need any help with your bags?"

"No. I traveled light. Only have one."

They went up the stairs together to his apartment, Clay stepping back to let him in. As soon as the door closed behind them, he was in Logan's arms, their mouths meeting in a passionate kiss. They parted after several deep kisses hello.

"I missed you, Sir." Clay said the title somewhat hesitantly. But it didn't feel strange to address Logan that way in his own home.

Logan kissed him again. "I missed you too."

Clay laughed a little. "It's crazy how I'm already used to being with you so much."

Logan gave him a roguish grin. "Aren't you glad you decided to give us a chance?"

"Yeah, I am," he replied. He rubbed his body against Logan's, making him groan. "Very glad."

"I want to be with you, baby. Now."

Clay nodded and turned to go back to his bedroom. Logan's arms came around his waist, pressing kisses to his neck as they walked. In his room, they fell onto the bed, kissing and touching, with Logan quickly taking control. In no time at all, Clay was naked underneath his Dom. Logan pushed deep inside him as he held his arms over his head. But this time Clay begged to be released.

"I missed you, Sir. Please let me touch you. Please?"

Logan looked down at him and Clay was so captured by those intense hazel eyes he almost didn't notice when he was let go. But he did and he stroked his hands down the thick muscles of Logan's back, caressing skin that was warm and slick with sweat under his palms. Clay kept going until he gripped Logan's firm ass, feeling the muscles there flex as his lover pumped into him. Clay bit his lip. His orgasm was rapidly building as the head of Logan's cock brushed that sensitive spot inside him over and over. He was surprised as Logan's big hand wrapped around his shaft and stroked him swiftly.

"Not gonna wait this time, baby. Come for me."

He squeezed the head of Clay's cock in the way that drove him crazy. Clay moaned and let himself go. As he came, Logan leaned down and bit his ear, thrusting hard with his own quick release. Clay smiled to himself. Clearly, Logan had missed him just as much.

****

Clay lay draped across Logan's chest as Logan lazily trailed his fingers up and down his back. "Thank you for helping me fall asleep this week."

Logan had called him each night he was at his grandfather's. Clay thought it was incredibly sweet Logan cared enough to call him and help him get some rest. Although the method he used had been anything but. Reminded of the phone sex they'd had, he grinned.

"My boyfriend has such a dirty mouth." Clay pretended to frown. "Although now that I think about it, *are* you my boyfriend or am I just being taken advantage of? You haven't taken me on any *real* dates yet. I don't even have your letterman's jacket. Maybe I should stop putting out."

Logan growled and squeezed Clay's ass. "Don't even think of denying me access to this." He leaned down and brushed a kiss across Clay's lips. "Or these."

As he met those teasing blue eyes, Logan knew he was falling hard for Clay. He wanted to press his hand to Clay's heart and tell him not to deny him access to that either. He didn't, feeling like it might be too soon. But he stroked a finger over the skin behind which his heart lay and the words he didn't speak hung in the air between them. Clay's eyes briefly widened but he didn't speak either. He just pushed himself up and kissed Logan softly. Logan pulled his lover completely on top of him and wrapped his arms tightly around

Clay. Clay kept kissing him and Logan let him take the lead, his heart beating hard as he gave himself up to their kiss.

23

They were back on rotation. They had a warrant to serve to a local drug dealer later that night. There were a couple hours before they had to meet in the strategy room so Logan had the team practicing hand to hand. Clay was paired up with Hector this time. Unlike Jody's calm patience, Hector was all wild energy, bouncing around, juking and jiving. Clay shook his head.

"How do you ever manage to calm down enough to make those long range shots?"

Hector grinned cockily and dropped his guard. "What can I say? I'm just that—"

Clay cut him off with a sharp jab to the gut.

Hector coughed and hunched over. "Way to play dirty, man."

Clay rolled his eyes. "Yeah, because the scum out there won't attack you when you have your guard down."

Hector straightened. The cocky grin was back in place but this time he kept his guard up. "I don't have to worry about mixing with the riff-raff. Snipers are above all that." He threw a punch, catching Clay in the chest. "See what I did there?"

Both of them got serious and got in some good jabs and take downs. When they were finished, they stepped off the mat, taking off their protective head gear. Hector headed to the locker room while Clay stopped to talk to Logan. He stood close, as close as he dared without causing any sideways looks. Logan kept his eye on the two sparring on the mats as he spoke.

"You want to go out for a drink after our shift tonight?"

"Sorry, I can't. I told Tiffany I'd hang with her." He finally made plans to talk with her about being in a D/s relationship.

"That's too bad. I was going to take you on that date you were asking for."

Clay arched a brow. "That late at night? I don't think so. You're just trying to get into my shorts."

Logan moved a step closer. "I can't help it. It's practically obscene the way they sit so low on your hips. Any lower and I'd be able to tell if you shaved or not."

Clay grinned. "You already know the answer to that."

"Maybe I ought to speak with the captain. Have him institute a dress code for training. All personnel must wear a shirt and shorts must stay at the natural waist at all times."

Clay glared. "You'd better not. You know he hates me. With that dress code in place he'd be following me around with zip ties to make my shorts stay up like I'm in middle school or something."

Logan laughed. "Well, try to keep those shorts up then. I don't want anybody getting a look at what's mine."

Clay opened his mouth, ready with a quick come back but Brady came up to ask Sarge a question. Logan's hazel eyes sparkled with humor because he knew Clay couldn't respond. He just barely restrained from childishly sticking his tongue out at Logan before he headed off to change.

****

Clay and Tiffany sat on the deck of her small but neat house. They were drinking glasses of lemonade and Clay was sharing his pack of Twizzlers. A potted plant bloomed on the table between them. Wind chimes tinkled in the breeze and the air was scented by the four o'clocks blooming along the fence. It was a sweet scene of Americana until you listened to the subject at hand. He'd just told her he'd had his first punishment.

"So the whole teasing thing. Is that poor sub behavior?"

"Depends on the Dom," Tiffany answered. "Some Doms like to have their subs under complete control and wouldn't tolerate that. Others don't mind when their subs play, because then they get to exert their dominance and pull them back in line. And if Logan made sure you felt pleasure in your punishment, then yeah, he's one who likes to be teased."

Clay's face flushed hot as he thought back to Logan spanking him with his belt and then making him work for his orgasm. That orgasm had been a long time coming – but he'd definitely felt pleasure that night. He snapped back to attention as he heard Tiffany talking.

"Going by the blush on your face – I can't believe you're blushing, how cute – I'm gonna assume Logan did make you enjoy your punishment."

Clay threw one of his Twizzlers at Tiffany, hitting her in the forehead. "Shut up."

Tiffany laughed and picked up the Twizzler from her lap to eat it. "Don't hate me for speaking the truth! But I hope you realize, you never know how inventive or intense your Dom's punishment is gonna be. So play at your own risk." Then she grinned. "But that's part of the rush."

Clay had to grin back. He could see himself taunting Logan just to see what he would come up with next. And he'd been hot with anticipation as he realized Logan was about to punish him for his handcuff stunt. "How do you know if Carlos wants you to be regular Tiffany or sub Tiffany?"

Tiffany took a big sip of her drink before answering. "Carlos gives me this look and I automatically know when he's in Dom mode. Actually with us, more often than not I'm submissive to him, but that's just me. And Carlos … well he can't help but be in control pretty much all the time. I don't mind, though, so I let him."

"What do you mean let him?"

"They might be controlling us but without us allowing them to, they couldn't do it. Dom's, well, good Doms anyway, don't want to take control. They want us to give it to them – to submit willingly."

Clay remembered the night when Logan told him he was a Dom and had waited patiently for him to make up his mind to submit and undress him. He hadn't forced him then and he hadn't at any time since. Clay looked over at Tiffany. She was laughing at her cat trying to catch a squirrel. He couldn't believe how at ease Tiffany was with her submission. She was so gleefully crazy sometimes, especially when she was setting bombs to blow a perp's door. He had a hard time envisioning her being submissive. "Does Carlos ever tell you …" He trailed off actually embarrassed to say it. "Does he ever give you praise?"

Tiffany cut her eyes over to him. "You mean does he tell me that I'm a good girl?"

Clay sat up. "Yes! Fuck! What is it about that that makes me feel like—" He stopped trying to find the best way to describe it.

"Like a puppy squirming for his Master's affection, desperate for a pat on the head and stupidly happy that you managed to please him?" Tiffany described in a dry voice.

Clay laughed. *Again with the dog analogies*, he thought. "Yeah, pretty much."

Tiffany shrugged. "When you truly submit to someone, all you want is to please them. When your Dom gives you praise, you know you've managed to do that and you feel proud that you've made them happy." Her fingers came up to touch her pendant.

"Did Carlos give you that?" he asked. "I always see him playing with it."

Tiffany smiled. "Yeah, he loves being reminded that I'm his."

At Clay's questioning look, Tiffany leaned over the table to show him what was on the silver medallion. It was a woman kneeling with a lit bomb in her extended palms. The words, *Carlos's Pet*, surrounded the figure in flowing cursive script. Clay was impressed at the detail in the engraving. "That's pretty sweet."

She grinned and sat back down. "He knows what I like."

Clay had to ask. "Is that your collar?"

"Yeah. Well, Carlos has my true collar. I wear this in public because it's a tad less conspicuous. A lot of subs who either can't wear their collars in public or don't have a collar that could just be seen as a necklace will get something simple from their Masters."

Clay inwardly flinched at the word Master. He was cool calling Logan his Dom, but Master felt like more than he was willing to accept. It might be strange to have Logan as his superior at work and then give up even more control to him when they were alone. He looked up and saw Tiffany watching him.

"You know Logan is going to want to collar you, right?"

Clay nodded distractedly, still thinking about having to call Logan Master.

"Are you cool with that?"

He bit into another Twizzler and shrugged. He thought he was but it seemed like a pretty big step. Clay changed the subject to what he'd been thinking of earlier. "I don't ever see you being submissive to anyone else."

"And you won't. I might be submissive sexually, but not in my work or any other part of my life. Besides, only my Dom can bring that out in me."

Clay was pretty relieved to hear it. Ever since he'd started this relationship with Logan, he'd been thinking about that.

Tiffany smirked. "Are you worried that if somebody on the team told you to kneel, you'd do it?"

Clay shot another Twizzler at Tiffany. "Fuck you. But, yeah, I guess I was."

"Don't worry. Your personality won't change. And if that did happen, be prepared for Sarge to punish you to the point you'd be ready to scream your safe word."

Reminded of his safe word, Clay laughed. Tiffany gave him a questioning look and he explained. "Just thinking of the safe word I picked – 5501." Tiffany laughed and he grinned. "That makes sense, right?" 5501 was the code for flashing red lights.

"Yeah, it does. But only you would be idiot enough to use a police code for your safe word."

The opening strains of Black Magic Woman sounded from Tiffany's phone and a second later, Clay's phone buzzed with a text. Clay checked and saw it was from Logan. Clay looked at Tiffany as she thumbed her phone to silence. "Was that Carlos?" At her nod, he asked, "What do you bet they timed that?"

Tiffany rolled her eyes. "I wouldn't take that bet. I'm pretty sure they were talking to each other and decided it was time they had our undivided attention back."

Clay agreed and stood up to go. He slapped Tiffany's outstretched hand. "Thanks for schooling me, Tiffany. I appreciate it." He really did. Logan had explained a lot to him but he still wanted to get info from somebody who was in the same position as him. He felt a little more at ease about some things … but not all.

"Anytime. And try to stay out of trouble."

Clay snorted. "Not in my nature."

24

Late the next morning, Clay was in one of the station's gyms on the row machine. He'd gotten a late start. He slept at Logan's last night and things had taken a very interesting turn. He'd teased Logan as he often did. But this time Logan got him back in an inventive way. He'd produced the gift he mentioned earlier, a chain designed to attach to his nipple rings. Logan had tugged him around by that chain all night, making his nipples sting with pleasure-pain. And that wasn't all. Logan also cuffed Clay's hands behind his back and made him do all the work in bed. Clay was completely aroused and into all of it. But when they were finished he'd been exhausted and fallen into a deep sleep. Clay woke this morning to Logan kissing the back of his neck, his hand already wrapped around his shaft and stroking him softly. He'd turned in his lover's arms, accepting his kiss and returning the erotic touch. They'd brought each other to climax that way and then lazed in bed.

Clay upped the intensity on his rowing as he thought about the night before. Even after the weeks he'd spent as Logan's lover, he'd still managed to surprise him. He just wouldn't have thought that straight-laced Sergeant Pierce would chain him by his nipple rings. But he liked it. The soreness in his nipples just reminded him of how much pleasure he'd taken in Logan controlling him that way. He had to laugh at Logan's two sides. At work, Sarge put up with his pranks and smart mouth. But in private... In private, Logan cuffed his hands behind his back and got a little sexual payback.

The gym door opened and he glanced up to see who it was. It was Officer Ryan Bennett. He was a little surprised. This gym wasn't necessarily assigned to SWAT, but they were generally the only ones who used it. He was even more surprised when Bennett came straight to him. They didn't normally converse. Still, he was friendly when the man came over. He was in too good of a mood not to be. "Officer Bennett. What brings you here this morning?"

"Here to get my workout in."

Clay waved his hand to indicate all the machines. "Gym is open, man. Have at it."

"Actually, do you mind if I work into your sets? Got some questions I was hoping you could answer."

"Sure, man. What's up?"

"You probably heard I'm looking to get onto SWAT."

The department was always hot with gossip. Sorority houses had nothing on them. And of course, the second someone expressed an interest in SWAT, all the guys knew about it. "Yeah, I heard." He got up from the machine, letting Bennett take his place.

"So can you give me any pointers on how to improve my odds? Like maybe, you know, how I can get on Sergeant Pierce's good side. You two seem pretty close."

Clay laughed lightly. "I guess you could say we've gotten closer lately." Clay was busy changing the pin on the next machine and didn't see the ugly look that crossed Ryan's face. "But as far as how to get on his good side, I probably don't know any more than anyone else. Besides, that won't be what gets you onto SWAT. Schmoozing with the other team leaders won't help either. If that was the case, I probably wouldn't be on a team. I have a hard time keeping my mouth shut. It's all about your skills, your attitude, and if you can work well as a team. On SWAT, we don't have time for superheroes. We're one solid unit there to get a job done."

"That sounds like good advice."

Clay laughed. "Oh, I'm full of advice. It's just not always helpful. Depends on what day you catch me."

Bennett laughed too. "Guess I lucked out."

Logan walked into the gym, looking for his lover. He had a class to teach but Logan knew Clay tended to lose track of time when he was working out. He spied him over at the lat pull down. Logan took a moment to admire the beauty of his lover's body as he worked out. His muscles moved smoothly in his arms and back to bring the bar down in a steady rhythm, his honey gold skin gleaming with sweat and health.

Logan's chest swelled with happiness that Clay was finally his. But that happiness dimmed somewhat when he saw who

Clay was working out with. Ryan fucking Bennett. His eyes narrowed as he glared at the man. Ryan saw him just then and smiled. Clay turned to see who Ryan was looking at and Logan wiped the glare off his face before Clay saw it.

Clay jumped up with a smile, looking like he was about to rush over to him before he remembered they were in public. He wiped his face off with his towel and walked over slowly. "Hey, Sarge. What's up?"

"Did you forget you're teaching a class this morning? It starts in about fifteen minutes."

Clay looked at the clock. "Shit, I totally lost track of time. Guess I had other things on my mind." Clay gave him a teasing look that let him know exactly what he'd been thinking about.

Logan barely managed to keep his face straight as he answered. "You need to be in uniform for this, not casual gear."

Clay wrinkled his nose and left, leaving him alone with Ryan.

"I thought I told you to stay away from Clay."

Ryan shrugged. "He was just here when I came in to work out. And I didn't say anything to him. Besides, what's the big deal if he knows? Everyone has exes, right? And you ended things with me before you took up with your current play thing." Ryan smiled and walked closer. "Well, except for that one night."

"Don't take another step," Logan snapped. Proving that he had at least some sense, Ryan stopped. "First off, unlike you,

Clay is more than just a play thing. He is *mine*. Second, nothing happened between us that night."

Ryan smiled again. "Really? If it was nothing, then why are you so worried about Clay finding out?"

Logan's insides clenched like he'd just been shot in the stomach with a bean bag gun. Ryan was right. Something had happened between them that night and he regretted the hell out of it. But it wasn't going to happen again so he was done talking about it.

"I'm not discussing this with you. Just remember what I said. Keep your mouth shut around Clay."

****

Clay took a deep breath before he went into one of the rooms used for conferences and lectures. This was his first time officially teaching a class. He'd taught out in the field before, but never standing at the front of the room like he was some sort of professor. He looked around at all the fresh, young faces, officers who were there to learn about SWAT.

"So how many of you are here because you think it would be cool to be a member of SWAT?" A few hands went up. Clay sat on the edge of the desk. "C'mon, don't be embarrassed. That's why I joined." Low laughter rippled through the room and all the hands went up. Clay grinned. He felt more at ease already. "That's more like it. Now let's talk about all the bad ass shit we get to do on SWAT."

25

Late afternoon sunlight spilled into the kitchen, warming the island where Logan sat. He was thinking over his confrontation with Ryan and what he should do about it. He needed advice so he picked up his phone. He scrolled through his contacts and tapped Carlos's number, but the line rang several times with no answer. He hung up only for his phone to ring almost immediately. Carlos was on the line, sounding out of breath.

"Sorry, man. I was busy."

Logan snorted in disgust. "You could have waited until later to call me back, Carlos. I don't want to hear you post-coital."

"Whatever. What's up?"

"Two things. First, I'm taking Clay out tonight to The Den. You two want to join us?"

"Yeah, we're in. Tiffany's been bitching that she wants to go dancing."

Logan heard Tiffany complaining in the background and then Carlos's deep voice apologizing. Logan rolled his eyes and waited but he'd had enough when it got quiet. He didn't even want to guess what they were doing. "Hey! I'm still on the phone."

Carlos came back on the line, laughing. "My bad. We'll meet you guys there."

"Alright, cool." He hesitated for a moment before he asked his second question. "Did you ever mess around before you got with Tiffany?"

Carlos laughed again. "Are you kidding? You know I couldn't keep it in my pants."

Logan grinned as he heard, "Oww! Fuck, Tiffany. That hurt!" Then indistinct grumbling from Tiffany. Logan cut in before Carlos could start apologizing to his sub again. "I meant while you were pursuing Tiffany."

Carlos told him to hold on for a moment. There was rustling and then a door closing. "What's this about, man?" Carlos asked, all joking gone from his voice.

Logan sighed in frustration. "Back when I was letting Clay think things over, I had a little encounter with Ryan."

"Oh for shit's sake, Logan! You fucked him?"

"No! Damn, Carlos. Why do you have to immediately assume that? But there was one night where some things happened. And now I don't know if I should tell Clay."

"Why are you even thinking about it? Has he asked or something?"

"No, but I've had a couple run-ins with Ryan and it has me thinking that he plans to say something."

"Look. Ordinarily, I'd say just leave it alone. It's over. You're with Clay now and there's no point in bringing up old shit."

Logan waited for Carlos to finish, the 'but' clear in his voice. When he remained quiet Logan finally prodded him to speak. "But?"

"*But*, Clay is a hair-trigger. And I don't know what you did with Ryan, but if it was more than a handshake *and* it happened while you were going after Clay *and* he finds out about it from someone other than you? Things could get ugly between the two of you. So my advice is just to tell him."

Logan held the phone with silence of his own before he finally thanked Carlos and hung up. His friend was probably right. Clay *was* a hair trigger and Logan didn't want to do anything to jeopardize their relationship. But he didn't want to ruin the evening he had planned for them or what he hoped was going to happen during their upcoming days off. So Logan would tell him. Just … not yet.

He leaned back against his kitchen counter and closed his eyes, unable to believe how stupid he'd been that night. Because even though he'd ended the evening drunk, he remembered everything that happened.

A group of them had gone out to a local bar for an officer's upcoming nuptials and baby. He'd been sitting at a booth in the back, Clay next to him. All of a sudden, they'd been by themselves at the table as everyone else left to go to the bar, bathroom, or were on the dance floor.

Logan had been so pleased to finally be somewhat alone with Clay that he dared to lift his arm from where it rested along the booth behind him and brushed his fingers up and down Clay's neck. When Clay didn't pull away, Logan grew bolder, massaging his neck, sliding his thumb underneath the collar of his t-shirt to stroke over his spine. Clay had relaxed into his touch and he started to get excited, thinking that something might happen between them that night. He scooted closer, just enough to brush his thigh against Clay's. And although the other man was still staring straight ahead, Logan saw his lips part, his tongue briefly darting out to lick them.

He applied the slightest bit of pressure to Clay's neck to get him to turn and face him. When Clay raised his eyes to Logan's, he saw the sweetest mix of desire and hesitation. He wanted so badly to just kiss Clay and show him how good it could be between them. But he hadn't. He told Clay he would wait for him to decide. And they were out in public. He was already pushing it with his hand on Clay's neck. That he might be able to shrug off as just an awkward moment if someone caught them, but there was no explaining away a kiss. So he'd waited, the air thick with tension between them, his fingers tingling with the urge to pull Clay closer. All he needed was for Clay to say yes, or okay, or even just nod his head. If he had, Logan would have had them out of that bar and back to his house in no time. But that didn't happen. Instead, Clay's phone rang. He'd looked startled for a moment and then dug it out of his pocket to answer it. He'd told whoever it was to hold on and then, with an apologetic and slightly relieved look at Logan, he slid out of the booth to take the call outside.

Logan groaned in frustration as he watched Clay's retreating back. But he had to choke back his disappointment when Clay came back to the booth and chose to sit on the other side next to Q instead of in the spot he'd been saving for him. A few minutes after that, Clay made his excuses and left with Q. And a few minutes after that, feeling defeated, Logan had already knocked back four shots and was on his second beer. He kept drinking, and soon after that, he'd been completely shitfaced.

Ryan had been there and he offered to drive him home. Logan said yes because he knew he had no business behind the wheel. Ryan walked him to the door, and once there, he asked if he wanted some company. Logan had been so frustrated, and drunk, and goddamn horny that he'd pulled him into the house. He'd slammed Ryan up against the door, kissing him hard and grinding their cocks together. But the whole time he'd been kissing Ryan, he wished it was Clay he was pressed against. With that thought in mind, he hadn't wanted to taste Ryan anymore. He turned so that his back was to the door and pushed Ryan to his knees.

The young man knew what he wanted. Ryan freed him from his jeans, stroking him to full hardness. And yeah, he'd definitely had his dick in Ryan's mouth that night. But as he'd leaned back against the door with his eyes closed, all he could see was Clay as he'd been earlier at the table. His eyes wide and his pulse beating fast in his throat as he tried to decide if he was ready. It had finally clicked in his alcohol soaked brain that what he was doing was wrong and if he couldn't be with Clay, he didn't want to be with anyone else.

He pushed Ryan off him and told him to leave. Ryan had been confused and probably a little pissed. But Logan didn't care, he just wanted him gone. The second he was, Logan staggered to the bathroom and stood under an icy cold shower until his head was somewhat clear and his hard-on was gone. After he finished and dried off, he collapsed on the bed in disbelief at what he'd almost done. He had a history with Ryan, but it would have been unacceptable to spend the night with him while trying to convince Clay to give him a chance. He breathed a sigh of relief that he had enough awareness not to go through with it. He had no intention of making a mistake like that again so he put it out of his head. He hadn't thought of it since. Until now with Ryan making noise like he planned to spill.

Logan decided to quit thinking about that whole mess. He already made up his mind to tell Clay after this week. And if Ryan decided to say something to his lover, well, then, he'd be happy to give him some training for SWAT – the most painful, brutal training ever. Logan would show him he meant it when he said to keep his mouth shut.

26

Logan walked into Clay's apartment. "I heard you did well in your class yesterday. High marks from all the attendees," he said as he settled on the sofa.

Clay sat next to him. "I did." He smirked. "My first lecture and I'm already the best speaker in the department. I'm adding that to my accolades of being the best scout HPD SWAT has ever seen." Clay climbed onto his lap, straddling him. "Let's celebrate."

Logan shook his head with a smile. "You're so modest."

Clay rolled his eyes. "Modesty is a false emotion. I don't believe in it."

Logan laughed. "The shit that comes out of your mouth. No wonder you're always in trouble. But doing well like that will be in your favor when it's time to talk promotion." He pushed Clay off his lap. "We'll celebrate. I even have a surprise for you."

Clay's hands came up and covered his nipples, an expression of mock horror on his face. "I don't think I can take any more of your surprises."

Logan gave him a stern look. "Careful or I'll show you just how much you *can* take."

Clay bit his lip, his eyes sparking with teasing and arousal. "So what's my surprise? A Prince Albert?"

"No." He let his eyes dip down to Clay's crotch. "But that might be something we revisit later." Clay grinned at him. "Your surprise is I'm taking you out tonight. Somewhere special."

Clay looked at him in surprised pleasure. "My boyfriend is taking me out on a date! I don't have to be ashamed anymore that he only wants me for booty calls," he joked.

"Enough with the sarcasm," he warned with a swift, hard kiss.

Clay laughed and gave him a much softer kiss. "Just ignore my smart ass mouth. So where are we going?" His face fell a little. "This isn't a fancy place is it? Because I don't do too well with fancy."

"It's not fancy. I promise," Logan reassured him. "But they do have a dress code. So go put on something nice."

About fifteen minutes later, Clay came out of the bedroom. "What do you think? I look good?"

Logan stood up. He thought his boyfriend looked more than good. He'd chosen a dark purple, short sleeved shirt. His jeans were a black rinse and fit him at the waist and straight down the leg. His tumble of black curls had been tamed and brushed so that they gleamed under the lights. Logan walked over and wrapped his arms around him.

"You look good alright. Good enough to eat." He rubbed his face into Clay's neck. "And you smell good enough to eat too." Logan kissed the soft skin there before running his tongue up to Clay's ear. Sucking his earlobe into his mouth, he bit down gently. Logan felt a shiver run through Clay and his hips moved against his. He lightly grasped his chin and kissed him, thrusting his tongue inside Clay's warm, sweet mouth. Their tongues stroked against each other soft and slow, Clay pressing close against him. Before things got too heavy, Logan pulled away. He grabbed Clay's hand and brought it to his cock. He was already hard.

"See what you do to me, baby?"

Clay stroked him through his pants and looked at him. "Maybe I can take care of that for you before we go?" he asked, biting at his bottom lip.

Logan was tempted as he gazed into those pretty blue eyes. But he knew if he felt Clay's hands and mouth on his cock, he wasn't going to stop. He'd want more. He always wanted more when it came to this man. He cleared his throat and took a step back. "No, we need to go. Carlos and Tiffany are waiting on us."

Clay groaned.

Logan frowned in confusion. "What? You don't want to hang out with them?"

"It's not that. It's just … I never get to finish my soda when we hang with those two."

Logan was still confused until he remembered what Clay was talking about. "I promise you'll get to finish all the root beer you want tonight," he said with a laugh.

27

Clay shared office gossip as they sped down the highway. "So Tony is staying home to take care of the kid while his wife goes back to work. Can you believe that?" Tony was a young black cop on the force. "I don't have a problem with it. I'm just surprised since Tony loved being a cop so much. But I guess stranger things have happened."

Logan's voice was low as he responded. "Yeah. Like me getting to spank your round little ass after all the time I spent lusting after it."

Clay shifted in his seat as he remembered the feel of Logan's belt cracking across his ass. He swallowed hard. "Right. Who'd a thunk it?"

Logan laughed and Clay changed the subject before he could say something else to get him even more turned on. "So where are you taking me?"

"To a BDSM club."

Clay sat up straight. "No shit! Will I see someone tied to a St. Andrew's cross and getting whipped? Do people wear ball gags there?" He saw Logan glance at him out of the corner of his eye.

"What have you been looking at?"

Clay smirked. "Wouldn't you like to know?"

"I would actually. But no, you won't see that. That all takes place behind closed doors in private rooms."

Clay's eyes widened. He'd sort of just been joking. Then he had a thought. "Aren't you worried someone will see us and we'll be outed?" That was the reason they hadn't gone on too many public dates.

"No. This place is very private. We'll be fine. Besides, anyone who is here probably wants to keep that a secret as well." Logan reached for his hand. "But would that bother you to be outed? Not as being into the *scene*, but with a man. We haven't talked about that much."

Clay didn't respond for a moment. He was in his head, seeing the look of disgust on his fellow sailors' faces. Including the face of the man he'd been with. He finally answered. "I don't know. But I guess eventually we're going to have to talk about that."

Logan took his eyes from the road for a moment and looked at him. "Yeah. We will."

Clay steered the conversation to lighter topics for the rest of the ride. They drove for a few more minutes until Logan pulled up to a clean and neat but fairly non-descript looking building. Rather than parking in the street, he drove down into an underground garage attached to the building. They came to a tall gate and Logan rolled down the window to enter a pin on the key pad, driving in after the gate opened. They parked and got out. Clay followed Logan over to the elevator, watching as he put in another code to start it moving.

Clay whistled low. "Damn, you weren't kidding about being secure. Do celebrities hang out here or something?"

Logan nodded. "Yep."

"Really? What about presidents? Have there ever been any presidents here?"

Logan smiled mysteriously. "I don't know about presidents, but there have been several Texas politicians here."

The elevator door opened and they stepped into a very nice lobby. The floor was black marble while the walls were painted a stark white. There were well-kept live plants and several chairs and couches covered in dark gray suede scattered throughout the area. They walked up to a … well, Clay didn't want to call him a bouncer even though he was big enough to be one. But he was dressed so classy, in a nice gray suit, sitting behind a white marble desk. Clay decided doorman fit the guy better.

"Good evening," he greeted. "Your membership numbers, please?"

Logan rattled off his number and Clay waited for him to say something like "and guest." Instead, he gave a second string of numbers. Had Logan gotten him a membership there?

"Thank you, Sir. I'll need you to check your cell phones. Will you need one drawer or two?"

"One is fine," Logan answered. He passed the doorman his phone and then reached out for Clay's. He handed it over without question. The doorman/bouncer locked them up in one of the little cubby drawers on the wall behind him and gave Logan the key. Logan took it and slid it into his pocket. Then he wrapped a hand around the back of Clay's neck as they walked across the lobby to a set of frosted glass doors.

"That was some top secret shit."

Logan nodded. "There are a lot of people into the scene that can't afford to have their tastes be public knowledge since BDSM is still considered pretty taboo. So, private clubs like this exist to meet that need. No names are given when visiting, only membership numbers. You have to be sponsored by another member and the credit card charge shows up as a health club on your bill. Cell phones are taken to make sure no one takes any pictures. Logan opened the heavy and, apparently, sound proofed doors and Clay got his first look at the club.

He'd been expecting it to be dark and broody with chains hanging from the walls and everyone dressed in black leather. Instead, he entered a room with more glossy black marble flooring. The walls were painted a soft gray and decorated with large black and white art photographs of people in various BDSM poses and outfits. The lighting was soft, especially at the booths. They were all circular with very high backs, offering the occupants privacy. And they were lit by a soft glow that came from the table instead of overhead. Clay kept looking around as he walked with his Dom.

Logan must have known where he was going since he headed in a straight line, still herding him along. But before they reached wherever their destination was, they came up behind Carlos and Tiffany. Logan reached out and tapped her on the shoulder.. Carlos immediately turned to see why she had stopped.

As the four of them greeted each other, Clay couldn't help but stare at Tiffany and Carlos. Carlos was dressed in a tight, black, short-sleeved shirt, his heavily muscled and tattooed arms on full display. His tee was only tucked into his dark gray pants in the front, a big silver belt buckle drawing attention to his hard abs. His hair was freshly buzzed and his brown eyes looked almost black in the dim lighting. Tiffany wore a pale blue bandage style dress that showed off her curves and great muscle tone. She straightened her curly hair and pulled it into a sleek ponytail that lay over her shoulder. But it was Tiffany's neck that his eyes were drawn to. The low cut dress showed off to perfection the thick, brushed-steel collar that circled her throat. In the dim light, Clay could just barely make out the engraved calligraphy that spelled out Ortega's Pet.

Clay leaned over and whispered in Logan's ear. "They make a good looking couple."

Logan turned to look at Clay and was surprised when he saw what looked like insecurity on his face. He wrapped an arm around his neck and pulled him close to whisper back, "Don't worry about that. You're perfect to me and you're the only one I want." Clay didn't react but Logan could tell that his words pleased him. They sat down at their reserved booth and a server immediately came over to take their drink orders. Clay ordered a root beer as usual, showing surprise when Logan did the same.

"You know I don't mind if you drink something harder."

"I know, but you don't like it when I taste like whiskey when we kiss." He brushed his lips against his lover's. "And I plan on kissing you tonight. A lot." Logan smiled. "In fact…" He kissed Clay right then, stroking his tongue across the seam of his lips until Clay opened with a sigh and let him in. Their tongues tangled together hotly, their passion heightened by the fact that they were finally somewhere they didn't have to hide their relationship.

Logan pulled back and looked at Clay. He loved seeing his lover like that, lips swollen and wet from their kiss, eyes soft and dazed with arousal. He would do anything to make sure he got to put that look on Clay's face every day.

"How cute," Carlos mocked. "The honeymoon phase where you can't keep your hands off each other."

Logan and Clay both looked at Carlos. He was brushing his fingers over Tiffany's bare shoulder and nuzzling her ear as they watched.

"Uh… then what's your excuse?" Clay asked.

Carlos smirked. "I'm a big horn-dog?"

Logan and Clay laughed as Tiffany elbowed him in the side. The four of them sat, talking and enjoying themselves. The music changed to a fast paced pop song and Tiffany started to leave the booth by scooting over Carlos's lap.

"Tiffany, what the fuck are you doing?"

"I love this song! I want to go dance," she replied.

"And that's the only way you could think of to get out of this booth?" Carlos growled.

Standing up, she gave Carlos a cheeky grin. "Not the only way but definitely the best way." She turned to Clay. "I'm only allowed to dance with other subbies. You wanna come with?"

Clay snorted. "Only if Uncle Jack is playing."

Tiffany looked confused when he named the local rap group. "Who?"

Logan laughed. "That was a no, Tiffany." Tiffany shrugged then took off for the dance floor, immediately finding a group to dance with. Logan gave Clay a quick kiss then excused himself from the table.

Clay turned to look at Carlos. He was watching Tiffany out on the dance floor with an amused expression on his face. Clay started to say something to Carlos but instead looked up as someone approached their table.

"Can I buy you a drink?"

"No, thanks. I'm set," Clay said, gesturing to his root beer.

"Alright, then, would you like to dance?"

Clay looked at the guy, starting to get annoyed. "No."

The guy persisted. "Why not? You're not collared."

Clay didn't know what the etiquette was for the place but he was about to snap on this guy. Before he could lose his temper, Carlos spoke up.

"He might not be wearing a collar, but you know he's here with someone because I saw you watch him as we walked over here. So fuck off and leave him alone."

The other man glared but must have decided he didn't want to square up against Carlos because he turned and walked away.

Clay looked at Carlos in surprise. "Thanks, man."

Carlos turned away from where he'd been staring after the obnoxious Dom. He shrugged. "Logan is my best friend, and he's been alone and fairly miserable for a long time. I've never seen him as happy as he's been since he got with you. As far as I'm concerned, I'll always have your back. Even more than before."

Tiffany came back to the table and sat down. Carlos immediately kissed and stroked his fingers over her collar. Clay looked away, not wanting to intrude on their moment. He caught the eye of someone else, but just as he started to look away, he realized he knew the person. It was Sam Roberts, a crime scene detective. Clay was surprised but raised his hand in greeting. Roberts acknowledged him with a small head nod, but didn't come his way.

Clay glanced back at the couple next to him and saw Tiffany smiling shyly at something Carlos said. He wondered what it would be like to wear Logan's collar and have the type of connection Carlos and Tiffany had. He was imagining a collar around his own throat when Logan came back to the table. Even though he knew Logan couldn't read his mind, his face flushed in embarrassment. Logan sat down and gave him a questioning look.

"What were you thinking about?"

Clay just shook his head, for once not letting his mouth immediately spew what was in his brain.

Logan smiled. "Don't make me say it."

"Say what?"

Logan put on a campy evil villain accent. "I have vays ov making you talk."

Clay laughed. "The more I get to know you, Sarge, the cornier I realize you are."

Logan just smiled again. "Yeah, but you like it."

"I like you."

That simple statement earned him another kiss from Logan. This time his big hand settled at the small of Clay's back, pulling him up against him until their chests pressed together. Clay wrapped his arms around Logan's neck letting him suck his tongue, moaning when his Dom bit his lip and then licked over the spot. They were so into it they didn't even notice when Carlos and Tiffany left the booth to go and dance to the slow song that had come on. When they finally stopped, Clay decided to bring up what he'd been thinking about earlier in a roundabout way.

"This guy tried to get me to go off with him while you were gone."

Logan sat up straight and scanned the crowd. "What? Who?" He looked like he was about to go and put a beat down on whoever it was that had bothered him.

"At ease, Sergeant. Carlos ran him off like a good guard dog. But he seemed to think that since I wasn't wearing a collar, I was fair game."

Logan turned back to Clay. "I'm sorry, baby. Most Doms in here aren't such blow-hards."

He shrugged. "No big." He paused for a moment before he asked his question. "But am I?"

"Are you what?"

Clay looked down. "Am I fair game because I'm not … since I don't have a collar?"

Logan wrapped a hand around the back of his neck, his thumb rubbing along his throat. "Of course not, baby. You're mine, you know that."

He bit his lip and nodded. "I know. I was just wondering …" Clay trailed off and didn't finish his sentence. He couldn't believe it. *He* was at a loss for words.

Logan knew what Clay was thinking about. He wanted to know if he was going to be collared. And that made Logan even more certain that he'd made the right decision on how he planned for them to spend the next few days. He moved his hand until he clasped Clay by the throat, pulling him closer.

"Do you think you're ready for that? To be completely mine? To really accept my dominance over you and acknowledge that I own you?" Logan felt Clay's pulse speed up under his palm.

"Yes, Sir," he whispered. "I'm ready. I want that."

Logan closed the last few inches between them and kissed Clay fiercely. He hadn't been kidding when he said he planned to kiss his sub a lot that night. After a few moments of their lips pressed together, Logan paused, resting his forehead against Clay's as they caught their breath. The music changed and Clay pulled back, tilting his head to the side as he listened.

"Is that who I think it is?"

Logan smiled. "The DJ is a big fan of the local music scene and he had some of their stuff."

A huge smile broke out on Clay's face. "You asked the DJ to play some Uncle Jack for me?"

Logan nodded, enjoying his lover's pleasure at such a small thing.

Just then, Tiffany came bouncing up to the table. "Alright, Clay, I know this is your kind of music. Come dance!"

Clay laughed and gave Logan a slight push to move and let him out of the booth. He didn't usually dance but since Logan had gone through the trouble to have one of his favorite rap groups played, he would match Tiffany step for step on that dance floor.

28

Early the next morning, the alarm clock on Clay's phone went off. He pushed his arm from underneath the covers, patting around on the nightstand until he found the thing. He sat up slightly to thumb it to silence.

Logan's arm came around his waist, pulling him back into the cradle of his big, warm body.

"Don't even think about trying to leave this bed. We've only been asleep for about three hours."

"I know, but I have to get back home." Clay shivered as Logan kissed the nape of his neck.

"No you don't. Stay the whole weekend with me."

Clay turned over to face Logan in surprise. "You're just now asking me to stay the weekend?"

Logan smiled without opening his eyes. "I was a bit busy last night. It slipped my mind."

Clay hesitated for only a moment. He knew the time would come when Logan would invite him to stay over for more than just one night. He'd been unsure if he was ready for it before but now that Logan was asking him, he realized he definitely wanted to. "Okay. I'll stay but you have to – oh crap!"

Logan finally opened his eyes and looked at him. "What?"

"I forgot that I'm being interviewed at the Leet Speak Magazine convention this afternoon for Ian's new game today. He used me as a knowledge base for a lot of stuff in the game and asked that I be there to lend some authenticity to the interview. So I have to go home but I can come back when I'm done."

"You'll come immediately after?"

"Yes, I promise."

"Good." Logan pushed Clay over onto his back. "The interview is this afternoon you said?"

"Yeah," Clay said slowly as Logan rubbed low on his belly.

"So that means you don't have to leave right now."

Clay took a little longer to answer this time. He was distracted by Logan's hand cupping his sac. "Umm… no. I guess not," he said, opening his legs to give Logan easier access.

"Then you'll spend the day here with me in bed."

It was a command not a question. As Logan squeezed his balls lightly, Clay gasped and gave the only appropriate response. "Yes, Sir."

****

The convention was packed. And loud. Vendors had demo booths set up all over the hall with their games and consoles on display for testing. Clay was impressed with Ian's booth. Two giant posters of the game cover flanked the set up. The crowd in line was excited, craning their necks to see the big screen where two con attendees played through a level. And of course Ian had a couple of models there. They were dressed in a sexy version of a SWAT uniform, smiling flirtatiously as they passed out swag like t-shirts, lanyards, and a key to download new gear in the game. Clay laughed at the good natured shit talking going on between the two currently playing.

He stepped to the side to talk with Ian while they waited for the Leet Speak Mag people to come around for the interview. "I'm in awe, man. Look at this shit. A crowd full of people waiting to play your game." He clapped his friend on the back. "This is awesome."

Ian grinned. "Yep. I'm so pro."

"I don't speak gamer, but I'm going to assume that means you're doing good."

Ian laughingly agreed and asked how things were going with Logan. Clay tried to play it cool. He shrugged. "Things are good."

Ian laughed again. "You are so full of shit, man. Just admit that you're in *love*." He dragged out the last word in an obnoxious voice and made kissy faces.

"Shut up, Ian. You're the one that's full of it." But Ian didn't shut up, not that Clay actually expected him to.

"Did you or did you not send me a text all giddy that Pierce asked the DJ at some club to play some rap group for you?"

"Yeah," he answered grudgingly.

"And I texted you a couple of times to see if you wanted to have breakfast before we met up, but I didn't get a response. Why is that?"

"Maybe I was tired and just wanted to spend the day in bed."

Ian burst out laughing. "I can't believe you just said that with a straight face."

Clay had to laugh too. "Fucker. If you already think you know how things are going with us, then why'd you ask?"

"I just wanted to see if you'd pass my test and admit it." He shook his head sadly. "Unfortunately, you failed."

Clay rolled his eyes. "I thought I was here to talk about your damn video game – not gab about my feelings like I'm some fifteen-year-old girl."

Ian let it go. "Alright, man." Then he smirked. "But I bet you don't make it twenty minutes into the day before you bring up Pierce."

"I'm a civil servant. I can't afford to gamble with you."

"Oh, this isn't a gamble. It's a sure thing."

****

Logan spent the day getting ready for Clay's weekend visit. He'd taken the time to watch the interview Clay and his friend Ian did at the convention. Clay texted him the link to find the live stream online. When the interviewer briefly asked about real life SWAT versus the video game, Clay made a comment about staying in peak physical condition. He joked it was hard for him and that he had to lay off the cookies and cream ice cream. Logan was surprised. He loved Clay's slender and lightly muscled body. He couldn't imagine that Clay would see anything wrong in the way he looked. He'd have to make sure his sub realized just how attractive he found him. Logan was even more surprised when Clay brought him up in the interview. He praised his leadership and skills, joking that the sergeant in the video game couldn't compete with him.

Logan heard a car coming up the drive as he took the garlic bread out of the oven. He started to head to the front door then remembered one thing he hadn't done. He was working on a project but he wasn't ready for Clay to know about it. He took off for the stairs, taking them two at a time and running down the hallway. He reached the last door on the right, locked it, slammed it closed then ran back down to the foyer. The doorbell rang just as he reached the front door. He opened it just a little out of breath. Clay noticed and gave him a curious look as Logan let him in.

"Why are you out of breath?"

Logan took Clay's bag from him and backed him up against the door. "Maybe I'm just excited to see you."

Clay's eyebrow rose. "Yeah, right. Tell the truth. You were playing with yourself, weren't you?"

Logan was laughing as he kissed his lover. "Why would I be playing with myself when I knew you were on your way here to do it for me?"

Clay wrapped his arms around Logan's neck. "Good point." They kissed each other hello, both of them glad to be together again even though they'd only been separated for a few hours. Logan sent Clay on to the kitchen while he went upstairs to put his bag away.

In the kitchen, Clay saw Logan made spaghetti with garlic bread and a salad. He offered to help bring everything to the table but Logan told him to sit down. He set a plate of food in front of Clay.

Clay took a bite to taste. "I'm impressed. This is good."

He snorted. "Don't be too impressed. Spaghetti is pretty much the only thing I can cook. Although, I do make a mean fried bologna and cheese sandwich."

Clay made a disgusted face. "Yuck. You'll be eating that by yourself."

They sat and talked about nothing in particular as they ate. Finally, Clay sat back in his chair after he'd taken his last bite. "That was really good." He smiled at Logan. "You take such good care of me. I want to be able to do something for you too."

"You can." Logan stood from his chair and pulled Clay up as well, pressing their bodies together. "I'm going to clean up the kitchen. And when I'm done, I want to come in my bedroom and find you kneeling on my bed, completely naked."

Clay's lips parted, his skin already warming with arousal. "I didn't mean something sexual but I'm okay with that."

Logan smiled. "It's not sexual. Well, not totally anyway." With that cryptic remark, Logan swatted him on the ass and pushed him out of the kitchen.

29

Clay kneeled on the bed, hands resting on his thighs as he'd been taught, wondering what Logan had in store for him. He didn't have long to wait before Logan came into the room, his presence so strong and commanding that Clay automatically lowered his head. Logan crossed to the bed and put a finger under his chin, tipping his head up so their eyes met.

"You told me yesterday that you were ready to wear my collar. Do you still feel that way?"

Clay's eyes widened, his heart pounding in anticipation. Was it about to happen? "Yes, Sir. I do."

"You understand that if you accept it, you are truly mine. I will be the one in control in this relationship. In return, I promise to always take care of you. If you ever need or want anything, all you have to do is tell me."

Clay nodded. He loved the way Logan took care of him. It was something he hadn't even realized he needed. Now that he had it, he didn't ever want to be without it. "I understand." He watched as Logan pulled a slim leather jewelry box from his back pocket. When he opened it Clay saw what the collar looked like but he didn't touch it. It wasn't his to touch until Logan gave it to him. The collar was made from the same stainless steel that was used to make their handcuffs. The clasp used a locking mechanism identical to that of their handcuffs also. Boldly etched across the front of the collar was PIERCE stamped in the straight clean lines that labeled SWAT on their uniforms. It was clean, simple, and beautiful. And Clay wanted it on his neck immediately. He looked up as Logan spoke.

Logan stroked a finger over the metal. "Do you like it?"

Clay nodded. "It's beautiful, Sir."

Logan cleared his throat. "Clay, I wanted you for so long that when I finally had you I could barely believe it. And watching you give up control to me is the most perfect thing I've ever seen. Your submission is so deep and real. So I'm asking you to wear my collar. To truly be my submissive."

Clay swallowed thickly before he responded. "Yes. Please, Sir. I want to be yours."

Logan smiled and took the collar from its box. He threw the box aside and placed the collar around Clay's neck. When Clay heard the clasp click closed, a shiver went through him. That sense of belonging that he'd been feeling was magnified a thousand times, echoing through every part of him. He belonged to Logan and that knowledge made him feel safe and secure. Clay touched his fingers to his collar and looked up at his Dom. "I belong to you," he said.

Logan nodded, a heady mixture of victory, desire, and possession swirling through him. He grabbed Clay by his upper arms and pulled him up against him. "Yes, baby. You belong to me." Then he kissed him, taking complete control of his lips and tongue. The thought that Clay was his raced through his brain. Everything Logan was feeling as Clay accepted his collar came through in his kiss. The kiss was hard with Logan smashing their lips together, thrusting his tongue into his sub's mouth. When they broke apart, Clay look dazed for a moment. He blinked slowly then bit his lip as a gleeful look came over his face.

"Can I go see what it looks like?"

Logan ran his finger along the new metal around Clay's throat. "Go ahead."

Clay hopped off the bed and ran into the bathroom to the big mirror there. Logan had to smile at how eager his sub was. He followed him in at a slower pace. Clay was in front of the mirror, his chin lifted as he traced his fingers over the lettering on the collar. He had an adorable mix of happiness and disbelief on his face. Logan came up behind him and wrapped his hand around Clay's throat, just under the collar. "You are so beautiful. Even more so with my collar around your neck."

Logan kissed Clay on his shoulder, his other arm coming up to circle around his middle. Logan closed his eyes and rested his forehead along the side of Clay's neck, feeling the metal of the collar cool against his skin. Clay was his now. He'd finally claimed the man that he wanted above all others. The man who accepted his need to dominate and gave him his submission so freely in return. Logan took a deep breath, inhaling Clay's scent. He would do whatever it took to keep his sub happy, because he was never letting him go.

He lifted his head and turned Clay's face to his enough that they could kiss over his shoulder. His let his hand drift down Clay's belly until he reached his cock. He was already semi-hard when Logan grasped him. He quickly stiffened further as Logan started to stroke. Clay moaned into his mouth and went to turn to face him completely but Logan shook his head. His sub immediately stopped and watched him, waiting to see what he wanted. Logan brought two fingers to Clay's lips. His lover opened up and sucked them in, still looking at him over his shoulder.

Logan pulled his fingers from Clay's mouth and trailed them down to his ass, slipping them between his cheeks. He sought and found his tight entrance, teasing and tapping against it, making Clay squirm before Logan finally pushed one finger in. Logan worked it in deep, thrusting slowly and maintaining the same pace with his stroking. He tried to take his time, but he was impatient to be inside his lover, to really feel him for the first time. So when Clay's breath started to come faster, Logan quickly pushed a second finger in, scissoring them to get that tight channel ready for his cock. Clay started moaning and Logan couldn't wait any longer. He removed his fingers to get a bottle of lube from the drawer. Unzipping his pants, he quickly covered his shaft in the silky liquid. With his own breath racing just as fast as Clay's, he pressed his cock to his entrance and pushed inside.

Clay gasped. "You're not wearing—"

Logan cut him off. "No more condoms, baby. I won't have anything between us again." He began thrusting. "From now on, when I take you, I'll fill you up with my cum." He sucked

Clay's earlobe into his mouth and bit down before releasing him. Logan whispered in his ear, "I've been dreaming about coming in your ass, watching my cum slide down those pretty thighs because you can't hold it all. Don't you want to feel your Dom's cum bursting inside you, thick and hot?" Clay's head dropped back against his shoulder as he moaned yes, his eyes drifting shut.

"No, Clay. Open your eyes. I want you to see what I see when I fuck you."

Clay obeyed and looked. What he saw was himself, naked, while Logan stood behind him fully clothed. Being undressed while Logan wasn't made him feel vulnerable and exposed, but in a way that was arousing instead of scary. Logan shook his head but kept up his slow thrusting.

"You don't see it. Don't see why I think you're so beautiful."

Logan let go of his cock and Clay whined in protest, but he shut up when Logan slapped him sharply on the thigh. Clay apologized and was rewarded when Logan guided him to wrap his own hand around his shaft. Logan moved their hands together on Clay's cock before he let go. Clay wasn't going to assume that Logan wanted him to keep going so he looked at his Dom in the mirror for permission. When he got a nod, he continued stroking himself at the slow, steady pace that Logan had set.

"What I see is this warm sexy flush that spreads from your neck up to your face."

Clay tried to concentrate on Logan's low voice whispering in his ear, but it was hard with the way he was pumping inside him. Goose bumps broke out on his skin as Logan lightly brushed his fingers over each place on Clay he described.

"I see your lips parted as you gasp, that bottom lip pouting and daring me to run my tongue over it. I see these pretty blue eyes hazy and dazed with arousal, especially as you start holding back your orgasm until I give you permission to come." Logan licked his shoulder. "I love to watch a sweat break out on your skin until I just want to lick all over your chest and your soft, sweet belly. He smiled. "And you know I love these," he finished, flicking his fingers over his nipple rings.

Clay couldn't tear his eyes away from Logan's as his Dom told him all those things. When Logan told him he was beautiful before, he hadn't really thought too much of it. They'd just been words to him. But now... now he saw what Logan saw. It made him feel good. Not just because Logan found him physically attractive, but because that attraction was tied to how it made Logan feel. That made him feel even more connected to his Dom. Logan started thrusting faster and the pleasure humming throughout his body dragged him out of his head.

"Stroke yourself faster, baby. I want you to see yourself come."

Clay followed Logan's instructions, pumping his fist quickly, his hand sliding slick and wet on his cock from the pre-cum beaded on the tip. His breaths were sharp, rasping in his chest as he felt his orgasm rising.

"That's it, baby. Come for me. And don't you dare close your eyes."

Logan closed his mouth around the skin just under his collar, sucking hard. Clay cried out as Logan bit him, his cock jerked in response, and he was coming. He kept stroking and Logan kept thrusting while he fought to keep his eyes open. He saw the flush on his skin darken. Saw his body shuddering – hips thrusting forwards, eyes heavy-lidded as he stared at himself in the mirror. Watching himself orgasm with Logan also watching was one of the most erotic experiences of Clay's life. His whole body tingled and his stomach clenched hard as he pulsed into his hand again and again. Finally, he was spent. His hand stopped moving and so did Logan.

He was breathing hard as Logan grasped his hand and lifted it to his mouth. Logan's tongue came out and licked at his fingers, catching Clay's cum and swallowing it down. Clay watched him in the mirror, his eyes gone wide, the sight making him hard again. But Logan didn't clean it all. Instead, he smashed their hands together, twining their fingers before kissing the back of his hand. Logan lowered their joined hands as his other came up and wrapped around his throat. He started to move again.

"You're mine now, Clay."

Clay whispered yes in response, his brain focused on nothing but the feel of Logan moving thick and hard inside him.

"Let me hear you say it."

It was a command, and Clay heard and responded even through the haze of pleasure in his head. "I'm yours, Sir."

Logan released their clasped hands and grabbed onto his hip, squeezing tight and holding him steady as he pushed faster and deeper inside him. He eased him forward with the hand at his neck, bending him down until he braced his hands on the counter.

"Say it again."

"I'm yours, Sir. Only yours." Logan moved even faster, pounding into him, his hips thudding against his ass, the head of his cock brushing his prostate with each thrust. Pleasure radiated throughout Clay's body from that spot and he lowered himself even further, silently encouraging Logan's hard, forceful thrusts.

"I own you, Clay."

Clay dropped his chin to his chest. It should feel wrong to take pleasure in another man saying that to him. But hell, Logan *did* own him. He owned every reaction of his body. Owned him so much that he simply closed his eyes and accepted whatever Logan chose to do to him. He knew what was best and Clay just wanted to be open for him, to take him into his body. Clay dragged his eyes back up to look in the mirror. He saw Logan watching him, a look of fierce possession on his face. A shiver chased down Clay's spine to be the object of such focus from another person. Yet at the same time, he loved the fact that that look was for him. Their eyes remained locked as Logan pumped into him with all his strength. A small, almost smug smile curled his firm lips.

"You love this don't you? Me fucking you. Owning you." Logan dug his fingers into Clay's hip, holding him firmly. "Giving you no choice but to take it."

Clay nodded, gasping for breath, his cock insanely hard at Logan's words. He was glad that Logan didn't ask him to say it out loud, because he didn't think he was capable of speaking right then. His hands curled into fists on the countertop as his balls started to tighten, his body trembling with another approaching orgasm.

Logan thrust into Clay again and again, his naked cock firmly gripped in his tight heat. It felt incredible to feel Clay's velvety channel directly on the skin of his cock. This was how he was meant to be inside his lover.

"About to come for you, baby. Gonna fill this tight little ass up with my cum."

He looked at Clay as he spoke. Logan could read it in his face, could practically hear him thinking that his sub wanted to come too. Reaching down, he grabbed Clay's shaft, pumping him fast and squeezing the head on each upstroke until he was fully hard again. "Come with me, Clay," he ordered.

They started to come together. Clay's ass clenching around his cock heightened the sensation. His balls drew up hard and tight until he shouted, "Fuck, Clay! Feels so good to come inside you." Logan ground his hips hard against Clay's, pushing deep within him as he came inside his submissive for the very first time. He felt as though he were marking and claiming Clay as his own in yet another way and he loved it. And from the way Clay was pushing back against him, moaning that it felt so hot and so good, Clay loved it too.

****

They stayed pressed together even after their bodies had nothing left to give. Their breathing slowed and their heart beats returned to normal. Logan pulled Clay up until his lover's back rested against his chest, his dark head lolling on his shoulder. Logan withdrew from him and just held his lover in his arms. He was tracing his fingers over his collar when Clay shifted against him. He felt a warm wetness on his skin and pushed Clay slightly forward. Looking down, he saw the backs of Clay's smooth thighs were wet with his cum. Without saying a word, Logan brushed his fingers over the wetness. He brought his hand to Clay's mouth, rubbing his fingers across his lips. Then he turned his lover around and kissed him slowly, sucking his lip into his mouth, the two of them sharing the taste of his cum. He wrapped his arms around Clay's waist, holding on to him as Clay relaxed and sagged against his body.

"You want to shower?"

Clay shook his head. "No, just want to lay with you."

Logan lifted him up and Clay's legs came around his waist automatically. His sub's breath was soft against his neck and he smiled as he walked them over to the bed. Clay was always so sweet after he'd come. It was so different from the way he usually was. Logan instinctively knew that even though he wasn't Clay's first, he was the only one to ever seen him like this.

30

Clay stood at the sink, rinsing dishes to put in the dishwasher. They'd just finished dinner after a movie. Logan was in the study, on the phone, talking to Captain Hayden so Clay got up to clean the kitchen himself. He came back into the room just as he was saying goodbye to Hayden.

Clay smiled without turning around as Logan's arms immediately came around his waist and his lips brushed the skin above his collar. All day, he'd been like that. Unable to keep his hands off Clay, holding him by the throat as he kissed him, tugging him closer with a finger hooked under his collar as he whispered *You're mine* in Clay's ear. It made Clay happy in a way he'd never felt before. He leaned back into Logan's embrace, tilting his head to the side to allow him easier access to his throat. "What did Hayden want?"

Logan sucked a kiss over his pulse before he asked, "Who?" in a distracted whisper.

Clay laughed. "Hayden. Captain Charles Hayden. Stuck up guy who runs the SWAT division and thinks he owns everybody in it."

Logan chuckled and stopped kissing Clay's neck. "Oh, him." He turned Clay around. "He wanted to talk about the numbers on our team. He's been after me to promote someone and bring in someone new since Mike is retiring."

Clay rolled his eyes. "He couldn't wait till you were back at the station for that?"

"You know Hayden. He wants all his *Is* dotted and *Ts* crossed on his schedule."

Clay grinned. "You should have told him to fuck off."

"I'll leave all the bucking of authority to you." Logan smoothed his hands up Clay's sides. "Especially since you look so pretty with these just within regulation silky curls tumbled all over your head." Logan watched as an adorable blush stained Clay's cheeks.

"I am not pretty," he groused.

Logan smiled at his sub's pouting. "You are. Do you want me to get you in front of the mirror and tell you why again?"

Clay lowered his eyes. "Maybe."

Logan tightened his arms around Clay's waist, pulling him up against him. He thought about telling Clay what it did to him when he lowered his head or eyes in submission like that but he wanted to keep that as his little secret. He pressed his lips to Clay's, sweeping his tongue inside. Logan savored the taste of his lover, barely noticing the cold water dripping down his back as Clay's arms came around his neck. He deepened the kiss, pressing Clay's back against the sink as he devoured his sweet mouth. When he felt Clay's hips moving softly against his, he ended the kiss. "Forget these dishes. Come shower with me."

Clay reached behind him to turn off the faucet that had been running the whole time. "I guess we should shower together to save water, seeing as how we were so wasteful just now."

Logan rolled his eyes. "Yeah, that's exactly why I want you to shower with me. Water conservation."

****

Clay leaned back against Logan's chest as they sat up in bed. He touched his fingers to his collar. "How did you choose what my collar would look like?"

Logan nuzzled his neck. "SWAT brought us together so I wanted it to influence the design." He tucked his finger beneath it. "And I chose metal because I worried leather would be stiff and chafe your skin."

Clay looked at his Dom over his shoulder. "Thank you, Sir." That caring nature Logan displayed for his team was such a part of him. He paid attention to the smallest details for Clay's comfort. It was no wonder he'd fallen so hard for Logan.

"So who do you think will get promoted this round of testing? Brady? He might be a goober, but he's great in the field."

"No clue. Maybe it'll be Brady. Maybe it'll be you."

Something in Logan's voice made Clay go still. "Logan," he began. Then he stopped and got up off the bed.

Logan looked at him, confused as Clay grabbed his hand and started pulling him from the bed. "What are you doing?"

"You said that in the bedroom you were in control, but you wouldn't restrict what I do outside of it, right?"

Logan nodded his head warily. "Yeah, to an extent."

Clay heard that qualifier but he let it go. "Then I need you to come with me." Logan finally got up from the bed and Clay pulled him into the hallway. Once they were out there, Clay let go of Logan's hand and crossed his arms over his chest.

"What the fuck, Logan? You'd better not make it a personal decision and push for me just because we're together."

"What's wrong with that? Of course I want to help you. Why wouldn't I?"

Clay was pissed. He didn't need or want help from Logan or anyone else. Everything he'd accomplished he'd done on his own and he planned to keep it that way. "Because goddamnit! If I get promoted it'll be because they're impressed with my work, not because my fucking boyfriend put in a word for me."

Logan's eyes narrowed at Clay's words and tone. Like he'd said, he would allow Clay his freedom to an extent. But that did not include being disrespectful when talking to his Dom. "Watch it, baby," he said with just a hint of dominance in his voice.

Clay lowered his arms to his sides and blew out a breath. "I'm sorry. I know that I get in my own way sometimes, but that's just something I'll have to fix on my own if I choose. I don't want to be that guy who uses you or anyone else for a step up."

"I know you would never do that. It's just one of the reasons why I love you." Logan brushed a kiss across Clay's lips. His sub didn't pull away but he didn't respond either. Logan refused to let it go. "Don't pout, Clay. If you want Brady to get that patch instead of you, I'll make sure to erase all your answers and fill in the bubbles to make a lightning bolt pattern before I submit your test to the paper pushers."

Clay huffed a laugh. "You don't need to do that. Just let our records and scores speak for themselves."

"Will do. Now give me a kiss." Clay's lips brushed against his in a ticklish kiss as he smiled. "Do I need to step back into the bedroom to be your Dom again?"

Clay shook his head, the smile still tugging at his lips. "No, Sir."

"Good. I want you to go down to the kitchen and fix us a big helping of what you find in the freezer."

Logan watched as Clay turned and went downstairs. He felt a slight twinge of guilt. He'd given a recommendation for Clay to be promoted because he loved him and wanted to see him advance. Like Clay said, he knew his contentious relationship with Captain Hayden held him back. He would do what he could to bypass that. But he understood how Clay felt, so he wouldn't do anything beyond what was already done.

Down in the kitchen, Clay was laughing as he stood there with the freezer door open. Clearly Logan had watched the whole interview with Ian because there was a big tub of cookies and cream ice cream sitting front and center in the freezer.

31

It was their last evening off. They were back on field rotation starting tomorrow. Logan had enjoyed every second of this time with his newly collared submissive. But to his shame, they'd gotten carried away in their love making. Overcome with passion, Logan let go of his control and took Clay a little too roughly. He'd apologized, only for Clay to look at him and say that he didn't mind. That he loved it. Honest emotion sparkled in Clay's gorgeous blue eyes as he spoke, so Logan knew he was telling the truth. But he still felt bad that he'd caused Clay any discomfort. He would make sure that they abstained from intercourse for awhile.

He'd run a bath for them so the hot water could soothe and relax Clay's muscles. They sat in the big spa tub, Logan with his back against the wall, warm from the heat of the water. Clay, as usual, was cradled between his thighs. He had a big sponge in his hand and used it to sluice water over Clay's chest, shoulders, and back. Logan was gratified to see Clay sliding down a little further into the water as he relaxed and rested his dark head on his shoulder. Then he tilted his face up to Logan's.

"Can I have a kiss?"

Logan looked down at the man he held safe in his arms. Clay's blue eyes were heavy-lidded, his face flushed and hair even curlier from the steam. Droplets of water clung to the steel of the collar around his throat. Emotion filled Logan's chest. This is what he'd wanted for so long. Clay as his submissive, wearing his collar, allowing Logan to care for him. To love him. Logan's heart pounded. He needed to tell Clay how he felt. Clay had accepted his collar, Logan hoped he would accept his love as well. He brought a hand up from the water to gently cup the side of Clay's face. "I love you."

Clay gave him a sleepy smile. "I know you do. I love you too."

Logan smiled back, happy at how simple, how *easy* it was to offer his love and have it returned. He lowered his head, brushing his lips lightly over Clay's. Logan kissed him softly and when Clay's mouth opened with a sweet little sigh, he just barely danced his tongue inside. Clay's eyes drifted closed during the kiss and when Logan ended it, they stayed that way.

"You wore me out, Sarge. I'm sleepy."

Logan tightened his arms around Clay and laughed lightly. "Go ahead and rest. I'll hold you up and get us out of here before the water gets cold."

"I love you, Logan," Clay whispered again as he started to fade into sleep.

Logan kissed his temple. "I love you too."

****

Logan finished checking to make sure the back door was locked. When he was done, he joined Clay by the front door. He tucked his finger under Clay's collar and drew him in close for a kiss. Then he pulled back.

"I'm sorry, baby, but it's time to take this off."

Surprise flashed across his sub's face as though he'd forgotten he couldn't wear his collar in public, followed quickly by a cross between ticked off and pouting. Logan hid a smile, pleased that Clay didn't want to remove his collar.

"I promise you can have it back as soon as we're alone together again."

Clay bowed his head, allowing Logan to open the clasp. When the weight of his collar fell from his neck, he felt as though he'd been cut loose and he didn't like it. He brought his hand up to Logan's chest, his fingers curling into the neckline of his t-shirt. "Logan, I…" He stopped, not even sure what he was about to say.

"It's okay, Clay. You're still completely mine."

"I know. It's just…" He stopped again, the fingers of his other hand touching his throat, a little thrown by how much he already missed the steel band that proclaimed him as Logan's. "I guess I just didn't realize how it would feel to go back out in public and pretend to be nothing more than co-workers when I really just want to tell every motherfucker out there that I'm yours."

Logan laughed. "Well you can't do that. Although I admit I'm looking forward to hearing the creative ways you tell those cops to mind their own goddamn business if we ever do come out at work. Now close your eyes and I'll give you a present."

"It's not a Marines shirt is it? Because I don't want people thinking I was ever a jarhead." Clay heard a metallic jingling before Logan spoke.

"Keep it up and I'll make you wear nothing but one of my old shirts for the next week whenever we're alone."

Clay shut his mouth. He really wouldn't mind wearing a Marines tee but he knew Logan would probably come up with something inventive to go along with that. He felt the kiss of cool metal against his chest and throat along with the brush of Logan's fingers against the back of his neck. At Logan's command, he opened his eyes and looked down. Around his neck was a set of dog tags. He was surprised at first, seeing his name and thinking they were just his tags from work. Because the work they did could be so dangerous, Houston SWAT issued all of its members military-style dog tags. Clay usually only wore his when he was out in the field. Logan nodded his head at the pendant.

"Turn it over."

He did and saw stamped in bold military lettering: PROPERTY OF SERGEANT LOGAN PIERCE. Logan touched the pendant with one broad finger. "Anybody who sees you wearing these will just think they're issued by HPD. But you and I will know they represent my ownership of my pretty little sub."

A sense of relief swept through him and he blurted out, "I fucking love you, Logan."

Logan's hazel eyes rose from the pendant and focused on his. "I love you too, baby."

Clay pressed forward and kissed his Dom briefly. "Thank you, Sir." He gave an almost embarrassed laugh. "I didn't know I would need that connection to you so badly. But this…" He gestured at his new public collar. "This makes me feel better."

Logan wrapped his arms around Clay, holding him close to whisper in his ear. "I told you, Clay. I will *always* take care of you."

32

"What the hell?"

Clay didn't look up at that loud exclamation. He'd just come out of the shower and wasn't fully dressed yet, wearing only a pair of boxers. He knew what had caused that outburst but he didn't acknowledge it. Too bad for him, his teammates wouldn't let him ignore them. They came over, surrounding him in a loose semi-circle.

"Damn, chico! Did you have an orgy or something?" Hector asked, his eyes wide with shock.

His partners were looking at the marks on his body. Clay knew each and every one of them, even the ones not visible to the guys teasing him now. Finger shaped bruises on his hips. Reddened marks on his wrists from restraints. A hickey on his neck. Another hickey on his belly. A bruise surrounding one of his nipples. His thighs … well, Logan had gone a little crazy on what he'd confessed was his favorite part of Clay's body. And, of course his throat was chafed slightly from his new collar. He finally looked up and saw them all gawking. His teammates clearly weren't going anywhere until they got something out of him so he finally answered.

"No, I didn't have a damn orgy."

Mike laughed. "Well, shit man, did you spend the night with Dracula's babes?"

Clay rolled his eyes. "Yes, I spent the night with fictional women and let them suck on my neck."

Hector choked on a laugh. "You let somebody suck on something!"

They all laughed and Clay felt heat rising in his face. He knew they were ribbing him and he didn't mind. He'd done the same or worse to all of them at some point so he let it roll off his back. He shrugged through his embarrassment. "I had a really great couple of days off."

A snort and "I bet" came from somebody in the peanut gallery. Clay pulled on his uniform pants just as Logan walked into the locker room. He saw Logan's eyes go straight to his belly before rising up to meet his. Clay stood there frozen at the intensity of that sharp hazel gaze. Someone noticed, but misinterpreted the look.

"That's crazy, right, Serge?"

"Yeah, that is crazy." His mouth curled in that sexy grin that Clay rarely saw outside their private moments together. "Somebody must have had a real good time for you to be marked up like that, Clay."

Everyone laughed thinking Sarge was teasing him. Well, he was. Just not in the way they all thought. Clay ducked his head to hide a smile and finally pulled on his shirt.

****

Clay walked into the strategy room. They'd been called in for a quick briefing for their operation that night. He passed Logan who was talking to an officer from Narcotics as he went to sit in the back row next to Tiffany. She had her head bent over her phone as she texted.

"What's up?" she said distractedly.

"Not much." Clay didn't really bother to answer since Tiffany clearly wasn't paying attention. Besides, he was busy watching Logan. He had to admire the way Logan managed to be so cool and in control all the time. That just wasn't in his genetic makeup. He needed to cut loose often, even when they were at work. Never in the field, obviously, but just about any other time was fair game. He also admired Logan's physique. Logan's broad shoulders and heavily muscled chest made that SWAT uniform look real good. He stood, braced by those thick thighs, his feet planted in a strong and confident stance. Clay really did love Logan's body, and now that they were together, he could admit it instead of hiding his attraction like he used to. Yet as much as he loved Logan's body, his Dom made sure Clay knew Logan loved his just as much, both with the interlude in front of the bathroom mirror and again with the ice cream in bed. He'd never be able to look at a bowl of cookies and cream ice cream the same way again. He was pulled from his daydream when he heard Tiffany talking to him.

"Well, well, well. You don't normally wear your tags when we're not out in the field. Why do you have them on now?"

Clay cut his eyes over to Tiffany. "Stop fishing."

Tiffany grinned. "Fine then, tell me. Is that your collar?"

"One of 'em."

Tiffany let out a whoop. "Congrats, man. Feels good to wear it, don't it?"

"Could you *try* to keep your damn voice down?"

Tiffany apologized but she kept on grinning. "Answer the question."

Clay answered with his usual bluntness. "Fuck yeah, it does. I even freaked out some when he took off the other one before we left his house. And I swear, right now I'm about two seconds from going over there and kneeling at his feet in front of everybody in this room."

Tiffany whistled low. "Shit, man, you've got it bad. I bet that makes Logan happy. Don't worry, I'm the same way."

Clay looked at Tiffany. "How do you deal with it and keep from letting that side of your relationship show when you're in public?"

Tiffany shrugged. "I can't always. Which is why we get teased so much about how close we are. People may not know what type of relationship we're in, but they do sense something different."

Clay nodded. He'd picked up on that himself before he learned of their Dom/sub relationship.

"But other than that, it's just through sheer force of will."

Tiffany said something else, but Clay didn't hear her because Logan was staring at him, even though he was still in conversation. From across the room, Clay could feel the heat in his gaze. He couldn't help but react. His body heated up, his own stare focusing right back on Logan's.

"Correct me if I'm wrong, but you guys haven't come out yet, right?"

"Nope."

"And you do realize that the eye fucking I'm witnessing right now between you two *might* give it away?"

"Yep."

"Do you even care?"

"Nope."

"You two are pathetic," Tiffany teased.

Logan broke their eye contact for a moment as he looked back at the officer. When the guy finished nodding like a bobble head and left the room, Logan looked right back at him. He was disappointed when Logan took his attention away to address the team. He watched with everyone else as Logan drew out the updated plans on the whiteboard at the front of the room. After going through the strategy with them, he asked if anyone had any questions. Everyone shook their heads so Logan dismissed them. For once, Logan left the room first. He hadn't made any gesture towards Clay, but he knew he was expected to follow. Clay stood.

Tiffany spoke again before he could leave. "Yep. Absolutely pathetic."

Clay looked down at her briefly. He didn't want to miss seeing where Logan was going. "Pretend I said something sarcastic and cruel in response and be offended," he joked to Tiffany. Then he took off to follow Logan.

Clay was walking down the hall, trying to decide where Logan had gone. It was either the storage closet or his office. He caught the door to Logan's office opening slightly and realized that's where he'd gone. No one was in the hall so he slipped inside. As soon as he was safely in the office, he was in Logan's arms, his Dom kissing him fiercely. They separated after a few moments, Logan taking small, nipping kisses at his bottom lip.

"I was not expecting to walk into the locker room and see you standing there like that, your pants open and all those pretty marks visible on your skin. Were you trying to drive me crazy?"

Clay's heart was still racing from their kiss. "No." Then he grinned. "But did I?"

Logan groaned and kissed him again. "You know you did. We might have to stop being in the locker room at the same time from now on. Don't think I'll be able to hold my response back if that happens again."

"Or you could just stop marking me up."

This time Logan kissed him hard. "I don't think so, baby. I love tasting you everywhere too damn much." He smoothed his hands down his back and cupped his ass. "Love the way your soft skin feels on my tongue when I suck you into my mouth." One hand raised to tug his shirt collar down while the other pulled him up close against Logan's hardness. "I guess maybe I could stop if you really wanted me to." Logan lowered his head, licking at his collarbone, grazing his teeth over the sensitive area. "Do you want me to stop, baby?"

Clay leaned his head to the side. "No, please don't stop."

Logan laughed, his warm breath blowing over his neck. He sucked at his collarbone lightly, still pressing their growing erections together. Clay rubbed back against him.

"Sir, we have an hour before go time. Do you think—"

Logan was shaking his head before he finished talking. "No. I meant what I said the other night. No sex for awhile."

Clay looked up at Logan and saw he was serious. He huffed out a sigh. "Fine. No sex." He sucked his bottom lip and looked up at Logan from beneath his lashes. "Does that include oral?"

Logan kissed him once. "No, it doesn't." The sexy grin from earlier made another appearance. "Get on your knees."

****

Clay came out of the gun cage after filling up on ammunition. As he headed up the dim hallway, he had a hard time keeping the pleased smile off his face. It was crazy. Just fucking crazy the way it made him feel to be with Logan. To be on his knees like that, sucking his cock while the whole of HPD carried on around them, completely unaware. He didn't really understand why, but he loved the way being Logan's sub made him feel. Clay laughed as he thought about how the team would react if they knew just who had left so many marks on his body.

"What's so funny?"

Clay snapped out of his daydream. Alison Crawford was there in front of him. "Nothing. Just imagining my team's reactions to something."

Alison smiled. "A secret? Can I be the first to know?"

Clay ran his hand over his hair. "Uh. No. Sorry."

"That's too bad. Could have been a great start to getting to know you a little better."

Clay cleared his throat, slightly uncomfortable. "Did you need something?"

"Just checking to see if you'd given any thought to the calendar idea. I think you'd be a great addition."

Clay's face heated. The thought of posing and trying to look sexy in front of a camera was slightly intimidating. "I'm still thinking it over."

"Well, take your time." She brushed her fingers over his bare forearm. "I just hope in the end you say yes."

Before Clay could respond, he heard Logan's voice behind him.

"Ms. Crawford. You're out of place down here, aren't you? Do you need help with something?"

"No, Sergeant. I was just trying to convince Corporal Foster here to be one of our models for the HPD charity calendar."

"I see. Well, we need to get ready to go do some important work so you'll have to excuse us."

Alison smiled politely. "Of course."

She stepped around them both and continued down the hallway. Logan turned and watched her go. When he turned back around, Clay was surprised by the hard look on his face.

"What's wrong?"

"What did I just walk up to?"

A frown crinkled Clay's forehead. "What do you mean?"

"I saw her touch you."

Clay's eyebrows shot up. "So? She touched me on the arm. It's not like she grabbed my ass or something. Besides, she doesn't know I'm in a relationship with anyone. As far as she knows, she wasn't encroaching on anybody's territory."

Logan looked to the left at a half open door. He stepped inside and pulled Clay with him. Clay found himself pressed up against a door for the second time that day.

"Maybe she should know. Maybe everyone should know."

Clay's breath came a little faster, his heart thumping hard at the way Logan was dominating his space. "We haven't really discussed that yet. But we won't have to if someone saw you drag me in here. You shouldn't have done that."

Logan's hand came up and wrapped around his throat in a firm grip. "Are you telling me what I can and cannot do, sub?"

Clay's belly swooped and a warm flush of arousal chased across his skin. He was definitely getting turned on from this possessive aggression his Dom was displaying. That stern voice always made him compliant. He stared up into the heat of Logan's hazel eyes and whispered his answer. "No, Sir."

"I didn't think so," Logan replied before kissing him hard. Clay opened up for his Dom, kissing him back while letting him dominate his mouth. He gave himself up to Logan's kiss, letting him press Clay even harder against the door. When Logan pulled away, Clay rested against it for a moment before he slowly opened his eyes to look at him. Logan ran a thumb over his lips.

"No one else is ever going to see this look on your face."

Clay couldn't manage anything other than a nod, his senses still mesmerized by Logan's kiss.

Logan smiled at him. "Go get geared up. I'll see you at the Bearcat in ten."

33

Several hours later, Clay was in the parking garage walking to his car with Q. The warrant had gone smoothly and he was ready to head home.

"Hey, man, we haven't hung out for awhile. You should come over."

"Your wife making pho?"

Q laughed. "For you, she'll probably make anything you ask, but you know you shouldn't."

Clay laughed too. He loved Q's wife like a sister, but she couldn't cook for shit. She tried to make traditional dishes for her Vietnamese husband, but she just couldn't get the hang of it. They stopped when they reached his car.

"Come on. We'll order a pizza, watch the game highlights."

Clay popped the trunk and started putting his gear in. "Alright. Let me just check with Logan first."

"Did I just hear that right? You need to *ask* Logan? Like for permission?"

Clay got his gear stowed and closed the trunk. "Yeah, that's what I said. What's the big deal? Don't you ask your wife before you go out with friends?"

"Yeah, I do. I guess I just didn't realize things between you two were so far along." He slung his bag around until it knocked him in the side. "Shit, man. Hope you enjoy being chained up."

Clay looked at his friend in shocked surprise. "What? What's that supposed to mean?"

Q laughed. "You're in a serious relationship for once. Guess that means no more running off to hang out with your friends whenever you want. You're chained up."

Clay relaxed. "You know, most people just say ball and chain for that."

Q scrunched up his face and pretended to gag. "I refuse to talk about balls when discussing you two."

"Don't be such a 'phobe," he shot back with a laugh.

****

Clay took a big bite of his last piece of pizza. They'd watched the highlights of all the basketball games. As always, the conversation had morphed into a hybrid of SWAT, sports, and video games. Now they were playing a round of basketball on Q's gaming console. Clay had just taken a shot, but Q managed to block it.

"So Logan put that little PR lady in her place today."

Q didn't look at him, his fingers still flying over the controller. "What? Who?"

"The lady working on our image. The one trying to get that calendar together."

Q laughed. "Oh yeah? What'd he say to her?"

"Nothing really. He just came up while we were talking and thought she was flirting with me." Clay lowered his voice to an exaggerated gossipy whisper. "He saw that little hussy touch me on the arm." He laughed. "Told her in his very strict sergeant's voice that we had *important work to do*. I think she got the hint that it wasn't the time to be peddling her wares." He shook his head at the memory. "Got to admit, it was strange seeing him jealous. He's always so damn calm."

Q took his attention off the game long enough for Clay to get in a game winning shot. Clay hooted in obnoxious excitement but Q ignored his antics.

"You don't think it's weird that he got upset over practically nothing? All she did was touch your arm."

Clay shrugged. "Nah, it was funny." He amended that to sexy in his head, remembering the heat in Logan's eyes when he pressed him up against that door.

Q shook his head. "Be careful, man. Jealousy can make people do some crazy shit. I don't want to see your ass wind up as a Lifetime movie."

Clay laughed hard enough that he nearly choked on the root beer he'd just swallowed. "Be serious, man. Can you see Sergeant Pierce doing something that wasn't above board?"

Q thumbed through the menu screen to start another game. "You're probably right. Besides, there's no way Lifetime could make a movie about you. I don't think they hire male models as actors, and they're probably the only ones pretty enough to play you."

34

Logan heard Clay pull up in the driveway. It was late, but he told him it was okay to come over when he was finished at Q's. Logan went to meet him at the door. He was a little nervous because he decided to tell Clay about things with Ryan. He wanted to get it out of the way so they could move on. But he changed his mind when he opened the door and saw Clay paused halfway up the walk, stretching out his back.

"What's wrong?" he called out.

Clay straightened and came up to the house. "Nothing. I think I just tweaked my back when I tackled that guy today. And sitting on the floor at Q's, hunched over a controller didn't help."

Logan let Clay in and shut the door behind him. He shook his head at the thought of his highly trained and skilled scouts sitting on the floor and playing video games like two little kids. "You two need to grow up."

Clay's lip curled. "No way. Grow up, grow old."

Logan shook his head again. "Come on upstairs and I'll massage your back for you."

Clay bit his lip. "You know…I might have other areas that need to be massaged."

Logan laughed and pulled him towards the stairs. "Stop trying to get me busted by Vice for giving out happy endings."

Upstairs in his room, he undressed Clay down to his briefs and pushed him onto the bed. Clay rose up on one elbow.

"Wait…"

Clay's hand came up to touch his throat and Logan knew exactly what he wanted. He went over to the nightstand and pulled out his collar along with a bottle of oil. He took the dog tags from around Clay's neck and put them on the nightstand then clasped the steel collar around his throat. Logan gave his lover a small kiss then pushed him back down. This time, Clay settled in, resting his head on his forearms. Logan stripped himself down to his boxers then climbed onto the bed. He straddled Clay's slim waist and picked up the bottle of oil.

"Maybe you should save the gaming for nights when you don't take down jacked drug dealers with flying tackles."

"Why? You trying to say I can't handle him because I'm scrawny?"

Logan laughed. "You are not scrawny." He leaned down and pressed a kissed to the bump of his spine. "You can take down whomever you want. Now be quiet and let me take care of you." He slicked his hands up with oil and pressed them into the muscles of Clay's back. He kneaded up and down the smooth flesh, digging his thumbs in to really work out any stiffness. Clay groaned and Logan knew he'd found a tender spot. Logan worked that area, kneading and rubbing until he felt Clay completely relax under his hands. Clay sighed in relief, but Logan didn't stop touching him. He stroked his hands over his torso, trailing his fingers lightly up and down his sides. Clay sensed the change in his touch and opened his eyes to look over his shoulder.

Logan leaned down, pressing his chest to Clay's slick back to kiss him. He brushed his lips up his cheek to whisper into his ear. "Do you feel better?"

"Yes. I feel better … everywhere."

Logan knew what Clay was trying to tell him. "Is that right?"

Clay nodded and started to turn over. Logan stopped him by squeezing with his thighs. "Stay like this. I want to rub you a little longer." He scooted back onto Clay's thighs and pulled his briefs down. Clay's hips rose slowly to help him get them off, the room so quiet the sound of cotton sliding down his legs was magnified. Logan's cock thickened as the firm round flesh of his lover's ass was revealed. He decided to exercise a little restraint and bypass that area so he could address the rest of the long lithe body beneath him.

Logan poured more oil into his palms and massaged his sub's thighs and calves. He rubbed him slowly, eventually stroking his hands everywhere until Clay's body gleamed with oil in the low lamplight. Leaning down again, Logan licked a path from the base of Clay's spine all the way up until he reached the strap of his collar. He sucked the skin there lightly, drawing a shiver from his lover. Logan slid a finger between Clay's cheeks, not penetrating, just stroking the sensitive skin. "I don't think it'll kill us to wait one more day."

Clay looked at him, his lips parted as though to protest, but Logan simply looked at him sternly and Clay didn't say anything. As a reward for that, and because his own cock was stiff and aching, he leaned down and whispered in Clay's ear. "No sex. But we can still play."

Logan stood up and pulled his boxers off. Clay watched him with those sexy blue eyes, heavy-lidded with arousal. He shifted on the bed as though he were about to change positions and Logan spoke up. "No, don't move. In fact..." Logan opened the nightstand drawer and pulled out a set of handcuffs linked by a long chain. He clasped one cuff around Clay's wrist before threading the chain through the slats of the headboard and closing the other cuff around his other wrist. Logan lifted Clay's chin to get his attention.

"Don't you dare beg me tonight. I don't want to have to gag you too." Clay's eyes flared in surprise and Logan figured the threat alone would be enough. Besides, he didn't really want to gag his lover. He enjoyed hearing the moans and sexy little gasps he made way too much.

Logan took a moment to just stare at his submissive. Clay was stretched out on his stomach, his arms raised over his head and chained to the headboard, every bit of his golden skin slick with oil. He was beautiful, lying there so patiently, waiting for his Dom. A hot streak of possessive pride sizzled through Logan's veins that this man belonged to him. Logan got back on the bed and straddled Clay again, picking up the bottle of oil one last time. He drizzled the liquid over Clay's ass, making sure some of it dripped into the crease of his cheeks. Then he capped the bottle and threw it aside. He ran his palms over

Clay's ass, cupping and squeezing the smooth flesh. He let his fingers play in between his cheeks, teasing at his opening, getting him slick there as well. Using his thumbs to spread his lover just a tiny bit, Logan blew a warm breath across the exposed area. Clay shivered but Logan didn't stop there. He traced his tongue inside, gradually stroking deeper until he reached his entrance. He licked the area but again he didn't penetrate. Just teased and circled his tongue against it until Clay was moaning and writhing beneath him. His hips pushed back against Logan's face and he allowed it, licking faster and deeper until Clay's ass was slick with both the oil and his saliva.

Logan rose up, his body sliding easily against Clay's oiled skin as he stretched himself out over his lover. He lined his cock up against the crack of Clay's ass and slowly moved his hips back and forth. "You have no idea how bad I wish I was inside you right now, fucking deep into your sweet ass," he whispered roughly in Clay's ear.

Clay cried out, jerking at his chains."Sir, please…"

"You're not begging me are you, Clay?"

Clay screwed his eyes shut. "No, Sir. But I can't…"

"Can't what?"

"I can't take it," he gasped as he continued to squirm underneath Logan.

Logan nipped at his ear lobe. "What? What can't you take?"

"I can't take feeling you against me, and listening to your voice, knowing I can't have you inside me." Clay trembled as Logan laughed low, the sound vibrating against his skin.

"You'll take whatever I want you to take. If I decide I want to rub against you like this all night, you'll take it. If I decide to tell you how much I love feeling your tight ass gripping every inch of my cock, you'll lay here like a good boy and listen. If I decide to take your cock into my hand and stroke you until I decide I'm ready for you to come, you'll let me. Do you understand?"

Clay sobbed out a yes, his hands twitching in their cuffs, his hips rising to meet Logan's slow thrusts. Logan slipped a hand underneath him and put his words to effect, grasping Clay's cock and pumping him with the lightest grip he'd ever used. It made Clay shake and tremble with the urge to somehow get Logan to squeeze him tighter. Logan whispered in his ear again.

"Clay?"

Clay licked his dry lips so he could answer. "Yes, Sir?"

"The first time I was inside you was the best thing I'd ever felt – that is until I made you mine and got to fuck you bare. Then I thought I'd died and gone to heaven."

Goose bumps chased across Clay's skin as Logan licked the shell of his ear, his cock still slipping up and down between his ass cheeks.

"I couldn't believe how hot you were. That luscious heat was amazing. And ever since then, all I can think about is burying my cock inside you again … and again … and again." Logan tightened his grip. "Pushing deep." He squeezed his fist around Clay's shaft. "Hitting your spot." Another squeeze. "Making you come." This time, the squeeze was accompanied by a brush of his thumb across the slick head of his shaft.

Clay moaned. "Oh my *God*. I need to come right now."

Logan licked his tongue up under Clay's collar. "I said I don't want you begging for my cock tonight, but I do think I want you to beg for your orgasm. So do it. Beg me."

Clay obeyed immediately. Pleading words tripped over themselves as he begged his Dom for release. He barely had any idea what he was saying other than the word please. But whatever he said must have been what Logan wanted to hear because the tightness of his grip and the speed of his pumping steadily increased until Clay was right on the edge. At the same time, he knew Logan was working towards his own orgasm as those hard hips flexed against him, driving that thick shaft in his ass crack. But then it happened. He pushed back and Logan pushed forwards. By that time, they were both so slippery with oil that the head of Logan's cock slid down smoothly into his entrance. Clay froze. Logan said he wouldn't be inside him tonight, but damnit, he was right there. Still, Clay didn't dare try to deepen the connection. He didn't even want to imagine the punishment Logan would come up with for that.

A desperate groan escaped him as Logan rose up to brace himself on his palms, pushing an inch further inside him. He stroked in the tiniest bit and Clay had to bite down hard on his lip to keep from begging Logan to fuck him. He looked back over his shoulder to see the muscles in Logan's arms bunched up hard and straining, his face tight with tension. Another shallow stroke.

"Fuck, Clay. You're so goddamn hot."

Then … he pulled out.

Clay bit down on his own arm to keep from protesting and begging. Thankfully, he didn't have time to be too miserable because Logan's hand gripped him again, resuming his fast pace as he stroked him. His lover came back down over his back and grasped his chin to turn his head to the side. Clay looked at him, his chest heaving with his racing breaths. "Sir?" he asked in a pleading tone. He wasn't quite sure what he was asking for, but he trusted that Logan would be able to give him what he needed. He always did.

Logan smiled slightly and whispered against his lips, "Come for me, pretty little sub."

Logan kissed him roughly, pumping him hard and fast. Once, twice more of that big fist moving on him and Clay was shuddering and moaning as he came in Logan's hand. When he was spent, Logan reached down and squeezed his cheeks tightly together as he continued to slide between them, faster and faster. Then, with a harsh groan, Logan came, spilling hotly on to Clay's skin.

****

Clay lay there, chained in his cuffs, and covered in sweat, oil, and his Dom's cum. By this point in their relationship, he didn't even find it strange that he liked the way he felt a little bit dirty, a whole lot possessed, and even more loved. Logan lay next to him and rubbed his back as they gazed at one another. "You bring something out in me that I never even knew existed," Clay said. "And I love it."

Logan kissed him softly. "Thank God for that. Because you're perfect for me and I don't ever want to go back to being without you."

35

Logan awoke with a start. He was wrapped around Clay, his thigh pushed between his sub's legs and his palm settled over the warm skin of his stomach. The bedroom was dark and quiet, so what had woken him? Then he heard it again. His phone was going off so he got up. Clay's protest, even in his sleep, made him smile. He was pulling on his boxers when he heard Clay's sleepy voice.

"Where are you going?"

"My phone is going off with a signal 90." Clay groaned and Logan just held back from doing the same. They'd just finished up a shift and it was early in the morning. It must be serious for him to get a call. He called in, getting the pleasant voice of Sandy at the switchboard.

"Sergeant Pierce. Good morning."

He sighed. "Is it?"

Laughter was in her voice as she responded. "It is morning, but I don't think it's good. There's a hostage situation in Willow Bend and your team has been personally requested by the captain to handle this."

Logan wanted to curse, but managed to hold it back. Willow Bend was a quiet area tucked away from the regular hustle and bustle of Houston. There were lots of big houses, lots of money, and lots of important people. That's why they'd been requested by Hayden.

"What's the address?"

She gave him the location but stopped him before he could hang up. "Oh, and Sergeant, I've managed to get a hold of everyone on your team except for Corporal Foster."

Logan looked towards his bed where Clay was still tucked in warm and safe under his bed covers. "I'll take care of him."

He hung up and walked back to the bed. Seeing Clay sleepy, with his hair mussed, in his bed, made him feel good. He wanted this to be a regular thing. He wanted Clay with him always. Logan sat down on the edge of the bed and Clay scooted close to him.

"We have to go?"

"Yeah." He repeated the information he'd gotten from dispatch.

Clay cursed. "Fucking Hayden. Somehow this is going to be good publicity for him and that's why he wants us there."

Logan pulled Clay up to a sitting position. "That's what happens when you're the best." He gave him a kiss. Clay looked at him and sighed.

"You're about to take my collar off, aren't you?"

Logan slid his hand up Clay's neck and into his silky hair. "Sorry, baby. I have to." He tugged Clay's arms around his neck then kissed him deeply, trying to convey all the love he felt. He unlocked his sub's collar, kissing his throat when the metal fell away. Logan pulled back and reached to the nightstand for the dog tags, draping them around Clay's neck. Then he got up and pulled him from the bed.

"They've been trying to raise us for awhile. Take a quick shower. I'll use the hall bathroom." He opened a dresser drawer for fresh clothes. Clay came up behind him and wrapped his arms around Logan's waist.

"Thank you, Sir. That helped."

Logan knew he was referring to the way he'd taken his collar off. "You're welcome."

Clay laid his face against Logan's back. "But now it looks like we'll have to wait even longer than you planned."

Logan groaned. "Don't remind me."

****

Hours after they were awakened by Logan's phone, they were in the Bearcat headed back to the station. Enough time had passed that the sun was sinking over the horizon. It seemed odd. The sun was coming up when he got into the truck that morning. They'd spent the whole day at what had indeed become a high profile case.

Two gunmen took the CEO of a major pipeline drilling company hostage. The gunmen were former employees of the company and were recently laid off after fifteen years. Their negotiator did an amazing job and managed to convince them to release the CEO's wife and child first then talked one of the gunmen out of the house. The other guy held firm, shouting crazy demands, including getting his job back. An hour ago, they heard a shot.

The team rushed the house to find the hostage splattered with blood and the gunmen dead at his feet. He was shaken at seeing the man commit suicide right in front of him, but was otherwise unharmed. They searched the scene and turned it over to the uniformed cops.

Back in the truck, they were talking about favorite movies. It was barely the end of summer, but somehow they'd gotten on the topic of Christmas movies. Clay brought up *Bad Santa*. Everybody was immediately into that one, laughing and shouting out their favorite lines from the movie. Everybody except Logan. Clay looked at him.

"You've never seen *Bad Santa*, have you?"

Logan shook his head. "No. I was too busy watching good movies like *It's A Wonderful Life*."

Clay rolled his eyes. "You mean old, lame movies."

Logan laughed. "You'll have to watch it sometime. You're missing out on a classic."

Clay smiled and lowered his voice. "Another movie night?"

Logan smiled back. "Definitely."

36

Clay waited on Logan's porch after knocking. Logan came and opened the door to let him in. "Hey."

Logan reached out and grasped him by the back of the neck. He pulled him into a kiss and into the house at the same time. "Hey."

Logan looked down at his bag and nodded. They were going to watch the baseball game then go straight to work from there so he'd brought his uniform like he was asked.

"Go put your bag up in my bedroom." Logan ran a finger over his mouth. "I want you naked today. Take everything off and I'll be waiting with your collar in the living room."

Clay was surprised but he went up the stairs to Logan's bedroom. He undressed, leaving his clothes on the bed. When he went back down the hall, he noticed that all the doors were open but one. Now that he thought about it, that door had been closed for weeks. Out of curiosity, he turned the knob but it was locked. Clay shrugged and went down the stairs. He walked into the living room where Logan was sitting on the couch. Logan smiled when he saw him.

"Beautiful."

Clay took the hand Logan held out to him, letting letting his Dom pull him between his legs. He kneeled, allowing Logan to fasten his collar around his neck.

"Snacks and drinks are in the fridge. Go bring them out for us."

Clay stood up. "The windows aren't open in there are they? I'd rather not have the neighbors see me naked."

Logan laughed. "No, the curtains are all drawn."

He grinned and went into the kitchen to grab two cans of root beer and a tray of finger foods. Clay went back into the living room and set everything down on the end table next to the couch where Logan pointed. When he was done, Logan pulled him into his lap. They sat together in the corner of the big sectional as the game got underway.

Logan stacked together a cracker, cheese, and meat and held it before Clay's lips. Clay opened up to let his Dom feed him. When he finished chewing, Logan gave him a grape. He bit into the fruit, the sweet juice bursting on his tongue. They watched the game while Logan continued to feed him until he was full. He licked his lips after swallowing the last bite. "Thank you, Sir."

Logan then ate some of the food himself. When he was done, he held his hand up to Clay's mouth. Clay licked Logan's fingers clean, catching all the crumbs. When the next commercial break came, Logan leaned down and kissed him. It was a soft yet deep kiss, Logan stroking his palm down his thigh. Clay wrapped his arms around Logan as he kissed him back. But when they returned to the broadcast, Logan immediately stopped.

Clay blinked in surprise. Logan asked him what he thought of their home team's chances to make it into the post season. After a moment, he dropped his arms from around Logan's neck and answered. Logan went on talking about the game, not mentioning the kiss. Until the next commercial break. Then Clay was kissed again. When the break was over, he released him and refocused on the TV. Clay quickly figured out the game. He gave his attention to the TV, but he found it hard to concentrate on baseball he was so filled with anticipation for each commercial break.

During a fifth inning commercial, Logan kissed him briefly then held a finger up to his mouth. Clay darted his tongue out, licking along the digit before sucking it into his mouth. Logan pulled the hand away and trailed it down his belly, past his cock, and dipped between his legs. He squirmed on Logan's lap as he teased the finger against his entrance before slowly pushing it in. Logan kissed him while he worked that finger in and out of him. Clay held onto Logan's broad shoulders, curling his hips up to meet every thrust. He was hard, his naked cock sliding across his belly from his movements. Logan pressed in deeper, adding another finger. He twisted them inside him, making Clay gasp into their kiss. Until the game came back on. Logan stopped kissing him and stopped pumping his fingers, but he left them inside him. And so it went until the seventh inning stretch. Logan pulled his fingers away and pushed him off his lap.

"There's a black box in my room on the nightstand. Go get it and bring it to me."

Clay quickly retrieved the box and brought it to Logan.

"Did you open it?" Logan asked.

"No." Clay grinned. "But I was tempted."

Logan shook his head. He opened the box and showed him what was inside. There was a tiny bottle of lube, a leather cock ring, and an anal plug. Logan took the cock ring from the box then leaned forward and sucked Clay's shaft into his mouth. Clay moaned, bringing his hands up to run through Logan's hair. Once he was fully hard, Logan stopped and snapped the cock ring closed behind his balls. Clay swallowed hard when Logan told him to turn around. He knew what was coming next. He stood there with his back to Logan, listening to the sounds of him taking the plug from the box and preparing it with lubricant. He moaned softly, his head dropping back on his shoulders when Logan slid the plug inside him. He turned back around to see Logan looking up at him.

"Take everything back to the kitchen."

Clay took a deep breath. "Yes, Sir." He grabbed up the tray and empty soda cans to go into the kitchen. As he walked, every step he took sent a surge of arousal through him. He felt full, his cock standing up hard and restrained. Clay had a feeling he would be wearing his Dom's toys for awhile.

He put everything away and returned to the living room. Logan yanked him back onto his lap. They were on another commercial break so he wasn't surprised when Logan started kissing him. He stayed with the pattern from before, immediately stopping the kissing when the game came back on. But this time, Logan played with the plug, pushing it in and out of him with tiny little thrusts, keeping him stimulated. Clay held back a groan. He knew nothing he said would make Logan end the torment. So he just had to wait until the next commercial break to find out what Logan would do next. When it came, Logan gave him an order before he kissed him.

"Open my jeans. Take me out."

Clay obeyed, his fingers fumbling with the button and zipper but he got them open. Logan groaned into their kiss as Clay wrapped his hand around his shaft, easing him out of his jeans. Logan yanked him down so he was flat on his back on the couch then shifted around to lay on top of him. Clay dug his fingers into the hard muscle of Logan's back. He loved the weight of Logan on top of him. When he started to move, grinding their cocks together, Logan slipped his hands down to grip the powerful muscles of his ass. Clay moaned and arched up to meet Logan's thrusts. His body was wound tight, but he knew he wouldn't come, not without Logan's permission and not while wearing the cock ring. He just savored the feel of Logan moving on top of him, working towards his own climax. Logan took his mouth in a deep kiss, and Clay gave himself up to it.

When Logan groaned, he knew his Dom was about to come. Clay squeezed his thighs against his sides and Logan rasped his name in a harsh whisper. Clay felt his hot release spilling onto the skin of his stomach and he shuddered, aching for his own release. Logan lay there on top of him for a few moments, kissing him lightly. When the announcer's voice sounded, he sat up and arranged them back in their original positions. Clay looked at him and bit his lip.

Logan smiled and traced a finger down his shaft. "Soon, baby. The game is almost over."

37

Clay had never been so happy to see a baseball game end in his life. He didn't even care that his team lost. He just wanted it to be over so he could get what he needed from Logan.

"Let's take a shower and get cleaned up."

Clay nodded quickly and stood up at Logan's gentle push. He followed Logan up the stairs to his bedroom, waiting as he stripped down. In the shower, Logan handed him the bar of soap. He started to wash Logan but before he made much progress, he was in his Dom's arms. Logan kissed him, licking into his mouth while his hands smoothed down his body to grab his ass. Clay's fingers clenched on the soap. He was so hard it was almost painful. He didn't know how much more he could take. Logan pressed him back against the shower wall, still kissing him. Clay cried out as Logan removed the plug and slid a finger inside him. With his chest heaving, he begged. "Sir, please."

"Not yet."

Clay bit his lip in frustration. Logan finally stepped back and let Clay wash them both. Once they were out of the shower and dried, Logan gave him another order.

"Dress me."

Clay went to Logan's closet and pulled out a uniform then got boxers and socks from the dresser. He started with the shirt, pulling it up Logan's arms and buttoning it over his broad chest. He dropped to his knees, feeling Logan's eyes on him as he helped him into his boxers and pants. Clay's arousal continued to build as he served his Dom. By the time he managed to tuck his pants into his boots and lace them up, his hands were shaking. When he was finished, he took a deep breath and bowed his head. Logan put a hand under his chin and lifted his head.

"Tell me what you need."

Clay stared up into the hazel eyes watching him so closely. "I need you inside me."

Logan pushed his head back further, stretching his neck. "Even though there's a soft bed right beside us, I want to fuck you right here on the hard floor."

"I don't care. I just need you. Please."

Logan gave him a slow smile. "Open my pants."

Clay reached up, undoing the belt and pants that he'd just closed. Once he'd pulled the zipper down, Logan grabbed the lube and dropped to the floor. He quickly prepared them both then pushed inside him. Clay cried out, his body bowing up off the floor. Finally, after hours of torturous teasing, Logan was inside him.

Logan thrust into him hard. "Is this what you wanted?"

"Oh fuck, *yes*."

Logan grabbed his wrists and held them down over his head. "You want it so bad you'll let me fuck you on the floor like a whore. You're a whore for this cock, aren't you?"

Clay pushed his hips up to meet every one of Logan's pounding thrusts. "Yes." Right then, he felt like he'd be whatever Logan wanted him to be. "Just please, don't stop."

Logan laughed. "I won't stop, little sub. I'll keep fucking you until I come deep in this sweet ass."

Clay moaned. He loved the way Logan was dominating him, holding him down and fucking into him so roughly. He loved it so much and was so turned on by it he wanted to shout and curse just to relieve some of the tension. Clay was still restrained by his cock ring, but with every movement of Logan's body over his, his stomach brushed his shaft. That friction pushed him further and further to the edge until he was panting, begging for an orgasm.

He didn't get one. But Logan did, groaning as he pushed deep inside him one last time. After he'd stilled, Logan pulled out of him and refastened his clothes.

Clay was in exquisite agony, his body stimulated beyond belief. He unashamedly writhed on the floor, running his hands through his hair and gripping it in his fists. He *needed* to come. "Please. Fucking *please* let me come."

Logan went and sat on the bed. "My boots are dirty," he said calmly. "Come and clean them."

Clay got to his knees. He crawled over to Logan so desperately turned on he wanted to scream. When he reached him, he saw that Logan's boots were spotlessly clean. He knew that didn't matter. Logan didn't expect him to go and get a towel to wash them. He leaned down and licked Logan's boot. The taste of leather was bitter on his tongue, but he didn't care. He wrapped an arm around Logan's leg, crowding in close and laving his tongue up and down both boots. Clay moaned, his fingers digging into the hard muscle of Logan's calf. He'd never felt so deep into his submission before. The act of cleaning Logan's boots with his tongue took him to a new high. He didn't want to stop.

Logan's voice sounded in a low whisper. "Take the cock ring off."

Clay continued to lick Logan's boots but reached down with one hand to unsnap the leather cock ring. He groaned as it fell from behind his balls, his orgasm immediately rushing to the tip of his cock.

"Make yourself come."

At those words, Clay groaned again in relief. He gripped his cock in a tight fist and pumped. He was so far gone that he was coming after only two strokes. He choked on a gasp, pressing his face against Logan's leg as he came. His head was bursting with pleasure, his stomach drawn in tight as he pulsed his release onto his thighs. It was the most powerful orgasm he'd ever had. The sensations coursing through him were so strong that he bit down on Logan's boot, shouting and cursing around the leather gripped in his teeth.

****

The intensity of the feelings rushing through Clay eased back. His head clearing, he let go of Logan's boot. Still, Clay stayed on his knees, gasping for breath. Logan stood and ordered him to do the same. Shaking, Clay pulled himself to his feet, crawling up Logan's body. Logan took the sheet and wiped the release from his thighs and ass. Then he slid his fingers into Clay's hair, holding him still for his kiss.

"You won't shower. You'll get dressed and go to work just like this with the scent of sex on your skin. Do you understand?"

Clay stared into Logan's sharp hazel eyes. They gleamed bright with fierce possession as Logan looked back at him. Clay nodded. "Yes, Sir, whatever you want."

"That's right. Whatever *I* want." Logan kissed him roughly. "Let everyone wonder why you smell like another man," he said in a harsh whisper.

Clay nodded again, pressing his body close against Logan's. Somehow he was both exhausted and exhilarated. He didn't even know how to describe the way he felt right then.

"Tell me who you belong to, Clay."

Clay exhaled on a long sigh. "I'm yours, Sir. Only yours."

38

Later that evening, Clay sat at his desk filling out paperwork. Being on SWAT had lots of adrenaline filled moments, but there was no escaping the drudgery of endless reports and forms. He looked up as Logan came out of his office. Clay smiled as Logan glanced his way. His fingers rose to touch his dog tags. Clay couldn't get their time together that afternoon out of his head. It was probably a good thing they weren't out in the field right then because his brain was filled with thinking about how good it felt to submit to Logan so completely. Shivers chased down his spine every time he remembered how Logan looked and sounded as he'd ordered him not to shower. He smelled like sex and he didn't care. Clay watched as Logan went over to the copier. He started to get up and go to him, but Q and Hector stopped by his desk.

"Hey, man, what's up? You want to hang out tonight? We're going over to Rudy's for a few drinks."

"Rudy's? That sounds good." He looked at Logan who gave him a slight nod. When Clay turned his attention back to Q and Hector, he noticed a strange look on Q's face, but his friend didn't say anything. "Yeah, count me in."

"Alright. Do you have your car or did your loco ass jog to work today?"

Clay laughed at Hector. "I drove so I'll meet you there. But it wouldn't hurt you to do a little running every now and then."

"How many times do I have to tell you? As a sniper, I'm above all that."

Clay looked at Q. "Can you believe this guy?"

Q shrugged. "Sounds like nothing but laziness to me."

Clay laughed and the pair left. Logan headed back into his office. Clay waited a few minutes before he joined him. "Do you want to come with us to Rudy's?"

"I can't. I've got too much stuff to get caught up on since I didn't take any paperwork with me to my grandfather's. And I've got something I'm working on at home."

Clay grinned. "You're such a stickler for doing the right thing."

"Somebody's got to be. Now lock that door and get over here to give me a kiss before you go."

****

Twenty minutes later, Clay had joined his team at the pub. At the bar, he paid and tipped the bartender who'd just passed him a giant mug of root beer. He cut through the mass of people playing darts, dancing, and just hanging out to get to his group. They pushed three tables together to fit everyone in.

With the exception of Carlos, Tiffany and Logan of course, the whole team plus a few others was there. Hector called out to him as he approached.

"Clay! Tell us about this new honey of yours. She must be good since you spend all your time with her."

Clay sat down and took a sip of his root beer, preparing to dance around his pronouns like he always did whenever he was dating a guy. "They're great. The relationship I have with them is different from any I've had before, but I love it."

"Is that right? Different how?" Brady asked.

"I don't think that's any of your business, buddy."

Everyone laughed. Jody smacked Brady on the back of the head, calling him nosy.

"Well, at least tell us what she looks like, man. I promise not to fap to her."

Clay's lip curled in mock disgust at Hector. "I don't know why I even bother to talk to you. Anyway, they've got dark blond hair, hazel eyes and a really good build. But I don't think they're your type." He made eye contact with Q. They shared a sly smile while Hector went on about how all blondes with good bodies were his type.

39

The next day, Clay sat in Logan's office. He didn't really have any purpose for being there. He was just watching him go through yet more paperwork, occasionally offering him unsolicited advice. Logan finally looked up at him in exasperation.

"Do you want to do this?"

Clay grinned. "Nope. I just wanna chase bad guys. I'll leave the boring parts to you, Sir."

Logan gave him a look at the address but turned his attention back to his work.

Clay waited a few minutes before he interrupted him again. "So when do I get to be in charge?"

Logan glanced at him with his eyebrows raised. "Come again?"

He leaned back and kicked his feet up onto Logan's desk. "You always control me. Do I ever get to control you?" Logan eyed his feet without saying anything. Clay grinned but he dropped them back to the floor.

"I think you're missing the whole point of the Dom/sub relationship."

Clay laughed and started to say something but the door opened. It was Mike.

"What are you two in here discussing?"

Clay kept his face straight. "I was just asking Sarge here if I'd ever get to be in charge." He flicked his gaze over to Logan. "But it doesn't look likely. He likes being in control too much."

Logan cleared his throat. "What'd you need, Mike?"

"Actually, I'm glad you're both in here. I'm just making sure everyone has the address and directions for my retirement party tomorrow."

"Yeah, I've got them."

Clay stood up. "I've got 'em too, but I hate driving. Sarge, can I bum a ride with you?"

"Yeah, sure."

Mike left and Clay turned back to Logan with a grin. "Now we can go on a date with no one the wiser."

"What am I going to do with you?"

Clay shrugged. "You could give me what I want."

"You're a brat. But I'll consider it. Now get out of here so I can get some work done."

****

The weather was nice. It was one of those gorgeous days with sunshine, low humidity, and a light breeze. Clay sat on a picnic table, sipping a root beer. They were at the lake house

Mike had rented for his retirement party. Lots of people came out to celebrate Mike's retirement and they all seemed to be having a good time. Mike and his family set up sand volleyball, horseshoes, and tables for card games. Logan was off playing a game of poker. Clay didn't know how to play, and he didn't want to seem like he had to be around Logan too much, so he sat with Tiffany, talking.

"You rode up here with Logan? How cute. You guys are on a date."

Clay laughed. "Yeah, a date no one knows about. Except you, Carlos and Q."

"Does that bother you?"

He took another drink. "Not really. I've hidden my bi-sexuality for so long it's second nature by now. And I don't want us to have any problems at work. Besides, it's kind of funny to get to tease him without anyone else realizing it."

Tiffany laughed. "Keep it up with the teasing."

Clay laughed, but quieted as he noticed Ryan coming over. He nodded at him. "Hey, Ryan. How's it going?"

Ryan smiled and stopped in front of them. "You guys talking about Logan? Don't stop on my account. I know what it's like to be under his control."

Clay paused with his soda halfway to his mouth. "What?"

Ryan shrugged nonchalantly. "You're playing with Logan, right? I've been there."

Tiffany jumped up from the table, telling Ryan to back off. But Clay got off the table slowly.

"No, that's alright, Tiffany. I want to hear this. When was the last time you *played* with Logan?"

Ryan looked like he was trying to think. "Let me see. Oh yeah, it was the night of Tony's engagement party."

Clay's stomach dropped. He remembered that party. And it made him both sick and angry because Logan had been pursuing him at the time.

Ryan kept talking. "I mean, I didn't really get to serve him the way I wanted to, but that's probably just because he was drunk."

Clay's hands clenched into fists. Now he wanted Ryan to shut up. He didn't want to hear anymore about him serving Logan while Logan had been after him.

Tiffany touched his arm. "Don't listen to him, Clay. You don't even know if he's telling the truth."

Ryan's expression changed, a smug smile crossing his lips. Clay turned around and saw Logan standing there with a guilty expression on his face. He knew in that moment that Ryan had been telling the truth. He went to walk off but Logan grabbed his arm.

"Clay, wait. Let me explain."

Clay jerked his arm away. "Let you explain what?" He was hurt and pissed and he wanted to curse Logan out. And punch Ryan in the face. But he couldn't do any of that because of where they were. He tried to storm off again but Logan called out.

"Clay, stop."

He automatically responded to Logan's order and stopped, which pissed him off so bad he wanted to fucking scream.

Logan spoke behind him. "Nothing really happened. I was drunk, you heard him."

Clay turned back around and looked at Logan in disgust. His voice was full of scorn. "Oh, I'm so sorry you were too drunk to let that little shit serve you."

"That's not what I meant, Clay. I was just trying to let you know that I was too drunk to know what I was—"

Clay cut him off. "You're really trying to put the blame for this on the evils of alcohol? With me?" He sneered. "I thought you were better than that, Sergeant Pierce."

Logan started to speak again but Clay was saved from having to listen to his bullshit when a few people came over their way. He knew they couldn't have this discussion in front of others and that was fine with him. He gave Logan one last angry look and walked off.

40

Logan watched Clay walk off for a moment. Then he turned around and saw Ryan still standing there. He waited until the people who'd come over wrapped up their conversation with Tiffany. They didn't stay long. The atmosphere between the three of them wasn't exactly welcoming. When they were gone, he went up to Ryan.

"What the fuck was that?" he asked furiously.

Ryan shrugged. "I guess Clay isn't as yours as you thought. Otherwise, he wouldn't have left you like that." Ryan came closer to him. "But I would never leave you, Logan. You know that. No matter how many times you send me away, I always come back when you call me. I can be a better sub to you than that hot-headed, disrespectful little punk if you'd just give me a chance."

Logan's hand clenched into a fist. The fact that they were at a party with so many of their co-workers was the only thing keeping him from grabbing Ryan by the throat and telling him just what he thought of him ever being his sub. Tiffany must have realized he was close to losing it because she jumped in front of him.

"Sarge, don't do anything you'll regret. He's not worth it."

Logan sucked in a deep breath and took a step back. She was right. He didn't want to start a shit storm by assaulting Ryan there. But he was still furious and he let Ryan know exactly how he felt.

"Tiffany's right, so I'm not going to choke the shit out of you. But I suggest you stay the fuck away from me and Clay. And if I lose him over your bullshit, I promise you, you will regret it both personally and professionally. You don't want to fuck with me on this again, Ryan." He looked him over, filled with self-loathing that he'd ever been with him before he left to find Clay.

Tiffany was left standing there with Ryan. "You don't know the first thing about being a submissive. If you did, you wouldn't hurt Logan – the man you claim to want to belong to – just to get what you want. A true sub would never be so selfish."

Ryan looked at her. "Shut up," he snapped. "Just because your crazy ass has been under Carlos's thumb forever, you think you know everything there is about being a sub. Well, you're wrong. Sometimes you have to fight to get what you want. Then you can submit. And Clay is the cockiest asshole I've ever met. There's no way he's going to stay as Logan's submissive for long. The newness will wear off and he'll be back to banging chicks. Or getting banged by some big bear.

Who knows with him." Then he gave that same smug smile from earlier. "I know how sad that'll make you though, since you'll lose your new little sub buddy."

Tiffany stood there listening to the hateful nonsense coming out of Ryan's mouth before she lost it. With a swift movement, she slammed her knee between his legs, catching him right in the balls. Ryan doubled over with a nearly soundless grunt of pain. She kneeled down like she was checking on him. But she grabbed his hair tight and pulled his face up to meet hers.

"I refuse to be all dramatic and tell you what that was for. Besides, if you can't figure it out, you're a bigger idiot than I thought." She smiled and stroked his hair. "You complain to anybody about this and I'll tell them I did it because you tried to cop a feel." She left him there bent over and gasping for breath.

****

Logan found Clay standing on the edge of the sand volleyball pit. "Can we talk?" Clay continued looking straight ahead, ignoring him. Logan wanted to touch him but knew he couldn't in front of all their co-workers. "Clay, please just let me explain."

Clay still didn't turn around, but he did answer him. "Sorry, I'm busy. About to play a game."

Logan clenched his jaw in frustration. He didn't like that Clay was ignoring him. But he was also worried. He didn't want to lose his lover over Ryan. He was determined to stay close to him until they worked it out. Someone on the other side of the net called out for a partner and he immediately volunteered. He jogged over, kicking off his shoes and pulling his shirt off. He stepped onto the court, feeling the sand warm beneath his feet. Clay looked at him through the net, his face set in hard, angry lines. Logan didn't let that scare him off. He knew Clay had a temper. He also knew he wasn't one to stay in a relationship when any drama got started. But he wasn't going to let that happen to them. Clay was going to talk to him.

The game started, Logan's team serving first. They went back and forth scoring points. The game was fairly relaxed until Clay went up and spiked the ball hard. Logan couldn't get his hands under it. He managed to jump back just in time to keep from getting hit by the ball. He eyed Clay, but he only stared back at Logan coldly.

"Point."

Logan let it go, picking up the ball to serve. The game went on with Clay continuing to spike the ball viciously hard whenever he was the one in play. He didn't say anything, not wanting to draw attention to Clay's anger. It was a private matter for them to settle. Logan heard someone loudly cheering and clapping from the sideline. He looked and saw Alison from PR jumping up and down and screaming every time Clay scored a point. He wasn't too thrilled to see that, but he was forced to give his attention back to the game when Clay sent the ball streaking towards his face.

When the game was over, it was Clay's team that came up with the winning score. He watched in shock as Alison ran onto the sand. She leaped up on Clay, hugging him tight, her legs wrapping around his waist. Clay's face looked just as shocked as he felt. He pulled her arms from around his neck.

"I didn't know you were that invested in the game."

Logan didn't hear whatever she said in response. He turned away and walked off a few steps to keep anyone from seeing his reaction. After a few moments, he turned back to the court to see Clay putting his shirt back on. Alison was nowhere in sight. He caught Clay's eye and jerked his head towards the tree line. Clay's chin came up but he obeyed the silent command and made his way into the trees. Logan waited a few moments before he followed, taking a different path.

As he approached, he saw Clay sulkily leaning against a tree, his arms crossed over his chest in a closed off manner. Logan went up to him, relieved that Clay agreed to talk to him. Worry that he might refuse to forgive him and the urge to spank his butt for his arrogance fought for space in Logan's brain. Clay spoke up before he could.

"So, what? Are you too fucking good to abstain or even masturbate for a few weeks while you go after someone you claim to want? Or does being a Dom mean you get to fuck whoever you want, whenever you want?"

"That's not what—" Logan started but Clay cut him off.

"And don't think because I'm the sub in this relationship that you can give me any lame ass excuse and I'll bow down and fall in line. Because I don't work like that."

Logan's jaw tightened in anger as he tried to stay calm and ignore Clay's angry sarcasm. The conversation would not go well if both of them were pissed off. "Are you going to let me talk now?" Clay swept his arm out, gesturing mockingly for Logan to speak. Logan ignored that too. "Yes, I fooled around with Ryan. And, yes, I was drunk. I'm not using that as an excuse, but I am saying that I made a really shitty judgment call and being drunk off my ass didn't help."

Clay hadn't been drunk or high for a long time, but he remembered the crazy shit he would do. Things he wouldn't normally do while sober. He knew alcohol turned people into idiots. Hell, that was one of the reasons he stopped drinking. But that didn't mean he was automatically going to excuse whatever Logan had done. "Tell me what happened."

Logan exhaled hard as he ran a hand over his head. "It was the night of Tony's engagement party and we were at the booth alone together for a few minutes. Do you remember?"

Clay nodded. He remembered that night very well. He'd almost given in to Logan that night even though he still hadn't decided if it was a good idea to get involved with him. But with Logan's hand on him and the look Logan had given him, like he was demanding that Clay say yes, he almost caved and kissed Logan right there in public. If his cousin hadn't called right then, he probably would have gone home with Logan that night. Still, remembering that didn't make him feel any better about the situation they were currently in.

"So what? You were pissed you couldn't get any from me and got some from Ryan instead?"

Logan stepped forward. "Stop assuming and let me tell you what happened. I wasn't pissed, but I was discouraged. I wanted you so bad, but it seemed like you were determined to keep us in the friend zone. Until that moment in the booth when it seemed like you were finally going to say yes. Then your phone rang and you left. I actually felt like maybe I should give up. And I'm not proud of this, but I started pounding shots and beers until I was pretty wasted. Ryan offered to drive me home. When we got to my house, he walked me to my door. He asked if I wanted company and …" He trailed off, hating that he had to admit to this. "And I pulled him inside and started kissing him."

"How far did it go?"

Logan closed his eyes for a second. "Like I said, we kissed. And he gave me head. But that's it. I swear. My fool brain finally woke up and I pushed him off me and told him to leave. I didn't come and I fucking swear we didn't sleep together."

Clay uncrossed his arms. "Why didn't you tell me?"

Logan laughed harshly. "I wanted to forget about it. I was embarrassed. But mostly because I was scared as hell that you'd be pissed and not want to be with me."

Clay cut his eyes at him. "You weren't wrong to be scared."

Logan's heart leaped into his throat. Was Clay about to leave him? Logan stepped closer and lightly grasped the back of Clay's neck. "Clay, look at me." When those blue eyes rose to his, Logan noticed they weren't filled with anger any more, but that didn't ease his worry much.

"I'm so sorry, baby. If I could take it back, I would. But I promise you it was a dumb, drunken mistake. One I won't repeat. *Ever*. I love you more than anything and I'll do whatever it takes to show you that. Please believe me when I tell you how sorry I am."

"That pissed me off, Logan, hearing Ryan say he'd been with you. But it hurt to hear him talk about serving you," Clay said in a quiet voice.

Logan understood. Subs could be just as possessive as Doms. "I know. And I'm sorry for that too." He stroked his hand up into the silky hair of Clay's nape. "You're the only one I want to control. The only one whose submission I want, need, *crave* with every part of me, every second of every day. I don't ever want to be with anyone else. Please say you forgive me?"

Clay looked at Logan and the sincere regret on his face. How could he stay mad at him after such an honest explanation and apology? And hearing him say how much he wanted his submission made Clay's heart race. All of Clay's anger drained from him. Christ, he had it bad for this stern man with his warm hazel eyes. He loved Logan and wanted to submit to him just as much as Logan wanted him to. Clay believed that Logan knew he'd made a mistake and that it wouldn't ever happen again. So there was really only one thing to say. He looked at Logan from beneath his lashes.

"I forgive you."

Logan's fingers clenched on his neck in obvious relief. "You do?"

"Yes. But you'd better not pull any shit like that again. I don't care how mad or upset or *discouraged* you get. If you're not sleeping with me, your new boyfriend is your right hand. Understand?"

Logan nodded that he understood before he smiled. "You've got an awful sassy mouth for a sub."

Clay snorted a laugh. "You ought to know by now that I've got a lot more to say than just, 'Yes, Sir,' and, 'No, Sir.'" Then he brought his hand up and caressed Logan's chest. "But how 'bout this? I love you, Sir."

Logan pulled him close against his body. "I'll take anything you have to say as long as I get to hear you say that. I love you too, baby."

He leaned forward and kissed Clay, almost weak with relief that he was still his. When their lips met, Clay opened and let him in as always. Logan stroked his tongue over his lover's, groaning with pleasure as one of Clay's legs came up and wrapped around his waist while they kissed. The kiss grew deeper and hotter, their chests pressing together, their grips on one another tightening. Logan finally broke away, mindful that someone could stumble upon them. He flipped Clay's dog tags over to the side that bore his name.

"Does this mean that you still want to wear these?"

Clay gave him a look that let Logan know he'd just asked an incredibly stupid question. Logan smiled and tugged on the chain. He looked up from stroking his finger over the metal when Clay asked him a question.

"There's nothing else you want to tell me, is there?"

Logan shook his head as he looked straight at Clay. "No, there's nothing else." He gave Clay a quick kiss. "You want to get out of here?" Clay nodded. "Me too. Let's say our goodbyes and head out."

Back at the house, the party was still going strong. Ryan was hovering near the volley ball courts. When he saw Clay and Logan walk over, he stormed off. Clay laughed to himself as he watched Ryan walk away. Clearly Ryan had waited around to see if he'd managed to break him and Logan up.

Clay wasn't stupid. He knew that asshole's nonchalant demeanor had been an act. He brought up that whole thing on purpose to cause trouble. When they reached Logan's car, Ryan had just gotten behind the wheel of his own. Logan got in on the driver's side and waited for him to get in. But Clay was going to let Ryan know that his play had failed. He whistled sharply to get his attention. His car window was down and he turned, hearing him easily. Looking straight at him, Clay pulled his collar from under his t-shirt and held it up for the other man to see. With his other hand, he popped up his middle finger, pressed his lips to it, and blew him a kiss. Then he turned his back on that little shit and got in the car. Logan grinned without saying anything and drove off.

41

Warm water streamed from the shower head. The air was thick with steam and scented with the spicy scent of body wash. Clay stepped into the shower. Logan smiled at him, the water sparkling on his eyelashes and giving his eyes a warm golden glow.

"Get your sweaty, sandy self over here so I can clean you up."

Clay grabbed the bottle of body wash off the shelf. "I can do it."

Logan took the bottle away from him. "True. But I want to do it for you. And you're going to let me."

Logan tugged Clay to stand in front of him, facing the shower head. Clay reached for his body sponge, intending to hand it to Logan.

"Leave it. We won't need that tonight."

Clay saw Logan set the bottle of wash back down and pick up his shampoo. Logan squeezed some into his hand and told him, "Get your hair wet." Clay ducked his head under the water for a few seconds, getting his hair wet like Logan told him. He pulled back, shaking the excess water off. Logan's hands came up and started to rub the shampoo into his hair. As he felt those strong fingers massaging his scalp, Clay released a long sigh of pleasure.

"Feel good?"

"Not at all," he answered jokingly. He hadn't had anyone wash his hair for him since he was a kid and it felt amazing. Logan's short nails lightly scratched across his scalp a few times before he heard, "Rinse." Once more, he went under the spray. When he pulled back he looked over his shoulder to see Logan rubbing shower gel between his palms. He turned back around and Logan's slick hands smoothed up his neck, washing the sweat away and massaging his tense muscles. Clay relaxed, forgetting about the drama with Ryan as Logan moved on to rubbing the soap into his shoulders.

"I'm sorry," Logan said as he pressed a damp kiss to his ear.

Clay could feel Logan's apology in every brush of his fingers on his skin. "You don't have to keep apologizing. It's forgiven and soon to be forgotten. Especially if you keep rubbing me like this."

More soap went into Logan's hands then he stroked down Clay's arms. "I just want to make sure you know I mean it. You're my everything, Clay."

Clay turned his head to look over his shoulder and kiss Logan on the jaw. "I know."

Logan rubbed his thumbs into Clay's palms, pressing into the fleshy pad of his thumb before sliding his soapy fingers in between Clay's. Clay moaned at how good that felt. He'd never considered his hands tense before, but he could definitely tell the difference in how relaxed they were now. More soap and then Logan was washing slow circles across his chest and belly, his fingers teasingly slipping down to brush his shaft. But Logan didn't grasp him the way he wanted. Instead, he stroked his hands around to his back, massaging all the soreness away before those wonderful hands slid down to his butt. He massaged there too, squeezing his ass in a firm grip, his palms rubbing and smoothing over him. A slick finger dipped inside of him the barest amount, making him gasp. "Logan…"

"Quiet. I'm not finished yet."

Logan came to stand in front of him, and to Clay's surprise, dropped to his knees on the shower floor. Logan soaped up his hands again then started to wash his legs. "Beautiful, beautiful legs. I would never do anything to jeopardize having the right to slide between them every night."

Clay's belly flipped and his eyes went wide as he watched Logan kneeling before him. He swallowed thickly as Logan's hands traced from his calves back up to his thighs, higher and higher until his knuckles lightly brushed his sac. "I know you wouldn't."

Logan wrapped a soapy fist around his cock. His hand slid back and forth, cleaning him, and in the process, making him so hard there couldn't possibly be any blood left in his brain.

"Do you? Maybe I'd better show you how much you mean to me just to be sure you really understand."

Logan leaned to the side, letting the spray wash away the soap from Clay's front. When Clay realized what Logan was about to do, he tried to stop him.

"Logan, you don't have to—" The rest of his protest was cut off with a sharp gasp as Logan sucked him into his mouth. Logan had given him head plenty of times before, but he'd never done it on his knees before. It was a position that Logan had never taken. Seeing his Dom pleasuring him like that was a huge fucking turn on, and made him realize that Logan would do anything to keep him happy. Clay looked down and saw those golden eyes watching him, those firm lips sliding back and forth on his cock. "Oh, god ..." he breathed out.

Logan grabbed Clay's hands and brought them to the back of his head. He pressed them there tightly, signaling without words that he was allowing Clay to take control. Clay was surprised again. Not once had Logan ever allowed him to take control, not even before he admitted to being a Dom. Clay was tentative at first, not sure how far Logan would let him go. He moved his hips slowly, just barely pushing into Logan's mouth. But Logan took his mouth from him long enough to command, "Do it." he reached around and dug his fingers hard into Clay's ass as he swallowed him back down. Clay gripped his lover's head, thrusting his cock in between Logan's lips. It felt different, like he was doing something bad, but he couldn't stop because it felt so good.

Logan's lips tightened on him as he sucked, his tongue flicking the sensitive side of his cock. Clay's belly tightened and he knew he wasn't going to last much longer. But before he could even think to get the words out Logan squeezed his balls tight and smacked him hard on the ass. His hips shot forward in surprise at the pleasure-pain. Clay lost it and exploded in a blinding, screaming climax that had every muscle in his body clenching as he pulsed into Logan's mouth. Barely realizing what he was doing, he pulled Logan close against him, holding him there as he kept coming. And every time he thought he was done, Logan would squeeze him again and suck him hard, drawing forth another rush of pleasure. When he couldn't take it anymore, he pulled his sensitive cock from Logan's mouth and collapsed against the shower wall. Clay stared down at Logan who was licking his lips with a devilish gleam in his eyes. He rose back to his feet and with an arm around his waist, pulled Clay up against his hard body.

"Did you like that?"

Clay gave a shuddering laugh. "Yeah. Didn't the screaming orgasm I just had clue you in to that?"

Logan smiled and pecked him on the lips. "You said you had a request yesterday. What is it?"

Clay remembered teasing that he wanted to be in control in his office the other day. With everything that had happened, it seemed like a long time ago. But if there was any night that Logan was going to give him what he wanted, this was it. "My request is for you to lie still for me and let me pleasure you the way I want, for as long as I want. Will you do that for me, Sir? Please?" Clay knew he was laying it on thick, but he didn't care. He'd bat his eyelashes if that's what it took.

"Yes." Logan pulled Clay in for a kiss. Clay's hand trailed over his hips, dancing along his pelvis.

"Thank you, Sir. I promise I'll make it good for you." His fingers teased over his shaft. "And if you don't like it, you can spank me afterwards. Is that okay?"

Logan cleared his throat. "Yes, that's okay."

Clay leaned up to whisper in his ear, his voice so low Logan barely heard him over the rush of the water. "Maybe I'll let you spank me whether you like it or not. Not that I could stop you from doing whatever you wanted to me with these big hands." His fingers tightened their grip on Logan's shaft, squeezing him roughly. "Or this thick cock. But until then, you'll have to lay there and let me do whatever I want."

Logan cursed and quickly shut off the water. "Let's go," he said, pulling Clay from the shower. Logan got them both dried off in record time and started pulling Clay towards the bed. Clay followed him without any resistance. Logan knew the smile teasing at his lover's lips was because of his eagerness, but he didn't care. He loved being in control of Clay, but after his whispered teasing, he was definitely willing to let his sub play like he wanted.

Logan lay back on the bed while Clay climbed up and straddled his waist. When his lover leaned down to kiss him, he parted his lips, gladly letting Clay slide his tongue into his mouth. Clay kissed him softly with slow, teasing licks of his tongue. He pressed his hips down, rubbing their shafts together. Logan stroked down his back and cupped his ass in his palms. Clay grabbed his wrists and tugged him away.

"No. No hands."

Logan pressed his hands flat to the bed, pushing his hips up to meet Clay's smooth thrusts. Clay ended their kiss too soon to suit him and pulled away. Logan tried to draw him back, but Clay shook his head.

"Uh-huh. The way *I* want, remember?"

Logan growled but he let Clay go. Clay licked up his neck, drawing his skin between his lips in tiny nips. His lover scooted down, licking across his chest until he reached one of his nipples. When Clay sucked him in, flicking his tongue against his sensitive nipple, Logan had to clench his fists in the sheets to keep from grabbing him and pulling his head tighter against him. Clay tortured him there, sucking and biting, rubbing his stomach across his cock until he was breathing hard and straining not to yank Clay underneath him. Then Clay stopped … and moved on to his other nipple.

Clay couldn't believe Logan was actually laying there for him. It was a heady feeling, having that big body there to do with as he pleased. He released Logan's nipple to move down his torso. He licked his way across those hard abs, stroking his tongue over the smooth muscles. He made sure to kiss and tease every inch of warm skin. He dipped his tongue into the indentions of his waist and his belly button, blowing a soft breath over the dampness he'd left. Logan shivered. Clay was heading for Logan's cock. It was so stiff and hot as it brushed against his face. But he took a few moments to torment the sensitive skin of his pelvis, licking and dragging his teeth lightly over the thin skin. Then he finally opened his mouth over Logan's cock. He licked his way from base to tip, slowly, slowly dragging his tongue up every inch of that throbbing vein.

Logan groaned as his cock was engulfed by the wet heat of his sub's mouth. Forcing himself to lay there and not take control while Clay sucked him was tough. But his lips felt so good gliding up and down his cock it was worth it. Clay palmed his balls and tongued the underside of his cock, pressing against the pleasure patch of nerves there. Logan's hips jacked up off the bed.

"Fuck! Baby, that feels so good. Do it again."

Clay obeyed and Logan started thrusting into his sub's mouth. He knew he was failing in letting Clay take the lead as he issued order after order on what he wanted Clay to do to him. But he couldn't help it. And with Clay following every single one, it just spurred him on. Finally Clay stopped and sat up, still straddling him. He watched Clay bring a finger to his mouth, licking at it with long wet laps of his tongue. He did the same with a second finger. Logan's breath was coming fast as he realized what Clay was about to do. Clay took his fingers from his mouth and trailed them down his torso before reaching around behind him.

"Did I do okay or do I get a spanking tonight?"

Logan cleared his throat. "You did more than okay."

Clay grinned and traced a finger down Logan's stiff shaft. "I kinda figured."

Logan couldn't see but he knew when his sub slid his fingers inside himself because he let out a soft moan. After pleasuring Clay in the shower and everything Clay had done to him tonight, and now watching his sub fuck himself on his fingers right in his lap, Logan was so hard he felt like he could fuck through a brick wall. "Clay, I want in you. Now." His voice was so thick with desire he barely recognized himself.

Clay shook his head, still riding his fingers and moaning. "My pace, remember, Sir?"

Logan dug his thumbs into Clay's inner thighs. "Clay..." he said warningly.

Clay gave him a sly smile and grasped his shaft. "It's not easy, is it?"

"No. But don't think that means I'll take it any easier on you after this."

Clay's smile grew. "I know you won't."

He leaned over to the nightstand for the lube. Logan lay there while Clay slicked him up purposely, *agonizingly* slow. Clay's tight heat slid on to his cock and he shuddered, just barely keeping his hips still to allow Clay to do as he wanted. When he was completely sheathed inside Clay's ass, he groaned deep in his chest. He couldn't stop himself from digging his fingers into Clay's hips, wanting to urge him on. Thankfully, Clay decided not to torture him further. He started moving, rising up and down on his cock, that sweet friction edging him steadily towards climax. Logan clenched his jaw, holding himself back to just enjoy the pleasure his lover was giving him.

Clay leaned forward and planted his hands on Logan's chest to give himself better leverage as he rode his Dom. Logan felt so good inside him, filling him and stretching him in the most amazing way. Clay was hard again and ready to come. But this time, he wanted Logan in control when he did. He lowered himself until his mouth was at Logan's ear. "I need to come, Sir. I … I need you to tell me to come."

That was all it took for Logan to grab him by the ass and roll them over until he was on top, slamming his cock into him so hard his whole body tingled from the pleasure. Logan snatched his wrists up and over his head, taking back control so fast it was clear he'd never really given it up in the first place.

"Get your leg up," he ordered in a husky whisper.

Clay obeyed, drawing a leg up. Logan hooked his arm under his knee and raised it even higher, opening him up more for his thrusts.

Clay arched back into the pillows. It had been fun to tease Logan, but this is what he loved, his Dom in control as he stroked inside him. He moaned as Logan's hand gripped his cock, pumping swiftly. Logan started pushing inside him faster, the head of his cock brushing over that spot deep inside him again and again. Clay shivered, his orgasm rising up his shaft. He silently gave thanks to all the gods when Logan spoke into his ear, breathing heavily.

"I want you to come for me, Clay. Right now!"

Logan rammed his cock into his spot harder than before and Clay couldn't help but let himself go as his Dom ordered. He trembled, his hands involuntarily jerking in the firm prison of Logan's fist as he released onto his stomach. Logan kept their hips pressed tightly together and a half second later, he felt the heat of Logan's orgasm flooding into him. Logan's big body jerked over his and Clay wrapped his other leg around his waist, needing to be as close to his Dom as he could.

****

When both their shafts stopped pulsing, but before their heart rates had slowed, Logan leaned down and kissed him softly.

"I love you, Clay." Clay wrapped his freed arms around Logan's neck and kissed him back.

"I love you, too."

42

Two days later, Clay walked into a warehouse downtown. The large space had been set up with props, lots of bright lights and camera equipment. Clay looked around. They brought in one of the big, black SUVs they used for transport and even a police dog – a mostly black German Shepherd named Sue.

Clay shook his head as he passed the makeup table. He couldn't believe he agreed to do this. But Hector had taunted and dared him until he'd finally given in. Of course, Hector wasn't there yet. The shoot had been set up in shifts to help move things along. Clay chose an early shift so he could get it out of the way. Hector had one later in the afternoon. He noticed Alison talking to the photographer and waved at her. She waved back and ended her conversation to come over to him.

"Clay! It's good to see you. I'm so happy you decided to be in the calendar." She smiled and tapped him on the chest. "I don't know what month you'll be given, but I can already guess it'll end up as the most popular."

Clay smiled back at her. He liked Alison. She flirted shamelessly, but he wasn't bothered by it. He appreciated a woman who was open and upfront about what she liked. "So what am I supposed to do for this?" He hefted his duffel bag. "I brought my uniform and gear."

Alison stepped back and looked at him for a moment then she led him over to a woman who stood in front of a rack of clothes. "Lisa, this is Officer Clay Foster. How would you like to dress him today?"

Lisa looked him over as well, but with a serious eye. "Put on your uniform pants, boots, and gloves," she told him. "I have a shirt and vest for you to wear." She pulled the two items off the rack and handed them to him, pointing to a curtained area where he could go change.

Behind the curtain, Clay pulled on his clothes first then the shoot clothes. The shirt was a short sleeved, black athletic style made with a silky nylon. When he put it on and looked in the mirror, he had to laugh. He was in shape, of course, but by no means was he ripped. The close fit and short sleeves of the shirt, however, made his arms and chest look a lot bigger and harder than they actually were. Clay pulled the tactical vest over his head and buckled it closed on the sides. It was smaller than his real vest and minus a lot of the pockets. It was also more streamlined and fit closer to his body. SWAT was printed in big white letters across the front instead of on the back. Clay shook his head. It was tasteful, like Alison had said it would be, but it was definitely designed to be sexier than the real thing.

Clay stepped from behind the curtain and went back over to where things were set up. Q, Tiffany and Carlos had arrived. Tiffany let out a long wolf whistle as he approached. Clay flushed in embarrassment. "Real mature, Corporal Jackson."

The three of them laughed. Surprisingly, Carlos had agreed to do the shoot and he was next. The wardrobe lady tried to give him a modified outfit but he turned his dark eyes on her and spoke one word in his deep voice.

"No."

She immediately backed off. Tiffany rolled her eyes at her boyfriend while he went to change into his regular uniform.

The makeup lady came over and offered to put some stuff on his face. He didn't know what it was but he put his hands up and backed away while Tiffany and Q laughed again. The lady looked exasperated but he held firm. Clay did let her brush his hair, not that he could imagine it would look any different. But when she held up a bottle of baby oil, Clay stepped away from her again. "What the hell is that for?"

At that point, Alison came over. She took the bottle away from the makeup artist and gently shooed her off. "Clay, this is just another prop to make the calendar look good."

Clay arched an eyebrow. "Somehow, I doubt being greased up will make me look better as a cop."

Alison smiled. "You'd be surprised. I promise it will help the camera pick up the definition in your arms and it won't look cheap or cheesy. Just trust me." She popped the cap on the bottle. "May I?"

Clay sighed and nodded. He'd agreed to it. "Fine. Besides, I guess I could use all the help I can get if I want my arms to look *defined*."

Alison poured a small amount of the oil in her palm and started rubbing it onto his forearms. "You don't give yourself enough credit."

Clay looked down at her with a grin. "I give myself plenty of credit. I just know I don't have bulging biceps."

Alison laughed and smoothed the oil the rest of the way up his arm.

****

Logan walked up to the warehouse. He wasn't participating in the calendar but he was there to show support for the team members who were being photographed. And since they weren't on rotation, when the shoot was done, they were all going out to eat and have a few drinks afterwards. Hector insisted on calling it a wrap party. He and Clay had done their best imitations of being models on a catwalk, strutting between the desks in the pen. Logan laughed at the memory. But when he opened the doors and walked inside, the laughter froze on his face.

He saw Clay standing there, looking especially good in a tight fitting black shirt and tactical vest, his black curls tamed and shining under the lights. That didn't bother him. What did bother him was the woman in front of him who currently had her hands all over his lover, running them up and down his arms. And Clay was letting her touch him while he watched her with a smile on his face. Logan didn't know what the fuck was going on, but he damn sure didn't like it. He strode over but before he reached them, Alison pushed Clay towards the camera.

Clay looked uncomfortable at first. But with Tiffany and Quan cracking jokes off camera, he soon relaxed. The photographer snapped away. After a few minutes, he seemed satisfied with what he'd shot. Clay came over, smiling when he saw Logan.

"Cripes. Glad that's done. Remind me never to quit my day job and become a male model."

"Can I talk to you for a second?" Clay frowned but he nodded and followed him off to the side. "What the hell was going on when I walked in here?"

Clay looked confused. "Can you be a little more specific?"

"More specific? Fine. I saw that woman with her hands all over you while you watched like you were enjoying the hell out of it. What was going on there?"

Clay laughed. "Oh that? She was just putting some baby oil on my arms. Apparently, it'll make me look more studly for the camera."

"And you couldn't apply that yourself?"

Clay frowned at Logan. He realized that he was actually pissed off that Alison had touched him. "I could have but I already had gloves on and she offered."

Logan's brow shot up. "That's your excuse? You had gloves on? I didn't realize it was such a struggle to take them on and off."

"Logan, what is the big deal? She rubbed baby oil on my arms. It was prep for the photo. And it's not like she was rubbing it on my chest or something."

"The big deal is I do not want some woman running her hands all over my property!"

Clay took a step back. He did not like Logan referring to him as property, not in that manner. He was starting to get mad, but he tried to stay calm and get Logan to see that it was ridiculous. "Logan. You're upset because the shoot organizer touched me in an impersonal way to get me ready for the photographer. She wasn't trying to get into my pants. Do you see how silly this is?" Logan stepped up close enough for their chests to brush together. Clay swore he could feel the angry heat coming off his furious lover.

"Don't feed me that impersonal bullshit, Clay! You and I both know that woman wants you. You're goddamn right I have a problem with her putting her hands on you while you fucking smile and encourage it! So yeah, I'm upset."

Now Clay was pissed. He didn't like the way Logan had referred to him as property, he didn't like the way Logan was talking to him, and he didn't like his absurd jealousy. He got right back up in Logan's face. "Well, you can calm the fuck down! Because I am not your goddamn property. And if *I* choose to let somebody touch me in an *impersonal* way, there's not a damn thing you can do about it!"

The two of them glared at each other until Tiffany came over. "Guys, this isn't the right place for this."

Clay sneered at Logan. "I don't think the place exists that is right for this nonsense." Logan's face was still hard with anger but Clay didn't care. He took the borrowed shirt and vest off, grabbed his stuff, and got out of there.

****

Logan started to go after Clay but Carlos came over and stopped him. "Let him go, man. Let him cool off for a few minutes." Logan took a deep breath and followed his friend's advice. But there was someone else he needed to talk to and he was doing that right now. He walked up to Alison.

"Do you have a minute, Ms. Crawford?" Anger must have still been on his face because she looked at him warily.

"Hello, Sergeant Pierce. I should probably stay over here and keep an eye on things."

Logan gave her a tight smile. "This will only take a few minutes." He stepped back to let her pass in front of him and they walked over to an empty area of the warehouse. "Ms. Crawford, I'm going to be clear and upfront with you. Corporal Foster is mine. We aren't out to the force but we are a couple. And I do not like watching someone put their hands on what belongs to me. Do you understand?"

Alison's eyes widened in surprise but she nodded. "Of course, Sergeant Pierce. I had no idea you two ..." She trailed off.

"Well, we are. Now that you know, I'm sure you'll stay away from him. And I think it would be best if Clay were removed from the calendar line up." He didn't need Alison's look of shock to tell him he'd gone too far. The voice in the back of his head told him that. But jealousy, ugly jealousy, wouldn't let him take it back.

Alison cleared her throat. "If that's what you think is best, I'll do so."

Logan nodded and Alison started to walk away. He called her back. "Ms. Crawford?" He waited for her to turn back around. "I'm sure I don't need to say this, but this conversation is not to be repeated."

She nodded and continued on.

Logan took another deep breath. He knew he'd overreacted. He needed to go talk to Clay and straighten things out with him.

43

Clay stormed out of the warehouse, yanking his shirt over his head as he went. He couldn't believe Logan had been so disrespectful to him! Logan didn't own him, not like that. He had no right to get upset over Alison touching him. Yeah, she'd been flirting but it didn't mean anything. Clay had no intentions of developing anything with her. He was heading to his car when he heard someone calling his name. He stopped and turned around. It was Tiffany. She came up to him, looking concerned.

"Are you alright?"

"Yeah, just pissed off. I can't believe Logan did that."

Tiffany shook her head. "I'm sure he didn't mean—"

He cut her off. "Save it, Tiff. He knew exactly what he was doing."

"Are you leaving?"

"Yeah. I'm too pissed off to stay and party after the shoot is done."

"Alright. I'll tell Logan you went home."

"I'm not going home. Gonna go hang out on my own for awhile."

"I don't think that's a good idea, Clay. Just go home and wait for Logan. Don't hide. If you do, you'll only make him madder."

"Fuck making him madder. I couldn't care less. Let me ask you something, Tiffany. Does Carlos trust you?"

"Yes. Why? You don't think Logan trusts you?"

"Clearly not! Otherwise he wouldn't have made me play Marilyn to his DiMaggio tonight. I can't believe he got that upset over some harmless flirting!"

Tiffany shook her head. "Clay, I'm not saying Logan was right to flip out the way he did but try to understand why he was upset. In his mind, you are his. And he was blindsided when he saw that women hanging on you. So he freaked out."

"Went ape shit is more accurate," Clay grumbled as he fingered his tags.

Tiffany ignored him. "All I'm saying is those tags around your neck that you keep touching means that you *are* Logan's property, Clay. And he's not going to like anyone else touching you."

Clay quietly stared at the building behind Tiffany as he thought about what she'd said. "Would Carlos have flipped out if he walked into what Logan saw?"

"I don't know. Maybe if he didn't have any warning he might have. But it's different with us. We've been together a lot longer than you and Logan. Your relationship is so new. It's going to take some time before Logan trusts deep down that you want to belong to him the way Carlos knows I want to be his." Then she grinned. "But I can guarantee you won't ever see him letting some other guy rub oil onto any part of me."

Clay huffed a laugh at that. He was still mad, but now he sort of understood where Logan was coming from. He looked at Tiffany. "Stop being so damn smart."

Tiffany smirked and buffed her nails on her shirt. "Beauty and brains in one petite package. That's me."

"Don't forget insanity."

Tiffany rolled her eyes. "Your jealousy is unfortunate. Now are you going home or hanging out here?"

"I told you I'm not going home. And before you say it, I'm not hiding. I'm just not ready to talk to him about this yet. I know you've had times where you needed a break from Carlos."

She smiled slightly. "Yeah, I have. Then go if you feel you need to. I just hope it's worth it when you can't sit down tomorrow."

****

Several hours later, Clay pulled up to his apartment complex. He wasn't surprised to see Logan's car parked in front of his building. He got out and went up the stairs to his unit. Logan was standing in front of the door. Clay didn't say anything, he just opened up. He didn't even consider trying to keep Logan from following him into the apartment. From the set expression on his face, he knew they were about to have it out.

"Where were you?"

"Out."

A muscle ticked in Logan's jaw. "Clay."

He dropped his keys on the entry table. "What? Am I not allowed to be mad now?"

"You're allowed to be mad. What you're not allowed to do is disappear on me, ignore my calls, and make me search for you all day."

"I didn't tell you to look for me."

Logan came up to him, crowding him backwards until he was pressed against the door. "Did you honestly think that I wouldn't?"

Clay didn't reply to that. He knew Logan would be looking for him. Looking at him, he saw how tense and upset Logan was. Surprisingly, he found himself wanting to soothe him. That was different for him. Normally in arguments, he was the one his partner was trying to calm while he was largely indifferent to their efforts. But he didn't say anything and Logan continued.

"I lost control today and that was unacceptable. I apologize. I should never have spoken to you that way. It just threw me to walk in and see her with her hands all over you." He shook his head as though he were trying to get rid of the memory. "Especially since I've known for awhile that she's interested in you. It threw me and I lost it."

Before Clay even knew he was about to speak, the words were out of his mouth. "It's okay, Logan. I understand. I'm sure that was a crazy shock to walk in to without any warning."

Some of the tension eased from Logan's shoulders. "Thank you for saying that."

Logan slipped his hand under the neck of his shirt and pulled out his dog tags. He looked at the pendant in his hands for a long moment before he looked back at Clay.

"This is going to sound insanely possessive but I don't fucking care. No one touches you but me. Not Alison, and not any other man or woman. Only me. It's bad enough that I can't claim you like I want to. That I can't let everyone know you're mine. But I'm not going to stand for having to watch while someone who isn't me runs their hands all over you. I'm not sharing you with anyone. Do you understand?"

Clay looked into the hazel eyes focused so intently on him. Angry Logan yelling at him he did not like. But this Logan, being so brutally honest about his possessive feelings towards him, had his heart beating hard and his breath coming faster. To have someone want him with such unashamed passion made him feel like he really belonged to Logan – like he was the center of Logan's world. And the fact that Logan desired him so much had him feeling as though he had power over his Dom. In fact, he *knew* he did. It was a potent mix that filled his head up, leaving no room for his earlier anger.

"I understand, Logan. And, honestly, I only want you to touch me. But please don't *ever* flip out like that again. Getting in my face like that without even checking to see what was going on or listening to me totally disrespected me and our relationship. I couldn't help but react the way I did." Clay shrugged. "I don't think I'm submissive enough to just accept you confronting me like that."

Logan smiled at him, all the anger gone from his eyes. "I know. And I don't want you to be." Logan kissed him lightly. "And I promise to never disrespect you like that again."

"Thank you. That's all I ask." This time, Clay was the one to lean forward and initiate a kiss. Their lips met, communicating their love and apology, their tongues sliding softly against one another until Logan pulled back.

"I like kissing and making up with you."

Logan raised an eyebrow. "Are you sure it's not just the kissing you like?"

Clay pretended to think. "You might be on to something."

Logan laughed and kissed him again. But when he ended the kiss, his face was serious. "You've earned a punishment tonight, baby."

Clay's eyes widened in surprise. "What? Why?"

"You hid away from me all afternoon, Clay—"

"I wasn't *hiding*," Clay started to cut in but with one look from Logan, he shut up. Besides, he *had* been hiding, even though he was too mule-headed to admit it to anybody but himself.

"You knew I'd be looking for you. Which is why you stayed away from your apartment. And you could have stopped Alison from touching you, but you didn't. Those were your choices, and now you have to accept the consequences." Logan stepped back and gestured down the hallway to Clay's room. "Let's go."

44

In the bedroom, Logan ordered Clay to undress. His order was obeyed but he could tell by Clay's sulky expression that he was upset at being punished. Still, when he stood there naked, the already half-hard state of his cock told Logan he was looking forward to it. "Come here," he said in a hard voice. After the barest hesitation, which of course he noticed, Clay walked over to him.

Logan pressed his finger to Clay's tags as he told him what his punishment would be. "You will not be allowed to orgasm tonight. And you'll be restrained all evening, even while you're asleep. Do you understand?"

After Clay's nod, Logan hooked his finger under his collar and dragged him closer for a kiss. He kissed him roughly, pushing his tongue between his lips. Clay submitted to him, his head falling back, but kept his hands at his sides like a good boy since he hadn't said that he could touch Logan. Logan ended the kiss with one last nip to Clay's bottom lip, but he grasped his lover's cock and slid his hand up and down in a slow stroke. "Undress me." He kept pumping as Clay undid his belt buckle then opened his pants. Logan squeezed Clay's shaft, making him gasp and hurriedly push his pants and boxers down to his ankles.

"Can you let me go so I can take your shirt off?"

"Are you asking me or telling me?" he said, squeezing harder.

Clay closed his eyes and bit his lip. "I'm asking you, Sir."

Logan moved his hand on his lover a few more times until Clay's hips started moving with him. Then he let him go and dropped his arm to his side. Clay took several deep breaths, clearly trying to calm himself. He unbuttoned Logan's shirt and pushed it off his shoulders and down his arms. But Logan wasn't completely undressed yet so he waited for Clay to finish. He saw a flash of defiance in his lover's eyes before Clay lowered his head and sank to his knees. Logan smiled to himself as Clay removed his socks and shoes and pulled his pants and boxers the rest of the way off. He'd have all that defiance out of his submissive by the end of the night.

"Get up and go lay down with your arms up over your head."

He watched as Clay moved just slow enough for it to be obvious that he was still ticked about his upcoming punishment. Logan didn't say anything. If Clay wanted to dig himself into a hole, making his punishment worse, Logan was going to let him.

While Clay got into position like he'd been ordered, Logan reached into the nightstand for a pair of black silk scarves he left there from a previous visit. He got on the bed and straddled Clay's waist, tying one end of each of the scarves to the headboard and the other ends around Clay's wrists. He tied the bonds tighter than he normally would have, giving them a jerk as he did so. Logan moved higher up Clay's torso until his cock was right in front of his lips.

"Suck me."

Clay's mouth opened, but from the expression in his eyes, Logan didn't know whether his sub was going to suck him … or bite him. Logan raised a brow in warning and pushed into Clay's mouth. He braced his hands on the headboard, moving his hips so he slowly slid in and out. Clay's tongue licked at him, but he still wasn't fully following his command. "I said suck me," Logan ordered again as he thrust hard.

Clay moaned and closed his eyes, raising his head up to do as he was told. Logan rested his weight on his knees as he indulged in the feeling of Clay's hot, wet mouth sliding back and forth on his cock. "That's good, baby. I like it when you do as you're told."

Clay's eyes flashed open at that, defiance still glittering in their blue depths. Logan felt Clay's teeth scrape the underside of his cock and he knew it hadn't been an accident. So he bucked his hips forward hard and fast until Clay was moaning and sucking him just as quickly, without any teeth. But soon, Logan could see Clay was straining to keep his head up so he pulled his cock out of his lover's mouth. He was surprised when Clay licked his bottom lip and whispered, "More." Logan denied him. "I won't be coming in that pretty mouth of yours tonight. Your tight little ass is gonna take all my cum." Clay's fingers clenched in his restraints and he smiled. Logan knew how his words affected his lover.

He moved back down Clay's body, grabbing the lube he put on the nightstand earlier as he did so. Logan lined their cocks up and drizzled the cool liquid over both of them before capping the bottle and throwing it on the floor. Clay gasped and his hips started rolling as Logan held both their cocks in his fist and started stroking.

"You're so hard, Clay. I want you to think about the fact that you have to stay like that all night. No matter how bad you want to come, I won't let you." Logan took his finger, slick with lube and pressed inside his lover. He leaned down to whisper against Clay's ear. "Even when I'm fucking you hard and coming deep inside you, you still won't be allowed to come." Logan added another finger as Clay moaned. "You'll have to hold it back ... all night."

Logan groaned as he sank into his lover. He reached down and grasped the back of Clay's thighs, pushing his legs up until his knees touched his chest. Logan moved his hips slowly. "Are you going to be kissing anyone besides me?" Clay shook his head, but when Logan slammed his cock into him hard, he gasped and answered appropriately.

"No, Sir."

Logan moved even faster, leaning down on Clay so that his legs bent even further back. "And will you be running away from me again?"

Clay shook his head quickly this time, panting and writhing beneath him. "No, Sir. I won't. I promise."

Logan released one of Clay's legs, but ordered him to keep it up. He took Clay's cock into his hand, pumping fast. "And will you be dragging your feet to follow my orders the next time you pout at getting punished?"

Clay bit his lips but desperate moans still spilled from between them. Logan moved both his hand and his hips even faster as he waited for Clay's response. Finally, those pale blue eyes opened and focused right on him.

"Actually, I probably will," he forced out.

Logan had to laugh. "Well, you get points for honesty," he said before kissing him fiercely. He thrust his tongue between Clay's lips, dominating his mouth just as he dominated his body. He ate up all of Clay's whimpers and moans as he pushed his sub hard. Pushed him right to the brink of release.

Logan broke their kiss so he could watch his beautiful sub struggle to hold back his orgasm. Clay was flushed and sweating as he strained against his bonds, but he was doing like Logan asked, like he'd *ordered*, accepting his punishment and fighting not to come. Knowing that Clay was doing it for him, that Clay willingly allowed him to control his mind and body, had his cock hard with love and power. He slammed into Clay with brutal strength and speed, doing his damndest to strike that sensitive bundle of nerves inside him with every thrust. At the same time, he jacked Clay's slick shaft even faster until he was shouting and cursing, begging to be allowed to come. Logan's back tightened and his balls drew up as Clay's ass clenched on his cock. "Don't you dare fucking come," he ordered from between gritted teeth. He thrust hard into Clay one last time, making his lover throw back his head and scream.

Logan's cock pulsed. He was coming in strong steady waves, releasing deep into his lover. He groaned into Clay's neck, savoring the pleasure coursing throughout his body until he finally collapsed on top of him. Logan sucked at his lover's neck as he enjoyed the last little aftershocks of his orgasm.

After a few minutes, he raised himself off Clay and let him drop his legs down. He could tell by the wild look of desperation on Clay's face that he managed to hold back. But Logan wasn't finished with him yet.

"Turn over."

Clay looked at him in disbelief but when Logan narrowed his eyes, he struggled to flip over onto his belly. "Up on your knees. And don't you fucking hesitate this time, Clay. I mean it."

Clay immediately got his knees underneath him, thrusting his ass up in the air. Logan rubbed his palm across that smooth ass before he slapped it hard. Clay jerked and gasped.

"I wasn't going to spank you tonight, but your little defiant hesitations gave me no choice." Logan spanked him again. "Do you understand, Clay?" He waited for Clay's affirmative response before he cracked his hand across his sub's ass again and again, spanking him until his cheeks were red and Clay's hips moved into his slaps. Logan smiled as Clay arched his back, pushing his ass up even higher, clearly taking pleasure in the punishment. Clay's wriggling and moans soon had him hard again. He stopped but he didn't give his lover a break. He pushed back inside him and wrapped his hand back around his cock.

Clay cried out as his cock jerked hard in his Dom's grasp. A thick drop of pre-cum slid down his shaft. Logan's punishment had him aroused to the point that he was shaking, gasping for breath, and aching for release. When Logan pushed back inside him, words he never thought he'd say burst from his lips. "If you're gonna fuck me again, please give me a cock ring." Logan started moving inside him and Clay begged desperately. "Please. I don't … I don't think I can hold back again. Please."

"You earned this punishment by yourself and you'll carry it out by yourself."

Clay groaned but he didn't ask again. He was surprised when Logan's hips stilled against him.

"Who do you belong to, Clay?"

He answered as he always did. "I'm yours, Sir. Only yours."

Logan's voice was deep and low as he spoke again. "Prove it. Put your pleasure out of your head and focus on mine. Make me come, baby."

Clay rested his head on his forearms for a moment, breathing hard. He didn't know if he could do like Logan asked, but he would try. Jesus, in that moment, he felt like he would do anything for his Dom. He began moving back and forth, fucking himself onto Logan's cock. But his movements were jerky and as Logan started squeezing his shaft again, he completely lost his rhythm. He hung his head, feeling defeated. He wanted to please Logan but his body was trembling with the orgasm he was still fighting to hold back and he couldn't concentrate on anything else. Logan's hand stroked up and down his back, calming him slightly.

"It's okay, baby. You can do it. Remember, you're pleasing your Dom. That's all you have to do."

Clay bit his lip and tried again. Logan kept rubbing his back and he fell into the rhythm of those strokes. He focused on Logan's breathing and as it started to come faster and heavier, he used that as his cue to speed up.

"That's it, baby. Just like that. Please me, Clay. I'm close to coming again."

Clay moaned and moved even faster. Logan was still stroking his cock, but his head was filled only with how he was making his Dom feel. He spread his legs wide and pushed back on Logan as fast as he could until Logan's fingers moved to clench his hips, helping him move.

"Fuck! I'm coming, baby! Gonna fill you up."

After that harshly voiced announcement, Clay began moving with him, driving deep until he felt the heat of his Dom's release spilling inside him. He pressed his face into the pillow to muffle his cry as his own orgasm suddenly shot back to the forefront of his mind. But Logan grabbed him by the hair and pulled his head up.

"I want to hear you. Scream for me, Clay."

That was one order he was happy to follow. If he couldn't come, he needed to have some sort of release. He screamed as Logan finished coming inside him then stayed there, gasping and shaking as he fought harder than ever before to keep from coming. A magnitude of emotions swirled through Clay as he kneeled there on the bed, Logan still inside him. He was frustrated, his body clamoring for release. He felt like he'd earned Logan's punishments of denial and the spanking. He regretted angering his Dom. He was glad that Logan had used his body the way he had tonight. And all of that confused and angered him. He'd never felt any of these emotions with a lover. There was so much going on inside him that he could barely contain it. A quiet noise escaped him. It wasn't a sob. Not quite. Regardless, Logan heard him. Logan pulled him up until Clay's back rested against Logan's chest. Strong arms went around Clay's torso, a big hand softly gripping his throat.

"Do you have something you want to say to me?"

Clay shook his head, not because he didn't have anything to say, but because he didn't know how to get everything he was feeling out of him. The frustration and anger and confusion and … *regret* rose higher and higher in his chest, nearly choking him. That sound came from him again, this time accompanied by the sting of tears. Clay closed his eyes and bit his lip, but a few tears still escaped him. He turned his head and pressed the side of his face to Logan's. "I'm sorry. Sorry that I disappointed you."

Clay wanted to be angry that his emotions were so out of control that he was crying in his lover's arms, but he couldn't. Not with Logan's thumb brushing the moisture from his face and Logan's voice in his ear, telling Clay that he was sorry too. Clay took a shuddering breath as Logan's arms hugged him close. The sexual frustration was still there, but at least he'd released everything else his Dom had brought out in him with his sexual punishment.

45

Once Logan was sure Clay had calmed, he pulled out of him and leaned forward to untie his sub. "Go get me a glass of water," he ordered. Clay nodded. His body was tight with unreleased tension, but he immediately followed the command.

Logan watched him as he left the room. His lover's back was damp with sweat and the backs of his thighs were wet from the cum he'd released into his ass. When he came back, Logan saw that his shaft stood up hard and straining, the head swollen and slick with pre-cum. Logan knew his sub was still on the verge of the orgasm that he wouldn't be receiving that night. To him, right then, with his hair a wild mess and his body sweaty and tight and hard, Clay had never looked more beautiful. That Logan was the one that caused him to look like that had him half-hard with possessive arousal.

When Clay reached the bed, Logan ordered him to kneel and again Clay immediately complied. Logan waited for a moment, not saying anything, until finally Clay realized what he wanted and extended the glass of water to him. This time,

Logan drank first and when he was finished, he didn't immediately give the water back to his lover. Instead, he brushed his fingers over Clay's flushed cheek and stroked his thumb over lips swollen from his kisses.

"I'm the only one who touches you, Clay."

Clay nodded, sucking his thumb into his mouth and rubbing his cheek against Logan's palm. "Yes, Sir. Only you."

Logan held the glass of water up for Clay to drink from. When his sub had finished it off, he set it on the nightstand. "Get up here." Clay crawled back into the bed and lay down, but he protested as Logan went to retie his bonds. "I said all night, baby," Logan said firmly. This time, he tied Clay's arms with enough slack to be able to move around and sleep comfortably.

When Logan was done tying him up, Clay rolled over to face him. He was still hard and aching for release. He wrapped his leg around Logan's hip, rubbing his cock against his stomach. "I need to come, Sir. Please." He kept thrusting his hips as he unashamedly begged, the friction of his cock rubbing against Logan's hard abs giving him some small relief. "Please, Sir. Please let me." He gasped as he felt another bead of pre-cum spill from his cock head. He looked at Logan, knowing his eyes were filled with pleading. "I swear I'm sorry. Please ... just let me come."

Clay saw a muscle tic in Logan's jaw, his hazel eyes heating with arousal. Logan's hand slipped down to his ass, pulling him up tight against him and trapping his cock between their bodies. Clay gasped again as Logan squeezed his ass hard and he thought his Dom was going to give him what he wanted. But Logan only kissed him softly on the lips and said no. He closed his eyes, wanting to scream and cry with frustration. His orgasm was there, just under his skin and it had his cock throbbing so hard it was all he could think about. Logan told him to turn over. Accepting Logan wasn't going to give in, he did, scooting up against his lover until his back was pressed to Logan's chest and he felt his semi-hard cock against his ass. He tried to put his orgasm out of his head, but cried out as Logan's fist wrapped around his shaft.

"I won't be able to sleep like this," he said in a shaky voice. Logan pressed a kiss to the back of his neck before whispering in his ear.

"Quiet. You'll be fine. Go to sleep, baby."

Logan stroked him lightly a few times and Clay bit his lip to stop a moan from escaping. Eventually, Logan's hand stilled and he just held him with a gentle grip. Somehow that comforted him and although he was still craving release, Logan's soft kisses on his neck and shoulders lulled him to sleep.

Clay's breathing deepened as he fell asleep but Logan was still wide awake. He thought about what he'd done that afternoon, telling Alison to cut Clay from the calendar. Was that the right thing to do? Then he thought about Alison wrapping herself around his lover twice now. He could see that she was a beautiful woman and admitted she was nice and intelligent. If she wasn't flirting with Clay, he would probably like her. But they had argued twice in over a week's time period. What if Clay started thinking he no longer wanted to be in a relationship with him? What if he decided he no longer wanted to be a submissive and would rather be with a woman?

That was a worry that plagued Logan often. He knew Clay's submission was deep and real. But he was so strong and submission was new to him. Logan knew Clay could, at any time, decide he no longer wanted to submit and just walk away. Alison's flirtations could lead to that happening. A tense knot of fear settled in the pit of his stomach as he imagined losing Clay. He tightened his arms around his lover, but he couldn't even smile when he snuggled back closer against him like he always did. He would do whatever he had to do to keep Clay as his own.

With that thought in mind, he couldn't help but think he'd done the right thing by telling Alison to remove Clay and to stay away from him. He relaxed thinking that he wouldn't have to worry any further about her making advances towards Clay. Yeah, he'd done the right thing. Logan closed his eyes and slept.

46

When Clay woke up, the first thing he noticed was that he was hard. Again. Or fuck, for all he knew, his erection from the night before had never really gone down. Logan was stroking him softly and when he shifted, he realized he was no longer bound to the headboard. Logan's voice sounded in his hear, low and gravelly with sleep.

"Good morning, baby."

Clay stretched. "Good morning."

Logan licked a slow path up his neck to his ear. "The night is over, Clay. Do you know what that means?"

Clay just moaned softly. He was hoping it meant his punishment was over but he was too distracted by Logan's hands on him to say.

"It means you don't have to hold back anymore, baby. You get to come. Would you like that?"

Clay pushed his hips back against Logan. "Yes, Sir. I would. I really, really would."

"I thought you might," Logan said with a husky laugh. He moved his hand faster and tighter on his shaft.

"That feels so good," Clay whispered.

"That's all I've ever wanted to do, baby. Make you feel good."

Clay reached back and tried to touch Logan as well, but he blocked him.

"No. This is just for you. Just want to make you happy right now," he said as he stroked him even faster.

Clay's hips were rolling, pushing his shaft through his Dom's fist and then pressing his ass back against Logan's hard cock. "I'd be happier if you were inside me, Sir." Logan groaned, making him shiver as the sound vibrated against the back of his neck.

"Don't say that, baby. I can't hold back if you tell me that."

"It's true," he gasped as Logan thrust his hips against him.

Logan groaned again and bit Clay on his shoulder. "Hand me the lube so I can fuck you and fill you up with my cum again. Will that make you happy, little sub?"

Clay was reaching for the small bottle of lube on the nightstand even before he managed to answer Logan. He passed it behind him quickly, eager to have his lover inside him and give him the release he'd been denied the night before.

Logan squeezed some of the slippery liquid into his palm then gripped himself to slick the lube over his entire shaft. He was definitely ready to be inside his lover again, but first he wanted to make sure Clay was prepared. He pushed one finger slowly inside Clay's ass.

"I need more, Sir. I need you."

Logan clenched his jaw tight as he kept his finger inside his lover. This time, he was determined not to give into Clay's begging so he could make sure he didn't hurt him. "Not yet, let me get you ready."

"I'm ready. Just, fuck me. *Please.*"

Logan strained to hold himself back from just shoving himself inside of his lover. "No. We're going to wait."

But Clay wasn't able to wait. He was so aroused from having to hold back his orgasm all night and with Logan's hand pumping his cock and his thick finger inside him, it was too much for him to take. With a choked cry, his hips shot forward and he was coming all over his Dom's hand … and without his permission. His release was so strong, he was aware of nothing but the throbbing pleasure coursing through him. He didn't realize he was screaming Logan's name. He didn't realize he was digging his fingernails into Logan's thigh so hard that he drew blood. All he knew was that his entire body was bursting with bliss and he just let it swell through himself, gasping and shaking until he was spent. When he finally came down, he realized what he'd done.

"Oh, fuck. I'm sorry! I didn't mean – I couldn't stop it—" He broke off his practically incoherent apology with another gasp as Logan suddenly pushed his cock inside him, filling him all the way up.

"It's okay, Clay," he said as he grasped his hip, holding him still for his slow, steady thrusts. "It's okay," Logan repeated as

Clay kept apologizing. Logan closed his teeth lightly on his earlobe. "Just don't do it again." Then he bit down hard.

Arousal streaked from where Logan bit him straight down to his cock, hardening him once more. Logan quickened his pace. Faster than he'd thought possible, he was back on the edge of orgasm and he was moaning, matching the movement of his hips to his Dom's. Thankfully, Logan was breathing hard in his ear, telling him to come again. And with Logan furiously stroking his cock as he pushed hard into that sensitive bundle of nerves deep inside him, he did. He clenched tight around his lover, drawing a harsh groan from him as he pulsed and came, filling him up with the heat of his release.

Clay blew out a deep breath. "Thank you."

Logan pulled his head around for a kiss. "You're welcome."

****

Later on that afternoon they were in the SWAT gym working out. Clay was doing lat pull downs when Tiffany came up to him.

"Wow, you can sit. I'm shocked."

Clay lowered the weights back to the stack and looked up. "Very funny."

Tiffany grinned. "I guess Sarge took it easy on you."

Clay picked up the weights again. "Fuck off, Tiff." He wouldn't classify the mega-super-giant case of blue balls Logan had made him go to sleep with as *taking it easy*.

But Tiffany didn't go anywhere. She stayed put, her grin widening. "Well, well, well. Guess he didn't take it easy on you after all. Hate to say I told you so, but I'm gonna."

Clay glared. "I hate to snitch to Carlos that sometimes you want a break from him, but I'm gonna."

The laughter faded from her face. "Alright, I'm sorry. I'll lay off." She backed away. "And people say I'm vindictive," she said with a sneer.

Clay laughed as she walked off. Finally, he managed to get the last word on her crazy ass. He was working on his last set when Q showed up.

"Hey, man."

"Hey."

Q cleared his throat, looking uncomfortable. "So Sarge lost his shit over that calendar shoot last night, huh?"

Clay snorted. "Just a little bit." He noticed Q didn't look at him as he asked his next question.

"Are you guys okay now?"

"Yeah."

Q looked at him, his brow creased with confusion. "And you just forgave him?"

Clay stopped. "I did. Why? What's up, man?"

"I heard what he said, about you being his property and you needing permission before you let someone else touch you."

Clay started lifting again. "I know you did. I've been waiting on you to say something. Surprised you made it this long."

Q looked at him strangely. "I'm surprised *you* didn't bring it up. I'm worried about you, man. You've changed since you got with Sarge. You don't joke around as much. You look to him first whenever someone asks if you want to hang out." Q's voice rose. He was clearly upset. "And you just forgave him for flipping the fuck out over a silly photo shoot? That's not you."

Clay was taken aback. He hadn't expected this reaction from his friend. He expected him to be surprised at what their sergeant had been hiding all these years and they'd both get a laugh out of it.

"Q, man. What's up? Why are you so worked up over this?"

"I just don't think you being in a relationship with someone who calls you his property is a good idea. You can't be equals if he's your Dom and you're just his submissive."

Now Clay was mad. "What do you mean *just his submissive*? It's not like that. He might be in control when we're in bed together, but he doesn't control me in any other way."

"That's not what it looked like to me. Besides, just wait. I bet shit like him getting jealous and pissed off will keep happening. And before you know it, he'll be telling you what you can and can't do all the time."

Clay didn't say anything to that. He couldn't help thinking that Logan had only promised he wouldn't flip out again, not that he wouldn't be jealous anymore.

"Think of all this now, Clay. Before you're in too deep and it ruins your career. If he wants to own you and you reject him, how will he take that? How will it affect your place on this team?"

Quan's words seemed to echo in his head as he stood there, the weights forgotten in his hands.

47

Clay sat in the arm chair in Logan's living room, trying to watch TV. Logan was on the couch across the room going through paperwork. He brought it home instead of doing it at the station so they could spend time together.

But Clay wasn't content to watch TV while Logan finished up. He was restless. He didn't want to think his conversation with Q was making him doubt his relationship. But ... a nagging feeling of disquiet was in his head. What *would* happen if things didn't work out between them? SWAT had a high turnover rate. Their team had been together longer than most, largely due to Logan. He checked on them, made sure they weren't getting burnt out. He was calm and he kept them calm. What would happen if they ended things? Would Logan show him that same treatment or would he be treated differently? Would Logan want him on the team? Would he even want to stay on the team?

He didn't have answers for any of those questions. And he didn't think he would get any by talking to Logan about it either. Even if Logan did think he'd be an asshole to him if they were to break up, he'd never admit it. There was no point in discussing it. So he was just left with that feeling of nagging disquiet.

He bit into a Twizzler from the pack Logan brought him, watching Logan instead of the TV. He looked so studious and intent as he went through his work. He didn't know what made him do it. Maybe because he was restless. Maybe because he was bored. Maybe because he wanted attention. He didn't know, but he did it anyway. He tossed the piece of candy at Logan. It landed in his lap. Logan looked up at him but he didn't say anything. After a moment, Logan looked back down at his work. Clay bit through his Twizzler quickly this time. When there was only one bite left, he again threw it at Logan. This time, it landed on the paper he was reading. Logan shook the candy off and glanced over at him in clear exasperation.

"What are you doing?"

Clay shrugged.

"Stop so I can get this finished."

Clay took a bite of the last rope of candy. "Sorry." Logan looked at him a little bit longer like he was waiting to see what he would do. He just sat there, slowly chewing on the waxy red candy and waited. As soon as Logan looked back down, he threw the last piece at him, hitting him right on the forehead. Logan's head snapped up, tossing the paper in his hand to the table in front of him. Clay bit his bottom lip. "Oops."

Logan grinned ruefully and shook his head. "You've got my attention. Now come here."

Clay stood and made his way over to him. Logan lightly grasped his hips, his thumbs sliding under his t-shirt to brush over his skin.

"What's wrong?"

Clay shrugged. "Don't know. Just feeling restless."

Logan tugged him down until Clay was kneeling in front of him. "You'd think I got all of that energy out of you earlier."

Clay laughed and rolled his eyes. "Very funny."

"You want to go swim for awhile? That ought to tire you out."

Clay perked up at the thought of getting into the water. "That'd be awesome. Especially since you made me eat junk food today. I need to work it off."

"I don't remember force-feeding you that bacon cheeseburger. And what about the package of Twizzlers you just scarfed down?"

Clay grinned. "Twizzlers are a fat-free candy." He jumped up to his feet. "C'mon let's go."

Logan grabbed his hand to keep him from rushing off. "Hold up. You don't even have any trunks."

"I can wear some of yours. Oh wait, anything that fits your tree trunk thighs will probably fall right off of me."

Logan gave him a roguish grin and ran his hand over his hip. "I'd be okay with that. But we can swing by the store and get you something to wear. That'd be faster than going back to your place. Actually, why don't you stay the next few days with me? I'm sure I've got some stuff here that you can lounge around in."

Clay leaned down and gave Logan a quick kiss. "Okay."

Logan studied him for a moment after he stood back up. "Are you sure there's nothing wrong?"

Clay pushed thoughts of Q and the doubts he'd raised even further back. "No, I'm fine." But even as he said the words, he knew that for the first time, he'd lied to his Dom.

****

Logan and Clay arrived at the gated pool. It was a nice sized free-form pool, well maintained with comfortable lounge chairs lined alongside and a small hot tub at the far end. There were a few people already in the water, but not many. His subdivision had another pool with slides and fountains. The kids and teenagers tended to frequent that one.

Logan watched Clay dip his toe in the pool. The calendar might say summer was coming to a close, but it was still hot in Houston. So he knew the water would still be warm from the day's heat. He ran his eyes over his lover, a smile tugging at his lips at the swim trunks he'd bought him. The selection had been picked over so they hadn't been able to find any of the long board shorts Clay favored. The only thing they'd found that fit him was a pair of very short trunks in a crazy pattern of bright orange palm trees and suns on a loud blue background. He'd griped then, but clearly he didn't care what he looked like now.

Clay threw a grin at him over his shoulder and with his body curved in a sleek arch, dived into the pool. He swam under water for almost half the length of the pool before he broke the surface and started a freestyle stroke. When he reached the end he flipped and pushed off the wall, swimming back to his side. Clay treaded water, staring up at him.

"You have to get in. I know you know how to swim. They make all you Jarheads learn so you can sneak up on people in the water, right?"

Logan slipped into the big pool. "I knew how to swim before the Marines got their hands on me. But that doesn't mean I like doing it. Unlike you. You clearly love it."

"Yeah I was on the swim team in high school."

Logan was surprised. He didn't recall ever hearing that before. "So what happened?"

Clay's face closed off. "I swam up until my junior year. Then I quit. Wasn't into it anymore."

"Really? That's hard to imagine with the way you're always jumping in the nearest pool."

"Things changed. Now I just swim when I want to."

Logan swam forward and stroked Clay's back. "Hey. Did I set something off? I didn't mean to, but you can talk to me about it if you want."

Clay took a deep breath and smiled. But it wasn't the easy one he'd had when he first got to the pool.

"It's okay. My baggage. You want to race?"

Logan let it go for now. "Is this an excuse to showcase Navy skill over Marines?"

Clay grinned, his face relaxed this time. "Maybe. You chicken, Jarhead?"

Logan couldn't let that challenge go. "Not at all. Let's see what you got, Squid."

****

The next morning, they were back in Logan's living room. They'd gone for a run to have breakfast tacos at the taco truck a few miles from his house. Now they were lounging on the couch after a shower, watching horse racing on one of the sports channels. Clay had his head in Logan's lap, cheering on one of the thoroughbreds. When the chestnut horse Clay had picked lost, he threw a piece of Twizzler at the TV.

"Hey, watch it."

"Sorry. I was really pulling for Be My Neigh-bor."

"You don't know anything about that horse. Or horse racing for that matter. And I'm pretty sure that was a replay from earlier this year."

Clay laughed. "Yeah, but I really got into it for that minute."

Logan snorted and picked up the remote to bring the channel guide up on the screen. Through it, Clay could still see what was playing. A paint commercial came on, showing people who looked way too happy to be painting. The last shot was of a bright blue door closing. As the image of that door faded, Clay was reminded of the locked door upstairs. He turned over and looked at Logan.

"Logan?"

"Yeah, baby. What's up?" He wasn't really paying attention since he was still paging through the guide, trying to find something to watch.

"Why is that door upstairs locked?"

Logan tensed underneath him.

48

Clay felt Logan's leg tense underneath him. Now he was really curious. "What's in there, Logan? I know it's not your mummified mother sitting in a rocking chair. Is it the chopped up body parts of your old boyfriends?"

Logan huffed a laugh. "You're disgusting."

Clay sat up. "And you're avoiding. What's in there?"

Logan looked at him for a long moment. "I'll show you." He stood up and held his hand out. "Come with me."

Clay grabbed Logan's hand and let him pull him up from the couch. He followed him up the stairs and down the hallway, beyond curious by that point. When they came to the locked door, Logan stopped.

"I wasn't lying when I said I was having some work done in here. I built this for us." He unlocked the door with the key he picked up on their way upstairs but he didn't open it. Instead, he turned and kissed Clay deeply, his thumb stroking the skin under his collar.

When Logan ended the kiss, Clay looked at him in confusion. What would Logan have built for them?

"You'll have to undress before you can enter this room."

Clay grinned. "Why do I almost always have to be naked for one of your surprises?" he said as he pulled his t-shirt over his head.

Logan's face remained serious at Clay's teasing, his voice hard. "You'll always be naked for this room, Clay. And you'll always have to remember your place as my sub. Do you understand?"

Clay's lips parted in surprise. It was rare that Logan was so stern with him. But he didn't mind. He lowered his head and finished undressing. "Yes, Sir. I understand." When he was nude, Logan pushed the door open. His Dom hooked his finger under his collar and pulled him inside the room. He turned on the lights and Clay got his first look at Logan's secret room.

He should have known what it was going to be when Logan asked him to remove his clothes, but somehow he was still surprised. It was a bondage playroom. His first thought was that the room was beautiful. And that may have been a strange thought, but it was true. The walls were padded with a honey-toned leather and the floors were cream marble threaded with veins of dark chocolate. Large windows let in the late afternoon sunshine, but Clay could tell from the tinting that you wouldn't be able to see into the room from the outside. A large bed dominated one wall of the room. Clay noticed immediately that the frame was made up of wrought iron bars with plenty of spaces to chain him up. On another wall hung a framed picture of him and Logan, blown up to poster sized and printed in sepia tones. In it, they were in their

SWAT gear at some location. They were standing close together, their expressions serious as they worked out whatever the problem was. Beneath the picture was a tall, dark wood cabinet that he guessed held things like lube and restraints.

But there were several other things that definitely caught his eye. A wall hung with whips, floggers, and paddles. A padded spanking bench. A large St. Andrew's Cross. And right in the center of the room was a heavy and solid looking frame that had black leather cuffs dangling from the top with a pulley system that would raise or lower the restraints as Logan chose.

He turned to look at Logan who was standing there watching him. "You built this for us?"

Logan nodded slowly. "Yes. I told you I've never collared anyone before, so there was no need to have my own playroom. But when I finally managed to catch you, I knew I wanted us to have a place to indulge ourselves."

Clay raised his hand to touch Logan, but he hesitated. Logan said he needed to remember his place as a sub which meant he wasn't allowed to touch his Dom without permission. But Logan grasped his hand and pulled him into his body. "Why did you wait so long to show me this?"

"I wanted it to be completely finished first. And … sometimes I still worry that all of this will be too much for you."

Logan didn't say, "and you'll leave." But Clay knew that was the real end to that sentence. He was surprised at the show of vulnerability from Logan. The doubts that had sprung up from his talk with Q fled even further from his mind. Right then, he wanted nothing more than to comfort his Dom and let him know he wanted to be with him.

"Show me, Sir. Show me what you want to do to me."

The vulnerability dropped from Logan as though it had never been, replaced by the commanding Dom presence that Clay expected. Logan wrapped his hand around his throat and walked him backwards to the center of the room. As he walked, Clay finally noticed that the floor, which should have been cool from the A/C, was warm under his bare feet. He mentioned it.

Logan smiled at him. "Heated floors. I want you focused on what I'm doing to you, baby, not shivering from the cold."

Clay couldn't believe how much this man cared for him. They reached the frame and when Logan raised his arms over his head to put the restraints on Clay's wrists, he allowed it without the slightest hesitation. Clay saw a pleased smile curl Logan's lips as he stared up at the black leather cuffs. Logan worked the pulley on the side of the frame and Clay was stretched up until he was standing on the balls of his feet. His breath came a little faster. Logan had never restrained him that way before. It was a little unnerving, but he trusted him.

He was held there, completely immobile, as Logan walked over to the wall where the toys hung. Clay watched, his mouth dry with anticipation as Logan trailed his fingers over a crop and a whip before finally settling on a black suede flogger. But that wasn't all he picked up. As Logan came back to him, he also had a black silk blindfold in his hand. Clay's heart was racing as he realized he wouldn't be able to see what Logan was doing to him. Before his Dom tied the blindfold on, he looked Clay in the eyes.

"Do you remember your safe word?"

Clay nodded. He'd never needed to say it but he remembered.

"Good. Use it if anything becomes too much, baby."

Then he tied the cloth around Clay's eyes. Clay immediately felt vulnerable. He couldn't see and he didn't have the use of his hands. There was no escape. He was completely at the mercy of his Dom. But he wasn't scared. Instead, he was hard, possibly more turned on than he had ever been. He liked knowing he was under Logan's control for everything he would feel. He heard Logan moving and turned his head, trying to follow the sound of his footsteps to figure out where he was. When Logan stopped, he only knew that he was somewhere behind him.

He jumped when he felt the flogger touch the skin of his back. But it wasn't the lash that he'd been expecting. Logan trailed the tails of his toy over Clay's shoulders and down his back. The soft material tickled him, raising goose bumps on his skin. He heard Logan move again and the tails of the flogger moved with him. They brushed up his side, down his stomach, and over his shaft. Logan kept the flogger there for a moment, sweeping it back and forth until Clay was gasping and raising his hips to meet it. Logan's thumb brushed across his cockhead.

"Hmmm...already hard and dripping wet. I think I'd better put a cock ring on you. I don't want to have to worry about you coming without permission while I play."

Clay dropped his head back with a moan as he heard Logan's footsteps walk away, pause then return. He didn't realize Logan was right in front of him until Logan's lips were on his, kissing him fiercely as he slid a cock ring down his shaft. Clay gave a sharp cry into Logan's mouth, but he didn't complain. This time, when Logan moved away, he forgot to track his movements, Clay's mind was focused on the way his cock throbbed in its restraint. So when the lash fell across his back, he jumped in both pain and surprise. The next lash fell in a different spot on his back, slightly harder, making his skin sting. The flogger continued to fall, never in the same place twice, with Logan varying the strength of each blow. Clay's body was all tripped up, sometimes rocking forward on his toes to escape the lashes and sometimes arching back into them, moaning as the heat of pain on his back caused a different type of heat to spread throughout his body. When the flogger moved down to his ass, he cried out but pushed his hips back into each stroke.

Suddenly, the flogger stopped. Clay twisted in his restraints, straining to hear where Logan was. He got his answer when he felt Logan's tongue stroking across his ass. His skin was overly sensitive from the flogger so the laps of Logan's tongue were almost painful. But he didn't care. And when Logan bit him, he shouted, but it was to ask for more. Logan sucked and licked and bit his way across both of Clay's cheeks until he was trembling and begging for Logan to stop, to bite him harder, to fuck him now. He jerked forward as Logan's palm slapped hard across his ass.

"Stop begging. You don't get to decide anything I do to you."

Clay apologized swiftly, but then Logan's tongue slid between his cheeks, and he had to bite his lip to stop from begging again. His Dom's tongue was slick and hot as he teased against Clay's entrance. When he felt it pushing inside him, he jerked hard on his restraints, wanting more. Logan tongue fucked him for long moments, his hand coming up and squeezing his sac roughly. Clay couldn't hold back any longer. "Oh god, please, please, Sir. Fuck me!" He should have kept his mouth shut. Because Logan squeezed his balls hard and swung the flogger around so it struck his cock. Clay screamed at that delicious pain.

"You disobeyed me."

Clay shook his head. "I'm sorry. I didn't mean to. I wasn't—" The flogger fell on his cock again and he heard Logan get to his feet.

"Be quiet. I guess I'll have to show you what happens to bad subs when they disobey their Doms."

Clay's fingers were twitching with anticipation, waiting for the flogger to strike him. But nothing happened. Instead, he heard the slow rasp of a zipper and the slide of cloth against skin as Logan undressed. He hung there, balancing on the balls of his feet, waiting for Logan to carry out his punishment. Clay didn't hear the sounds of Logan undressing anymore. It was quiet, so quiet that it felt as though his ears were filled with noiseless sound. He turned his head, wondering if Logan had left the room. And that's when the flogger struck him across the belly. He gasped in pain but he arched towards the blow. That did him no good, because Logan moved on. The flogger hit his thighs, his ass, his cock. The pattern of where the tails landed on his body was unpredictable as was the interval in between each stroke. Finally, Clay stopped trying to determine any pattern. He just let his Dom carry out his punishment as he would.

As the flogger met his skin, sometimes in soft brushes and sometimes in stinging slaps, Clay was lost in his own dark world. Nothing existed to him but the sounds of Logan's breathing and the flogger as it fell sharply against his flesh again and again and again. But there was no longer any pain. Instead, his body relaxed and welcomed each lash and the pleasure it brought him. His head dropped back on his shoulders with a sigh.

Clay didn't understand what was happening. He just knew that he felt so good and so peaceful and he never wanted Logan to stop what he was doing to him or to let him down from his cuffs. He heard Logan calling his name but it sounded as though his Dom was very far away. He had to struggle to lift his head up and answer him. "Yes, Sir?"

Logan's hand lightly grasped his shaft before he spoke. "You know that you are mine, don't you, Clay?"

He nodded, just barely remembering to whisper, "Yes, Sir" so he didn't anger his Dom.

"And you admit that I own you?" he asked, slowly pumping his fist on Clay's cock.

Clay shivered as he answered. "Yes, Sir. You own me. All of me."

Logan squeezed his shaft. "So why don't you call me Master?"

Clay felt a small flicker of … something in his head at that word. But he was so deep into the sensations he was floating in that he couldn't think of any reason why he shouldn't do as Logan said. "I'm sorry, Sir – Master. I didn't know that you wanted me to."

"I do. Very much. I want to hear that from your lips while I fuck you, little sub."

Clay nodded slowly. "Yes, Sir … Yes, Master. Whatever you want." Clay gasped as he felt Logan's naked cock brush against his. "I'll do whatever you want."

"Such a good boy," Logan told him before kissing him slow and deep. Clay moaned as Logan sucked on his tongue. Logan ended the kiss and pulled off his blindfold. Clay blinked as the light hit his eyes. Logan was the first – the only thing he saw.

"I want to see those pretty blue eyes while I'm deep inside you."

Clay's head was fuzzy as he responded. "Thank you. You're pretty too."

Logan laughed softly and grasped Clay's chin. He looked at his sub, saw the faraway look in his eyes and heard the slower cadence to his speech. He realized Clay was flying, that he'd drifted into subspace. Logan felt a rush of pleasure at the knowledge that his sub trusted him enough to let go and submit to what he did to him so completely. That *his* strikes against Clay's smooth skin had sent him into a place of euphoria.

He picked Clay up by his thighs. It would have been easier for him to take him from behind, but now more than ever he wanted to see his lover's face. He wrapped Clay's legs around his waist, telling him to hold on. Logan fit his cock against Clay's entrance and pushed inside slowly. Clay moaned softly, his breaths coming in soft little pants.

"Please … Master. I need you inside me."

Logan kept his eyes locked on his sub's, making sure he was okay as he drifted, but also because he just wanted to watch those beautiful eyes that he loved so much. He pushed up hard until he was deep inside his lover. "Like this, baby? Is this what you want?" Clay nodded and his eyes started to drift closed. "No. Look at me, Clay." He started to move. "Don't take your eyes off me." Clay's eyes blinked open. They were hazy and dazed. But they stayed on his.

Logan's fingers clenched tight onto Clay's thighs as he fucked into his sub slow and steady. Each time he stroked into him, he went deeper and deeper until finally Clay gasped as Logan tapped his spot. Logan pulled Clay tighter against him as he kept thrusting at that angle. He increased the strength and the speed of his thrusts, watching as that beautiful flush rose on Clay's face and sweat dampened his chest. Logan could have stayed like that forever, watching his sub, feeling the sweet friction and luscious heat of Clay's ass on his cock as he pushed deep inside him. But he felt Clay's channel start to grip him tighter and knew that his sub was close to orgasm. And he wanted to let his sub have his release … as long as he did one thing.

"I can feel you trying to come, baby." He took his hand from Clay's thigh to lightly brush his fingers up and down his cock. "Do you want me to take this cock ring off you and let you come?"

Clay moaned. "Yes, Sir. *Please…*"

Logan let his fingers tease at the cock ring as he continued to pump his hips against his lover's. "I will. But you know what you have to do."

Clay breathed in and out slowly before he answered him. "May I come, please, Master?"

Logan slipped off the cock ring and increased his speed even more. "Say it again." Clay obeyed him and Logan smiled fiercely. He started moving his fist on Clay's hard cock, working him closer to the edge. "Again, baby. Let me hear who owns you." Clay's stomach muscles were clenched tight as he moved his hips at his pace.

"Master, please. I need to come, please let me."

Logan pumped his fist on Clay fast, squeezing the head on each upstroke. "Come for me, sweet sub. I want to feel this ass squeezing me tight and your hot cum all over my belly." Clay moaned softly and then he was coming just like Logan wanted, shooting even higher as he did. Logan held his own orgasm back just so he could see his beautiful sub reach his pleasure. It wasn't until Clay sighed and went limp that he groaned and pulsed into his lover, his body humming with the intensity of his release.

Logan released Clay from his cuffs, catching him as he fell against him. He wrapped his arms around his sub tight, kissing him again and again as he walked him backwards to the bed. After pulling back the covers, Logan helped Clay lie down then stretched out beside him. He pulled the covers up over his sub and wrapped an arm and a leg around him. Clay's face was tucked into his neck and he felt his slow, shallow breaths against his skin. Logan rubbed his back in slow circles. "Come back to me, baby. Come back down." He kept talking softly to Clay, telling him how much he loved him and how beautiful he was until finally Clay shuddered and lifted his head. Logan looked at him and saw that his eyes were clear and focused.

Clay licked his lips. "What…what happened? What was that?"

Logan brushed a soft kiss across Clay lips. "You went into subspace, baby. It's what happens to a sub when they get a rush of endorphins from what they are experiencing and completely let themselves go."

Clay's brow creased. "I didn't think that was real."

"It is. And to see you like that … flying so high…" Logan kissed Clay again. "It was a beautiful gift. Thank you."

Clay was exhausted. He had no energy to do anything other than accept Logan's kiss, his Dom's lips soft and gentle against his.

****

Later that night, Clay lay in the bed, back in Logan's master suite. Logan was up, getting him a glass of water. All night long, Logan had done everything he could think of to make sure Clay was comfortable. Clay could tell that Logan was happy and he was happy too. But … he was also a little bothered by what happened in the playroom. Going into subspace had been unexpected for him. Like he told Logan, he'd read about it, but he didn't think it was real or at least not that intense. He hadn't been prepared for that floaty spacey sensation. He hadn't been high or drunk for a long time, but he remembered the feeling. What he'd just experienced with Logan was different, but still gave him the sense of being out of control. He thought of how he used to crave that feeling and what his life was like before he cleaned himself by joining the Navy. Clay admitted to himself that it *had* felt good to let go like that and to call Logan 'Master' for the first time. He rolled over and stared at the ceiling. But he learned a long time ago that just because something felt good didn't mean he should do it.

49

The next day at work, Clay slowly laced up his boots. They had a warrant to serve that evening but he wasn't filled with the normal anticipation he had before they hit the street. Instead, he was tired. Not necessarily physically, but mentally he felt like he wanted to curl up in his bed and sleep for a day. He was just … tired. And now that he was off by himself and not under the spell of whatever it was he felt when he was with Logan, the doubts Q had raised came rushing back.

Those doubts filled his head up with questions, especially since he experienced going into subspace. That feeling unnerved him. It was too close to what he experienced back in his days of getting high. He also couldn't help but worry that he would lose too much of himself with Logan in control of him in private and as his superior at work. He couldn't help but think that maybe he was in over his head with this Dom/sub relationship with Logan. All of those thought just made him … tired.

Clay shook himself. He needed to get that shit out of his head. Worrying about it wasn't going to solve anything and he needed his head clear for work. The best thing he could do was talk about it with Logan after work. He considered going to get a root beer or a cup of coffee for a quick shot of caffeine when Q walked into the locker room. He saw Clay sitting there and came over.

"Hey, Clay. Listen, man, I'm sorry if I overstepped my bounds talking about your relationship. I just noticed things were different with you and I was worried. That's all."

Clay looked up at his friend. He couldn't be mad at Q for being concerned about him. "Don't sweat it. I appreciate you looking out." He held his hand out to shake and Q grinned.

"What? No fist bump?"

Clay laughed and bumped Q's fist, glad things were comfortable between them once more. It would have been rough to work so closely with him if they had friction between them, but it would have bothered him most because they were friends. The door opened again and Logan walked in. Clay saw immediately that he was still in that good, almost hyper mood he'd been in ever since their time in the playroom the previous night. He almost seemed to vibrate as he noticed Clay and came over. He smiled at Clay and gave Quan only the briefest hello before his attention shot right back to him. That was unlike him. Normally, he made sure to check on everyone, especially if they were going on a call out.

"I want to see you in my office, Clay."

Clay looked up at Logan and without even thinking replied, "Yes, Sir."

He could have put it off on just being respectful to his superior. But going by the shocked look on Q's face, and the possessive one on Logan's, it hadn't come out that way. He didn't know what to think. If he needed proof the boundaries were blurred, he'd just provided it for himself. It was clear his automatic response made Logan happy. He, on the other hand, was almost ashamed of himself. Was he so deep into this relationship that he couldn't even remember to call Logan by his name in public? The confusion and doubts in his head came rushing back, pounding against his brain in a constant swirl of confusion. Still, when Logan stepped back and left the room, Clay followed.

****

In Logan's office, Logan sat in the chair behind his desk and pulled Clay in between his legs.

"Why did you want to see me?" Clay questioned him.

Logan smiled. "I just wanted a few minutes alone with you before we go out tonight." He pulled his t-shirt from the waist of his pants, running his hands underneath and lightly gripping his waist. "Can't help how much I want to be close to you."

Clay nodded. Even though he was confused about everything, he couldn't deny that he wanted to be near Logan.

Logan smoothed his hands up his sub's back. "Can't wait to get back from this warrant tonight, knowing once we're alone, I'll have you naked and writhing beneath me." He laughed. "I don't know if I'll be able to stand it. Whoever this asshole is, he better not resist or I'll have to put him down hard so I can hurry up and get back to what's important." He pushed Clay's shirt up further and pulled him even closer. He rubbed his face against his belly, inhaling the sweet scent that was uniquely Clay.

He looked up at his lover, thinking how this time last year he'd been so lonely. And how he spent so much time thinking of how to or if he even should approach Clay. Now that Clay was his, he was so happy. He could hardly believe how lucky he was. "I love you, baby," he said before placing kisses along the soft skin just above his waistband.

Clay's hand brushed lightly over his head. "I love you, too."

Logan smiled and slowly unbuttoned Clay's uniform pants. Clay's lips parted as he pulled the zipper down, but he didn't try to stop him. Logan slipped his hand into Clay's pants, smoothing his palm over the curve of his ass. "Be careful out there." Logan put a hand to his mouth to get a finger wet before slowly pushing it inside of Clay. "I want to get you home and hold you close tonight."

Clay gave a tight nod as Logan kept working his finger deep inside him. "Yes, Sir. I will." He thrust his hips back hard against his hand. "Sir… we're alone…" Logan's finger rubbed over his prostate and he shivered. "So can we … will you…?" Clay cut off with a sharp gasp as Logan pressed hard against that sensitive area. A surge of pleasure went through him, hardening his shaft even further. He had to take a deep breath before he could talk again. "I need you inside me."

Logan nipped at Clay's cock sharply. "Mmm… I don't think so. Gotta make sure my point man is sharp out there tonight. Besides, can't have everyone seeing you all soft and sweet after your orgasm. That's for my eyes only."

Clay made a sound somewhere between a moan and a laugh as Logan slowly pulled his finger out of him. "You are evil," Clay said.

Logan smiled. "I thought I was corny."

Clay laughed for real this time. "That too."

"But you love me."

Clay looked at Logan for a long moment. His lover's hazel eyes were bright and sparkling, his normally stern face relaxed and happy as he smiled. "Yeah. I do."

Logan brushed his thumb over Clay's stomach. "I want you wearing my mark tonight. If I had my way, everybody would know I owned you." He sucked the smooth skin just above his waistband into his mouth. He stroked his tongue over the spot, closing his eyes and breathing in Clay's scent as he suckled. Clay's fingers clenched on his shoulders and Logan sucked even harder, rubbing his hands up and down Clay's smoothly muscled back. When he finally lifted his mouth and looked down, he saw a deep bruise rapidly rising on that lightly tanned skin. Logan pressed a kiss to the spot. "You are completely mine, Clay." He was tugging his pants back into place when Clay spoke.

"Why did you want me?"

Logan smiled as he zipped up his pants. "You know why. Because I admire the way you've turned your life around. Because you're so strong in your beliefs. Because even though you can be the biggest prankster, you're serious and get the job done when it's go time. Because your sarcastic attitude cracks me up. And because you're fucking gorgeous." He was surprised to see a frown on his sub's face.

"But all those things were true about me since I joined this team. Why did you wait until you did to approach me?"

Logan shrugged. "It just wasn't the right time." He knew Clay's track record, knew he'd been in and out of relationships, none of them sticking for long. And, of course, he had to take his own lifestyle into consideration. But he didn't say that and Clay looked like he wasn't satisfied with his answer. He asked him another question.

"If things don't work out between us, would we still be able to work together? Would I stay on this team?"

A frown creased Logan's forehead as he answered. "You don't need to worry about that. Where is this coming from?" Clay started to respond but Logan's office phone rang. Logan picked it up, just barely refraining from rudely barking into the phone at the interruption. It was someone from Narcotics, letting him know their team leader wanted to go over a few more things before the raid. Logan sighed and hung up.

"Duty calls." He stood and gave Clay a slow kiss. "We'd better get out there." Logan left the office with Clay, putting their conversation on hold. He'd have to find out what was on Clay's mind later.

50

Clay slowly walked into Logan's office after they returned to the station. He didn't even know why he was following him instead of going to his desk or to the locker room. Logan had beckoned and he followed. That bothered him. But he was too tired to question it. Logan was so full of energy, probably even more so with the adrenaline of the raid still pumping through him. But Clay just felt ... tired. Tired and conflicted. Doubts swirled through his head so fast he couldn't focus on any one of them to think about it or try to voice it. He allowed Logan to pull him into his arms and kiss him. His body responded, kissing him back, but his mind was elsewhere. He couldn't get those doubts out of his head.

Why did Logan feel the need to control him? Why did he not only respond to that taking of control, but get off on it? Was he becoming nothing more than a slave to Logan? How long before Logan wanted to control him beyond the bedroom? Was a BDSM relationship healthy and normal for him to be in? How could he be his own man if he was calling another man 'Master'? Was he so weak that he was changing to suit Logan's wants? Was he so weak that he so easily gave up every part of his control to Logan?

He remembered what it'd felt like when he "flew" as Logan called it. He'd felt loose and relaxed, like he had absolutely no control over anything. Like he didn't *care* about anything but how good he felt. Just like when he'd been high or drunk. And the horrible part was that he wanted to feel that again. Could see himself becoming addicted to and drowning in the things Logan did to him. Just like if he were an addict. Again. Logan's hand closed around his throat at that moment and he snapped.

"Don't touch me like that!" he shouted, knocking Logan's hand away from him.

Logan's face was shocked but that was quickly replaced by his sternest Dom expression. "What did you just say to me?"

Clay's breath came hard and fast. "I said don't touch me like that! You can't make me feel like that again."

Logan looked shocked again. "Clay, baby, what's wrong? Talk to me." Logan reached for him but Clay stepped back.

"I can't do this. It's too much. This isn't me, goddamnit!"

Panic crawled through Logan. He didn't know what had set Clay off. "Baby, calm down. Whatever is wrong, we can talk about it and fix it. I promise." He held his hand out. "Just come sit down and let me take care of you." But Clay was shaking his head furiously.

"No. You can't fix this and I don't *need* you to take care of me. I just need out of this."

Logan froze. His heart stopped beating for a tense moment before racing and slamming so hard it felt like it would bruise his ribs. He didn't want to believe what Clay was saying. His lips barely moved as he spoke. "Clay…" He had to force his next words past his throat even though it was tight with fear. "Are you asking me to release you?" Logan didn't want to say those words, but he had to. He couldn't keep Clay if he didn't want to be kept.

Clay looked at Logan and saw the devastated look on his face. *What was he doing?* He needed to calm down like Logan said. But he couldn't. His heart was pumping furiously and crazy sick adrenaline rushed through his system, blurring his vision, forcing his lungs to work double time to keep up with his heaving breaths. He felt ill and he knew he was losing it but he'd rather lose it now than lose himself completely later. He had to look away from Logan's sad eyes, all of the happy sparkle from earlier completely wiped out. He slowly turned his back to Logan and bowed his head.

Clay didn't hear any movement behind him for the longest time. Then he felt Logan's fingers brush his skin as he removed the dog tags from around his neck. As soon as the chain was clear of his body, he choked on a breath and tears stung his eyes. He immediately felt cut off from Logan – the feeling sharper and insanely more painful than when Logan normally took his collar off. But he didn't turn around and ask for it back. Clay felt lightheaded as he walked across the room just as slowly as he had entered it. He stood with his hand on the door knob for a long time, unable to bring himself to open it. Logan called his name softly.

"Clay, I love you. Don't do this to us."

Clay didn't reply. He didn't know what he would say if he opened his mouth. More shouting? Apologizing? Begging for his collar back? So he just stood there, staring at the wood in front of him, refusing to turn around. Finally, he worked up the energy to open the door and leave. But once he was on the other side, he collapsed back against it, his hand at his throat, gasping for breath.

51

Logan stood frozen in the middle of his office. He didn't understand what had just happened. Clay was no longer his. Within the space of a few hours, he'd gone from telling his sub he loved him to removing his collar. Logan shook his head, unable to comprehend. But he forced himself to put his own feelings aside. Clay looked just as shocked as Logan felt. And whether he wanted him to or not, Logan had to make sure he was alright.

He forced himself to move, to leave his office and head out to the pen. Thankfully, Tiffany was still at her desk.

Tiffany looked up as Logan approached. She started to smile but it turned to a worried frown when she saw his face. "Sergeant, what's wrong? Is everyone okay?"

"Yes. Everyone is fine. But I need you to do me a favor."

She stood up. "Of course. What do you need?"

Logan paused for a second. When he spoke, his voice was dead, lacking its usual commanding snap. "Clay is upset. I need you to make sure he gets home okay."

Tiffany was confused. Why didn't Logan check on him himself? "Sure I can. But what's going on?"

"Just... just do it for me, please."

His hand moved slightly, drawing her eye. She noticed a ball chain dangling from his fingers and immediately realized he must have a pair of dog tags in his hand. In a flash of realization, she understood what that meant. Clay had been released. Tiffany walked around the desk and touched Logan on the arm.

"I can do that. But are you okay?"

He stepped back. "I'm fine." He turned and went back into his office. His movements weren't as precise as usual, but stiff and tight. When he closed the door to his office, she finally snapped into motion. She secured her desk and grabbed her keys. She was almost out the door when she ran into Ryan.

"Where you rushing off to Jackson? Chasing after your buddy? He sure looked torn up when I passed him just now." He grinned. "I wonder what that means? I'd better go check on Logan and make sure he's alright."

Tiffany glared at him. "You fucking vulture. Leave him alone."

The grin didn't budge from his face. "What kind of friend would I be if I did that? But you don't have to worry about following after Clay. I'm sure he'll be alright. He'll find some skeevy chic to bang before the week is out."

Tiffany shook her head in disgust. "Logan won't fall for your shit."

Ryan stepped out of her way. "We'll see."

Tiffany continued on to the garage. She didn't have time to deal with that asshole. But she pulled out her phone to send a quick message to Carlos. She came across Clay just as he was throwing his bag in the trunk.

"Hey, Clay."

He looked over at her. His face was pale. He looked just as shell shocked as Logan, if not more so.

"Hey."

"I just thought I'd come check on you."

He blinked. "I'm fine. Just headed home."

"Why don't you let me drive you?"

"Why would you ask that?"

"You look like you could use some company. And you've been trying to open that car door with your house key this entire time."

Clay stood there and looked down at the keys in his hand. Tiffany took them from him and pushed the button to unlock the car. He went around and got in the passenger seat while she slipped behind the wheel. She didn't say anything else until they were out of the garage. "Did something happen between you and Logan?" She thought Clay wasn't going to answer. But he took a deep breath and spoke.

"I had him release me."

She'd figured as much but it was still hard to hear. Especially in Clay's low, lost sounding voice. "That was pretty sudden. Did something happen?"

This time, Clay didn't answer her. He just turned and stared out the window for the rest of the quick drive to his home. When they got to his building, Tiffany walked with him up to his apartment. She'd have to wait there for Carlos to come and pick her up. Inside, Clay dropped everything in the middle of the living room floor.

"Can I get you anything, Clay?"

"No. I'm just gonna lay down." She expected him to go back to his bedroom. But he went over to the couch and curled up on his side, still in his uniform and boots. Tiffany's heart was breaking as she looked at him laying there, just staring at nothing. She went over to him and kneeled down.

"Clay. Do you want me to call Logan over so you guys can talk about this?" she asked as she brushed her fingers through his hair.

Clay looked at her for a second before he went back to staring at nothing. "No. I did the right thing. This is what's best for me."

Tiffany followed his wishes, even though he voiced them in the most unsure voice she'd ever heard him use.

****

Carlos walked into one of the bars frequented by HPD. After Tiffany's message telling him that Logan and Clay had separated, he'd immediately started trying to get a hold of his friend. Logan finally replied to his texts and voice mails. He let his eyes and ears adjust to the smoke, music, and loud conversations before he headed straight for the long bar. Logan was sitting there with a shot glass in his fist … and Clay's dog tags laid out on the bar in front of him.

"*Christ.* Logan, buddy, you need to put those away."

Logan ignored him and threw back his shot.

Carlos sighed and sat down on the empty bar stool to Logan's left. "If you don't put them away, you might spill liquor on them. You don't want that to happen, do you?"

Logan gave him a look that clearly showed he knew Carlos was bullshitting him. But after signaling the bartender for another shot, he tucked the tags in his pocket.

"What happened?"

Logan tossed his shot back before he answered in a voice harsh with pain. "It was too much for him. I should have known this was gonna happen. I should have just been with him without all of my kinky bullshit."

"That would never have worked Logan."

Logan laughed bitterly. "Well, this didn't work either so it doesn't fucking matter, now does it?"

Carlos sighed as he watched his friend hold up two fingers, signaling for two shots this time. When they arrived, he downed them one after the other. "Logan, you need to stop. You're going to make yourself sick."

"Carlos, I just lost the most important thing in the world to me. And it's my fault for being such a freak. So I don't give a shit if I wake up tomorrow with a fucking hangover." Logan pounded another shot. He slammed the glass on the bar and stared at it. He was suddenly quiet. "I just wanted him to be mine so I could love him and take care of him. I should never have tried to control a man as strong as Clay."

Carlos hated pointing out the obvious but Logan was so bombed and upset he couldn't see the truth. "Logan, Clay let you control him for what? Three months? He wouldn't have done that if he didn't want to give up control to you. Stop blaming yourself for being who you are."

Logan took his keys out of his pocket and slid them across the bar top to Carlos. "I only let you know where I was so you could drive me back to the house. Will you do that for me and stop talking?"

Carlos grabbed the keys. "So you're ready to go?"

Logan shook his head and raised his finger at the bartender. "Nope. I just want you to let me drink in peace."

Carlos didn't have much patience to begin with and he lost what little he had with his friend. "You can stay here if you want, pounding shots and hiding away from your problem like a fucking pussy. Or you can go home, sleep this shit off, and wake up tomorrow ready to figure out how to get your sub back. Either way, I'm going home right now and I'm taking your keys. You can go with me or I can leave you cash for a cab. What's it gonna be?"

Logan looked at the newly arrived shot in front of him but he didn't pick it up. Carlos waited until his friend looked at him with blood shot eyes.

"You think I can get him back?"

Carlos didn't know what had happened and he didn't want to give out false hope so he spoke the truth. "I think you can *try*. But you're not going to be able to do that if you're too drunk to even talk. Do you think Clay would respect you enough to want to be under your control again if he saw you like this?"

Logan's fingers touched the glass … then he pushed it away. "He asked to be released, Carlos. You really think I should try?"

Carlos got the bartender's attention so he could close out Logan's tab. "People break up and get back together all the time. Even Doms and subs. And Clay is new to BDSM. I bet something probably scared the shit out of him and he panicked. You need to figure out what that was and fix it."

The effects of the alcohol were finally kicking in and Logan's words came out slurred. "He said he didn't want me to fix it."

Carlos clamped his hand on his friend's shoulder and waited until he looked at him again. "You're the Dom. Fix it."

52

The next night, Logan was still confused as to what had caused Clay to end things so abruptly. Clay hadn't spoken to him since. And as they rode back to the station after serving that night's warrant, Clay wouldn't even look at him. In fact, the mood in the Bear was uncharacteristically quiet. Logan was tense and he knew his mood was influencing the team. He tried to shake it off but he couldn't. He just kept glancing at Clay who sat without engaging anyone in conversation. He might as well be alone for all the interaction he had with them. Logan wanted to reach out to him, but he couldn't with everyone looking. But then he became aware of just how closely everyone was watching them. He noticed eyes darting back and forth between him and Clay. Clearly, they realized something was up between them with the tense moods they were both in. Logan forced himself to look away from Clay and strike up a conversation with Jody.

****

Clay ignored everyone as he walked back into the station after the Bear dropped them off. He'd come out of the fog he'd been in last night after ending things with Logan, but he didn't feel any better. He felt that he'd done the right thing. Staying as Logan's submissive was wrong for him. As much as he loved being with Logan and enjoyed the things he did to him, he couldn't let him take over his life the way he was doing. And he was ashamed ... and scared at the way he'd so easily gone into subspace in Logan's playroom. That loss of control felt so good when it was happening. But it terrified him afterwards. And now, now he cringed when he thought of the way he crawled at Logan's feet and licked his boots. He didn't like what his enjoyment of that said about him. And he didn't want to go down that path any further. He was determined to hold firm and not allow himself to get sucked back into Logan's world.

So he'd made his decision but he didn't feel any better. His mood was shit and his attitude was shittier. Q had borne the brunt of his bad mood out in the garage. They'd gotten out of their cars at about the same time and Q caught up with him so they could walk in together like usual. Q asked him where Logan was and Clay lost it. He'd stopped and furiously yelled that he didn't know where Logan was because he'd broken up with him just like Q wanted him to do.

His friend stood there staring at him in shocked surprise as he unloaded on him, saying that he was right, that Logan was controlling him like a slave and he was so weak he was falling for it. But when he shouted, "Are you fucking happy now?" Q walked off, leaving him standing there in the garage alone.

He'd taken a few minutes to calm himself as much as he could before he went into the station. He knew yelling at Q like that was a real dick move. And although they'd worked together as seamlessly as always, the air between them was hard and uncomfortable. He knew he should apologize, but he just didn't have it in him to do so. Right then, he didn't want to talk to anyone on the team. So he kept his back to everyone as he geared down in the locker room. Thankfully, they sensed he didn't want to be bothered and left him alone.

****

Logan walked out of his office. He was headed for the coffee machine when he saw that Clay was at the copier. Looking around, he noticed the pen was fairly empty. He went up to Clay, taking in how miserable he looked. He looked just as unhappy as Logan felt. He tried to set a light-hearted mood as he made Clay aware of his presence.

"Working on your after action reports, I see. Trying to make my life easier so I don't have to hunt you down for them?"

Clay's head snapped up. A hard expression overtook his face. "I don't do anything *for you*. I'm doing this because it's my job."

Clay saying that he didn't do anything for him hurt but he didn't let that stop him. "Clay, can we talk?"

Clay shrugged and looked back down at the copier. "There's nothing for us to talk about."

"There is. I'd like to know why you ended things between us. I thought our relationship was going well, that you liked what we had together."

"I told you that wasn't me. Why can't you just accept that?"

But Logan couldn't. Clay's voice might read indifference but his body language told another story. Clay looked so lost and sad as he stood there, his shoulders curled in protectively and refusing to look at him. He was tense and his mind clearly wasn't on task. His hand hovered over the keypad but he hadn't pressed any buttons or made a single copy since Logan walked over to him. It took everything Logan had not to reach out and pull Clay into his arms and ease the pain he was obviously feeling. He didn't, but he couldn't help moving a little closer.

"Clay, you told me just hours before we broke up that you loved me. Was that a lie?" When Clay shook his head, Logan took another step closer. "And you told me just days ago, when I held you as you fell asleep, that you loved wearing my collar. Was *that* a lie?" Clay shook his head again and Logan moved closer still, close enough to touch. He raised his hand, but this time Clay backed away.

"It doesn't matter what I said before. What matters is what I'm saying now. That type of relationship isn't me. Isn't *for* me. I can't lose myself like that."

Logan started to ask Clay what he meant by that comment but Clay talked over him.

"Look, Logan. We have to work together and we agreed when we started dating that if we ended things, we'd keep it professional. Let's just keep that in mind and forget about everything else."

Logan tried one last time. "Clay, are you sure you don't want to talk? I can give you more time if you need …"

Clay was already shaking his head before Logan could finish his sentence. "I don't need more time and I don't need to talk. I just need you to understand that we're over."

Clay grabbed all his papers from the machine and walked away. Logan didn't try to stop him. Clay couldn't have made things any clearer. It wasn't just a moment of panic that caused him to ask to be released. He no longer wanted to be Logan's submissive. They were done.

53

Clay sat up in his bed. It was three o'clock in the morning. He'd pretty much given up any thought of getting any real sleep. Which made that the third night in a row he'd be nice and cozy with meaningless late night TV. A commercial came on and Clay glanced at his phone. It sat on his nightstand, its screen dark. He looked back at the TV. He should watch something on his DVR so he didn't have to sit through the commercials, but he didn't feel like bothering to check and see what he had in there. When another commercial came on, he looked over at his phone again. It was still dark. After he glanced at the stupid thing for the fifth time, he admitted to himself that he was waiting for Logan to call. Ever since that first time Logan helped him get to sleep, Logan had called him every night they were apart.

He loved those phone calls. Sometimes they talked about work, sometimes random stuff, and sometimes Logan convinced him to indulge in phone sex – something he'd never really done before. But always it had been Logan's deep voice telling Clay that he loved him that had lulled him to sleep.

Was he crazy to leave someone who obviously cared for him so much?

Clay reached over and picked up his phone. He was tempted to call Logan, even at that hour. But he just held the phone in his hand – not even thumbing it awake. Logan loved him and Clay definitely loved him back. But he couldn't live Logan's lifestyle. He couldn't give up control like that. With his history of abusing alcohol until he lost control and wrecked lives, it wouldn't lead to anything good for him – he knew it.

He tossed the phone back onto his nightstand and lay down. Switching the channel off the sports network, he flipped through until he found infomercials. Maybe he just needed to watch something really boring to fall asleep. Clay snorted. After the past two sleepless nights, he knew that wouldn't work. He gave it a try anyway.

Logan sat up in his bed. It was three o'clock in the morning. He knew he probably wasn't going to fall asleep any time soon. He gripped his phone in his hand wanting to call Clay. To talk, to try and work things out, to help him fall asleep. But Clay had been clear. They were over. Still, he had Clay's number up on his screen and he kept rubbing his thumb across it to keep it lit.

As he sat there, an ugly thought crept into his mind. Maybe Clay wasn't alone. Maybe he'd found someone to spend the night with. Someone, he'd had sweaty, mindless sex with to help him forget about Logan. Or maybe Clay *was* alone that night, but he wouldn't be for long. Now that he'd had a taste of being a submissive, maybe he would want more – just with someone who was better for him than Logan was.

Logan stopped staring at his phone's screen as ugly pictures began filling his head. Clay kneeling at another Dom's feet. Clay chained up for another Dom's lash. His grip on the phone tightened. Another Dom pushing into his sub, making him moan. Logan squeezed that little piece of technology harder still. Another Dom holding Clay in his arms as he trembled in the aftermath of his submission. Logan cursed and swung his arm out, slamming the phone against the headboard. He heard a snap and looked down. He'd cracked his phone's screen. Logan pressed his head back against the headboard, his throat working rapidly as he tried not to cry. He hated himself for thinking like that, but he couldn't help it. He knew Clay's dating history, knew he wasn't one to stay alone for long. He just couldn't believe that *their* relationship would end like this.

How had he fucked things up so badly? Clay said *he couldn't lose himself like that.* Logan must have overwhelmed Clay in some way for him to say that – he just didn't know what he'd done. Logan ground the heels of his hands into his eyes. He more than likely had no reason to fear that Clay would get with another Dominant. He'd probably done a great job in scaring Clay away from the scene for good. But what did he do wrong? Logan admitted to himself that it was his fault. He should have talked to Clay more, made sure he was okay. But his beautiful lover had been doing so well and his submission had come so naturally that he hadn't thought... No, that wasn't an excuse. He was a terrible Dom and it was *his* fault. *He should have checked to make sure Clay was really okay.* And now Clay wouldn't even talk to him so he could find out where he went wrong and fix it.

Logan looked at the time on his cracked phone. 3:45 am. His thoughts circled right back around to wanting to call Clay. But he didn't because Clay didn't want him to. Logan slammed his fist down on the bed, angry at himself, at Clay, at the whole goddamn situation. He was going to go crazy if he sat there any longer thinking like this. He got up, threw on a t-shirt and a pair of sweats, and stuffed his feet into tennis shoes. He headed downstairs into the dark and silent living room.

Logan stood there for a moment. He could probably still get a few hours sleep. All he had to do was go into his kitchen, pour himself a couple drinks and let the alcohol do its job. But that was something someone weak would do. And he had to stay strong so he could try to get Clay back. He went through the kitchen into his garage.

Flicking on the lights, he started to head for his favorite classic car, a black 1970 Ford Mustang Boss. But when he reached it, he touched the hood, remembering the things he'd done to Clay ... and the things he'd made Clay do to him on the hood of that car. It had to have been that shit that sent him running. Fuck! If he wasn't such a goddamn kinky asshole, Clay would still be his. Logan angrily turned away from the black car and got into the driver's seat of the sky blue '67 Chevy Camaro next to it. With a total lack of the care he normally took with his vehicles, he twisted the key viciously in the ignition, stomping hard on the gas and revving the engine while he waited impatiently for the garage door to go up. Once he had enough clearance, he tore out of there, driving one handed while he searched Sirius for the angriest, loudest metal he could find, turning the volume way up. He shifted, making the engine roar as he flew down the streets of his subdivision. He was probably pissing off every neighbor he passed but he didn't care.

When he was out of the quiet and primly manicured area, he went tearing down the freeway. He was being a huge fucking hypocrite by breaking the speed limit, but he didn't care about that either. At that speed, he had to really concentrate on what he was doing – which meant he had no room in his brain left to torture himself with thoughts of Clay.

Clay managed to drift off into a light doze but his mind didn't shut off the way he'd hoped. No, he was dreaming. Dreaming of being with Logan. Dreaming of how Logan had used a bowl of ice cream to let him know that he was perfect in his eyes.

"I can't believe you're going to eat so much of this stuff."

Logan raised an eyebrow. "No we're going to eat this."

Clay shook his head. "No way. My body wants to be fat. I eat that and it will be."

"You're not fat, Clay. You're beautiful, just like I told you last night." Logan held the spoon up. "Here, have a taste."

Clay turned away but he was smiling. "Please don't do the airplane."

Logan smiled and ate the spoonful of ice cream himself before setting the bowl down on the bed. "Do you know how many calories are in a serving of cookies and cream, Clay?" he asked, tugging Clay's boxers down.

Clay raised his hips to help his Dom. "No."

"About three hundred." Once he was naked, Logan started stroking his cock. "Do you know how many calories you burn with an orgasm?"

Clay was starting to breathe a little faster, his hips slowly moving along with Logan's fist. "No," he said again.

"A hundred. So tell me, Clay, how many times would I have to make you come for you to burn off your share of this ice cream?" Logan kept up his smooth pumping as he spoke.

Clay moaned and thrust his hips up. "Three."

Logan laughed softly. "You're so smart." He used his free hand to grab the spoon and scoop up some of the cookies and cream. This time, when Logan held up the spoonful of ice cream, Clay parted his lips and let Logan feed it to him. Logan alternated between feeding him and himself. He kept stroking Clay the whole time, keeping him just shy of that delicious gasping urge to release until there was only one spoonful left. Then he took his hand off Clay's cock. He gave a sharp little cry of protest, thrusting his hips forward to seek Logan's hand. But Logan ignored him.

"I'm not going to give you any orgasms to burn off this ice cream, Clay. Do you know why?"

Clay shook his head, his body still craving Logan's touch.

"Because you are beautiful. I love your body. You don't need to be ripped with muscle to be great at what we do. You prove that every time we go out in the field. Your slender arms? Perfect. Your sweet little round ass? Perfect." Logan touched him again, but this time it was to smooth his palm down Clay's thigh. "These thighs *that I love feeling wrapped around me?" A drop of the melting ice cream fell on the thigh Logan was caressing. He leaned down and licked it up, lightly sucking the spot into his mouth. Clay watched as Logan looked up at him with those beautiful hazel eyes. "Perfect," he whispered. Logan held the spoon of mostly melted ice cream up to his lips and without a moment's hesitation, Clay ate the last spoonful. Logan dropped the spoon, raising back up to kiss him, telling him he tasted extra sweet. He started stroking Clay's shaft again.*

"I won't make you come for that, baby. But I will give you three orgasms. One because you're gorgeous when you reach your pleasure. One because I want nothing more than to make you feel good. And one because I lo—"

Clay wrenched himself awake. He'd prefer to stay awake for the rest of his life if that's what was waiting for him on the other side of consciousness. It was bad enough he couldn't get Logan off his mind while he was awake. He couldn't stand to dream of him too. Throwing off the covers, he got out of bed. He pulled on the first pair of shorts he found in a drawer, tied on a pair of running shoes and grabbed his headphones. The sun wasn't up yet, but there were plenty of street lamps to light the way for a run.

54

It was early in the morning. So early it was still dark outside. He didn't have to be at work for hours, but just like the previous two nights, Logan was unable to sleep. So he was in the station gym getting a work out. He knew it was dangerous to drive at such reckless speeds. So after that initial drive, he stopped. But he still needed a way to take his mind off things. A workout was as good a way to do that as any.

He was switching the heavy dumbbell to his other hand when the door creaked open. He only gave a cursory glance to see who it was until he saw it was Clay. Logan's heart skipped a beat and he forgot about the weight in his hand. Clay came into the gym but when he noticed Logan sitting on the weight bench, he froze. Logan knew Clay was about to turn around and leave so he spoke up. "You can come in, I don't bite." Clay gave him a look and Logan huffed a small laugh. "Maybe that was a poor choice of words. But I won't bother you if you want to work out." He watched Clay stand there for a moment before he went over to one of the treadmills without saying anything a word.

Clay was surprised when he walked into the gym and noticed Logan. He'd almost stepped right back out but he figured them being alone was going to happen sooner or later. Might as well dive off that cliff now. He stepped up on the treadmill but he was flustered. He pulled his t-shirt off like usual and then thought that might not be a good idea. But it would look stupid to put it back on so he left it off, draping it over the handrail. He fumbled with his headphones a bit but managed to get them on without dropping them like an idiot.

He'd used that machine probably dozens of times, so despite his awkwardness, he had it going pretty quickly. But he couldn't get into a good rhythm. Logan said he wouldn't bother him, but he could feel the other man's eyes watching him. He knew that if he looked onto the big wall mirror in front of him, he would see those hazel eyes focused on him. Clay tried to find his pace without raising his eyes to the mirror. But he couldn't resist the pull he felt and eventually he looked up. Just as he thought, Logan was looking straight at him while he slowly curled the weight in his hand up and down. Their eyes met in the mirror and Clay stumbled. He grabbed the handrails to steady himself, but he didn't resume his run. He hit the stop button twice and stepped off the treadmill. Clay was shaking but trying not to show it as he snatched off his headphones and picked up his shirt to leave. He was almost to the door when he Logan called his name.

"Clay, wait."

Like an idiot, he stopped … and waited. He heard Logan approaching and turned around to face him. Logan came close, closer than he should have allowed, but he didn't step back.

"You look tired, baby."

Clay started to snort and give a flippant response. But he didn't. Logan at least deserved his honesty. "I haven't been sleeping well," he said, shrugging. "But I'll be okay."

Logan's hand came up and lightly touched his lower back. "You need to take better care of yourself."

Clay looked down at the ground between their feet. "Logan, don't," he said in a low voice.

Logan noticed Clay didn't say anything about him calling him baby, nor did he back away from his touch. He stroked his hand over Clay's slightly damp skin. "Don't what, Clay? Don't miss taking care of you? Don't miss being inside you and holding you afterwards?" His fingers dug into the smooth muscles of Clay's back. "Don't love you?"

Clay shook his head. "I told you I can't—"

Logan cut off the rest of whatever Clay was going to say with a kiss. He wrapped his arms around the man he loved more than anything and pulled him up tight against him. Clay's lips remained closed at first, refusing to kiss him back. But Logan kept trying, kept kissing him. Clay was there and he couldn't give up that chance. Finally, Clay's lips parted, a whisper coming from him. *"Logan."* Logan heard that whisper, felt Clay stop resisting and relax against him. He swept inside, tasting the sweetness that had been denied him. Now Clay kissed him back. Logan felt the shirt Clay had been holding brush his legs as he dropped it and wrapped his arms around his neck. Their kiss was hot, rough and desperate, all the pain, loneliness, and heartache they were both feeling coming out as their lips met.

Clay pulled back and looked up at him with wide eyes. "We shouldn't do this. We're going to get caught."

Logan looked at the man in his arms. It was right. It was where Clay was supposed to be. That was all that mattered to him. "I don't fucking care if anyone walks in here. I don't care if anyone sees us." He tugged Clay close again. "I just want you."

Logan wrapped his arms even tighter around his love and walked him backwards to the wall behind him. He pressed Clay against the wall, kissing him deeply again and again until they were both gasping for air. He finally gave them a chance to breathe, but he didn't stop touching him or kissing him. He couldn't. He trailed his lips up Clay's jaw until he reached his ear. "Clay, please…" His voice broke and he had to stop and clear his throat. "Please, come back to me."

Clay was quiet for several seconds. Logan held his breath, hoping he would get the response he wanted.

"I'm sorry, Logan, but no. I can't."

Disappointment surged through him in a bitter wave. Logan kissed him again, this time out of frustration, but Clay turned his face aside.

"I said no."

Logan pulled back and looked at Clay. His lips were swollen and wet from his kisses, his eyes soft, his face flushed.

He looked like he always did whenever they kissed. Then he lowered his eyes. Logan had to push himself away. He couldn't take seeing that sweet sign of what had once signified Clay's submission to him while Clay was telling him no. Logan turned his back, clenching his fists tightly.

"I thought I could be alone with you without trying to make you mine again. Obviously, I was wrong. So you'd better leave. Now. Because I'm about five seconds from pushing you up against that wall and fucking you till you agree to come back to me." He looked up in the mirror and saw Clay standing there with his eyes wide and his chest rapidly rising and falling. "And right now, you look like that's exactly what you want me to do. So go. Unless you *want* to be here with me." He closed his eyes, not wanting to see Clay walk out on him again. But his ears worked just fine and he heard his feet crossing the room, the door opening and closing.

When he opened his eyes, he was alone … and he just lost it. He picked up one of the heavy iron dumbbells, and in a rage, threw it at the mirrored wall. The thing shattered instantly and Logan just stood there, watching the pieces fall.

Clay heard the crash from the other side of the door and he flinched. That wasn't his problem to deal with. He shook his head hard. He *wouldn't let* it be his problem to deal with. No matter how badly he wanted to go back into that gym and walk right into Logan's arms, he wasn't going to do it. Clay put his headphones back on and left the station. He couldn't run on the treadmill but that was okay. He'd just run outside again.

Logan was back at home. He'd made up some bullshit story about how he'd lost control of a weight and broken the mirror. They didn't look too closely when he paid for it. Now he was sitting in his bed. Alone. He held Clay's collar in one hand, rubbing his thumb over the letters etched into the metal. In the other, he held the shirt Clay had dropped and forgotten when he left the gym.

He didn't get up to turn off the light so he could sleep. He just sat, staring at the collar. He didn't turn on the TV for noise to distract him from his thoughts. He just sat, staring at the collar. He didn't get undressed or take off his shoes to get comfortable. He just … sat.

55

"You look like shit."

Clay looked up and saw Tiffany standing in front of his desk. Normally, he would have shot back a snide reply but he just wasn't up to it. So he didn't say anything. Besides, he knew what he looked like. He hadn't slept much ... or at all since his encounter with Logan in the gym the day before. The pale and drawn face that greeted him that morning was the result.

Tiffany sat down on the corner of his desk and handed him a bottle of water. Her voice came out low to keep anyone from hearing their conversation. "Now that you're no longer practically comatose, you want to tell me what happened between you and Logan?"

Clay took a sip of the cool water. He hadn't talked to anyone about this. He'd had lunch with Ian and mentioned that he'd broken up with Logan. But when his friend tried to talk to him about it, he shut him out. Ian didn't know about their BDSM relationship and Clay wasn't comfortable discussing it. And, of course, Q knew they were done, but his out of control screaming tirade – which he still hadn't apologized for – did not count as talking about it. So maybe he should get things off his chest with Tiffany. He drank deeply from the water bottle before giving her his full attention.

"I just realized that being a sub wasn't for me. And since that's Logan's thing – I had to end it."

A confused frown creased Tiffany's forehead. "You don't just realize that being a sub isn't for you. What happened to make you think that?"

"It was nothing. Logan and I had an argument and I decided it wasn't right for me to be submissive to anyone."

Tiffany's expression was clearly disbelieving. "Come on, Clay! Don't bullshit me. If you don't want to talk right now, that's fine. But don't put me off with a half-assed story. I know how you felt about belonging to Logan. Remember what you told me when he first collared you?"

Clay remembered. *I swear right now I'm about two seconds from going over there and kneeling at his feet in front of everybody in here.* He should have known then he was in trouble. Clay sighed. He might as well tell Tiffany the truth. "Have you ever gone into subspace?"

Tiffany smiled slightly. "Yes. I love it when Carlos takes the time and does things to get me there. I just relax and let go. It feels so good, almost like I'm high" Tiffany cut herself off mid-sentence and looked at Clay. "Oh."

Clay snorted. "Yeah… *oh* is right. Last weekend I experienced that for the first time. I liked it. Fuck, I more than liked it, but I just can't give up that much control. And I can't accept something that makes me feel like I'm high." He didn't mention the doubts he had about how uncomfortable he was at work – not wanting to bring Q into the mess anymore than he already was.

Tiffany looked confused again. "Okay, I'm not a recovering addict so I'm not sure how to help you with that part. But if you liked giving up control to Logan, why would you walk away from it? You're safe letting Logan take control when it's just the two of you. There's nothing wrong with that. It's not like Logan asked you to be a lifestyle sub."

Clay blew out a frustrated breath and laced his fingers together over his forehead. "Because it wasn't just in the bedroom that I was letting him take control. I called him Sir in the middle of the goddamn locker room with Q sitting right next to me, for fuck's sake. If that isn't a sign that I was losing too much of myself to him, then I don't know what is."

"Clay, when did you two have your session in Logan's playroom?"

He dropped his hands. "Saturday. Why?"

Tiffany ignored his question. "And afterwards, did you feel sort of tired, like you just didn't want to deal with anything?"

Clay nodded. "Yeah. I just wanted to sleep for days, it felt like."

Tiffany gave a sad little laugh. "Clay… what you experienced is totally normal. If you felt like you were high, it makes sense that eventually you would come down, right?"

Clay looked at Tiffany. Where was she going with this? "Yeah… so what?"

"So your defenses were lowered. Everything you felt afterwards was because of that. Doubting your role as a submissive, slipping up and calling Logan Sir in public, asking to be released… All of that was a result of coming down. It takes a lot to let go enough to go into subspace. And sometimes, once you come out of it, it's like your equilibrium is off. And that feeling can really mess with your head until you're back on track. You can't let that come between you and Logan. It's not worth it."

Clay responded swiftly, almost forgetting to keep his voice down. "It is worth it, Tiffany! If I stayed with Logan, we would have wound up in that playroom again and I'd be high as a kite. And if what you say is true, then that means each time I'd be weak and tired after that – like I'm coming off a fucking bender – and I'd be calling Logan *Sir* in front of every damn body. I might as well wear my collar in public." Clay felt a small thrill of pleasure at the thought of walking with Logan so clearly marked as his, but he pushed it down. "And I've come too fucking far to let myself get addicted to anything ever again. Besides, Logan was just … He was crossing the boundaries we set. It was just too much."

"Clay, it can be hard to keep those boundaries in place, especially for someone who is new to BDSM. And Logan might not be new to being a Dom, but he's never had his own submissive before. You guys are both learning your way through this. You should talk to Logan about this. Did you even let him know how you were feeling when you were recovering from subspace?"

Clay shook his head. "No, I didn't realize the way I was feeling was tied to that."

Tiffany sighed. "Always talk to your Dom about how you're feeling, Clay." Then she frowned. "But Logan should have noticed how you were feeling and helped you."

Clay was about to say something but he stopped as Logan came into the pen. For some reason, he felt the need to avoid him. "Thanks for the talk, Tiffany, but I've got some stuff to take care of."

"Wait, are you going to talk to Logan?"

Clay shook his head. "No. I just don't think that type of relationship is for me. I've got to go." Clay hustled out of there. He didn't look back to see if Logan had seen him.

****

"Sergeant Pierce, can I see you in my office, please?"

"I'll be right there." He sighed and put the phone down. Earlier in the pen, he'd seen that Clay was avoiding him. That sent his mood plummeting to even lower depths than he thought possible. So he didn't feel like dealing with whatever bullshit Captain Hayden had on tap for the day. He headed down the halls until he reached Hayden's office.

"Close the door," Hayden told him once he arrived. "I'm going to get right to the point. Fix whatever is wrong with your team."

"What?"

"You think I don't notice stuff like that in here? Well, I do. Your team has been tense and strained these past few days. Whatever is the cause of it, take care of it. We've got the HPD convention coming up and we need your team on point.

That's why these law agencies are paying us and it's what will bring them back next year." He cleared his throat. "And it's what will keep your team safe out in the streets," he tacked on almost as an afterthought.

Logan fought not to roll his eyes at the captain's priorities. "You seem to be the most tense of all." He narrowed his eyes. "You and Corporal Foster. There a problem between you two?"

Logan straightened. "No. Sometimes people just get out of sorts. We'll get it together. *I'll* get it together."

Hayden leaned back in his chair. "Make sure that you do."

****

Logan went looking for Clay. The convention was in two days. They needed to get things cleared up between them so their team could gel once more. He entered the pen but Clay wasn't at his desk. Hector sat at the desk next to Clay's. "Have you seen Foster?" he asked.

Hector nodded towards the locker room. Logan thanked him and went that way. Pushing the swinging door open, he walked to the back until he reached the bay of lockers where Clay was. When he saw him, he came to an abrupt halt.

Clay was there with his back to him. He was shirtless and Logan could see the marks he'd left on his smooth skin from the flogger. They were faded, nearly gone, but still visible to his hungry gaze. He remembered putting them there. Remembered every single lash and Clay's passionate reaction to them. He wanted to reach out and trace his fingers over them. But he no longer had that right. Their relationship was gone, the fading marks on Clay's skin nothing more than a taunting reminder of what they shared. He cleared his throat and Clay spun around.

Logan swore he saw a welcoming expression on his face before it was replaced with the closed off one Clay now wore whenever he saw him. Or maybe that was just wishful thinking. He needed to stop doing that. He pushed that out of his mind so he could do what he came to do.

"We need to talk. And not about us together but about us at work."

Clay nodded but he didn't meet his eyes. "Okay."

Logan took a deep breath. "What's going on between us is affecting the team. We need to reach some sort of peace between us so everyone stops picking up on our tension."

Clay nodded again. "You're right." He ran a hand over his hair. "We both promised that we'd keep things professional if we ended it. But I know I haven't tried very hard to do that."

Logan smiled slightly. "I haven't either." They were quiet for a moment. "So maybe the first step would be to stop avoiding eye contact with one another when we talk."

Clay finally looked at him. "I can do that."

Logan forced himself to ignore the emotion that went through him as he looked into those bright blue eyes. There was so much he wanted to say but it would serve no purpose. Clay had made that clear. "I know it won't be easy, but we were friends for much longer than we were lovers. We might not be able to get that relationship back, but at least we can behave like friendly co-workers."

"Yeah, we can. I'm sorry."

"It's okay. We both fucked up." An uncomfortable silence fell between them but at least it wasn't as tense as it was before. "So we're good." Logan looked at Clay, waiting for his answer. He was surprised at how long Clay stood there, silently watching him before he finally answered.

"We're good."

There was nothing else to say so he left the locker room.

56

The HPD Criminal Justice Convention had arrived. HPD had taken over the same convention center that held the Leet Speak con that Clay attended for Ian. But this event was different. It was just as loud and crowded but the technology was different. Instead of video games and computers, there were weapons, ammo, and body armor. And these con goers were people who either worked in the criminal justice system or aspired to do so. Their team had already put on two small training sessions that day, teaching the latest in SWAT techniques. It was almost time for their big demonstration, a run through a course that had been created especially for the convention.

Clay came out of the area they were using to change and saw Q standing there in his gear. He needed to quit being a dick and apologize to his friend. The tension between him and Logan wasn't the only thing affecting their team. Q heard him approaching and turned to him with a wary look on his face.

"I should be the one looking like that. After what I said to you last week, I wouldn't be surprised if you punched me in the throat right now."

Q relaxed a little bit. "I'm thinking about it."

Clay gave a lopsided grin. "And I'd deserve it. But I'm hoping you'll hold off on the throat punching to let me apologize for being such an asshole."

Q crossed his arms over his chest, but a smile was already tugging at his mouth. "Go ahead."

"I shouldn't have said any of that. None of what went down with Logan was your fault. I shouldn't have screamed at you like a lunatic. And if I missed anything, I'm just gonna issue a blanket statement to make sure I cover it all. I'm an asshole and I'm sorry."

Q laughed. "That was the craziest apology I've ever heard." He held his hand out to Clay. "But I accept it."

Clay shook his hand and pulled his friend into a one-armed hug. They embraced for a second, Clay glad to have his friend back. Then they shoved each other back laughing and joking. "You want to hang out tonight after this madhouse?" Clay asked.

"Actually, I was going to head over to Carlos's party. You should come with me."

Clay had forgotten about Carlos's party. He was having a big bash at his house to celebrate his birthday. Clay originally planned to go, he and Logan making plans to attend together several weeks ago. Obviously, he wasn't going with Logan anymore but he should still stop by. Except Logan was Carlos's best friend. Which meant that he would definitely be at the party. He hesitated, wondering if he should go or avoid situations like that until he and Logan had both moved on. Q knocked him on the shoulder.

"What's up, man? You going or not?"

Clay looked at his friend. He really should stay away from Logan outside of work. He opened his mouth to tell Q he was just going to head home afterwards. At least that's what he planned to say. Instead, he answered, "A party sounds like a great idea."

****

Clay stood in a line with the rest of his team. Logan was in front of them, speaking to the crowd about being safe and effective as a SWAT team. Clay looked around. Logan had them hanging on his every word and they all looked excited for what was to come. With their reputation for being the best, Clay hoped they would deliver tonight. Clay hefted his M16 and raised his chin. They were the best. He *knew* they would deliver.

"Alright, this was specially designed by Sergeant Mitchell. So you know it's going to be tough and have some surprises."

The training run was created to resemble multiple armed assailants in a crowded shopping area. Officers from HPD played the role of the bad guys. Volunteers from the convention were invited in to be onlookers and hostages. Logan went over the intel they'd been given and they came up with their plan. He looked at Clay and Q.

"Get us in fast and safe. We've got your back."

Clay nodded, his adrenaline already pumping. He loved his job and the chance to showcase his skills, whether it was for real in the field or in demonstrations like this. He and Q moved into place, taking out the two guys guarding the entrances. From there, the rest of the team swarmed in. Everything went as smooth as gravy. Using paint filled bullets, they managed to "kill" or subdue all the gunmen. They didn't lose a single hostage, and by the end of the run, their uniforms were free of the paint that would have indicated they'd been hit.

The applause when they were finished was thunderous. The whole team laughed and acknowledged it. Getting recognition from their peers like that felt amazing. Logan grabbed the microphone again and said a heartfelt good bye to Senior Corporal Mike Dorsey. Clay and Hector pushed Mike forward to accept his own round of applause from the crowd and everyone there from HPD. Mike smiled and waved sheepishly then quickly rejoined the group.

Once they were off the convention floor, they all high-fived each other. Clay turned from slapping Jody on the back to see Logan was right in front of him. Without thinking, he moved closer and wrapped one arm around Logan's neck. It could have been just a friendly congratulatory hug. But he pressed a little closer than was expected for just friends. Logan's arm went around his waist and Clay's stomach lifted lightly at the touch. He turned his head, whispering, "*Good job,*" in Logan's ear. Then he stepped away. The entire thing took about three seconds, but he couldn't meet Logan's eyes when it was over.

****

Clay was next to Q, gearing down. He noticed Officer Ryan Bennett approaching. Bennett was trying to get on SWAT and had served as one of the baddies in the demonstration. Clay narrowed his eyes as the blond went up to Logan. Clay couldn't hear what the two were talking about, but from the smile on Bennett's face, it wasn't hard to guess. Clay was suddenly glad he'd been the one to pop Bennett with the paint bullet earlier. He hoped it hurt. Clay glared at Bennett as he walked off. When he looked back at Logan, he saw that his sergeant was watching him. Clay quickly looked away.

57

Logan lay back on one of the lounge chairs on Carlos's upstairs balcony. The night air was muggy and hot, only the barest hint of a breeze blowing every so often. He took another sip of the beer he'd been nursing for the past thirty minutes. Carlos's party was in full swing, the sounds of thumping music and people talking and laughing took over the quiet neighborhood. But Logan was alone. He didn't really feel like partying – not even to celebrate his friend's birthday. Of course, he'd go down and join the party later. He just wasn't ready yet. Logan kept going over Clay's hug and the angry jealousy he'd seen on his face when Ryan had come up to him.

He didn't want to be a crazy-stalker-ex who looked at everything as a reason to try and get back with his lover, but something told him those actions shouldn't be ignored. Was Clay signaling that he wanted to come back to him? Or was Clay taunting him with the reminder? He didn't think Clay was one to play games like that. But even without playing games, Clay's mixed signals were still messing with his head.

He was lifting the bottle of Bud Light to his mouth again when his phone buzzed with a text from Tiffany.

Clay is here.

Logan squashed his immediate urge to go down and find Clay. Just because he was there didn't mean he wanted to see him. If he did, all he had to do was call. Or catch up to him after the convention. He'd done neither. Clay was probably just there for the party like everyone else. Another text came.

He looks really sad.

Logan's fingers clenched around his new phone. He needed to stick by his decision. Clay would have to come to him to try and work things out if that's what he wanted. Logan wasn't going to put himself out there to be rejected again. His phone lit up his little corner of night with another text from Tiffany.

He keeps staring at my collar.

Logan was out of his chair in a flash. He set the bottle down on the balcony railing and headed downstairs.

Clay watched as Tiffany put her phone away. "Who do you keep texting?"

"Oh, just someone who needs direction."

"You mean direc*tions*."

Tiffany rolled her eyes. "Yeah, grammar police. That's what I meant to say."

Tiffany resumed the story she was telling about the fit Carlos threw when he realized his little sister had gotten a tattoo, but Clay was barely listening. All he could think about was Logan. He knew Logan was at the party somewhere since Tiffany had not so casually mentioned he was staying there. He looked back at Tiffany and tried to pay attention to their conversation, but his gaze was caught again by the silver medallion around her neck – her public sign of belonging to Carlos. Without him realizing it, his fingers came up to his own neck, missing the feel of Logan's collar around his throat. Clay had to look away from Tiffany's collar, realizing he wanted his own back so badly he hurt.

But when he looked up, his eyes immediately clashed with Logan's. He was standing across the room, watching him. Clay dropped his hand, but he knew it was too late. Logan had seen the gesture. Clay stood there frozen, unable to tear his gaze away from Logan's. When Logan jerked his head towards the hallway then headed that way, Clay followed immediately, not even noticing that he was leaving Tiffany mid-sentence.

Logan waited for Clay inside Carlos's spare room. When he arrived, Logan stepped back and let him into the dimly-lit room. After closing the door, he stared at Clay without saying a word. Clay dropped his eyes and lowered his head. "Do you want to talk?" Logan asked. Clay shook his head slowly still not looking at him. "So you're just here for sex then? You want the physical pleasure of submitting to me but nothing else?"

Clay finally looked at him. Logan saw the struggle on Clay's face and the answer to his question. It wasn't the one he wanted, and it pissed him off. But he was even more pissed at himself, because he knew he wasn't going to walk away from it and he wouldn't allow Clay to either. He knew it wasn't a good idea for them to have sex with the way things were between them. But he couldn't pass up the chance to be with Clay once more. And he hoped … No. He pushed that aside.

Logan wrapped his hand around Clay's throat in the space where his fucking collar should be, struggling to push down his anger at the situation they were in. It helped that Clay didn't resist him, he just allowed Logan to tilt his head back, his eyes wide as he waited to see what he would do. Logan pulled Clay in close, wanting to kiss him, but decided at the last second he wouldn't.

Instead, he walked Clay backwards, guiding him further into the room. With a bit of pressure, he forced Clay down onto his knees. Releasing his hold on Clay's neck, Logan unzipped his jeans, pushing them down just enough to pull his cock out. He was already half-way hard and throbbing just from looking at Clay on his knees before him. Logan didn't speak, he just grabbed Clay by the back of the head and held him as he rested the head of his cock against Clay's bottom lip. Smart boy, he opened up immediately and Logan pushed into Clay's hot, wet mouth. Logan's other hand came up to hold Clay's head completely still as he thrust over and over, fucking into Clay's mouth, taking what he wanted instead of allowing Clay to give it to him. But even with his rough treatment, he could feel Clay using his tongue to rub against the sensitive underside of his cock.

He gripped Clay's head tighter, thrusting faster. Clay moaned, the sound sending vibrations tingling along Logan's shaft. Logan groaned and pushed himself in deep until he hit the back of Clay's throat and held himself there. He looked down to see Clay's eyes closed, the expression on his face was one of peaceful bliss. Logan loosened his grip and stroked his thumb over Clay's cheek. "Clay." At his whisper, Clay's eyes opened and met his. For a moment, Logan saw the sweet submission that he'd grown accustomed to seeing whenever Clay served him. But then Clay blinked and the look was gone. Clay closed his eyes again and Logan's anger came surging back.

Logan pulled himself away from the pleasure of that mouth. He put his foot in the middle of Clay's chest and pushed until he tumbled onto his back. Logan followed him down, spreading Clay's legs with his hips so he could rub their cocks together. He ground against him and it felt good but it wasn't nearly enough. He sat up and pulled Clay's shirt over his head before yanking his shoes and the rest of his clothes off until he lay there naked. Logan looked at Clay. He was tempted to take him dry, but even in his anger, he couldn't hurt him. "Don't you move from this spot," he ordered. Logan went into the attached bathroom and found a small bottle of lotion. He took his time, letting Clay know they were doing this on his terms. When he came back, Clay was just as he'd left him, flat on his back, his legs still open for him. Logan dropped back down to his knees between those spread thighs and tossed the bottle of lotion to him. "Get me ready."

Clay sat up and squeezed the cool liquid over his cock. He set the bottle aside and slowly pumped his fist over Logan's shaft, spreading the lotion around. Then his fingers slid lower to cup his balls, squeezing them lightly and rolling them in his hand. It felt good so Logan allowed it for a moment before he knocked his hand aside and pushed Clay back down.

"That's more than I asked you to do and you know it." Logan stretched himself out over Clay. He didn't remove any of his own clothes. He just fisted his cock and lined himself up against Clay's entrance. Without any preparation, he started to work himself inside. Clay groaned but Logan just snapped, "You can fucking take it." Beads of sweat popped out on his forehead as he pushed the head of his cock past that tight ring of muscle. The way Clay's ass gripped him was amazing, but when he was only half way inside, he stopped.

"Why did you hug me tonight, Clay?"

Clay's eyes slid away from his. "I was just celebrating that the demonstration went well. That's all."

Logan wasn't buying it. And although his cock was throbbing, his balls aching, he wasn't going any further until he got his answer. "Don't lie to me. I'll leave you here on this floor by yourself if you do it again." He pushed in another inch, drawing a moan from Clay. "You didn't hug anyone else. So why did I get one? And why were you glaring at Ryan?" Clay's jaw set stubbornly so he started to withdraw. "Answer me!"

Clay's eyes snapped back to his. "I don't know, damnit!"

Logan stared down into blue eyes, stormy with both confusion and passion. He wanted Clay to admit the truth so he gave him a calm, quiet order. "You do know. Tell me."

Clay hesitated, chewing his lip before he gave his answer in a low voice. "Because I still think about being yours."

Logan froze, thinking that was it. Clay was going to come back to him. "Then why aren't you?"

Again, Clay closed his eyes, obviously hiding from him. "Logan, please... I told you ... Can we just ..."

He tightened his inner muscles, squeezing his shaft and Logan had to stifle a groan. He clenched his jaw in frustration but he gave in to what Clay was asking and his body was demanding. He pushed forward again. He kept going until he was balls deep in Clay's ass.

Logan braced his hands on the floor. His breath came quick and harsh and he had to fight to keep his hips still. Clay was so damn hot and tight and he missed being inside him so much that he had to push back the urge to come immediately. After he regained a bit of control, he began thrusting slowly. Clay's hands came up to rest on his back but he yanked them off him. "You don't get to touch me," Logan hissed. "Keep your hands on the floor." When Clay complied, Logan kept up with his slow pumping, wanting to savor the feeling of being inside his love again for as long as he could. He pushed deeper until he was striking Clay's pleasure spot, watching as Clay writhed beneath him. His teeth bit into his bottom lip, obviously trying to hold back from speaking. Logan wasn't going to allow that. It was bad enough Clay wouldn't talk to him about their relationship. He wasn't going to let him be silent during this.

"Stop holding back. Talk to me." He thrust almost brutally hard several times and Clay moaned.

"I … I want…"

When he trailed off, moaning again, Logan leaned down and bit his nipple, tugging the tender flesh into his mouth and pulling. Clay cried out, his legs coming up to squeeze tight against his sides. Logan released him. "Tell me, right now, what you want." He slowed his thrusts even more, dragging his cock out of Clay's hot, gripping channel before pushing back in at the same deliberately slow speed. "Do you want me to go faster?"

Clay shook his head and opened his eyes to look up at Logan. "I want … oh god… I want whatever you want, Sir," he gasped.

Fuck! Logan loved hearing those words from Clay and they set him off like nothing else could have. He rose up on his knees and grabbed Clay's thighs, pulling him closer and throwing his legs over his arms. Logan dug his fingers deep into those sexy thighs, holding on tight as he slammed his cock into Clay's ass over and over again. Clay was moaning and gasping and crying out his name beneath him, his back arching off the floor, his skin gleaming slick in that sheen of sweat that Logan so loved. He saw that his lover's cock was hard and stiff against his belly but as much as he wanted to, he didn't touch it. He didn't lean down to lick up that gorgeous sweat from his lover's chest or kiss his lover's mouth. In his anger that Clay had spooked and asked to be released after always submitting to him so beautifully, he denied them both those things. But Logan could barely stand the temptation. So he pulled out and dropping Clay's legs, he flipped him over onto his belly. Yanking him up onto his knees, Logan rammed his cock back into Clay almost before he could take a breath. His hips pistoned back and forth as he fucked Clay so hard he would feel the reminder for a week, Clay's cries for more urging him on.

Clay was in ecstasy. The rough carpet abrading his knees and palms didn't matter. All that mattered was that he was beneath Logan again. That Logan was inside him again, his thick hardness stretching and filling him up. His breath came in quick pants and he tingled from head to toe as the broad head of Logan's cock struck his sensitive bundle of nerves over and over again. The pleasure he felt was so intense that he was light-headed. It made him moan. Made him spread his legs wide and bend down, thrusting his ass in the air so Logan could reach even deeper inside him. But it wasn't just the physical pleasure that had him feeling so good. Being dominated by Logan like that was what he wanted. He'd never understood it – barely questioned it- and maybe he should have. But right then he *needed* to let Logan control his body. His cock was heavy and stiff, swaying from the force of Logan pounding into him. He wanted to stroke himself off – but even then he obeyed the command that Logan had given him months ago and he didn't touch himself. He was about to ask for permission to do so when Logan pulled his hair and scattered his thoughts.

Logan's head was buzzing with pleasure that Clay was submitting to him again, but he needed to hear Clay admit it. He reached up and twisted his fingers in Clay's dark hair and pulled back until his spine arched. "Who do you belong to?" Clay answered in a voice too low to satisfy him. Logan yanked on the hair in his grasp. "I said, who do you *fucking* belong to?" This time the response was loud and clear.

"You! I'm yours, Logan – Sir. Please … take me. Own me."

As the words poured out of Clay's mouth, a possessive growl rumbled from deep in his chest. Hearing that admission had him pounding into Clay, deep and hard, again and again. Clay was *his* goddamnit!

Clay took the rough thrusts without complaint, chanting softly, "I'm yours. I'm yours."

Logan couldn't take it anymore. He reached down and fisted Clay's cock, finding it hard and slick with pre-cum. He jacked him furiously, not letting up or even giving him the chance to ask for permission to come. His fist slid up and down that wet cock faster and faster until Clay screamed, his cum gushing over Logan's hand in hot, steady pulses. Sweat ran down his spine and his shirt stuck to his back while he fucked Clay through his orgasm. His fingers clenched tight on his lover's hips as he yanked them back to meet his thrusts. Clay's channel clenched so tight around his cock with his release that it practically pulled Logan's orgasm from him. He meant to pull out, to deny Clay the pleasure of feeling his ass filled with his Dom's cum, but when the time came, he couldn't do it. Clay felt too damn good wrapped so tightly around his cock, and he refused to miss the satisfaction that *he* experienced in marking his sub that way. Logan sucked in a deep breath as his orgasm rushed up his shaft. He pulled Clay's hips back so his ass was pressed close against him. Logan's balls tightened almost painfully and as his cum exploded from his cock, he threw back his head and shouted. "Damn you, Clay. You are mine!"

58

Clay lay wrapped in Logan's arms, shaking and trying to catch his breath. As Logan's big hand stroked down his back, he was surprised that he would take the time to calm him like he always did when, by all rights, Logan should've just left him there on the floor. He tucked his face into Logan's neck, knowing he was probably taking advantage of his kindness, but he didn't care. He didn't know if he was going to get to be held like this again. Expelling one last sigh, he finally relaxed. Only Logan ever got him so worked up that he needed so much time to come down.

He bit back a protest as Logan released him and got up. When he saw him going to the en suite bath, he just laid there, still too weak to move. Logan came back with a damp cloth, directing him to turn over. When he did, he felt the warm towel wiping up the release that had seeped out onto his legs. Clay lay there quietly, letting Logan clean him. He couldn't help but think of how Logan used to take care of him when they were together. He missed that. When Logan was finished, he tossed the towel aside and stood, pulling Clay to his feet as well. He took the clothes Logan handed him and re-dressed himself as Logan zipped his pants and went to sit on the bed. Clay hesitated, unsure if he should leave or not.

"Did you mean everything you said or was that just heat of the moment bullshit?"

Clay's head snapped up to find Logan's sharp gaze focused intently on him. He opened his mouth but when nothing came out, Logan continued.

"Because this is me. I am a Dom. I can't change that. I want you as my sub. And I think you want that too."

He had to force himself not to back away as Logan got up and walked over to him until they were chest to chest. Logan's voice lowered to a whisper.

"You submit to me so sweetly."

Clay's heart was racing and he felt that now familiar funny lift in his stomach.

"I love hearing you moan when I'm inside you." Logan's lips brushed his. "Calling me Sir." Another brush of the lips. "Telling me you're mine." Logan cupped the back of his neck and brushed his thumb over his throat. "And I know you miss my collar." Logan let him go and stepped back. "But I can't force you to wear it. So you need to decide what you want. I don't know what made you change your mind but I'm here for you to talk to anytime."

Logan looked at him expectantly. Clay knew he was waiting for him to say what was going on in his head. But he was so tangled up, he couldn't think of what he wanted to say. He didn't want to have this conversation with Logan until he understood what he wanted a little better. He loved the way submitting to Logan made him feel. But at the same time, he was wary of the way it made him feel. The memory of him licking Logan's boots tried to put in an appearance, but he pushed it back. A look of disappointment crossed Logan's face at his silence before he pulled him in for a quick, hard kiss.

"I love you, Clay." Logan turned and left the room.

Out in the hall, Logan laced his fingers over the back of his neck, seething with frustration. *Why wouldn't Clay talk to him?* As people walked past him, laughing, Logan remembered that he was at a party and tried to relax so he could make nice. He spied Carlos and Tiffany in the living room and went to join them. As he walked up, Carlos smirked.

"There's a shower in that guest room, you know."

Logan looked at Carlos. "What?"

"You smell like you've been fucking that sub of yours."

Logan shrugged. "Yeah. Sorry."

Carlos laughed. "It's whatever, man. I would ask if you guys straightened things out but I can tell from the look on your face that you didn't."

Logan shook his head. "He won't talk to me. I still don't know why he left, even though I can tell he wants to be with me."

"Obviously. Hence the fucking."

Logan narrowed his eyes at Carlos, ready to curse his friend out. But Tiffany spoke up.

"I know why he freaked and had you release him."

Both of their heads snapped around to her. "What?" they asked in surprised unison.

Tiffany rolled her eyes. "Are you guys going to harmonize next?"

"C'mon, Tiffany. If you know something, please tell me," Logan urged.

"I don't know that it's my place to share. If Clay isn't talking, he probably wouldn't appreciate it if I blabbed."

"Jesus! Tiffany—"

Carlos cut in. "Logan, Tiffany's right. We can't ask her to break Clay's confidence." Carlos turned and looked at Tiffany. "But maybe she can give us a hint?"

Tiffany chewed her bottom lip as she considered. "I guess I can do that. It has to do with what happened in your playroom, Logan."

Logan's brow creased in concentration as he tried to think of what could have bothered Clay that night. "Can you give me a little more than that?"

"What happened in your playroom … and Clay's past." Tiffany looked away for a moment. "I'm sorry to say this Logan, please don't be angry, but you should have taken better care of him afterwards. And maybe prepared him before."

Logan drew in a deep breath, but not because he was angry. It was with a sense of realization. His mind was working, figuring it all out when Carlos spoke.

"Um… Logan? Clay's leaving."

Logan followed the direction of Carlos's gaze and looked out the window to see Clay getting in his car. "Shit!" He rushed through the mess of people, trying not to knock anybody down until he burst through the front door and onto the lawn. But Clay was gone, the rear lights flashing bright as Clay braked at the stop sign down the street then disappearing as the car rounded the corner.

****

After Logan had left the room, Clay sat down on the bed more confused than ever. If he really wanted to get away from Logan, then why did he so easily find himself back with him? Was it just that last itch that needed to be scratched before he could truly end the relationship? Or did he want to try to work things out with him? Or maybe … maybe something in him just wanted to submit. That thought was in his head again as he sped down the highway. But maybe the person he submitted to didn't have to be Logan. Clay put that last thought out of his head. He was nowhere near ready to think about being with anyone else. His phone beeped with a text but he didn't check it until he pulled into his complex's parking lot. It was from Logan, as he expected.

Remember what I said. I'm here for you to talk to any time. And I want to apologize for not being there for you like you needed me to be.

Clay reread that last sentence. It sounded like Logan was shouldering some of the blame for their break up. He didn't quite know what to say, but he didn't want to ignore Logan's message. So he just replied *Thank you*. Clay got out of the car, grabbed his bag, and went inside.

Logan had squashed his first impulse to get in his car and follow Clay. It didn't make sense to chase him down. Clay obviously didn't want to talk to him right then. And maybe after what had happened in that guest room, they needed to take a moment apart to just breathe. Rather than running after him, he sent him an easy, no pressure text, letting Clay know that he was there for him. Logan turned to go back into the house. Although the party was still going, he was headed back up to his solitary balcony. But when he walked through the front door, he came face to face with Ryan. He was standing there with an inviting smile on his face and a bottle of Jack Daniels in his hand. Trent, a guy he knew from the BDSM scene, was with him. Ryan extended the bottle of Jack towards Logan.

"Hey, Logan. Would you like to and come and play with us … Sir?"

59

Logan looked at the two men standing there. He reached out and took the bottle of Jack from Ryan. "Do I look like an animal? Go get me a glass. With ice." Logan smirked as Ryan rushed off to do as he'd said. Logan looked at the handsome young red head. "Still don't have a Master, Trent?"

Trent shook his head. "No."

"So what are you doing here with Ryan? Shouldn't you be putting yourself in a position to let Doms know you're available?"

Trent shrugged. "I guess. But there's nothing wrong with having a little fun while I'm unattached, right?

Logan didn't say anything to that. Ryan walked back up with a glass full of ice and Logan took it from him. "Let's go," he said. He led them not to the room he'd just been in with Clay but to Carlos's small study. He walked casually so as not to draw attention to the fact that he was going off with two men. Once inside, he sat on the edge of the desk. "Trent, take a seat." He waited until Trent sat down in one of the brown leather armchairs before he turned to Ryan. "Kneel," he commanded.

Ryan followed his order slowly, looking as though he wanted to say something. Logan poured himself some of the whiskey. He set the bottle down before taking a sip. Finally, he spoke. "Let's ignore the fact that you pulled this stunt in public when you know that I'm not out. I thought I told you earlier today that I wasn't interested."

"Yes, but you shouldn't have to be alone tonight. I just thought Trent and I could make you feel better. Make you forget about ... him."

Logan took another drink. "Is that right? This is all for me? It has nothing to do with you trying to become my submissive?"

Ryan had the grace to flush. "No. I mean ... yes. You know I want to be yours, Sir."

Logan set the glass down. "Don't you think if I wanted you for my own, I would have made that happen by now? Before I got with Clay, I played with you off and on for what, two years? And in all that time, I never once offered you my collar. Does that tell you anything, Ryan?"

The embarrassed flush on Ryan's face deepened to a dark, angry red. "That's because all that time, you were thinking about Foster! I saw you always watching him. And sometimes even with me, he was all you would talk about! You think I didn't know that you were wishing you were with him instead of me? It made me mad. Clay wasn't even a submissive, he barely even gave you the time of day outside of work, and still you wanted him."

Logan wasn't bothered by Ryan's little outburst. Everything he said was true. But Logan had been very clear that it was just a casual play session with Ryan every time he called him or Ryan had come to him. Those times were just for them to take the physical pleasure they needed from each other and nothing more. He crossed his arms over his chest. "So if you knew all that, why do you keep thinking that I'll take you as my own?"

"Because you always called me when you needed release! No one else, I know."

Logan sighed. That had been more about not wanting to sleep around with a bunch of people than any desire to collar Ryan, but he didn't say that out loud. "What about when I collared Clay?"

"I honestly didn't think it would last," Ryan answered with a shrug. "And I thought once you got him out of your system, you would see I was the one for you."

Logan snorted. Clay would never be out of his system. He looked down at Ryan. "Ryan, I'm sorry you thought something more would develop between us. You did a real good job of pretending to be on board with our casual relationship. But this time I need you to listen up and really understand what I'm saying to you. As long as there is even the *slightest* chance that Clay will be mine again, I will do everything I can to get him back. And if he comes back to me, I have no intention of ever being with anyone else."

Logan stood up. "Clay is the only one I want." He glanced at Trent who was looking extremely uncomfortable. "Not Trent." He looked back down at Ryan. "Not you. No one but Clay. So not only do I find your play to entice me with liquor and the promise of a threesome extremely forward and unattractive in a submissive, I also find it completely useless because I have zero interest. *I do not want you.* Do you understand that?" Ryan had tears in his eyes but he nodded. Logan ignored the evidence of Ryan's emotions. He hated to be so harsh, but he knew if he offered Ryan even the slightest amount of comfort, it would undo everything he'd just said. "Good. Now both of you need to leave."

Ryan immediately jumped to his feet and stormed out. Trent got up slowly.

"I'm sorry, Logan. Ryan made it seem as though you would be open to the idea of us spending a night together."

Logan wasn't angry with Trent. He knew he hadn't been a part of Ryan's scheming. "Don't worry about it. But, Trent, I hope you'll take this advice. If you want to belong to someone, you need to stop listening to Ryan and going along with what he says. No Dom will take the right kind of interest in you if all they see is you following his influence."

Trent smiled slightly. "Thank you, Logan. You're right."

Logan clapped him on the shoulder reassuringly and Trent turned to go. But just as he was reaching for the doorknob, the door flew open and Carlos burst in. Logan looked at his friend in surprise. "What the hell?"

"Tiffany told me she saw you go off with Ryan and Trent." Carlos glanced around the room as if he was expecting to see Ryan hiding behind some furniture.

Logan looked and saw Tiffany peeping around the door frame. He laughed. "And so ... what? You're here to join in?"

"Don't be a smart ass, Logan. I'm here to make sure you don't do something you'll regret."

Logan laughed again before he said goodbye to Trent. The poor guy left the room looking relieved. Logan headed back over to the desk to pick up his drink.

"Come on in, Tiffany. I promise there's nothing happening in here that Carlos doesn't want you to see."

He took his seat on the edge of the desk again, smiling at his friends as he sipped the smooth whiskey. "Carlos, I just got finished fucking that sub of mine, as you so romantically put it. And I'm determined to get him back. So why would either of you think I'd have a threesome with those two?"

Carlos sat down in the wing chair and pulled Tiffany onto his lap. "What were we supposed to think when you went off alone with them and a bottle of whiskey? Besides, when you got here, you said you accepted that Clay didn't want to be with you anymore."

Logan nodded. "True. I came in here with Ryan to set him straight once and for all. But as far as what I said earlier, you can forget that. That was just me being a pathetic loser. I'm not giving up so easily. Clay is mine. I know it and he knows it. I may have made some dumb mistakes both before and after we broke up. But we're going to sit down and talk this out."

Carlos smiled and kissed Tiffany's cheek. "Never give up, huh, Logan?"

Logan smiled back. "Damn straight."

60

A week later, Logan was struggling to maintain his positive attitude on winning Clay back. He'd sent Clay a few texts asking if he wanted to talk. He called him once. He approached him at work once. But so far, he hadn't convinced Clay to really talk to him. Clay always replied to his texts with one word responses, *Thanks. Okay. Soon.* Clay did answer his call, agreeing that they needed to talk and that he *wanted* to talk, but Logan couldn't get him to give a definitive answer on when. And when they spoke at work, Clay had been skittish, at first seeming as though he were ready to talk, but then quickly backtracking and leaving.

By this point, Logan was frustrated. He wasn't going to give up but he didn't want to cross the line and come off as harassing Clay either. What he *wanted* to do was find Clay, drag him off, tie him up if he needed to, and force him to talk things out with him. But he worried that might freak him out even more. Especially since he'd run off after their crazy angry sex at Carlos's. Instead, he planned to find Clay and *gently* tell him he'd be waiting whenever he was ready. Logan dug his thumbs into his temples in frustration. And if that didn't work after a few days? He'd go with Plan B and chain Clay to his bed.

****

"Corporal Foster. How are you?"

Clay was in the cafeteria, grabbing a sandwich when he the heard slow Texas drawl behind him. He grabbed a napkin and fork before he turned around. "Doin' good, Detective Roberts. How 'bout yourself?"

"Well, I've only had one person ask me if my job is just like one of those crime shows on TV, so I guess it's a good day."

Clay laughed. Detective Sam Roberts worked in crime scene investigation. Clay paid for his meal and went to find a table. He didn't say anything when Sam joined him. The tall detective had made a point to speak to him several times over the past week. He'd been coming around Clay, making small talk and doing a little bit of flirting. Clay wasn't stupid. Roberts had seen him at the BDSM club the night he'd gone with Logan so he knew he'd been Logan's sub. He must have figured out they were done and was making his play.

Clay didn't encourage Sam, but he hadn't told him to fuck off either. He couldn't help thinking he needed to see if he would have the same reactions to another Dom that he did with Logan. He'd gotten deeply involved with Logan so damn fast and he never stopped to think about what he was experiencing. He wanted to know if the intensity he felt when submitting was because something in him wanted to submit, or because something in him wanted to submit to *Logan*. He needed to understand that a little better before he talked to him. He figured the only way he could find that out was to be with another Dom. Sam was clearly interested in him. And Clay felt Roberts could be a good candidate for him to explore. He was tall and good looking with skin a healthy tan from the sun, faded denim blue eyes and dark hair touched by silver at the temples. Sam's eyes flicked over his shoulder but before he could turn to see what he was looking at, the big man touched his hand.

"Would you like to go out with me tonight, Clay?"

Clay hesitated for only a second. If he wanted to find out the answer to his question, there was the opportunity to do so. "Yeah, that'd be great."

"I'd like the chance to talk to you privately so why don't we—"

Sam abruptly stopped talking and stood up. Clay knew without turning around that it was because Logan was behind him. He was proven right when Logan stepped up and stood toe to toe with Roberts.

"What are you doing here, Roberts?"

Roberts looked down his nose at Logan. "Not that it's any concern of yours, but Clay here has just agreed to go out with me tonight."

Logan's nostrils flared in anger as he bowed up to Sam. "He's not going anywhere with you."

Sam smirked. "Is that right? I don't see your mark of ownership anywhere on him. So I don't think you're in a position to say anything about who he spends time with."

Clay saw the rage come over Logan's face and knew things were about to get ugly. Logan shoved Sam hard, making him stumble back. But Roberts wasn't cowed and his hand clenched into a fist.

"Don't put your hands on me again, Pierce."

"Listen up you stupid redneck—"

Clay jumped up and cut Logan off. "Jesus fucking Christ! Are you two kidding me? Is this the part where I say, 'Easy, boys, there's enough of me to go around?'" Both men turned and looked at him, their faces still hard with aggression. "Would you guys cut this out before you embarrass me anymore than you already have?" Looking around, Clay could see several officers avidly watching their little drama.

Clay spoke quietly to Logan. "Logan, Sam's right. I'm not yours so you don't get to say who I spend time with."

Logan's lips parted as though he wanted to speak but he didn't say anything. Instead, an awful look of hurt and sadness bled across his face. It made Clay feel like shit and he hurt for Logan deep in his chest. But he had to do it. He looked up at Sam. "I'll find you after my shift." Then he left. He didn't bother to bring his food with him. He wasn't hungry anymore anyway.

Logan looked at Sam. He was shaking he was so furious. "Don't you fucking dare hurt him."

Sam smirked again. "It ain't your concern what I do with sweet little Clay. Besides, we both know if he didn't want to be hurt just a little bit, he wouldn't have agreed to go out with me."

Logan reigned in his urge to punch Roberts in the jaw. "Hurt him and I will hurt you so bad you'll wish you'd never laid eyes on him."

Logan stormed off, his blood pumping furiously through his veins. He was so damn pissed off he could barely see straight. He needed to work out his anger and aggression somehow or he was going to fucking explode. Back in the pen, he came across Carlos sitting at his desk. "Come spar with me."

Carlos looked up at him. "Oh fuck. What happened?"

Logan forced the words out past the tight ball of hurt and anger in his throat. "Clay is going out with Sam tonight."

Carlos looked dumbfounded. "And you're going to let him?"

Logan clenched and unclenched his fists. "He's not mine, Carlos. I can't stop him from doing what he wants," he said, almost choking on the words.

Carlos closed his eyes and sighed. "Let's go. But please remember that I'm not Roberts once you have those gloves on."

Logan nodded tightly. He needed to destroy something. Since that wasn't an option, he'd settle for knocking Carlos around on the mats.

****

Clay finished the last of his steak. They were at Sam's house, eating out on his enclosed patio. Sam wasn't out either so they decided not to go to a restaurant. He felt a flash of annoyance when Sam first suggested they eat at his house. He was getting tired of hiding who he was. Clay watched as Sam took the last bite of his steak then neatly wiped his mouth.

"Did you enjoy your dinner, Clay?"

"Yeah, it was good. Thanks."

Sam smiled. "You're welcome." He sat back in his chair and gave Clay a long look. "You're real far away over there. Come and sit by me."

Clay recognized the order in Sam's request. He didn't feel that urge to obey like he did with Logan, but he still got up and moved his chair until he was right next to Sam.

"Tell me, Clay. How'd you get into the scene?"

Clay shrugged. "I was seeing Logan. After a few weeks, he told me he was into BDSM. He asked if I wanted to try it and I said yes."

Sam raised an eyebrow. "Just like that?"

"I tend to jump into things feet first," Clay answered.

"I'll admit that I've been attracted to you for a long time, Clay. I just didn't realize you were open to the scene. If I had, I might have asked you out sooner."

Clay didn't say anything in response. He couldn't help but think that if Sam had been the one to ask him, he might not have said yes.

"So tell me, Clay. Did you enjoy submitting?"

"Yes." He was honest but he didn't elaborate.

Sam traced his fingers over the back of Logan's hand. "Hmmm… I'd like to see that. I bet you're beautiful restrained and awaiting your Master's pleasure."

Clay remembered Logan tying him up and telling him how beautiful he was but he pushed the thought away. He was there with Sam. He didn't need to be thinking about Logan right then.

Sam's fingers circled his wrist. "I want to kiss you, Clay. Will you let me?"

This time, it was Clay's turn to look at Sam. When he did, he didn't see anything but open and honest desire. And Clay did feel a slight attraction to him. He nodded, thinking that could be his chance to understand a little more about his feeling of submission.

Sam stood, pulling him up as well. He pressed his hand into the small of Clay's back, pressing their bodies together lightly. Sam's lips were warm as they touched his. Clay parted his almost immediately, not waiting for Sam to get to that point. He felt like he wanted to hurry things along so he could get his answers. Sam took advantage of what he offered, sliding his tongue into Clay's mouth. Clay rubbed his tongue against Sam's, feeling a slight tingle of desire. But ... he couldn't help but think of how eager he'd been to accept Logan's kisses. And of the pleasure he felt in allowing Logan to dominate his mouth. He didn't feel any of that with Sam.

Clay tried to stop thinking of Logan and accept the pleasure of Sam's kiss. The man was a good kisser, taking his time. But when Sam grasped him by the back of the neck Clay froze, wanting to pull away. He tried to relax and when Sam told him to put his arms around him, he did. But it felt awkward and uncomfortable to hold on to him. Sam must have sensed something was off because he pulled back from their kiss and looked at him as though he were searching for answers of his own.

"If I told you to kneel for me, right now, would you do it?"

Clay blinked. "Why? That's not necessary for me to do right now, is it?"

Sam chuckled ruefully. "That answers my question." He went and sat back down in his chair, leaving Clay standing there confused. He took a sip of his drink before he looked back at him. "Clay, I don't know why you and Sergeant Pierce are apart. But you can't submit to anyone else when your soul has already found its Master."

61

Logan sat on the couch, flipping through the channels. He was looking for something, anything, that would hold his attention and take his mind off the fact that Clay was out with another Dom right then. His doorbell rang. He was tempted to ignore it but figured he might as well take care of whoever it was. It might at least give him a few minutes distraction. When he went over and looked through the peephole, he saw Ryan standing there. He opened the door in annoyed surprise.

"Really, Ryan? So nothing I said to you at the party stuck in your head?"

Ryan raised his hands up in a defensive posture. "Hear me out before you yell and slam the door in my face. You said as long as there was a chance you could get Clay back then you wouldn't think about being with anyone else. But I know Clay is out with Sam right now. I figure that's got to be a pretty clear sign that he's moved on."

Logan's jaw clenched in anger. He didn't want to admit it, but Ryan might be right. "That doesn't mean that I want to be with you, Ryan."

"I know. But I know you're upset. I saw you boxing with Carlos. And I remember that you don't like to be alone for too long."

Ryan was right again. He remembered all those times Logan called him to his home because he got fed up with being alone and the need to dominate someone became too strong for him to ignore. "So? What's your point?"

"My point is that I could be with you tonight. You could take some of your anger out on me."

Logan braced his hand on the door frame. He was actually considering letting Ryan in. To just lose himself in punishing him so that he could forget about everything for a couple of hours. After all, Clay was out on a date with Sam fucking Roberts.

Ryan sensed he was about to give in because he came closer and touched Logan's hand. And suddenly Logan remembered Clay's smart ass remark back from their first fight. *I don't care how mad or upset or* discouraged *you get. If you're not sleeping with me, your new boyfriend is your right hand. Understand?* Logan smiled at the memory.

"I'm sorry, Ryan, but the answer is no. I might be discouraged right now. But I'm not willing to end things with Clay for sure by sleeping with someone else."

Ryan sighed and shook his head. "I hope Clay knows how lucky he is."

Logan laughed. "Trust me. It's definitely the other way around." Ryan just shook his head again and stepped off the porch, heading to his car.

Logan watched him go for a moment. He didn't quite understand why Ryan was so determined to be with him. He was about to close the door when he noticed a dark car parked a few houses down. Looking closer, he realized Clay was standing next to it. When he saw Logan looking at him, he turned, about to get back in the vehicle. But Logan wasn't going to let him go that easy. He jumped off the porch, forgetting that he was only in his boxers.

"Clay, wait!"

Clay stopped and slowly turned around.

"You're not going to make me shout down the street, are you?" Clay hesitated for a moment before he walked up the street to his driveway. When Clay reached him, he tried not to be obvious as he looked him over in the light from the porch to make sure he was alright. He couldn't help it. He knew Sam's predilection for doling out pain.

"Do you want to come in?" He stepped onto the porch, holding the door open. Clay didn't move. He just looked Logan up and down. Logan looked down at himself. He'd forgotten again that he was naked except for a pair of boxer briefs. "I can throw on some clothes. It'll only take me a second." Logan wanted to grab Clay and pull him into his arms but he was determined not to give him any reason to run off. Logan kept his voice soft and calm as he entreated again, "Come in, Clay." Clay came up the porch steps and into the house without saying a word. Logan closed the door behind him. "Take a seat while I get dressed."

Logan tried to keep his cool as he rushed upstairs to put on the first pair of sweats and t-shirt he found. But his heart was racing and his hands were shaking. Clay had come to see him! He thrust his feet into his sweats and yanked his tee over his head. He knew he was rushing, but Clay looked like he was ready to bolt. He had a feeling if he took too long, Clay wouldn't be there when he went back downstairs. When Logan was dressed, he joined Clay at the kitchen table.

"What's up?"

Clay rested his folded forearms on the table. He'd gotten some of the answers he wanted after his time with Sam that evening. He'd been attracted to the other man. And at another time, he might have thought it was fun to have a little bit of kinky sex with Sam. But that was all he felt. He didn't feel like he *needed* to submit to Sam the way he felt with Logan almost from the beginning. And that told him just how much he felt for Logan. It wasn't just any Dom that could make him feel that way. Sam's comment that he couldn't submit to anyone else if he'd already found his Master had been a little dramatic, but it did help him to realize just how much he wanted to be with Logan. So he quit running and now he was there.

"I wanted to talk to you."

Logan smiled. "I'm glad to hear that. You know I've wanted to talk to you."

Clay laughed a little at that before quieting again. "Here's the thing, Logan. I miss you."

Joy burst in Logan's chest and he reached over to touch Clay's hand encouragingly. "I miss you too." Clay pulled his hand away.

"I miss you and I want to be with you, but I don't want you to swallow me up. You overwhelmed me before. Right now, I just want to spend time with you."

Logan was determined for them both to be very clear with each other about everything. "What do you mean by that, Clay?"

Clay sighed. "I want to spend time together. I want us to talk about what went wrong. But I don't think we should have sex yet." He looked at Logan before his gaze flicked away. "And I don't think we should continue with our Dom/sub relationship." He looked back at him. "For right now at least. Is that okay?"

Logan nodded. "Of course. I want you to be comfortable, Clay. But most importantly, I want us to work things out so we can be together again. Both of us did a pretty poor job of communicating before."

Clay nodded. "Yeah. That's true."

Logan braced his elbow on the table. "Why don't you tell me what made you freak out that night?"

Clay had to laugh. Freak out was the perfect way to explain his actions. "Going into subspace played a big part in that. And I wasn't ready for how I felt afterwards."

"I'm sorry. I should have prepared you better. Told you what to expect. That was a huge mistake on my part." They were both quiet for a moment until Logan asked him a question. "You didn't like the way it felt?"

"No! I loved it. It felt so good, Logan. *You* made me feel good. But afterwards, I couldn't help comparing it to being high or thinking that it felt so good I would crave the feeling all the time. And I just ... I don't know. It felt wrong."

Logan was quiet for a moment. "It might help if you tell me a little more about your addiction problem."

Clay took a deep breath. He didn't want to, but he needed to come clean. That part of his past had played a big part in his decision to leave Logan. It wouldn't be fair to either of them if he didn't get it out. He wasn't sure where to start so he just blurted out the worst of it. "I was responsible for my brother's death."

Logan's eyes went wide with shock. "What?"

Clay ran a hand over his head. "I was a typical spoiled rich kid. My parents weren't that involved in our lives so we got away with doing a lot of shit. My brother, Alex, was only a year younger than me and we were both on the swim team. When we hung out with our friends we'd do coke and drink. Just get wasted and do dumb shit with no sense of possible consequences." Clay stopped for moment. Thinking back to that time in his life was rough. And he was embarrassed to admit to Logan what a waste of space he'd been. He could see that Logan was anxious to hear the rest of the story but he didn't push him. Clay was thankful for that.

"One night we wanted to go swimming, but our parents had already closed our pool for the year. We were all out of control as usual and someone came up with the idea to sneak into a neighbor's pool. Everybody laughed and jumped up to run over and hop the fence. Alex reached the pool first and dove in. But he was high and not paying attention and dove into the shallow end." Clay stopped again. Even after all these years he could barely stand to think of the night he'd lost his brother. Logan touched his hand and this time Clay didn't pull back.

"You don't have to finish this story if you don't want."

Clay looked into Logan's caring and sympathetic eyes and shook his head. "No. I need to finish this." Clay gathered his courage to tell the rest. "Alex hit the bottom head first. I hadn't made it over the fence when it happened and the two who were on that side didn't realize anything was wrong at first. One of them screamed Alex's name and the sound of terror in their voice when they said my brother's name sobered me up immediately. I stopped fucking around, jumped the fence and into the pool. By the time I pulled Alex out he was already unconscious. I started CPR while one of my friends ran to get help." Clay swallowed hard, emotion thick in his throat. "We tried, the paramedics tried … but we couldn't save him." He looked down at the table. "I wish I could say I got clean right then, but I didn't. Instead I quit the swim team and fell even more heavily into drugs and alcohol. I was a wreck and almost didn't graduate on time."

Logan whispered a curse under his breath and squeezed his fingers. "So what did get you clean?"

"Graduation day came up. I'd told my parents I didn't want any kind of party or trip and I wasn't planning to walk across the stage. Then one day I went into Alex's room. I sat in there looking around at his posters of the Navy. He'd wanted to be a Navy Seal. I realized that Alex's dream, that *life* for Alex was gone and it was fucking selfish of me to keep wasting mine. It could just as easily have been me that crashed head first into that pool. I decided at that moment to get myself clean. It was hard, even with rehab. Once I'd kicked those habits I enlisted in the Navy, partly in Alex's honor and partly because I knew I needed the structure to finally get my shit together." Clay finally looked back at Logan. "I haven't had any illegal substances or alcohol in my body since that day in Alex's room."

"And when you went into subspace the feeling of losing control reminded you of how you used to feel."

It hadn't been a question but Clay answered him anyway. "Yes."

"Clay, I've never had a problem with substance abuse or experienced a tragedy that terrible, so I'm not going to say I completely understand how you felt. But I ask you this. When we go out on a call and the adrenaline is pumping, don't you feel really good about it?"

Clay thought about how he felt after some of their missions. When they'd done their job, bringing down whatever scum they were after, he felt like he was on top of the world. And that feeling of euphoria sometimes lasted for hours. "Yes."

"Well, you probably love that feeling and look forward to experiencing it again, but you don't crave it or feel like you can't function without it, right?"

Clay answered yes again.

"I'm not saying that going into subspace is the same as that. But I am saying it was your own mind and body that made you feel that way in both situations not anything you took. So you're no more likely to become addicted to the things I do to you than you are to the things you do for our job. Does that make sense? And you're safe with me when you let go and drift. You're not out of control or at risk of doing anything dangerous."

Clay nodded. After he calmed down, he'd had similar thoughts. It was just such a shock for him that he'd needed time to come to grips with it.

Logan smiled. "I'm not trying to solve that problem for you right here and now or trivialize your loss, but I just want to give you something to think about. You beat that problem a long time ago, Clay. You're not the person who lets his impulses rule him anymore."

Clay was relieved that he'd finally told Logan how he felt and was happy Logan didn't make light of the situation. He understood Clay's problem with going into subspace and tried to help him relate it to something positive in his life. But Clay wasn't ready to talk about that yet. "Thank you, Logan. I'll think about what you said. Like I said, I just wasn't ready for that and … well, shit, it scared the fuck out of me, to be honest."

Logan squeezed his fingers again. "I'm sorry I wasn't there for you like you needed me to be while you were struggling. I should have checked to see if you had any triggers and I'm ashamed that I didn't." This time it was Logan who looked down at the table for a long moment. "Was there anything else about that night that bothered you?"

Clay started to shrug then stopped himself. He needed to admit to Logan the things that bothered him. Otherwise, they would never stand a chance of moving on. He looked Logan in the eye. "I don't think I was ready … No, I definitely wasn't ready to call you Master." Clay saw a hurt and disappointed look cross Logan's face before he hid it.

Logan leaned back in his chair. "Okay. I wasn't expecting to hear that."

Clay squeezed Logan's fingers, repeating the words Logan once said to him. "Don't hide from me, Logan." When Logan's lips curled in a small smile, Clay continued. "Tell me what you're thinking."

Logan sighed. "I won't lie, Clay. It hurts to hear that. I thought you accepted your submission to me."

"I did. But you *know* there is a big difference between calling you Sir and calling you Master. It means something more, something deeper. It felt like I was giving up so much to you. And even though I loved it and it felt right, it also felt wrong, like I must be weak to allow myself to call another man Master." Clay laughed softly and scrubbed his hands down his face. "You probably think I'm crazy for not being able to make up my mind on that."

Logan shook his head. "No, I don't. It's not easy submitting, Clay, especially for someone as strong as you. I should have seen that you were conflicted and helped you. And I shouldn't have asked you to call me Master. So that's my fault too."

"No, it's not just your fault. I could have told you how I felt about calling you Master."

Logan scoffed in disbelief. "Not while you were flying like that, you couldn't have. I shouldn't have asked you then." Logan wouldn't look at him and a frown turned down the corners of his firm mouth. "I'm sorry, Clay."

Clay felt bad. Logan was hurting and shouldering all the blame for their problems himself. "Logan, I could have spoken up before. You told me to never hide what I was feeling from you and I did. So I'm just as much to blame in this."

Logan stroked his fingers over Clay's arm for a moment before he looked at him with somber hazel eyes. "But I was your Dom. I should have noticed you were struggling. I wasn't a very good Dom to you, was I?"

"Don't say that, Logan. You always took good care of me."

Logan smiled softly. "That's because I loved doing it." He sighed and looked away. "As much as I hate to admit it, I went too fast for you. I was so caught up in having you as my own, I rarely stopped to think. You were just … so goddamn beautiful and intense in your submission and I had wanted you for so long that I had to experience everything with you. Everything that I'd been dreaming of for months."

Clay's heart raced as Logan looked straight at him.

"I can see why you felt like I swallowed you up, because that's exactly what I wanted to do. I wanted to take you and lock you away with me so I could indulge myself in dominating you in every way that I'd imagined. And I loved the way you trembled in my arms after your release, Clay. If anyone was going to become addicted to something, it would have been me with the way I craved having you turn to me for safety and comfort." Logan took a deep breath and exhaled slowly. "I did overwhelm you and I'm sorry for that."

Clay was caught up in the impassioned regret of Logan's admission. Logan was right, they had gone too fast. But after listening to him and admitting to himself how he felt in submitting to Logan, he couldn't really blame him. Clay looked down. "Don't take on all the blame for us going too fast, Logan. I've never felt anything like what I felt when I was with you. And the more you gave me, the more I wanted."

After Clay finished talking, they both sat there quietly without looking at each other. Finally, Clay looked back up and tried to lighten the mood. "So this was a pretty intense talk. Are we capable of doing anything lightly?"

Logan laughed a little. "This *has* been a heavy talk. We should stop now before we're listening to sad country music and crying into our drinks. We can talk about everything else later. But one last thing. I didn't do anything with Ryan. He showed up at my door and offered but I turned him away."

"I know. I mean, for a second I thought you might have been with him and that's why I started to leave. But when you called my name, I knew you hadn't." Clay cleared his throat. "I'm sorry for going out with Sam tonight. I needed—" Logan cut him off before he could finish.

"I don't care, Clay. Whatever happened or didn't happen doesn't matter. All I care about is that you're here with me now."

Logan caressed his arm again. As they looked at each other, Clay knew Logan wanted to kiss him. He didn't even hesitate before he gave his answer. "Yes." Logan leaned closer, his hand coming up to cup his cheek, his lips brushing lightly over Clay's.

"Thank you for coming to see me tonight, Clay," he whispered. "You don't know how happy you've made me."

"You're welcome," he whispered back. He closed his eyes as Logan softly pressed his lips to his. When Logan kissed him, he felt the biggest sense of relief. He didn't have to keep fighting and avoiding his feelings any more.

Logan kissed Clay sweetly, not asking for anything more than to express his love. He was beyond happy in that moment. Clay had come back to him and they were going to work things out.

62

Clay was over at Logan's again. They decided it would be best if they stayed in and talked through Clay's issues with submitting. He was happy they were doing it. Logan never made him feel pressured into anything, but like they both admitted, they'd gone very fast before. Clay was new to being in a D/s relationship and he needed time to come to grips with the dynamic between the two of them.

Clay sat in the armchair as they talked, just like every other night since they decided to work things out. Logan was on the couch, the open space next to him a clear invitation for Clay to join him whenever he chose. So far, Clay hadn't made that choice. It's not that he didn't trust Logan. He did. And, of course, he trusted himself. But he knew how explosive things were between the two of them. He figured it was best not to risk it until they'd truly solved all their problems. He just admitted he'd been embarrassed when he called Logan 'Sir' in front of Q.

Logan looked slightly confused. "Quan already knows about that part of our relationship. Why was that so bad?"

Clay lips twitched. Logan was being a block head. "It's not a problem for you because you wanted everyone to know I was yours."

He saw Logan's mouth tighten and knew it was because of his use of the past tense. So he wasn't surprised when Logan deliberately used the present tense when he responded.

"And you *don't* want everyone to know that you're mine?"

Clay had to look away for a moment. He thought of how much he hated to take his collar off and of having to ignore the feeling of wanting to submit to Logan no matter where they were. But that wasn't the point and he wouldn't let Logan steamroll over him on this. He looked back at him and spoke with a hint of warning in his voice. "Logan…"

Logan sighed and slouched down slightly on the couch. "I'm doing it again, aren't I?"

"Trying to swallow me up? Yep."

Logan rolled his head over to look at him. "You did a good job of stopping me just now."

Clay paused for a moment. A single word from him and Logan backed down. Was that all it would take? He remembered his realization that Logan would do anything to keep him happy after Logan had apologized for the drama with Officer Bennett. Had he held more power in their relationship than he knew? That was something he'd have to think about on his own. For now, he just answered, "We haven't come out to the department yet." Clay shook his head. "Although, with the way we've been acting, it's probably a moot point. However, it's important to me that we keep that part of our relationship private. I think that's something we both need to work on. Tiffany told me once that sometimes it's just through sheer force of will that she doesn't let the true nature of their relationship show. We both need to practice that and remember the boundaries we set." Clay coughed lightly. "If we go back to that, that is."

Logan looked at him from beneath lowered lashes but he didn't address his last remark. "We'll work on that together."

Clay's throat was a little tight as he answered. "That sounds fair." *Jesus*. How did Logan affect him so much with just a single look? He changed the subject, stopping the conversation before it got too heavy like he always did. He still hadn't brought up the biggie that was weighing on his mind. He would get to it. Later.

"Let's watch some cop shows." Logan turned the TV on and flipped until flashing blue lights and a doped up looking criminal filled the screen.

"It's always funnier watching this stuff on TV than when we're the ones taking somebody down."

Logan rolled his eyes. "Maybe because we're not the ones on guard that some wacko is about to try to take one of us out."

Clay snorted. "You might be right." They watched quietly after that, only talking to comment on the stupidity of the criminal. When the episode ended, Clay stood up to go. "I'd better head home to get some sleep." That was a joke. He wasn't sleeping much, but he wasn't going to tell Logan that. It was his problem to take care of and he knew if he mentioned it, Logan would want to try and help him.

Logan stood up too. "Alright, Clay. I'll see you tomorrow."

He came closer and Clay's heart rate sped up. He didn't know why he got so worked up when Logan kissed him goodnight. But he did, his pulse pounding every time. Logan stroked his back, pulling him up against his broad chest.

"Good night, Clay."

"Good night."

Logan kissed him, pressing their lips together lightly. He didn't part his lips and Logan didn't try to get him to do so. It felt good to be held against Logan's warmth, feeling his heart beating just as rapidly as his own. Logan kissed him softly again and again until Clay couldn't stop a low moan from escaping him. He wrapped his arms around Logan's back, curling his fingers and pressing them tight against the hard muscles there. He wanted to open for him, to let Logan dominate his mouth like he always had before. Instead, he forced himself to pull away. He saw the tension in Logan's clenched jaw. But Logan didn't try to stop him. Clay said goodnight one more time and left.

****

The next night, Logan was on the couch waiting for Clay to come over again. When the doorbell rang, he went over to open the door. It was Clay and he looked exhausted. Logan stepped back to let him in. "Are you alright?"

"Yeah, it was just a little tiring being stuck in that crawl space for so long today. The fucking heat didn't help either."

They worked a bust and buy earlier that day. Clay and Q had been tasked with entering the building early and keeping an eye on the undercover Narcotics officer who was inside alone with the mid-level heroin pusher. The only way they were able to do it was to hide in the ceiling crawl space of the old house. But Logan didn't think that was all that was bothering him. Clay looked worn out. So when Clay went to collapse in the armchair, Logan took control of the situation. "No. You're not sitting in that chair tonight."

Clay looked over at him in surprise. "What?"

Logan pulled him away from the chair and with a slight push, got him walking towards the staircase. Clay protested but he kept going until they were in Logan's bedroom. "You're going to get in the bed and be comfortable tonight." He gently pushed Clay so he was sitting on the edge of his bed then Logan kneeled down to take off his shoes.

"Logan …"

Logan looked up at the tired man above him. "Just so you can relax, Clay." After a moment, Clay nodded and Logan continued untying his laces. Once Logan removed both his shoes, Clay scooted over to the center of the bed. Kicking off his own shoes, he joined him and grabbed the remote. "What do you want to watch?"

Clay yawned. "We can watch that Iraq War show you were telling me about."

Logan wasn't surprised when a few minutes into the show, Clay slid down and laid his head on a pillow. And a few minutes after that, when he heard a light snoring, Logan smiled. Clay obviously needed sleep. He leaned over to turn off the lamp and turned the volume down low on the TV. Logan changed the channel. He wasn't that tired so he'd save the show to watch with Clay later on and watch baseball highlights instead. The sports casters started talking about the playoffs. He loved this time of year. End of summer baseball was always exciting, even if his team wasn't in the —.

63

Logan woke up slowly. He was curled around Clay, his back warm against Logan's front. In his half-asleep state, Logan didn't see anything wrong with that. He slipped his hand underneath Clay's shirt, caressing the soft skin of his belly. He wondered briefly why Clay had fallen asleep in his clothes but the thought went out of his head when Clay shifted, his ass pressing lightly against Logan's groin. His body hardened in response and he pressed a kiss to the nape of Clay's neck. Clay shifted again and Logan responded by smoothing his hand up Clay's chest to brush his thumb across a nipple, feeling it tighten under his touch.

Clay gave a sleepy little moan. "Logan, we shouldn't be doing this."

Logan trailed his lips along Clay's neck, breathing in his sleep-warmed scent. "Mmm… why not?"

"We said we would wait. But if that's not what you want …"

Clay gasped as Logan tugged at his nipple ring.

"I'll do whatever you want. Shit! Logan … we shouldn't."

Logan came fully awake at hearing Clay struggle to ignore his desire to submit and stay on track with what they'd agreed. Logan snatched his hand from underneath Clay's shirt and sat up. "Clay, I'm sorry. I wasn't all the way awake."

Clay rolled over onto his back and looked up at him. "That's okay." He stretched. "I can't believe I fell asleep. I guess I needed that more than anything else."

"You don't have to come over when you're tired, Clay."

Clay shrugged. "It's not a problem. But I'd better go."

He didn't move to sit up and Logan waited to see if there was anything else he wanted to say. Clay gave him a lazy smile.

"Since I didn't get my good night kiss, do I get a good morning kiss?"

Logan smiled too and leaned down, kissing him lightly. Clay softly brushed his fingers across his cheek.

"Give me a real kiss, Logan."

Logan clenched his jaw tightly. He didn't think that was a good idea. They were in bed and his body was hard and desperate for his lover from waking up with him in his arms. But as he looked into Clay's blue eyes, still soft and heavy lidded with sleep, he couldn't say no. Besides, what was the point of being a Dom if he couldn't control himself?

He slid back down until he was lying next to Clay. Cupping the back of his head, he pulled Logan closer. This time, when their lips met, Logan stroked his tongue over Clay's until they parted. He swept inside, kissing him deeply for the first time in weeks. Clay moaned, his tongue rubbing against his. The kiss went on, growing hotter, Logan drawing gasps from Clay as he sucked and nibbled on his bottom lip.

Clay wrapped his arms around Logan's neck. Logan followed his body's natural inclination without even thinking. He slid on top of Clay, his hips resting against his lover's, Clay's thighs splitting wide to accept him between his legs.

Logan groaned as he felt Clay's hard shaft against his. He lightly pressed his hips down, groaning again when Clay pressed back. He did it again, and by the third time, Clay caught his rhythm, his hips rising so their shafts rubbed together. Logan told himself it was okay as long as they were only kissing and kept things light. He released Clay's lips to brush his mouth over his smooth jaw and further to kiss and tongue his throat.

Clay's leg shifted, drawing his attention. Logan ran his palm down the outside of Clay's shorts until he reached the hem. He teased his fingers just underneath and when Clay didn't protest, he stroked his hand up inside, just wanting to feel that warm thigh, promising himself he would stop as soon as he reached Clay's briefs. But Clay wasn't wearing any. His hand met nothing but naked skin until he reached that sweet indention between thigh and pelvis. Logan's palm tingled, knowing there was nothing between his hand and Clay's bare cock. It took all of his control not to grasp that hard flesh, but he couldn't resist briefly sweeping his thumb across it. Clay gasped and his hips jerked up.

Logan abandoned kissing Clay's neck and moved back to his mouth, kissing him hard. He slipped his hand around to cup and squeeze Clay's ass. He knew things were getting out of control. They'd gone past just kissing, their hips no longer pressing lightly, but instead moving faster and grinding their cocks together hard. But he could still keep things from going too far. He would stop … just not yet.

He pressed the tip of his finger into Clay's entrance. Clay winced and Logan whispered an apology in his ear. Quickly pulling his hand from under Clay's shorts, he sucked his fingers, getting them wet. Returning his hand to that warm skin, he slowly eased a finger inside Clay's channel. This time, Clay didn't complain. His body was relaxed and welcoming so Logan carefully added another finger. He pumped them in and out until Clay was gasping, rocking his ass back on his fingers and thrusting his hips up so their cocks continued to grind together.

Logan was hard and aching as Clay's ass flexed and squeezed around him. All he could think about was taking Clay, right here, right now. Clay was his. The tight heat gripping his fingers was his. He could fuck Clay if he wanted to. As soon as that last thought crossed his mind, he knew they'd gone too far. He pulled his fingers away.

"We need to stop," Logan said, breathing hard. But he looked down at the man beneath him and saw his lips parted, that sexy flush on his cheekbones. Clay's tongue darted out, licking his bottom lip, and sucking it into his mouth before he slowly released it.

"Fuck," Logan breathed out. "Just one more kiss…" He lowered his head again and took Clay's mouth fiercely, stroking his tongue in slow and deep. Clay responded to him, kissing him back with equal passion. Still, he managed to end their kiss then went to raise himself up. But Clay's leg came up and wrapped around his waist. Logan shuddered at the feel of that sweet thigh holding him captive. He needed to stop things now if he was going to be able to stop them at all.

"Baby, we need to stop." And he meant to. But somehow he found himself pressing his hands into the mattress to balance himself as he thrust his hips fast and hard, the bed creaking as Clay matched his movements. The friction he felt was amazing, but he wanted more. He hooked the fingers of one hand into the waistband of Clay's shorts. "Just want to feel you against me, okay? That's all."

Clay nodded, his chest heaving as he panted underneath him. "Okay."

Logan started pulling Clay's shorts down. Then he paused. He was kidding himself. There was no way he would be able to stop once he had Clay naked. He would be deep inside him, riding him hard until they both were shaking and shouting with their release.

"Damnit!" Logan threw himself off Clay, rolling to the side and onto his back. He rubbed his hand over his eyes, trying to bring himself back under control. That hardly helped so he grabbed himself at the base of his shaft, trying to rein in his urge to thrust inside of Clay. He looked over at him, seeing him clearly in the same aroused state. "I'm sorry. I let that get way out of hand."

"That's alright. I didn't exactly try to stop you."

Logan looked at Clay lying there. From the expression on his face, Logan knew that if he were to reach out and strip Clay naked Clay wouldn't stop him. But Logan didn't want Clay to make that decision with a mind clouded by passion. Of course he wanted Clay, wanted him so bad that he ached.

But he loved him more and would wait until Clay made the choice to fully resume their relationship on his own. He didn't want Clay to do anything he would regret later. Logan ignored his erection and got up from the bed.

"Why don't you head home to shower and change? Then we can meet for breakfast before we head in to the station."

"Sounds good," Clay said, getting up.

Logan waited for him as he put on his shoes. When he was ready, they went downstairs to the front door. Logan pulled Clay in for a quick kiss, but he jerked back.

"Don't!" he said in a shaky voice.

Logan looked at him in surprise.

Clay closed his eyes. "I'm close, Logan. If you touch me again …"

He didn't finish his sentence but Logan understood. He couldn't let Clay leave like that. "Clay, look at me." He waited until Clay's eyes slowly rose to meet his before he continued. "Let me take care of you, baby. I promise we won't do anything else."

When he got a nod in acceptance, Logan pressed Clay against the door. He gently tugged down his shorts and wrapped his fist around Clay's shaft. His lover cried out and thrust his hips forward. Logan groaned. He really was close. Clay's cockhead was already slick, his shaft pulsing in his grasp. He didn't waste any time teasing. Logan immediately started pumping his fist up and down, encouraging Clay to move with him. "Hold on to me, baby."

Clay wrapped his arms around Logan's neck, one leg winding around his waist as well. Logan buried his face in

Clay's neck. He cupped Clay's ass with his free hand, pulling him up as tight against him as he could get while still leaving room for his hand to move on Clay's shaft. He stroked faster, Clay's sweet moans driving him to make sure he helped his lover reach his pleasure. He squeezed his hand around Clay's cockhead and felt Clay start to shake.

"Logan … Can I … oh god! I'm coming!"

Logan's own cock was throbbing for release as he spoke against Clay's damp neck. "Go ahead, baby. Whenever you want." All of a sudden, Clay bit his neck hard. Logan's body jerked, slamming Clay back against the door. "Fuck! Harder, Clay!" Clay bit down even more, Logan tightened his grip on the straining shaft in his fist and Clay's hips pumped high and hard against him as he moaned with his orgasm. Logan loved the feel of Clay's release spilling thick and hot in his hand once more and he kept going until he coaxed forth every last drop.

Clay clung to him for a few moments before he dropped his leg and eased his arms from around Logan's neck. They stayed pressed against one another until their breathing returned to normal. Logan finally pulled away. He used his own shirt to wipe up the pearly drops of semen on Clay's stomach then tugged his shorts back into place. He stepped back. "You'd better hurry if you want to be able to have breakfast." He saw Clay look down at his obvious erection.

"Do you want me to …"

Logan cut him off. "No. I'm okay." He gave him one last kiss. "Go ahead and get cleaned up."

Once Clay was gone, Logan leaned his forehead against the door. *Christ.* The first time he got Clay relaxed enough to join him on the bed, he dry-humped him like a horny teenager and then jacked him off against the door. Not exactly the best way to show that he was on board with Clay's request to wait. It had taken everything he had not to pick him up and carry him back to the bed. He wanted nothing more than to be inside his lover again. Going by the stiff hard-on in his shorts, his body was not happy about his self-control. But that wasn't happening so he moved to the next available option.

He went upstairs to the bathroom and turned the shower on cold. The spray was icy and uncomfortable as it hit his skin, but it did nothing to stop his erection. Logan looked down at his hand and laughed to himself. Then he palmed his cock and started to stroke.

64

"I'm sorry. I let that get way out of hand."

Logan's voice echoed in Clay's head as he swam laps in his apartment's pool. He had the pool to himself so he swam at a relaxed pace, the familiar routine of stroke, kick, flip helping him to think. His response to Logan's apology had been absolute bullshit. Not trying to stop him? Hell, he'd been full on encouraging Logan. From the moment he asked Logan for a real kiss, he'd known what would happen. He knew what Logan was like when he woke in the mornings. How many times had he been awakened by Logan kissing and stroking him to readiness? How many times had he been awakened with Logan poised and ready to enter him? He knew what would happen when he asked for that kiss. The question was, why did he ask for it? Was he horny? Fuck yeah. But ... maybe he'd been testing Logan. He'd agreed to wait and even with as far as things had gone between them, Logan kept to that promise. He hadn't tried to push for anything more. He'd only given Clay pleasure, denying himself that same chance for release. Clearly Logan cared about making him happy. But

Clay already knew that too. Why, then, was Clay still holding back? He flipped and headed back across the pool on his last lap.

He had to be honest with himself. Even with the realization that he didn't have to let Logan run roughshod over him, that he had the power to guide Logan to do what he wanted, he just wasn't sure he wanted to be Logan's sub again. But he definitely wanted to be with him. Maybe they could be together without that aspect of their relationship and instead just have a little light bondage sex every now and then. But could Logan ever be satisfied with that?

****

Logan was up watching TV. Clay was in his bed with him, already curled on his side and asleep. Again, Logan was wrapped around him. But this time, he was propped up on one elbow and better armed to stay awake, thanks to a late night Starbucks run. It was the routine they'd fallen into. Clay would come over in the evenings. They would talk – sometimes about their relationship and sometimes not. Logan would see Clay getting tired and encourage him to lie down. And once Clay was asleep, he'd turn off the lights and turn down the TV. But he always stayed awake. He wanted to make sure they didn't have a repeat of what happened the first night Clay fell asleep with him.

Around seven in the morning, he would wake Clay up, send him home, then go back to bed to catch a few hours of sleep himself. Was he insane? Probably. But he wanted to spend that time with Clay and he loved having the chance to hold him in his arms at night. Besides, he knew Clay had been having trouble sleeping but when he stayed at Logan's house, he slept with ease.

Logan smoothed his hand over Clay's hip and dropped a kiss on his shoulder. Yeah, he was insane, but Clay trusted him enough to sleep with him. He knew that soon Clay would be his again. A few days of sleep deprivation was worth it. As he continued to rub Clay's leg, he heard a soft moan come from the sleeping man. Logan stopped, thinking he was disturbing Clay's sleep. He quieted for a few moments before moaning again. Logan started to move his hand off Clay's leg completely but the next whispered moan stopped him.

"Logan…"

All of him froze, except for one part that was rapidly thickening and hardening. Clay moved restlessly in his sleep. If it wasn't obvious what he was dreaming about before, his next words made it clear.

"Sir, please…"

Logan groaned quietly. Hearing Clay call him that while he was asleep and didn't know what he was doing was torture. Still, he responded to his sub's subconscious plea. Logan carefully pulled down Clay's shorts, trying not to wake him. He hardened even further when he saw that, yet again, Clay didn't have on anything beneath the loose shorts. It probably wasn't the smartest idea, but he lightly grasped Clay's hand and guided it to his shaft. As much as he wanted to feel Clay in his hand, he didn't trust himself to touch him without waking him and taking it further. He moved their hands together for a few strokes until Clay was doing it on his own.

He let go, watching as Clay pleasured himself. His hand moved slowly up and down on his shaft, his lips parted as he panted lightly in his sleep. From the small beads of sweat dotting Clay's forehead and his faster breathing, Logan knew that Clay was on the verge of release in his dream. He was glad that it was nearly over. It was difficult listening to his soft moans and watching him stroke his stiff cock, knowing he couldn't wake Clay and give him what he was experiencing in his dream. Until there was a whisper that almost shattered his resolve.

"Sir, please, may I come?"

Logan's fists clenched in frustration as he held himself back from touching Clay. In his sleep, Clay submitted to him. When would he do so while awake? He couldn't help it. He had to be a part of this in some way. Leaning over Clay's ear, he whispered back, "Come for me, baby." Logan lightly traced his tongue over the rounded shell of Clay's ear and watched as Clay's hips pumped his release.

Logan's cock throbbed, desperate to push inside of his lover. Desperate to feel those hot walls clenching him tight as he came, drawing forth his own climax. Logan dared to kiss Clay's neck lightly, his tongue lapping at his sweaty skin. He managed to hold himself back from doing anything else and finally Clay was done.

Clay sighed, snuggling back even closer against him. His body relaxed as he fell back into a deep sleep. Meanwhile, Logan was so tense it felt like he was vibrating. With a shaking hand, he grabbed a corner of the sheet and cleaned Clay up as best he could before pulling his shorts back up. Then he scooted back to put space between his body and Clay's. He wouldn't be able to get his erection under control with Clay's ass cradled between his hips. Unfortunately, Clay scooted back with him, keeping his body pressed tight against Logan like he always did. Logan tried to move once more but Clay followed him, a frown creasing his forehead. Logan gave up and stayed where he was. It would have been comical if he wasn't so goddamn hard.

He looked at the clock. 6:05. He only had to suffer for 55 minutes. Then he could wake Clay up. Logan fixed his attention back on the TV, now even more determined not to fall asleep. If he did, he was likely to wake up with his cock already buried in Clay's ass.

Logan stared at the TV for 10 minutes before he realized he was watching an infomercial about women's hair straighteners. He left it there, watching the transformations from curly haired and sad to straight hair and ecstatically happy. When it was over, Logan looked at the clock. Seven am. Thank fuck. He shook Clay's shoulder. "Clay. Wake up."

Clay woke up, stretching and yawning. As he stretched, he arched his back, pressing his ass against Logan, bringing his erection surging back. Logan hissed in pained pleasure. He grabbed Clay's hip, holding him tight as he pressed back, his throbbing shaft rubbing between Clay's clothed cheeks. His voice came out in a harsh whisper. "Clay... don't do that."

Clay went still and then all but leapt from the bed. Logan sat up slowly, swinging his feet down to the floor. Clay looked at him, an embarrassed flush spreading across his face as he noticed Logan's erection.

"Sorry about that," he said.

Logan shrugged. "Don't worry about it." He continued to look at Clay until he lowered his eyes. At that, Logan got up and went to him. He pulled Clay to him by his upper arms, ready to kiss him goodbye like always. Softly with lips closed and no tongue. But this time, he wanted more than that. He didn't know if it was Clay's dream or if he was just tired of waiting. Whatever it was, when their lips met, he kissed Clay hard. He traced his tongue over Clay's bottom lip before he nipped him sharply.

Clay drew back and looked at him in surprise. "Logan, what…"

Logan shook his head, not allowing Clay to finish. He grasped him by the back of the neck. "Kiss me back, Clay."

Logan heard the dominance enter his voice. That hadn't been his intention, but he wouldn't take the words back. He wanted – no, he *needed* that from Clay. He tightened his fingers on his love's neck. "Kiss me *back*." The surprise and confusion on Clay's face melted away, replaced with desire … and submission. Clay's eyes drifted closed, his lips parting as he tilted his head back. Logan made him wait for several heart beats. Then he slowly licked into Clay's mouth, curling his tongue against his. He slid his hands up under Clay's shirt, rubbing the smooth muscles of his back. Logan kept up with the light stroking, refusing to deepen the kiss until Clay was pressing tight against him, chasing after his tongue. Only then did he kiss him rough and hard, sucking his tongue into his mouth, lightly dragging his teeth across it before letting him go. He bit at Clay's lip again. Clay gasped, pushing his hips against Logan. Logan did it again, wanting that same reaction, making a sound of satisfaction when he got it.

He rubbed his hands along Clay's slender body until one grasped the back of Clay's neck and the other palmed his ass. He held him tightly against him just like that, thrusting his tongue into his lover's sweet mouth over and over until Clay was breathing fast and clutching at his back, whimpering almost desperately. Logan was just as affected, just as turned on. His shaft was throbbing and he circled his hips, grinding slow and hard against Clay, who moaned and rubbed back against him.

Logan broke their kiss before things escalated. He pulled back slightly, watching Clay as his eyes slowly opened, his still parted lips swollen and wet from his kisses. *That* was what he wanted. To see that beautiful look of surrender on his lover's face. Logan smoothed his palms down Clay's sides to lightly grasp his hips. He tucked his thumbs into Clay's shorts, sweeping them back and forth over the soft skin of his pelvis. His voice was low in the quiet room. "What are we doing, Clay? Why aren't we fully together again?"

Clay chewed his lip, indecision clear on his face. When he spoke, it wasn't what Logan expected or wanted to hear.

"Logan ... I don't know if I can be with you as my Dom. Can you be with me without it?"

****

Logan sat in the strategy room with Carlos and Tiffany. He was attempting to go over the plans for that night's raid. They were talking, about what he didn't know or really care. He was only paying enough attention to respond when they directed a comment or question to him. Otherwise, he tuned them out.

It was taking him much longer than usual to complete their strategy. His concentration on his work was shit. Logan was angry and confused. Clay didn't know if he wanted to be his submissive. He thought talking about Clay's concerns was leading to them being together the way they were before. And after all they'd discussed, to hear Clay say that … He didn't know what to do. Clearly something was holding Clay back. Maybe he wouldn't ever be okay with submitting to him. Would he have to let go of his dream of owning Clay? The thought depressed him, especially after he experienced what it was like to have Clay as his own. But he couldn't and he *wouldn't* force Clay to submit to him. So if Clay didn't want to be his submissive, there was nothing he could do. He heard someone calling his name and looked up. It was one of the guys from Narcotics.

"Excuse me, Sergeant Pierce. But Sergeant Lee wants to know if you can change—"

Logan cut the young officer off. "Don't even bother finishing whatever you're about to say because I don't want to fucking hear it. Tell him I'm not changing anything else and he better not send you back over here with anymore bullshit."

Everyone around him quieted. Tiffany looked at him like he'd grown a second head while Carlos studied him with narrowed eyes. The officer spoke first, stuttering in apprehension.

"I'm sorry, Sergeant Pierce … umm … Sir. But I don't think I can say …tell… relay that message."

Logan took a deep breath. He was out of line and he knew it. He dug through his memory to come up with the man's name. "I apologize, Officer Holtz. You caught me at a bad moment." He forced a smile. "Just let Lee know I'll be ready to go over things soon. Thanks." The officer nodded then actually saluted before he left.

Tiffany's voice was chock full of what the fuck. "Damn, Sarge, what was that?"

Carlos put his hand on Tiffany's arm. "Tiffany, go get us some water."

She nodded, lightly touching Carlos's fingers before getting up and leaving. Once she was gone, Carlos leaned back in his chair and looked at Logan.

"What's up?"

Logan blew out a harsh breath. "Clay told me this morning that he doesn't know if he wants to be my submissive. And he wants to know if I can be with him without being in a D/s relationship."

"Can you?"

Logan looked at his friend. "Honestly? I don't know. I think I could try. I'm just not sure how long I would be successful in ignoring that part of me." He needed the calmness he got controlling his partner, and the sense of fulfillment that came when he took care of him after. He leaned his head back against the wall behind him. He was frustrated and confused and fucking *tired*. "I don't get why Clay is resisting. We've been talking through things. And he *always* submits to me. It's only afterwards that he seems to regret it."

"Do you want me to talk to him?"

Logan shook his head. "No. I don't think a Dom telling him how wonderful it is to submit would help."

Carlos laughed. "Yeah, you're probably right about that." He sobered before he spoke again. "I'm sorry you guys are going through this. I know how badly you wanted him to be yours."

Logan didn't answer. He was beginning to think Clay might not ever be his.

****

Clay looked up as Tiffany suddenly perched on the corner of his desk.

"Hi! So Logan just bit the head off some cop."

Clay's eyebrows shot up in surprise. "*Logan* did that?"

"Yep. Why's your Dom so cranky? You not putting out?"

Clay nearly choked on the bottle of water he was drinking. "Logan isn't my Dom, Tiffany."

Tiffany tilted her head and looked at him, confusion evident in her dark brown eyes. "I thought you two were working things out?"

"We are. It's just … we might not go back to that part of our relationship." Tiffany stared at him for so long that Clay's felt his ears turning red. Finally, she shook her head.

"Clay, as long as you and Logan are together, he will always be your Dom."

65

Clay waited for Logan to open the door. He considered staying away that night. After what Tiffany had told him, he watched Logan and noticed he was a little short with people at work instead of cool and calm like usual. And after admitting to Logan that morning the doubts he still had, he felt like he needed to think things through on his own. So spending the night apart for each of them to think about things might have been a good idea. But when it came down to it, he'd rather be with Logan than alone in his own bed. He was just raising his hand to press the doorbell again when Logan opened the door.

"Sorry about that. I heard the doorbell ringing when I was in the shower and got down here as soon as I could."

Logan stepped back from the doorway and Clay stepped inside. He didn't quite catch what Logan said. He was too busy looking at the pale skin of Logan's bare torso. Those hard muscles were only an arm's length away. All he had to do was reach out and touch. He wanted Logan so much. He wanted to be beneath him again. He wanted to be his again. And it was driving him crazy that, for whatever reason, he couldn't seem to either give in to Logan … or walk away from him. Logan noticed him staring and gestured at the shirt in his hand.

"I was just about to finish getting dressed."

The words popped out of his mouth before he had a chance to think them through. "You don't have to put on a shirt." Logan turned back to look at him. "I mean … if you're more comfortable like that, it's okay." Clay's heart raced as they stared at each other, nothing separating them but ten feet of air… and Clay's indecision. He shouldn't have said that. He didn't know what he wanted yet so he shouldn't be encouraging anything physical between them. *Especially* after that kiss this morning.

Logan took a step towards him and Clay backpedaled quickly. "Although, I guess you're probably cold. Maybe you should wear a shirt." Logan's face seemed to freeze before he abruptly turned away and roughly yanked the shirt over his head. He didn't turn back around when he was done. He stayed facing away from Clay, his head lowered.

"Come upstairs, Clay."

Clay followed him up the staircase. Logan was clearly aggravated. Logan was obviously frustrated and cranky like Tiffany had said. In the bedroom, he settled himself on the bed with Logan sitting next to him. Logan laced his fingers through his.

"Do you want to talk tonight?"

Clay looked into Logan's hazel eyes, noting the lines of tension around them. He needed to decide what he wanted. He knew he wanted to be with Logan. He knew he loved how it felt to submit to Logan. But his brain kept shying away from the image of him licking Logan's boots. And he just couldn't fucking bring himself to say, 'Yes. You are my Master.' And that was just something he was going to have to work through on his own.

He shook his head in answer to Logan's question. "Can we just hang out tonight?" A muscle ticked in Logan's jaw, but he nodded in agreement. Clay scooted down and laid his head in Logan's lap. The hard muscle of Logan's thigh was strong and warm against his cheek. And Logan smelled good, the scent of his body wash familiar. Clay closed his eyes, thinking about how good it would feel to have nothing between him and Logan's warm skin.

Logan stared blankly at the TV. He'd known from the moment he laid eyes on Clay that it would be a challenge to win him. He just hadn't realized how much of a strain it would be to have him, lose him, and then be in this fuzzy and confusing no-man's land with him. They didn't say I love you anymore. They weren't together physically. And he was tired of it. He wanted things to be the way they were and he fucking wanted it now. He was trying his best not to show his impatience, but after what Clay said that morning, he wanted to know. Was Clay his or not?

Clay's head moved in his lap, his face rubbing across his shaft and Logan grit his teeth. He didn't know if he could deal with another night of laying there aroused while Clay slept on, peaceful and oblivious. He started to move Clay off him, but as he looked down and saw him so relaxed, Logan felt a wave of emotion for the sleeping man and let him stay where he was. And he stuck by that decision … for all of two minutes. Because Clay kept rubbing his cheek softly against the growing bulge in his sweat pants, back and forth, his warm breath seeping through the cotton and heating his shaft. He couldn't take it. He shook Clay's shoulder lightly. "Clay, baby. You need to wake up."

"I'm not asleep."

66

Logan's heart pounded, his mouth going dry. Clay wasn't asleep. Then what was he doing? He asked his question out loud. "What are you doing, Clay?"

Clay turned his head and brushed his lips across his shaft. "I was thinking that I could repay you for what you did for me the other night." He brushed his lips over him again. "Since you didn't get to come."

Logan shifted his hips in an attempt to get away from Clay's teasing mouth. "I took care of that myself." He made a hoarse attempt at a laugh. "Just me and my right hand." Clay rolled so that he was between his legs and Logan automatically made room for him.

"But that's not what you really wanted, is it?"

"No. But that's what we agreed to."

Clay lowered his lashes. "Yeah, but ... I want to taste you, Logan."

Logan cleared his throat, shifting his hips again. He was unbelievably hard and desperate to take Clay up on his offer. But he hadn't said anything about what he'd decided, which meant they were still on their sex ban. "I don't think that's a good idea."

"Why not?"

"You know I won't want to stop with just that, Clay."

Clay trailed a finger down his shaft. "But we used to stop. Before. Why can't we this time?"

Logan swallowed hard. Before he'd been able to stop, but that was before he knew the mind blowing pleasure of burying himself deep inside his lover. Fuck. How was he supposed to refuse Clay's offer when he wanted it so bad? He didn't say anything because his brain couldn't think of an argument to deny what his body wanted. Clay must have taken his silence for agreement because he curled his fingers into the waistband of Logan's sweatpants and boxers and pulled them down. And Logan … let him. It was almost embarrassing how hard he was. His shaft stretched up his belly, the head swollen and dark, already slick with pre-cum, the vein underneath standing out strong and prominent.

Clay looked down at his cock and then back up at him. He held their eye contact as he leaned forward, his tongue coming out to slowly lick across his cockhead. Logan inhaled sharply and pressed back against the headboard. Just that one lick and he was ready to lose it. "Clay …"

Clay didn't say anything. He just wrapped his hand around his shaft and sucked him down. Logan groaned in pleasure. It had been so long since he'd felt anything besides the touch of his own hand. And his hand definitely didn't compare to the delicious wet heat of Clay's mouth sliding up and down his cock. Clay moaned, sending vibrations tingling up and down his shaft. Logan fisted his hands in the comforter. He wanted to touch Clay, to slide his fingers into his hair and hold him still so he could thrust up into his sweet mouth. But he didn't. Clay wanted him without Logan taking control. So he would try. He let Clay suck him as he wanted, keeping his mouth shut and not giving a single order. And he kept his hips still. It didn't take long before his belly was clenching tight and he knew he'd be coming soon. He tried to get Clay to stop, unsure if his lover wanted him to release into his mouth.

"Clay, that's enough." Clay ignored him and kept going, moving his mouth even faster. Logan groaned again, gripping the comforter tighter as he strained not to move. "Clay ... no more. I'm close." Clay dug his fingers into his thigh and continued. Logan drew that leg up and Clay wrapped an arm around his thigh, crowding in even closer against him. Logan couldn't take his eyes off him. His reddened lips were stretched wide around his cock and the sounds he made were driving him crazy. The wet sounds of his sucking. The laps of his tongue against the sensitive underside of his cockhead. The moans that made it seem as though Clay loved what he was doing. The sounds, the way it felt, all of it combined was just too much. His balls were tight and his cock was throbbing. Logan couldn't hold back any longer. Just before he erupted he tried one last time to get Clay to stop.

"I'm about to come baby. You need to st—" He cut off with a shout as Clay squeezed his sac and rapidly tongued his slit. Logan's orgasm shot up his shaft into the welcoming mouth of his lover, sending waves of breath stealing pleasure coursing throughout his body. Logan gripped Clay's shoulder, his body shaking as he kept coming, his hips thrusting up against his will. But Clay didn't complain. His lover drank him down, not letting up until the tension in his body eased and he collapsed back against the headboard. Clay slowly slid his mouth up his shaft one last time before he finally released him.

Logan's body was relaxed but his chest was still pumping with harsh breaths. He looked down at Clay and saw him watching him. They stared at each other, the desire on Clay's face plain to see. Logan's heart pounded as he tried to convince himself that he could stop from taking this any further. But then Clay reached for him.

"Logan …"

That was all it took. Logan grabbed Clay by the upper arms and yanked him up so that he was straddling his lap. Smashing their lips together in a frantic kiss, he sucked at Clay's bottom lip. "I can taste my cock on your lips." Logan licked into Clay's mouth. He cupped Clay's ass in his hands, pulling him even closer. "And my cum on your tongue." Clay moaned and pushed his hips into him, his hardness rubbing across Logan's stomach.

"You taste good, Logan," he whispered against his lips.

Logan quickly rolled Clay underneath him, kissing him deep and hard. Fuck waiting. He wanted Clay now. He roughly pushed Clay's shirt up his chest, his head and his body focused on nothing but getting inside his lover. Still, Logan tried to let Clay know they didn't have to do anything else.

"Tell me to stop and I'll stop, Clay."

But he ground his rapidly hardening shaft against Clay's as he spoke. And Clay just raised his arms to help get the shirt off. Logan hurriedly kissed his way down Clay's chest and stomach until he came to his shorts. As he tugged them down, he tried again, his words coming out in a desperate whisper against the soft skin of Clay's belly.

"Tell me to stop, baby."

But Clay lifted his hips so he could slide the shorts down his long legs. Logan looked at Clay, naked beneath him. He was as beautiful as ever and being without him had been torture. But no more. Clay was finally there with him.

He moved down Clay's body, gripping his thigh and pushing it up. He sucked kisses along that smooth flesh until he met the crease where his thigh ended. Trading kisses for long laps of his tongue, he licked across Clay's lightly muscled ass. "Clay ..." He reached his entrance, lightly teasing it with the tip of his tongue. "Tell me to stop and I will." But Clay only moaned and pushed his hips forward. Logan tightened his grip on Clay's thigh and speared his tongue inside him.

Clay gasped. Logan's hot breath against his skin and his tongue thrusting inside him felt so good there was no way he would tell him to stop. Clay grasped his own shaft and stroked. But with a low growl, Logan knocked his hand away. He felt the loss of Logan's mouth for a moment, just long enough for him to lick up his shaft, getting it wet. Then Logan wrapped his big fist around Clay, pumping smoothly. Logan returned to what he was doing before, licking deep into him over and over again. Clay lifted the leg that Logan wasn't holding and wrapped it around his shoulders. He wanted to keep Logan close against him, making him feel that way forever. It seemed as though he would get his wish as Logan worked him higher and closer to climax. Until his tongue withdrew. Clay sat up, a protest ready on his lips. He didn't voice it however, because one of Logan's thick fingers pushed inside him. He shuddered, pushing his hips down to capture more of it.

Logan pushed another finger in and Clay fell back on the bed, crying out Logan's name. He couldn't stop his body's writhing as Logan twisted his fingers deep inside him. He couldn't stop his whispered pleas as he clawed at Logan's shoulders, trying to pull him up. But Logan was immovable. Clay had to lay there and take it as those fingers pressed against his spot and that hard hand continued to pump his cock, making his whole body spark with pleasure. How had he managed to stay away from Logan and the way he made him feel?

Logan had reached the end of his control. Clay's pleas and squirming fed his need to be inside of his lover. Now. He couldn't wait anymore. Rising up over Clay, he fit the head of his cock to Clay's entrance, ready to push himself inside. But he forced himself to slowdown. To stop and *think*. If they did this and Clay wasn't ready … he didn't want to do this if it would set them back. Breathing hard, he brushed a hand over Clay's silky hair. "Clay, do you want this?"

Clay nodded with his eyes closed. That wasn't enough for him. He needed to make sure this was what Clay wanted.

"Clay, open your eyes and look at me." He waited as Clay's eyes drifted open. "I need to hear you say that you want this."

Clay licked his lips and nodded again. "Yes. I want this. I want you."

Logan leaned down and kissed his lover. "I want you too." He started to push inside, but even though he'd prepared him, Clay was tight. Logan hated to part from his lover for even a second but he had to. He snatched open the nightstand drawer to retrieve the lube. He cursed, his fingers clumsy and fumbling on the bottle as Clay cupped and squeezed his balls while he prepared them. Finally, Logan was able to throw the bottle aside and lower himself back over Clay. Again he started to enter him, going slow, ignoring the urge to just push forward until every inch of his cock was gloved by that snug channel. He blew out a harsh breath as he inched in, damn near shaking with the strain not to hurt his lover.

Clay rubbed his palms down Logan's chest to get his attention. "You won't hurt me, Logan."

Logan kissed him, rough and full of passion to distract him from any pain as he pulled back and thrust past that first ring of muscle. When he was all the way in, they both cried out. Logan held still for a moment, breathing hard, just savoring the feeling of being inside his lover again. Clay started moving restlessly beneath him, his hands roughly stroking his back.

"Logan, please. Move now."

This time it was he who obeyed Clay. He moved. Slow. Deep. "Is this okay, baby?"

Clay nodded and Logan smoothed a hand up Clay's arm, stretching it over his head. Clay brought his other arm up and Logan went to wrap his hand around his wrists. But he remembered what Clay had asked him. He closed his eyes for a moment to get the sight of restraining Clay out of his head. Logan brought his hand back down, caressing his thigh instead. He gently lifted Clay's leg, urging him with a whisper to wrap it around his waist.

The air was filled with the sultry symphony of soft curses, heavy breathing, and the creaking of the bed as he slowly rode his lover, sliding deep inside him again and again. Clay's hips rose to meet every one of his thrusts, the expression on his face was one of blissed out pleasure. Logan lowered himself until their heated bodies were pressed tightly together. He buried his face in Clay's neck while he kept thrusting slow and easy. Clay squeezed his inner muscles around him and Logan groaned.

"You feel so good, baby." The heat. The tightness. Logan wasn't going to last. Already he could feel his muscles clenching, his shaft pulsing with the urge to come. "I'm sorry, Clay. I don't want this to end but it feels so goddamn good to be inside you again." Clay pushed his hips up, digging his fingers into Logan's back. His breath washed over his shoulders as he spoke in between moans and cries of pleasure.

"That's okay. I'm close too."

Logan sped up his thrusts slightly. He reached between them and grasped Clay's shaft, stroking in time to his thrusts so Clay felt as much pleasure as he did. Those velvety walls rhythmically clenched on his cock, spurring on his need to come. He licked Clay's neck, tasting the damp saltiness of his skin. "Can I come inside you, Clay?"

"Yes. I want to feel you coming inside me, Sir."

Logan was shocked and from the way Clay froze stiff beneath him, he was too. Clearly, he hadn't meant to address him like that. He pushed himself up to look at Clay. Panic crawled across his face. Logan dropped a slow kiss on his lover's mouth and reassured him. "Don't worry about that. Just stay with me, baby."

Logan didn't mention it again and after a moment, Clay started to relax. Logan kept pumping and stroking Clay, squeezing him hard, making *sure* he stayed in the moment. And it worked. Soon, Clay was moving with him again, his hips rising faster and faster until he was moaning out his orgasm, his cock throbbing and pulsing in Logan's fist. Clay's release spilled out onto his belly, getting Logan's hand slick and wet. Logan smiled and kissed him, happy he was able to give Clay that pleasure.

He tried to maintain his slow pace but Clay's walls were squeezing him and it felt so good he finally just let go, letting his hips jerk tight and fast against his lover's as his cock pulsed with his release. He kissed Clay as he came, groaning into his mouth, breathing in the moan Clay gave him in return. As the pulsing pleasure subsided, he had to let Clay know how he felt.

"I love you, Clay," he whispered against his lips.

Clay was still moaning and breathing hard, but he whispered back, "I love you, too."

67

Logan rolled to Clay's side and went to pull him up against him. Clay put his hand on his chest and stopped him.

"I'm sort of a mess here."

Logan didn't care about that. It crossed his mind that Clay never used to either but he was still enjoying what they just shared too much for his brain to focus on the change. He scooted closer to Clay. "That's alright. But we can take a shower together if you want."

Clay shook his head. "No. I just need a towel."

Logan rose up on one elbow finally noting that Clay seemed to be withdrawing from him. "Is everything okay?"

"Yeah. I'm fine. Just ... will you get me a towel?"

Logan wasn't sure about Clay's mood. But he got up and pulled on his boxers before going into the bathroom to get a warm, wet towel. He took the time to clean himself up and couldn't help smiling, thinking they were together again. When he came back out, Clay was already sitting up in bed, his shorts and shoes on and his t-shirt in hand. He obviously used the sheet to clean up because it was balled up and thrown on the floor. Logan stopped short. "Are you leaving?"

Clay didn't look at him as he pulled his shirt on over his head. "Yeah, I should get home."

Logan carelessly dropped the wet towel on the floor and went over to him. "You've slept with me nearly every night for a week. Why are you leaving now?"

"Because we shouldn't have done that," Clay said, standing and gesturing at the bed. "I'm sorry. That was my fault."

Logan just managed to keep from cursing out loud in frustration. *Damnit, he'd asked if that was what Clay wanted.* He couldn't take much more of his indecision. "First of all, don't ever apologize for us being together. But why do you even feel like you need to? I wanted you and you said that you wanted me. So where is the problem?"

"Because I told you, Logan! I don't know if I can be with you the way you want me to be!"

Logan grabbed Clay and pulled him up against him. "Fine! We don't have to be together like that. I want you more than I want anything. *Including* being a Dom. So if that's what it takes to get you back, I'll trash every toy and restraint I own. I'll tear down the playroom. I'll throw out your collars—"

"No!" Clay protested, curling his fingers against his chest.

Logan stopped and studied the man in front of him. "You don't want me to throw your collars away? Why not?"

Clay took a deep breath. "I just meant that I don't want you to give up something that's a part of you. That's all. You think I don't know you were holding back tonight?"

"Now that's not fair, Clay. You asked me if I could be with you without dominating you. And I tried. I'm willing to keep trying if that's what you want." Logan studied Clay again. "But I don't think that's what you want. Going by your slip, I wasn't the only one holding back."

Clay looked away from him. "That *was* a slip. But just from habit."

"Really? I heard you last night, Clay."

Clay met his eyes again. "What?"

"I heard you while you were dreaming." Logan pulled Clay even closer against him. "You were submitting to me in your dream, baby. Asking me, asking *your Dom,* for permission to come." He brushed his lips against Clay's. "And, God, you have no idea how bad I wanted to wake you up and give you that permission … after I worked you up just as much as you were in your dream."

Clay flushed hot both with embarrassment and desire. He had vague memories of that dream, but hadn't realized he said anything out loud. Or that Logan had been awake to hear him. Before he knew it, his body was relaxing against Logan's, his hands smoothing over his broad chest. He bit his lip as he looked into Logan's sharp hazel eyes. Eyes that watched him with so much love and desire. In that moment, he knew he was going to be with Logan again. There was just one last thing he had to admit.

"Logan, the day we watched the baseball game together …" He trailed off.

Logan prompted him when he stayed silent. "What about that day?"

"It was just when we were here in your room, I…" His face heated again. "When I made sure your boots were clean." He dropped his eyes to Logan's chest. But Logan wouldn't let him hide. He put a finger under his chin, raising him up until their eyes met again.

"You mean when you were being submissive and licked my boots?"

"Yeah." He felt open and vulnerable discussing it, but Logan's arms tightened around him, helping him feel at ease. "That was one of those things that felt good while I was doing it but bothered me later."

"Bothered you how?"

Clay shrugged. "I don't know."

Logan frowned. "Be honest, Clay. We can't move past this if you aren't."

Clay knew Logan was right. He quit being a pussy and said what he felt. "I was embarrassed."

"Why?" Logan asked calmly.

"What would people think? A grown man groveling at the feet of another, licking his boots? They'd think I was less of a man."

"First of all, our sex life is private, so no one will ever have any reason to know or think about what we do behind closed doors. But, more importantly, you were not groveling. Being on your knees for me represents the dynamics of our relationship and it does *not* make you lesser than me. But I do understand how you feel. When I first entered the scene I worried that if anyone found out what I was into that they would think I was some kind of deviant or liked to abuse my

467

lovers. I had to get that out of my head and understand that if dominating made me feel good, that's what I would do, regardless of what others might think."

Clay looked at his lover, at the sincerity in his face. Logan wasn't just saying these things to bullshit him. "Why do you feel the need to dominate? You never told me."

Logan stroked his back as he answered. "It's a part of my personality to be in control and to take care of others. But I'd say it really started when I was in Iraq. You know what it's like out in the field. You plan assignments and you have contingency plans, but you still can't control everything. Things get out of control and people get hurt or killed. Once I earned command of my own unit that was hard for me to deal with, sending those boys out there and not being able to control everything to make sure they came back safe. I internalized all of that angry frustration and it stayed with me once I returned to civilian life. I thought I'd lose that urge to control everything but I didn't. I was restless and angry. The relationships I had weren't satisfying me. I was talking to Carlos about the problems I was having and he suggested I try learning about BDSM. We'd been friends since high school, so I trusted him and tried it."

"And it worked for you."

"Yes. I had to experiment to find what I liked. But I quickly figured out that having that control over a lover calmed me. And taking care of them afterwards gave me a satisfaction I'd never had." Logan kissed him. "That's why I love the way you turn to me, Clay. Taking care of you, holding you in my arms is better than anything I've ever experienced.

And I think the way you feel when you submit to me gives you the feeling of release that you need."

Clay nodded, taking in what Logan said. But he must not have looked totally convinced because Logan asked him a question.

"Tell me truthfully, Clay. Did you like cleaning my boots with your tongue?"

A shiver of arousal went through him at the memory. "Yes."

"And were you turned on by serving me?"

Clay thought of how hard he came, stroking himself off while licking Logan's boots. "Yes, I was turned on."

Logan kissed him. "Then that's all that matters. What makes you, *us*, feel good. You can't keep yourself from enjoying what I do to you and what I have you do because of what other people *might* be thinking. They'll never know the things we do anyway."

Clay nodded. He felt better now that he'd admitted what had been bothering him, but he still needed to think things over.

"Okay, Logan, I admit it. I want to be with you. And if you're willing to consider being with me without being in a D/s relationship, I'm willing to consider being with you as your sub again. But let me think. Just give me until tomorrow night."

Logan smiled, his happiness at Clay's statement evident. He brushed another kiss across his lips. "I can do that." He started walking him backwards. "Now come back to bed."

Clay laughed. "No, Logan. If I'm going to think, I need to do it without you distracting me." Logan's lips nuzzled his neck and his hand slid into his shorts to cup his ass.

"I won't distract you." His hand slid around to his front to teasingly brush low on his belly. "Well, I might just a little bit."

Clay moaned softly, and before his next breath, Logan's lips were on his. It was getting harder to resist as Logan kissed him, the slow licks of his tongue almost making him forget why he was leaving. "Logan... I mean it ... I need to be alone." Clay felt the vibration of Logan's protesting growl against his chest, but he let him go.

"Okay." Then as Clay tried to walk away, Logan pulled him back by his t-shirt. "Have lunch with me in my office tomorrow?"

Clay laughed again. "You don't give up, do you?"

"In general? No. When it comes to you? Never."

Hearing that, Clay had to turn back and give Logan a deep kiss of his own. He ended it quickly and dodged Logan's hands as he walked across the room.

"Tease," Logan said.

Clay turned back, a secret smile playing on his lips. "Sometimes." Then he was out the door.

68

Clay finished up his After Action Reports for the week. It felt good to be done with them. He was also feeling good because he knew what he wanted. No more confusion. No more going back and forth with Logan, afraid to commit because he didn't know what he wanted. Clay had thought over everything about his relationship with Logan long and hard last night. And when he took worry over what people might think out of the equation, he realized he *did* love the dynamics of his relationship with Logan. The way he was able to let go of his control and let Logan take over, take care of him, gave him a peace that he'd never had before. They could work on his fears of going into subspace and keeping the D/s aspect of their relationship private. Together.

Clay looked at the clock. It was time to meet Logan for lunch. He'd made his decision, but he hadn't decided if he was going to tell Logan during lunch or wait until later that night. Clay grinned. He figured he'd just play it by ear.

Logan sat in his office, waiting on Clay. The sandwiches he ordered were on his cleared off desktop. He was pleased they talked the night before and glad Clay was ready to commit to them being together. And Clay would let him know later what he decided about resuming their Dom/sub relationship. He knew what he preferred – but he'd take Clay no matter what he decided. He sat up straight as the door opened and Clay came in.

"You're trying to woo me and all I get is a sandwich?"

Logan had to smile. He loved that smart ass so much. "Not just a sandwich. There's also chips and a drink."

Clay laughed and sat down. "Be still my heart."

They mostly talked about work as they ate. When Logan was done, he tossed his trash away and sipped his drink as he waited for Clay to finish.

"So will you be over tonight after work?" Clay looked down at his plate. Logan noticed the smile tugging at his lips before he looked at him from beneath his lashes.

"Yes, Sir."

Logan sucked in a breath, afraid to believe what he just heard. "Is that your answer?"

Clay looked at him directly, the blue of his eyes clear. "Yes, Sir."

Logan's heart raced. So many emotions swirled through him at that moment. Joy. Pleasure. Relief. Love. He wanted to pull his sub to him and kiss him until he couldn't think of anything but submitting to him. But Clay hadn't locked the door when he came in. So, instead, he trailed his fingers over the back of Clay's hand. "And you're telling me this now?"

Clay's eyes glinted with mischief. "Well, I didn't think you'd want to wait to know my answer."

Logan laced his fingers through his lover's. "I didn't. And I don't want to wait to celebrate your answer either."

"That's too bad. We've got a long night ahead of us before we can leave and do that."

"You little tease."

Clay gave him a smile that almost lured Logan out of his chair so he could kiss that pretty mouth.

"Maybe. What are you going to do about it, Sergeant?"

"Hmmm... I think I'm going to go over, lock that door and—" The sound of the aforementioned door opening kept him from finishing his sentence. He dropped Clay's hand just as Captain Hayden walked in. With a sigh, Logan leaned back in his chair.

"Captain. How can I help you?"

Hayden looked back and forth between them. "You two look cozy in here."

Logan's hackles went immediately up. "So? Is there a rule against us having lunch together?"

"Not at all. Actually, I guess it's a good thing that Corporal Foster is here. I'm here to tell you that the promotion you wanted has been approved." He looked at Clay. "Congratulations, Foster. You're now a Senior Corporal. It was against my recommendation, of course, but Sergeant Pierce here pushed for it."

Logan clenched his jaw in anger. The way Hayden worded it made it seem as though he pulled some strings to make it happen. He looked at Clay and he saw exactly what he expected to see. Growing anger.

"I'm sure you'll manage to prove me wrong. Or maybe you won't." He left the office but Logan barely noticed. His eyes were locked on Clay. As soon as the door closed, Clay jumped to his feet, his chair screeching back over the linoleum. "You lying piece of shit!"

Logan saw Clay looking down at him with an expression of absolute fury on his face. He stood up and went around the desk to him. "Clay, listen."

Clay stepped up in his face. "No, you listen! I fucking told you to let the department decide if they wanted to promote me or not. You had no goddamn right to interfere! I told you I didn't want any special treatment and to stay out of it!"

"I did! I may have given my opinion that I thought you were ready for a promotion but that's all. That's hardly special treatment."

"Bullshit. You didn't say anything for any of the people you weren't sleeping with, did you?"

Logan closed his eyes for a moment. He couldn't believe they were fighting when they'd just gotten back together. "Clay, I'm sorry. I just wanted to make sure you have the career you deserve."

Clay was so pissed off he lost it and shoved Logan hard in the chest. "I don't need you to make sure I get anything! You think I'm talking out my ass when I say I'm the best this department has ever seen? I know that the only thing holding me back from being promoted is not being a stuffy yes man with a stick up his ass like you!"

Clay knew he'd gone too far with that comment but he didn't care. He couldn't believe what Logan had done. He turned his back on Logan and headed for the door. "Just stay the fuck away from me."

"Clay, wait!"

Clay spun back around. "No! You don't get to ask me to do anything. If it isn't about work, you don't even need to talk to me."

Logan went after Clay anyway. He slapped his hand on the door, preventing him from opening it. There was something else he'd done behind Clay's back and he might as well get it out now. "Clay. Please, just wait for a second."

Clay turned back around, his fists clenched in anger. "What?"

"Back when we fought over Alison touching you … I told her that you weren't to be put in the calendar." Logan hadn't thought Clay could get any angrier. But going by the angry red flush creeping across his face, Clay was about to explode.

"You did what?"

"I told her to leave you off the calendar." He spoke fast, wanting to get the rest of it out while he still could. "I only did it because—"

"Shut up! Just fucking shut up! I don't want to hear you attempt to explain why you did it. Because let's be honest, Logan." A disgusted sneer curled his lip, the blue of his eyes bright with fury as he spoke. "You did it because you're jealous and possessive. You don't respect me as your partner if you think you have to sneak around behind my back pulling shit like that to keep me with you. I should have listened to Q when he tried to warn me."

"Clay, please just let me explain."

"Forget it. You can keep your explanations and your fucking collar. Because I don't want either of 'em." Clay turned back around and jerked hard at the door, making it clear he wanted out.

Logan stepped away to let him leave. All he could do was watch as Clay stormed off, not once looking back. Logan stood there in disbelief. In all the years he'd known Clay, he'd never seen him so furious. He figured it was pretty safe to say that they were over.

69

Clay left the station. He was furious. Fucking Logan and his goddamn interference. It was *his* career! Logan had no right to use his influence one way or another. And fuck! They hadn't exactly been secretive lately, he was pretty sure people were starting to put it together that they were seeing each other. How would that look if people found out he was dating Logan and then received a promotion almost immediately afterwards?

He was so mad, his stomach churned and he couldn't relax, his muscles grabbing down hard onto his bones. He needed to do something to take the edge off. He could have run or sparred or gone for a swim. But instead he was there at his barber. It was the middle of a weekday so he was able to get in the chair almost immediately.

"Cut it off."

The mirror showed his barber's surprised reflection. "Are you sure?"

"Yes, I'm sure."

The man grabbed the clippers and buzzed them on. "Alright, just tell me how low you want it."

****

A few days later, Clay slouched on his couch. The TV was tuned to a show on the military channel but he wasn't watching it. Instead, he glared at the Senior Corporal patch that he'd been given. He wished it wasn't there in his apartment, sitting on his coffee table. Wished there were a way he could give it back so he wouldn't have to have it sewn onto his uniform. He didn't want it there with all the other offices and awards he'd actually *earned* over his time in the military and police. That patch had no place on his body because that rank wasn't his.

He was done with Logan. Done with being his submissive, his lover, his anything. Logan clearly didn't respect him and since that was the case, he would have to find somebody else to play his kinky games. He couldn't believe that Logan had lied to him and manipulated things behind his back.

Clay snorted in disgust, thinking of Logan's promise not to betray him. Clearly, they had two different opinions on the meaning of betrayal. He was distracted from his righteous anger when the doorbell rang. He looked at the door, the glare still on his face. If it was another fucking delivery man with another fucking bouquet of flowers, he was going to take the stupid flowers and bash the delivery guy over the head with them. *Jesus*! Did Logan think he was a female crying because he'd forgotten their anniversary? Clay got up and snatched the door open.

"What?" He stopped as he saw his friend standing there. "Oh. What do you want, Ian?"

"Well, hello to you too, haircut."

Clay self-consciously brushed his hand over his shorn hair. He'd had the barber cut it all the way down to a buzz cut. "Now's not a good time, man."

Ian just grinned. "Yeah, I figured. But..." He pushed forward and shouldered his way into the entryway. "You've been avoiding me."

Clay rolled his eyes to the ceiling and let his friend knock him aside. He was there, so Clay might as well deal with it. He shut the door and headed back over to the couch, leaving Ian standing there.

"Aren't you going to offer me something to drink?"

Clay didn't even look back. "You invited yourself in here. You can get your own damn drink."

"Somebody's being a cranky asshole today."

Ian's footsteps faded as he went into the kitchen. After a few minutes, he came into the living room, twisting the cap off a bottle of iced tea. He noticed the patch on the table.

"Well, lookit there. You earned a new rank. Congrats, man."

"I didn't earn that rank."

Ian dropped down into the armchair across from him. "What do you mean you didn't earn it?"

Clay hadn't planned to go into it, but he wanted to get it off his chest. He wanted to tell someone what an asshole Logan had been and he knew that Ian would understand. "I didn't earn it because Logan pushed for me to get it. That patch and the rank it represents isn't mine."

Ian took a sip of his drink. "Yeah, so? That doesn't mean it's not yours."

Clay looked at his friend with a frown. "Did you hear what I said? Logan interfered in my career."

Ian took another sip, his face perfectly calm. "And this has you pouting because…"

Clay's eyes widened in surprise at Ian's cluelessness. "Are you fucking kidding me? Logan interfered in my career! He had no right to do that."

Ian leaned forward and rested his elbows on his knees. "So let me get this straight. You're pissed because your boyfriend–"

"He's not my boyfriend anymore." Ian closed his eyes and mumbled under his breath. Clay only caught, "Dumber than I thought," before Ian opened his eyes and spoke out loud again.

"You're pissed because your *ex*-boyfriend cared enough about you to want to see you advance in your career and used his influence to make sure that happened."

Clay didn't care how his friend worded it, Logan was still in the wrong. "I didn't need him to use his influence. I'll earn everything I have in that department on my own. All they need to do is look at my track record to decide if I'm worth an advancement in rank."

Ian laughed. "Now *you're* kidding , right? This is the HPD we're talking about. An organization filled with politics. A game that you refuse to play. And you have a captain who, from what I've seen and heard, appears to hate you." Ian shook his head. "Shit, you were fighting an uphill battle my friend. I think it was a good thing you had someone like Logan on your side."

Clay cut his eyes at Ian. "Don't even try to make it seem like Logan had good reasons to do what he did."

"Don't *you* keep being so damn mule-headed," Ian said as he pointed at him with his bottle of tea. "Logan did what he did because he cares for you. And, hopefully, because he was smart enough to know it was a good decision for the team. Besides, if the brass didn't feel you were deserving of wearing that patch, they wouldn't have gone for Logan's suggestion. If you'd get over yourself for two fucking seconds, you'd see that."

Clay crossed his arms over his chest. He wasn't going to argue this with Ian anymore. He knew once his friend got something in his head, he stuck with it. But he knew what would make him understand his anger. "Fine. Let's forget about Logan sticking his nose in on this. You want to know what else he did? He told Alison to cut me from the calendar. Explain how that was good for the team."

Ian shrugged. "I can't."

"Exactly! Can you believe that motherfu—"

Ian cut him off. "I can't explain how it was good for the team, but I know why he did it."

Clay snorted. "Doesn't take a genius to figure that one out. It was jealousy!"

Ian gave him a long look before he spoke again. "Remember that time you were dating Laurie and then broke up with her right after you met that MMA fighter at the gym? Or when you left that MMA guy high and dry for that asshole bike mechanic? And when that didn't work out, you consoled yourself with Lisa for about a month? Should I go on or do you need a few more flashbacks from your quick silver love life to see my point?"

Clay spoke from between clenched teeth. "I see your goddamn point."

"Then why are you still pissed?"

"Because he should have trusted me."

Ian shrugged again. "Can't blame the man for being spooked by your relationship hopping history."

"That's ... that's irrelevant. If Logan wants me to be with him the way he wants me to be, I need to be able to trust him."

A confused frown crossed Ian's forehead. "What?"

"Nothing. Just ... he shouldn't have lied to me about my promotion or that stupid calendar."

"So Pierce isn't perfect. Tough shit. I'm pretty sure you aren't either."

Clay narrowed his eyes. "Aren't best friends supposed to come over with ice cream or something when shit like this happens?"

Ian laughed. "You don't need ice cream. You just need a swift kick in the ass."

70

Two weeks had passed since Clay walked out of Logan's office in a rage. They'd continued to work together, managing to do so well. They kept to their word this time and put their personal stuff on hold while at work. Except for tonight. Tonight was different.

The team had taken one of the large unmarked SUVs for this operation. On the ride back, Clay was seated next to Logan. Without meaning to, Clay looked over and made eye contact with Logan. Once he had, he found it difficult to look away. They ignored the conversations of the others in the vehicle with them as they gazed at each other, while the two feet separating them felt like nothing. Logan's eyes dropped to his mouth. Out of habit, Clay bit his lip. Logan's eyes flashed back to his. Even in the semi-darkness of the truck, Clay could see that there was heat in that gaze. Hot sexual heat. Clay didn't have to be a mind reader to tell what Logan was thinking. He was thinking of touches and kisses and bodies coming together. Clay's breathing shallowed, his skin prickled with anticipation. He saw a muscle tense in Logan's jaw and realized he was holding himself back. Clay cursed under his breath and turned to stare out the window for the rest of the ride.

That was stupid of him. He knew Logan would take what had just happened as encouragement. And he was right. Inside the station, Logan casually stood outside his office door, talking to their team members as they passed. But when Clay came abreast of him, Logan's hand closed over his wrist before he could pass. Clay stopped and turned. He pulled his arm out of Logan's hold, both for appearances sake and because he couldn't take Logan touching him, holding him in his firm grip. It made him think of other times … of Logan holding him down, restraining him while he—

Clay forced himself to put that out of his head. He directed his question to Logan's chest, refusing to look at him.

"Did you need something, Sergeant?"

Logan didn't answer. He just stood there quietly. Clay knew what he was waiting for. He tried not to look at Logan. He tried. But he couldn't stop himself. He looked up to see Logan's hazel eyes focused directly on him. That heat was still there. Heat and *longing*. For him. Clay fought to keep his face neutral, not wanting Logan to read the same in his expression. He repeated his question. Now that Logan had what he wanted, he answered him.

"I need…" He cleared his throat. "Need to see you in my office."

Clay stepped back. He knew Logan didn't want to see him for anything work related. And he wasn't going there with him. "Sorry, but I have to go shower."

Logan took a step towards him, closing the gap he put between them. "I can wait."

Clay shook his head. He took a few more steps back. "Don't."

"I will, Clay. Right here in my office. I'll wait for you."

Clay dragged his gaze away from Logan's. "Don't," he said again. Clay turned and walked off, refusing to look back.

Logan watched Clay walk away from him. He wanted to be with him. He ached for him. But it wasn't just the physical side of their relationship that he missed. Logan missed Clay. Missed his teasing. Missed holding him in his arms. He missed just *being* with him.

He could tell Clay missed him too. And he'd easily seen his physical desire. That gave him hope. He saw how fast Clay hopped from relationship to relationship in the past. But this time, he hadn't done that. Logan hoped that meant Clay didn't want to move on. He knew he majorly messed things up between them and he desperately wanted an opportunity to set things right. Logan knew if he could just get Clay to spend some private time with him, he would have a chance to apologize again and get Clay to talk to him. So he planned to wait there in this office, hoping Clay would show up.

****

Clay sat at his desk. They returned from serving the warrant an hour ago. He was showered, his gear bag packed.

He could go home. But he didn't. He waited at his desk, pretending to work on his After Action Report. But really he was waiting for everyone to leave.

Logan was in his office, expecting Clay to join him. And although there were a dozen reasons why he shouldn't, he was going to. He changed his mind while he showered. It was obvious they both had an itch that needed to be scratched. Clay decided there was no harm in a quick one-off between them to take care of that itch. Exes did it all the time.

Once the pen was nearly empty, he got up. Clay reminded himself that he was just satisfying a physical need as he went to Logan's office door. That was all. He turned the door knob and stepped into the office. Logan was sitting behind his desk. He smiled when Clay walked into the room.

"I knew you would come." He got up and came over to him.

Logan was still in his uniform and boots. Clay couldn't help but notice how good he looked. He thought back to Logan having him lick those boots. But this time, the memory didn't make him burn with embarrassment. No, this time his skin heated with the flush of arousal and he found himself wanting to be at Logan's feet once more. But that wasn't why he was there. As Logan reached him and pulled him into his arms, he stated that fact both for himself and for Logan.

"I don't want to be here."

"But you are."

"Yeah. But I'm not here to get back with you."

Logan's gaze was direct on his. "Then why are you here?"

"You know why."

"Maybe I don't. Why don't you tell me?"

"I know I didn't come here to play games," he snapped. He turned out of Logan's arms and grabbed the door handle. But Logan's hand slapped onto the wood, preventing him from opening it.

"Tell me why you're here, Clay."

He turned back around. "Because I want you. Physically. Nothing more."

A small smile quirked up the corners of Logan's mouth. He watched him quietly for a few moments before he spoke again. His response wasn't what he expected.

"Take off your clothes."

Clay stood there, surprised for a moment. But when Logan didn't say anything else, only continued to watch him silently, Clay did as he asked. When his clothes were in a pile at his feet, Logan wrapped his hand around Clay's shaft and started to stroke.

"I want you too, Clay. Want you so bad I was tempted to go out to the pen and drag you in here in front of everybody."

Clay's eyes widened at that confession.

"Does that sound crazy? Well, you *make* me crazy."

Logan reached for his hand, slowly bringing it to his mouth. He watched silently, his hips rising in rhythm with the hand that continued to pump his cock, as Logan sucked two of his fingers into his mouth. The sight of his fingers disappearing between Logan's lips, his pink tongue coming out to slowly lick at the sensitive pads of his fingers held him entranced. With one last lick, Logan released his fingers from his mouth. He lowered his arm back down to his side and guided Clay to slide one of his own slick fingers inside himself. Then he let go, bracing his hand on the door above Clay's head.

"Prepare yourself for me, baby."

Clay did, but he made it clear he was doing it because he wanted to not because Logan had any control over him. "Don't think I'm following your orders. I'm doing this because I want to."

"Does it matter? You're still doing what I want you to do." Logan squeezed the head of his cock, making him gasp. "Add another one."

Clay obeyed, pushing in another finger to join the first, twisting and scissoring them.

Logan leaned in close, Clay catching the scent of his cologne. He whispered in his ear, "Tell me when you're ready," while trailing kisses along the sensitive underside of his jaw.

Clay moaned, his hips curling up to meet Logan's pumping fist. "I'm ready now."

Logan leaned back and shook his head slightly. "I don't think so. Got to make sure you're able to take me. All of me." He dropped his arm from the door to grab Clay's hand and push his fingers in deeper. "One more, baby."

Clay again did what Logan ordered. Preparing himself for Logan while Logan stroked his cock had him hard as fuck. But perversely, he wanted to deny Logan the full satisfaction of knowing how affected he was. So as he slid a third finger inside himself, stretching his channel for Logan's cock, he bit his lip to stop the moan that rose up his throat from escaping. Logan immediately noticed. Clay should have known he would.

"So you're going to deny letting me hear the sweet noises you make? Let's see how long you can stick to that." Logan let go of his cock. "Turn around."

Clay pulled his fingers from himself and turned, bracing his forearms against the door. He heard the sounds of a belt opening and a zipper going down. Logan's chest pressed to his back, the hot, hard flesh of his cock brushed against his ass before slowly sliding inside him. Clay bit his lip again, stubbornly holding back the moan that wanted to come out. Once Logan was all the way inside him and his hand was again stroking his cock, Clay pressed his forehead to the door, losing himself to the feeling of Logan pushing hard and strong deep inside him.

"Clay, you're lying to yourself."

Clay roused himself from the mind numbing pleasure coursing through him to question Logan. "What?"

"If you think the only reason you're here with me right now is for sex, you're lying to yourself. You can get sex from anybody." Logan kept pumping into him, his strokes getting harder and harder as he spoke. "But you followed me in here because you want to be with *me*. You want *me* inside you. You want what *we* have together. You want to *submit* to *me*."

Clay shook his head, wanting to deny what Logan was saying, but he couldn't get the words to come out. He couldn't think past the pleasure that had him shaking and pushing back to meet Logan's thrusts. Logan thrust hard against that sensitive spot inside him and he clenched his fists against the wood of the door as he fought to hold his moan back.

Logan laughed softly, his breath tickling his ear. "So goddamn stubborn. But that's okay. It just makes it all the sweeter when you finally give in."

Logan's fist left his cock and he almost, *almost,* cried out to ask for it back. But he remained silent. Logan grabbed his arms, stretching them high above his head. He wrapped a hand tightly around Clay's wrists, squeezing firmly while the other returned to pumping his shaft. A soft cry escaped him, thankfully too low for Logan to hear. Logan licked a slow path up his neck to his ear, making him shiver.

"No one else can make you feel like this, baby. Only me."

Clay squeezed his eyes shut in frustration. Damnit, Logan was right. He loved the way he felt right with Logan pressed tightly against him, pushing so deep inside him, holding his arms down so he had no choice but to accept the pleasure Logan was giving him. Logan was in control. And it was what Clay wanted. Logan's voice was husky and low in his ear as that big fist squeezed him tighter, pumped him faster.

"Give me what I want, baby. Let me hear you moan."

Clay couldn't hold back anymore. He dropped his head back against Logan's shoulder, the moans and cries Logan wanted to hear spilling from his lips as bone-deep pleasure made his cock pulse and sent delicious tingles throughout his body. Logan growled softly in his ear, "There's my sweet sub." Clay tried to say that he wasn't Logan's. But Logan's hand was moving faster on him and his cock was throbbing with his rising orgasm. He wanted to say, "I'm not yours," and he managed to get the "I'm" out. But with his climax approaching fast, against his will it turned into, "I'm coming!"

Logan slammed his cock into him fast and hard, again and again, his grip on his wrists tightening almost brutally. Clay gasped as he took everything Logan had to give, spreading his legs for him. As Logan hit that sensitive spot inside him with each thrust, he cried out, just barely remembering to keep his voice low. "Oh god, Logan! Fuck me! Fuck me, Logan! Please, I need to come. Make me come!"

Logan groaned. "I like hearing that, baby." His hand slid down and squeezed his balls at the same time that he ground the head of his shaft against Clay's spot. "Come for me." He squeezed again and Clay erupted. He shuddered and moaned with his release as Logan's hand returned to his shaft, stroking him swiftly until he'd released everything he had into Logan's hand. Finally, his head started to clear from the pleasure that had fogged his brain and his body eased. Logan released his wrists and Clay sagged against the door, his heart racing. But Logan hadn't finished yet. He gripped Clay's hips as he continued to slide his cock in and out of his body.

"No one else can make you feel pleasure so intense, Clay. Only me. Accept it."

Logan's comment sparked one last bit of defiance in him. "Don't come inside me."

Logan's fingers tightened on his hips. "Why not?"

His head was clear enough now that he was able to say what he tried to earlier. "Because I'm not yours." He was surprised that Logan didn't protest. Instead, silence was his response. Logan withdrew and Clay yanked his hand around to grasp his shaft and finish him off. He was glad to do it, loving the feel of Logan pulsing his release into his hand. But he couldn't help feeling empty that Logan hadn't come inside him even though he was the one that prevented it.

Logan rested against Clay's back, both of them breathing hard as sweat dried on their skin. Logan's low voice sounded in his ear.

"We need to talk. Come home with me tonight."

Clay almost said yes. But just because they'd had sex didn't mean that he'd forgiven Logan. "I can't."

Logan spun him around. "Can't? Or won't?"

"Does it matter? Either way, I won't be there."

Logan narrowed his eyes at Clay's continued stubbornness. If Clay wouldn't talk to him then he would take advantage of their time to make him *see* what they felt for each other was still there. "Fine. Then I want you again. Right now."

Logan pulled Clay into the center of the room. His face showed his reluctance, but he followed. Dropping down to the floor onto his back, he tugged Clay on top of him. "Ride me," he ordered. Clay's eyes closed and he sat there, straddling his hips for a long moment. Then he reached behind him, grasping Logan's shaft and stroking him until he was hard again. It had been so long since he'd been with his lover that it didn't take any time at all. Clay lifted his hips. and slid down onto his shaft slowly. Logan groaned, thrusting up until he was all the way inside him. Clay started to ride him. Logan groaned deep in his throat as those hot walls squeezed him tight. His heart pounded with joy that Clay was with him. The way he felt, and the way he knew Clay felt, *how* could Clay think it was only physical?

Logan rubbed his hands over every patch of Clay's smooth skin that he could reach. He caressed his arms, stroked his belly, smoothed his hands up Clay's back. And again and again he returned to those beautiful thighs, stroking them, squeezing them, feeling the muscles working as Clay moved his body up and down on his cock. He watched Clay the whole time, saw his lover with his head thrown back, lost in the pleasure he was feeling. Saw his lips part with his gasping breaths. Saw the pulse beating fast in his throat and his stomach muscles tightening. He knew Clay was about to climax, but he was filled with surprise when he spoke.

"Fuck! I need to come! May I come, Sir?"

Logan's eyes flashed to Clay's face. He waited a heartbeat to see if Clay would panic or go back on what he'd said. He didn't, he just continued to move, his face tight with tension. Logan sat up, wrapping one arm around Clay's back. With his free hand, he grasped Clay's shaft and started to stroke. "Come for me, Clay. Come all over your Dom." Logan kissed him fiercely, thrusting his tongue into his lover's sweet mouth, not letting up or letting him pull away as Clay started to gasp with his orgasm. He swallowed Clay's moan as his release jetted out in hot pulses onto his stomach.

When Clay calmed, Logan lay back down, his hips thrusting up as his spine tingled with his own coming climax. "You're so sweet and tight, Clay. Gonna come for you, baby."

Clay made as if to move off him. "No, not inside me."

Logan clamped his hands firmly on Clay's slim hips, holding him down. "Yes. Inside you. Every drop, baby." Clay made a slight sound of protest and attempted to rise up again. But as Logan started to come, pushing up hard, Clay stopped moving. He dropped his head to Logan's chest, his fingers digging into his shoulders. And Logan heard him whisper, "Feels so good." Logan groaned and completely let himself go. His sub was stubborn, but he made him feel like no one else ever had.

****

Logan lay there, uncaring that the floor was cold and hard against his back. It didn't matter because Clay was resting on top of him, his legs folded on either side of his waist, their chests pressed together and Clay's face in his neck.

"I told you not to come inside me."

Logan smiled to himself. He knew Clay's strength and knew he hadn't tried very hard to stop him. He caressed Clay's ass, letting his fingers slide in the wetness there and on the backs of his thighs. "Sorry. Guess you'll have to stay in here with me until it all runs out of you."

Clay made a wordless sound of annoyance but he didn't say anything. It was quiet for a moment before Logan spoke again. "Clay?" He wasn't surprised at the surly, "What?" that came back at him. "You called me Sir." Clay went still on top of him. "And you asked me for permission to come like a good boy." Clay immediately rolled off him and stood. Logan sat up and watched as Clay went over to his desk for a tissue. "Why are you running away from me again?"

Clay quickly wiped himself off. "I'm not running. I told you I was only here for sex and we did that. So now I'm leaving."

He headed towards the door and his clothes but Logan called out for him to stop. The muscles in Clay's shoulders were bunched up hard with tension, but he stopped. Logan stood up and walked over to him, uncaring that he too was naked. He stepped close enough that he could feel Clay's body heat and he knew Clay could feel his too. "You missed a spot."

Logan swiped his finger in the lone streak of cum left on Clay's leg. He turned Clay around to face him and held his finger up before those sensuously full lips. Logan didn't say anything. He just stared into Clay's eyes and waited. Finally, Clay's lips parted, his warm breaths blowing across Logan's hand for several heartbeats before Clay's tongue came out and slowly licked his finger. He moaned softly, his eyes closing, and sucked Logan's finger into his mouth. Triumph streaked through Logan but he didn't say anything. Instead, he pulled his finger from between Clay's lips, sliding his hand down so he held him lightly by the throat. Logan kissed him slowly, softly, stroking his tongue inside to rub against Clay's. Clay succumbed to his kiss, his head falling back as he let Logan suck on his tongue. Then he abruptly turned his face away.

"Don't. This doesn't mean anything."

"Really? So after this, you can honestly say you don't want to be mine?"

A hard expression settled on Clay's face as he set his jaw stubbornly. "I could never belong to anyone who lies to me and doesn't respect who I am."

"You know I'm sorry. And I know that I was wrong in what I did. I made a mistake and I regret it. I deserved to have you unleash that temper of yours on me. But you're keeping us apart unnecessarily by holding on to that anger, Clay. Why can't you see that?"

"You're wrong. I'm not keeping us apart. We *are* apart, because of you. And we're going to stay that way."

"No. We're fighting. Couples fight. But I love you, Clay and I know you love me. And that means we work through our problems until they're resolved. And if I have to apologize a hundred different times a hundred different ways until you forgive me, then that's what I'll do. I'll do whatever it takes to make you see that I do respect you and that you can trust me."

Clay shook his head but Logan didn't let him say whatever he was about to. He tightened his hold on Clay's neck a fraction and kissed him hard. "You want to belong to me, Clay. And I'm going to reclaim what's mine."

Clay stepped out of Logan's hold and hurriedly finished dressing. He fumbled with the door knob before he got it open. Logan could think what he wanted. Clay wasn't running. But he got out of there as fast as he could.

71

They were out for a routine, high-risk warrant. It was late at night and from what they could see, everyone in the house was sleeping. They'd already settled on doing a break and rake followed by tear gas to drive the guy outside. Logan gave the signal and Q smashed the hooligan into the window using the hooked end to clear the frame of all glass. The suspect woke up, quickly rolling out of bed and dropping to his knees. Clay stepped up and aimed his gun at the ceiling. The weapon was designated for tear gas bullets only. The bullets exploded and released the gas when they made contact. He popped off two rounds and the room quickly filled with smoke. But the guy was fast and managed to get to a gun he had under his bed. Clay got out of the way, taking cover on the side of the house just as a bullet flew out the window.

He heard a crash and knew it was Logan and his group smashing the front door in. His heart pumping, Clay peeked around the broken window and saw the suspect running from the room. Yelling for Q to cover him, he swung himself up and through the window. He landed in a crouch. The thud of another pair of boots hitting the floor behind him let him know Q was inside too. They set off, Q watching his back while he fired off more tear gas bullets at the ceiling, forcing the guy towards the front of the house where Logan and the others waited.

Everything was shouting and chaos and smoke, but Clay heard Logan curse loudly, his voice harsh with pain. He spun around just in time to see Logan's left arm fly out from his body. He stumbled back a few steps before he fell on his ass.

Fear punched him in the gut. "Officer down! Officer down!"

Logan remembered his training. He kept his gun up and scooted out of the way and behind the couch for cover. Seeing that helped Clay keep calm. He closed in with the rest of the team on the suspect. The suspect had dropped his gun and was kneeling on the floor. Clay resisted the urge to kick him in the face. He let the rest of the team get him cuffed and the rest of the people out of the house while he ran over and crouched down next to Logan. He knocked his own helmet off before gently removing Logan's.

"Where are you hit?"

Logan's face was already pale and drawn with pain. "Just in the arm. I'm alright."

"You're not alright. You've just got adrenaline pumping through you." Logan's uniform sleeve was soaked. "You're losing a lot of blood." Clay pressed a hand over the wound to try to slow the bleeding. He looked up, wondering why no one was tending to Logan yet. "Get a fucking medic over here!" A heart beat after he finished shouting, the sound of rushing feet and jangling equipment signaled the arrival of the EMTs.

Logan touched his arm. "Clay, calm down. I'm alright."

Clay looked at him and saw he was telling the truth. There was pain tightening the corners of his hazel eyes, but they were still clear and sharp. He nodded and got out of the way to let the EMTs take over.

****

Carlos stood up from his desk. He looked around the pen where their team was all still gathered. "Sarge is in recovery. The bullet lodged in his arm but they got it out with no trouble. He's going to be out for a few hours. But when he wakes, I'm sure he's going to want to see some friendly faces. So make time, plan out a schedule, do whatever needs to be done. But everyone is to visit him." Carlos's dark eyes flicked to Clay. "Everyone. Does anyone need anything?" A low murmur of *no's* came from the group. "Alright, then. Get home to your families."

Everyone stood up, gathering their things, talking in quiet voices as they headed out. Clay got ready to go as well. Tiffany came up to him.

"Are you okay?"

Clay nodded. "Yeah, of course."

"Don't be bull headed. I know that had to be tough for you to see him hurt like that no matter what's going on between you two. Make sure you go see him, but take care of yourself too. Call me if you need anything, Clay. I mean it."

Clay nodded again. "I will. Thanks, Tiffany."

Tiffany pulled him in for a quick hug before she went off to join Carlos. Clay watched the two of them together for a moment. Then he grabbed his bag and headed out.

72

Clay had been circling the neighborhood for a good while. He didn't know what to do. He'd set out with the purpose of going to check on Logan at his home. But before he'd gone a third of the way, he changed his mind. He hit a u-turn and headed back to his apartment. Then he changed his mind again and made another u-turn. As he drove, he went back and forth on what he should do. He was leaning towards just going back home once and for all when he thought of the last delivery he received.

It was a cactus. It had come the morning after Logan was shot. He must have ordered it before that cluster fuck of a shift. He accepted it from the delivery man, devoid of the usual snarkiness with which he'd received Logan's other gifts. Tucked into a little plastic stem in the pot was a card. He'd pulled it out, immediately recognizing Logan's precise handwriting.

Cactuses are prickly fuckers and it's not easy getting close to them. But you can't help but want to reach out and touch one, especially when there's that one perfect bloom, taunting you with its beauty.

He looked again at the cactus, noting that there was one bright flower on top of the plant. Logan had been wrong in his actions. But maybe he'd been too harsh in his refusal to talk things over with him. He had to sit down for a minute and process. The flowers Logan sent him had all ended up in the trash. But he had a feeling that spiky plant would be with him for awhile.

Clay roused himself from his day dreaming when he realized he was approaching Logan's street. He made up his mind. If there were cars parked in front of Logan's house, indicating he had visitors, then he would go back home. If there was no one there, he would stay. He drove down the quiet, tree-lined street, going well under the speed limit as he drove up to the house. No cars in the driveway. No cars parked on the street near his house. That meant Logan was alone and Clay was staying. He pulled into the driveway.

Clay got out of the car, went up to the door, and rang the bell. He was there now. No sense pussy footing around. He waited with his bag slung over his shoulder. He stood there for so long that he started to think Logan might not be home. Maybe he was recuperating at someone else's house. He should have called first. He was reaching into his pocket for his phone when the door swung open. There Logan stood. He had on a sleeveless tee and sweat pants, his feet bare, a black sling holding his arm protectively against his body. He looked tired and in pain. And just like that, Clay was very glad that he'd come.

Logan couldn't have been more surprised when he looked through the window and saw Clay standing in front of his door. He thought for a moment that maybe he was asleep, the meds making him dream of Clay. But the constant throbbing pain in his arm let him know he was awake. "What are you doing here?"

"Making you let all the a/c out. You gonna let me in?"

Logan stepped back and allowed Clay in, still in disbelief. Clay shut the door and looked at him.

"I thought you could use some help for a few days."

Logan swallowed hard so he could speak past the emotion in his throat. "Yeah, I could. Being a one-armed man ain't easy."

Clay headed into the living room and Logan followed behind him. He'd forgotten about the mess he'd made until Clay remarked on it.

Logan shrugged his good arm. "I've been camped out here. It was easier than making trips up and down the stairs every time I needed something, especially with that morphine still in my system." He started to sit back on the couch but Clay grasped his good arm and stopped him.

"Go upstairs and go to bed, Logan. I'll clean up this mess and bring you something to eat when you wake up."

Logan didn't move towards the stairs. He just stared at Clay before he cupped the back of Clay's head, rubbing the soft fuzz there. "I can't believe you're here."

Clay met his gaze for a moment then lowered his eyes. "Go rest, Logan. I'll be here when you wake up."

Logan rested his forehead against Clay's. "Promise?"

Clay touched his chest briefly before his hand dropped away. "I promise."

****

When Logan woke up, he felt rested, his head almost clear of the fog left behind from the anesthesia and pain meds. He immediately remembered that Clay had come to his house. Again he thought it might have been a dream. But as he sat up, he saw his bedroom floor cleared of the stuff he'd left laying around. The light in the bathroom was on, lighting the way in the darkened room. He knew he hadn't turned it on before he went to bed. He strained his ears and heard the low sound of the stereo playing music he would never listen to on purpose. He hadn't dreamed it. Clay was there. He got up and went in to the bathroom to relieve himself and freshen up. When he came out, Clay was just walking into the room with a tray.

"I figured you'd be up about now."

"Yeah, I was just about to head downstairs."

"Pretty sure I told you to stay up here and I would bring you what you need. Although, I guess I need a way to know when you need something."

Logan settled himself back on the bed. "I could get a little silver bell and ring it when I need you."

Clay gave him a look. "Don't even think about it."

"Well, you could stay close to me. Then I could just tell you when I need you."

Clay didn't say anything to that. He just settled the tray on Logan's lap and backed away. Logan looked at the tray in surprise. There was a steaming hot bowl of what looked like fresh soup, oranges, and crackers. And a big glass of water. "Did you make soup?"

Clay snorted. "I *ordered* soup. I know you probably want something more substantial, but until those meds are completely out of your system, you won't have much of an appetite. So I figured sick people food was best."

Logan popped an orange slice in his mouth. "No, this is great," he said after he swallowed. "I keep thinking I'm starving but when I go to eat, I leave half of it on the plate."

"Yeah, I saw."

Logan smiled sheepishly. "Thank you for cleaning that up for me. Sit down and keep me company."

Clay looked around but the only chair was way on the other side of the room. So he sat at the foot of the bed. The two of them talked while Logan made his way through most of the food. He downed his glass of water and Clay stood up.

"I'll get you another."

"Thanks. Those pain pills are terrible. I've got a serious case of cotton mouth going."

Clay took the glass and put it back on the tray. He went back downstairs with his load, dropping it off in the sink before refilling the glass. But when he walked back into

Logan's room with the water, Logan was sound asleep. He set the glass down on the nightstand and pulled the covers up over him. He watched Logan sleep for a moment. When it was obvious he wasn't going to wake up, Clay went down the hall to the guest room he'd chosen for himself. Clay quickly prepared for bed and turned out the lights. He turned the TV on but kept the volume low. And he left the door open so he could hear Logan if he needed him in the middle of the night.

73

For a man who just had surgery, Logan had a pretty awesome day. When he'd woken up that morning, Clay was still there. He helped him shower and get dressed, joking about hiding his blushing eyes. They had breakfast together. Clay even drove him to his follow up appointment to have his wound checked. Then they just hung out at his house for the rest of the day. Clay didn't make any mention of needing to leave, he just played cards with him and watched TV. Logan was humbled. He was hopeful for their future. And he was more in love than ever. They hadn't discussed their recent fights, but that was okay. Right then, he was just enjoying his time with Clay. The discussion could wait.

Now the hour was late and he was sitting up in bed. He should've turned out the bedside lamp and gone to sleep, but Clay was still up somewhere in the house. And he didn't want to go to sleep until Clay did. Eventually, he heard Clay come up the stairs. He waited to see if he would come into his room or continue down the hall to the guest room. He did neither. There was no movement for a long time then Logan heard a lock click and a door swing open. Again there was silence. Logan knew Clay was looking into their playroom. He sat there quietly, wondering what Clay was thinking. Was he regretting their time in there? When the door closed again Logan called out to him.

"Clay. Can you come in here, please?"

Clay appeared in his doorway. "Did you need something?"

Logan shook his head. "Just some company."

"I've kept you company all day." But he came into the room anyway.

Logan scooted over and patted the empty spot next to him. "Come sit with me for awhile." Clay kicked his shoes off and settled on the bed. Logan gave him a grateful smile. "Thank you very much for coming to take care of me, Clay."

Clay shrugged and looked away. "You always took such good care of me. It was the least I could do."

Logan lightly grasped Clay's chin and turned his face back to his. "Is that the only reason you're here? To repay a favor?"

Clay lowered his eyes. "No. But it's the only one I want to discuss right now."

He leaned in and brushed his lips softly against Clay's. "I can accept that."

"Logan ... don't."

He gave him another soft kiss before he whispered against his lips, "Don't what?"

"Don't kiss me."

"Why not?"

"Because you know it'll lead to something more. And lately, every time it does, nothing good comes from it."

Logan stroked his thumb across Clay's cheek. "I don't agree with that. I think every time we're together, you open up to me just a little bit more." Logan kissed him again, a little longer this time. Clay's lips parted beneath his, but he didn't take advantage of it. He pulled back and looked at Clay, who swallowed hard.

"I'd better get back to my room." He started to get up.

Logan put his hand on Clay's leg to stop him. "Don't go. Stay a little longer. I promise not to touch you." Logan grinned as Clay looked down at his hand on his thigh. He moved it away. "Starting now."

Clay relaxed again. "Alright, I'll stay. What do you want to do?"

"I was hoping you could do me another favor."

Clay looked at him with curious eyes. "What?"

"Well, I have this fantasy of you pleasuring yourself right in front of me."

Clay laughed. "Logan... you're crazy."

He shrugged "Maybe. But it would make me feel better. And I promise to go to my physical therapy tomorrow if you do this for me."

Clay shook his head, the smile lingering on his mouth. "You're going to go anyway."

"Yeah, but this way I'll go with a smile on my face." He lowered his voice to a husky whisper and looked at Clay from beneath his lashes. "C'mon, Clay. Do this for me. I promise not to touch you."

Clay sat there silently for a few moments just gazing back at him. Then he reached down and grabbed the hem of his t-shirt, slowly pulling it over his head. He tucked his fingers into the waistband of his shorts and briefs and lifted his hips to pull them off. Then he lay down on his back on the bed.

Logan scooted down too, propping himself up on his good arm. He made sure to keep space between them. "You're so beautiful," he whispered.

Clay closed his eyes, his hand drifting down his belly to grasp his semi-erect cock. He bit his lip as he made contact and started to stroke.

"Clay, I want you to do something for me."

Clay's voice was a hushed whisper in the quiet room. "Okay."

"I want you to think of one of our times together while you touch yourself. Will you do that for me?" Clay nodded, his eyes still closed. "Good. What are you thinking of?"

"My first visit here, when we were in your garage ... on top of your Mustang."

Surprise and arousal jolted through Logan. Arousal because he remembered that time, remembered how Clay had let him do whatever he wanted to his body. And surprise because he thought for sure that was one of the things that caused Clay to run from him. He cleared his throat. "Tell me what you remember from that day."

"You took me into your garage to show me your cars."

"I cannot believe you have these! You should let me drive one."

Logan laughed. "I don't think so. I've seen the reports you filed after you banged up department issued cars..."

"Ha-ha." Clay laughed dryly.

He led Clay to the blue Thunderbird first, showing him all the restoration he'd done. After Clay was finished admiring it, he brought him to his favorite of the two, a 1970 Ford Mustang Boss. It was painted a glossy black with very little embellishment on either the interior or exterior.

Clay rubbed his hand over the hood. "I like this one. It doesn't need stripes or anything else to show how bad ass it is. And I'm pretty sure it's snarling at me," he said with a laugh.

Logan was immediately filled with desire, watching Clay's hand caress his favorite car as he described it in the exact same manner that Logan would. "I want you."

Clay laughed again. "You always want me." He nodded towards the house. "Let's go then."

Logan shook his head. "Uh-huh. I want you right now." He backed Clay up against the grill of the black Mustang. He leaned forward to put his hands on the hood of the car on either side of Clay, forcing him to lean back. "Right here."

"And then what happened?"

"You laid me on the hood of your Mustang and you took all my clothes off."

Logan scooted a little closer. "I did. Did I tell you anything, baby?"

Clay nodded, his hand still slipping up and down on his cock. "You told me I was beautiful."

"Mmmm… I can see why I said that. What else happened?"

Clay moaned, his hand moving a little faster. "You fucked me … first with your tongue then your cock."

Logan scooted even closer, close enough that he could feel Clay's body heat. "And did that feel good to you?"

"Yes … yes. I loved it."

Logan slowly pushed Clay down until he lay on the hood. He told him to scoot up until his head rested on the windshield, his legs hanging over the grill. Logan pulled Clay's shorts and briefs down and off and stroked his hand up a bare thigh. "You. Naked. On top of my favorite car. I think this is the most beautiful thing I've ever seen in my life." He stretched the leg he was caressing up in the air, gripping Clay's thigh tightly as he bent his head to suck at his smooth skin. He dropped slowly to his knees, sucking more kisses as he went down until he reached his ass. With no warning, no teasing, Logan thrust his tongue inside him. Clay cried out, his body jerking and almost slipping off the car. But Logan held him steady and tongue-fucked him, cupping and squeezing his balls until he was writhing and moaning with pleasure. Logan looked up at Clay. Sunlight streamed down from the sky light in the garage, falling onto Clay's body, making his skin glow golden against the black backdrop. His heart pounded. Sometimes he still couldn't believe Clay was finally his. He just knew he wanted to keep him with him always.

Logan stood up straight and undressed then pulled Clay down until he was in the position he wanted him in. Fitting his cock to his sub's entrance, he pushed inside. Logan thrust into Clay's snug heat slow but hard. His pace was steady and unchanging, drawing desperate little moans from Clay, his back arching up off the hood. He squeezed his thighs around Logan's hips, clearly wanting him to go faster. Logan laughed deep and low. "Look at you, stretched out on the hood of my car with my cock deep inside you. I bet I could open this garage door and let anybody who goes past see me fucking you and you wouldn't care, would you?" Clay shook his head wildly, staring up at him with passion filled eyes. "That's right. You wouldn't care. Because you know who owns you. And you'll do whatever I want you to do. Won't you, sweet sub?" Clay nodded, his fingers sliding on the hood as he tried to keep himself steady. Logan leaned down and sucked at Clay's neck. "You're such a good boy, Clay. My good boy."

Logan purposely let his stomach brush against Clay's cock as he thrust inside him with bruising strength. He brushed against him hard enough for Clay to feel it and like the friction. Soft enough that it didn't satisfy him. He watched as Clay rubbed his hands down his stomach coming closer and closer to touching his cock. But he knew the rules, so he didn't touch it. Purposely at least. But the force of his body slamming into Clay's sent his shaft sliding across his belly and his fingertips brushed his cockhead. He bit his lip, blue eyes flashing to Logan's to see if he noticed. Logan pretended that he didn't. He grabbed him by the backs of the thighs, pushing his legs up, folding that limber body in half beneath him. He continued to thrust, loving the way Clay's walls squeezed him. But he didn't want either of them to get too close to climax. Not yet. Logan pulled out and yanked Clay down, his sweaty skin sliding on the slick metal. Once Clay's feet hit the ground, he turned him over. "Put your hands on the hood."

Clay followed his order immediately, pushing his ass back towards him. Logan smacked his hand on one of those smooth cheeks. "Are you trying to rush me?"

"No. I ... I just want to feel you, Sir."

"Is that right? Which do you want to feel more?" He lightly stroked his hand down Clay's shaft. *"My hand on your cock?"* He let go and brushed the head of his cock against Clay's ass. *"Or my cock in your tight little ass?"*

Clay moaned. "I want … I want whatever you want, Sir."

Logan was close enough that he leaned over and whispered in Clay's ear. "What happened next, Clay, after I fucked you with my tongue and my cock?"

When Clay noticed how close he was, he jerked and made as if to scoot away. Logan stopped him. "It's okay, baby. I won't touch you, I promise. Just tell me what happened next."

Clay raised his knee, his foot planted on the bed as he fucked up into his fist. "You made me come."

Logan scooted Clay closer to the car, groaning as he pushed back inside his sub. "Good boy." He held those slim hips tight enough to leave bruises as he stroked into him. After a few moments, he worked his hand around to grip his lover's cock in his fist. He stroked fast and tight until Clay was gasping.

"I need to come, Sir!"

Logan smiled a secretive smile behind Clay. "Go ahead, baby. Come for me." Clay cried out and then he was coming, his body trembling as he released. Logan enjoyed those sweet pulsations on his cock as Clay came. When he eased to a stop, Logan slowed his thrusts until he was barely moving. "Clay?"

Clay was breathing hard as he answered. "Yes, Sir?"

"Did you just come on my car?"

Clay went still. "Shit, Logan. I'm sorry."

"*Don't worry about it,*" *he replied silkily. He waited a moment for Clay to relax.* "*Just clean it up.*" *Clay made as if to push himself up, but Logan stopped him.* "*With your tongue.*"

Clay didn't hesitate. He lowered his head to the hood of the car. Logan thrust in deep again, watching Clay as he turned his head and looked at him over his shoulder. Those pretty blue eyes stayed locked on his as Clay's tongue came out and very slowly licked through the spill of pearly cum. Logan growled deep in his chest at the sight. "*You are so fucking sexy.*" *A wicked glint lit up Clay's eyes as he did it again. Logan grabbed him by the back of his collar and yanked him up. Twisting Clay's head around, he kissed him roughly, sucking his tongue into his mouth, tasting his cum. He shoved him back down. Hooking his arm under Clay's knee, he stretched his leg up until it was tucked next to his body on the hood of the car. With his other hand, he gripped his sub's collar, pulling it just tight enough for him to feel it and know he was owned. He laid almost all of his weight on top of Clay, fucking into him roughly, the Mustang bouncing underneath them. He angled to hit his sub's spot, knowing he was successful as Clay trembled and gasped, his fingers clenching and clawing on the windshield. Logan's orgasm was coming, but he wanted to make sure his sub found his release too. He spoke into Clay's ear, his voice harsh with arousal.*

"*Come for me, little sub. I won't come until I feel this sweet ass gripping me tight with your orgasm. And I want to come. Want to come bad.*" *He licked Clay's ear.* "*Want to fill you up. So don't make me wait.*" *He thrust as hard as he could into that sensitive spot again and Clay shouted out,* "*Oh, fuck yes! I'm coming, Sir! I'm coming!*"

Logan groaned. "I can feel you." Clay's channel squeezed him tight, and Logan bit his lover's neck as his release burst from his cock. He pressed his shaft deep inside him, flooding Clay with his heat, making him moan …

Logan was hard, his entire body strung tight with tension as he listened to Clay's description of that day, his mind filling in anything he didn't mention. Watching his lover stroking himself, his hand wrapped tightly around his thick cock, his hips thrusting up, had him ready to lose it.

Clay gasped, "I'm coming!"

Logan didn't touch him. But if he were any closer, he'd be on top of him. "Come, baby. Let me see you."

"Kiss me!"

Logan's eyes shot to Clay's face and he saw that his eyes were open, looking straight at him. He didn't have to be asked twice. He leaned over Clay, sealing their lips together, thrusting his tongue into his mouth. But Clay tore his mouth from his and Logan was disappointed that he ended their kiss so soon.

"Logan … I need to feel you on top of me. *Please.*"

It was awkward with one arm, but he rolled on top of Clay immediately. Clay's hands went to the waistband of his sweatpants, frantically pushing them down. Logan lifted himself with one arm, aiding Clay so his pants ended up around the middle of his thighs. He kept his good hand planted on the bed, thrusting his hips so their cocks slid together. Clay's legs came up and wrapped tight around his waist. He kissed Clay again, shuddering as Clay squeezed his hand around both of their cocks, pumping them swiftly. He knew Clay was close and so was he. As he felt the silky wet heat of Clay's release against his shaft, he let himself go too.

****

Logan collapsed back to Clay's side. Clay looked at him, his chest still heaving.

"Every time… every time I feel like I'm supposed to be with you. That I'm supposed to belong to you."

Logan's heart pounded at Clay's remark. "Does that bother you?"

Clay took a deep breath. "I try to tell myself that it does. Or that I don't really feel that way, that it's only good sex." He laughed softly. "Well, fucking great sex. But even though I'm a hard-headed motherfucker, I have to admit that I'm bullshitting myself."

Logan smiled at Clay's blunt confession. "Well, I have to admit that I'm glad you feel that way."

Clay looked at him a long moment. "You lied to me, Logan. And you kept things from me."

Logan sobered. "I know. I was wrong no matter how I try to justify it. And I really am sorry. I promise you, nothing like that will ever happen again. But I want you to know, what I did had nothing to do with me being a Dom. It was just me making bad choices. I don't want you to think the two are related. If it's not just us behind closed doors, I won't ever interfere in or try to control anything again."

Clay shook his head. "This time I'm not just being stubborn, but just because you say that doesn't mean that you won't. Or at least, doesn't mean that I *believe* you won't. And I have to trust you if you really want me to be yours again."

Logan nodded. "I know. Until you trust me, I won't ask anything from you, except for the chance to spend time with you." He smiled. "I can't show you that I'm trustworthy if you won't let me near you."

"That's fair. But it won't happen overnight, Logan."

Logan brushed a finger along Clay's jaw. "What we have is too important to me to care about how long it takes."

Clay smiled slightly, lowering his eyes. He got up and Logan just managed to keep from asking him to stay with him. Clay went into his en suite bathroom. Logan listened as he heard the water running. He came back out with a towel and cleaned their mixed release off his stomach and his softened cock then helped him pull his pants back up. Then Clay returned the towel to the bathroom. He came back out and walked towards the doorway. When he turned off the switch, Logan tried to keep the disappointment out of his voice. "Goodnight, Clay."

But Clay's footsteps crossed back to the bed and Clay lay down in front of him. "Is this okay?"

Logan curled his body around his love's. Happy was barely adequate to describe the way he felt. "Yes. Why wouldn't it be?"

"I don't want to accidentally hurt your arm in the middle of the night."

Logan pressed a kiss to the nape of Clay's neck. "My arm will be fine."

It was quiet for a few moments before Clay spoke again.

"Logan?"

"Yeah?"

"I can hear you smiling."

His smile grew. "That's because I am."

Clay was quiet again and then Logan felt the lightest caress on the fingers of his injured arm.

"Me too."

74

"Are you sure you're up for this?"

Logan looked at Clay. "What do you mean?"

"It's been less than a week since you were shot, Logan. And you kind of look like you'd rather be at home."

Clay was right. His arm was hurting, but he had a job to do. Besides, he was only there to get caught up on paperwork. He tried to set Clay's mind at ease by teasing him. "Since when did you become such a mother hen? First taking care of me at home, now concerned I need to take a sick day."

Clay's eyes narrowed. "Fine. Next time you get shot and have a bullet dug out of your arm, I'll leave you there to deal with it on your own."

Logan laughed. He wouldn't trade Clay's visit to him for anything. He lightly touched Clay's arm and lowered his voice. "I like you as a nurse. But maybe next time you can wear a cute little nurse's outfit?"

Clay laughed too. "I don't think so."

Logan smiled. "Are you sure? I think you'd look good. I'd even pick it out for you." Logan playfully rubbed Clay's buzz.

"Although I'm not sure how you'd get the nurse's cap to stay on this bald head."

Laughing again, Clay ducked from under his hand. "Keep on dreaming, Sergeant Pierce."

The rest of the team started to trickle in, including Carlos, who was in charge while Logan was out. Logan sat off to the side while Carlos went over the operation for that night. When they were ready to go, everyone filed out.

Clay stopped at his side. "You missing it yet?"

"I was already missing it the second I was shot. Be careful. We can't have you getting hurt. I'd look too silly in that nurse's outfit."

Clay grinned. "I will."

Once the team was gone, Logan headed for his office. But he paused before he went in. There was something he needed to do.

****

"Can I come in?"

Alison looked up in guarded surprise. "Sergeant Pierce. Of course. How can I help you?"

He didn't blame her for looking wary. The last time he'd seen her, he hadn't exactly been Officer Friendly. "I wanted to apologize to you." Her pretty face went from wary to shocked so fast that he couldn't help but laugh. "Yes, you heard me right. I'm sorry that I was so hard on you when I warned you off Clay. I could have handled that a lot more diplomatically than I did."

"I can understand that." She blushed. "I was coming on sort of strong."

Logan grinned. "He sort of inspires that reaction."

She smiled back. "Yep. How's your arm?"

He looked down at it, moving it slightly. "It's healing nicely. Should be able to get back in the field soon." He was quiet for a moment, gathering his thoughts. "I know I don't have any right, but I have a favor to ask if it's not too late."

Alison gave him a knowing grin. "You want Clay included in the calendar?"

"Yes. Is it possible?"

"I'll have to make nice with the guy working on it, but I should be able to get him in."

"Thanks, Alison. Feel free to use my name and threats of bodily harm if you need to." He stood up to go. "Thanks for speaking with me."

"You're welcome."

Logan reached across her desk to shake her hand before turning to leave the room.

"Oh, and Sergeant Pierce?"

He turned back.

"You guys make a cute couple."

Logan grinned. "Thanks."

75

Logan looked at the clock, considering whether or not to call Clay over. They were in Laredo for a training demonstration. Laredo was a border town and close to the problems Mexico was having with the drug cartels. The city was determined to let its residents and the nation know they were safe. The team had been brought in to take a small, well-trained force and ramp them up to the next level in SWAT techniques. The day had been long. It was after ten o'clock, but they'd only been back at the hotel for about two hours. He knew Clay needed his sleep but he really wanted to see him. He'd just decided to let him rest for the night when his phone buzzed with a text.

WIRED! Wanna come over for a while? Room 1126.

Logan smiled to himself. Clearly, Clay was not at all ready for sleep. He got up and threw on fresh clothes before grabbing his wallet and room key to head out.

Clay sat in the hotel chair with the remote in his hand, flipping through channels. He wasn't really looking for anything to watch. Instead, he was thinking about Logan. Thinking about everything from the time they spent together over the past two weeks, to the phone calls, to the gifts Logan had sent him.

Last Monday was the last day Logan missed going into the field with them. So he thought it funny that when Clay got to his desk, he found a small SWAT toy figurine. Logan had even taken a metallic marker and written PIERCE across the figure's back. There'd been a note under the toy. *I'll be back out there with you soon. This guy will watch your back until then.* Clay laughed and put the toy in his pocket. He started to go into Logan's office to thank him but he'd changed his mind and sent him a text from the Bearcat. *I guess I can trust this little guy to keep a lookout since you're still carrying on about that scratch on your arm.* Logan texted him back, promising that he'd be back in the field with him by the weekend. Clay put his phone away, knowing Logan would keep that promise.

When he got back to his desk at the end of the night, there was another gift. He opened it to find a book with a plain black cover. Inside, there was a picture of a bound woman and the title, *Screw the Roses, Send me the Thorns*. The book was a detailed discussion on Dominance and submission. That night, he started reading it, continuing whenever he had a little downtime. It was enlightening, helping him to understand both his and Logan's roles in their relationship. And it was almost comforting to see the things he felt and experienced with Logan written about by others in such a personal, yet matter of fact way.

Reading that book, Logan's gifts, their long conversations both on the phone and when they were together, all combined to help him get back to that point where he felt like he could be with Logan again. Little by little, he was giving in to Logan, letting him take control. If Logan called him on the phone, he dropped what he was doing to talk to him. When Logan called him over to his house, he went. If Logan told him to take his clothes off, he did. He laid there as Logan caressed him everywhere but where he wanted it most, kissing him only on the mouth, before finally following his order to stroke himself off. And every time he tried to touch Logan as well, he denied him with, "Not till you're mine again."

By that point, he was ready to fall at Logan's feet and give him whatever he wanted just to be able to touch him. And he knew Logan had to be going just as crazy, if not more so. He never gave himself a release during their times together. Which meant it probably wasn't a good idea for him to invite Logan over to his room where they'd be alone. But he was bursting with energy and he wanted company. Well, he wanted Logan's company. When the knock at the door came he hurried to answer it. Logan was standing there just as he expected.

"Thanks for coming over. You sure you don't mind? I know it's late."

"No, it's fine."

Clay rubbed his hand over his shorn hair and stepped back. "You'd think I'd be dog tired after the work we put in today, but I am completely wired. It'll probably be awhile before I calm down enough to go to sleep."

Logan came all the way into the room and closed the door, watching as Clay practically bounced over to the table.

"Look, I got Candy Land!"

Logan chuckled. "Where did you get that?"

Clay sat on the bed and started setting up the game. "Some of the guys are having a game night. That's where Quan is. They ran out to the store up the road to get some games. My choices to take were Scrabble or Candy Land." Clay grinned at him. "I figured you'd have a better chance at winning if I got this one."

Logan ignored that last bit. "So Quan is out with the others. And you're here with me."

Clay looked up at him. "Yes. I wanted to play with you." An embarrassed flush crept up Clay's cheekbones. "I mean I wanted it to just be us."

Logan smiled and kicked his shoes off to sit on the bed. "Let's play."

****

Three games in and Logan was holding back a smile. Clay had lost twice already and the frustration was clear on his face. Logan was going to let him win this one, but he couldn't resist teasing him first. "Hmmm… looks like we should have played Scrabble."

Clay looked up from the board with his eyes narrowed. Then he smiled … and tipped the game over.

Logan just smirked. "Sore loser?"

Clay didn't say anything but his smile grew. He pulled his bare foot back and kicked the whole game off the bed.

Logan's eyes widened. "You brat!" Clay shrugged carelessly, and without thinking, Logan launched himself across the bed and tackled him. Clay landed on his back, all the air going out of him with a soft whoosh as Logan fell on top of him. He grabbed Clay's wrists and held them over his head, grinning down at him. "I guess being a brilliant smart ass doesn't help with this game."

But the teasing smile fell from his lips at Clay's expression. He stared up at him, his lips parted. His eyes were wide and soft with desire, and in them Logan saw the look he always had as he waited for his instructions. He'd denied them both the physical intimacy they wanted as he waited for Clay to trust him again. But right now, with Clay looking at him with such an obvious desire to submit, he knew it didn't make sense to deny them any longer. Logan squeezed Clay's wrists once and those pretty blue eyes drifted closed, a soft sigh escaping his lips.

"What do you want, Clay? Do you want me to get off you so we can play another game?" He pressed his hips down, rubbing their growing erections together. "Do you want me to leave?" Logan squeezed his wrists again and Clay's hips thrust softly against his in response. "Or do you want me to show you again how good it feels to submit to me?" He brushed a gentle kiss across his lips. "Tell me what you want."

His eyes still closed, Clay bit his bottom lip for a moment before he answered. "I want you ... want you to show me."

Logan groaned, Clay's words making him think of that first night when Clay had asked him to show him about BDSM. He kissed those soft lips, sliding his tongue slowly inside when they parted. Logan kissed him over and over, taking in each of Clay's breathy little moans. Finally, he released his mouth and started to loosen his grip on his wrists. Clay protested.

"Logan, please. Don't let go."

But Logan knew he couldn't just give Clay what he wanted. If he wanted to experience the pleasure he felt in being restrained, he was going to have to earn it. So he let him go.

Clay's eyes sprang open. "Logan…Why?"

"I think you've forgotten the way things work. I decide what happens between us, Clay. And I know what you need, when you need it. Do you understand?" Clay nodded, his breath coming a little faster. Logan rolled off him. "Get up and take your clothes off."

Clay stood up and reached for the hem of his t-shirt. He pulled it over his head and dropped it on the floor, his pants and briefs following. Logan looked at Clay, standing there naked, aroused, and waiting for his next instructions. He stood up himself and reached for Clay's erect shaft. Clay's eyes closed in clear anticipation of Logan stroking him. So just to keep him on his toes, Logan merely brushed his finger over his cockhead before he dropped his hand. "Undress me."

76

Clay opened his eyes and looked at Logan. He wanted this. Wanted to hear Logan's deep voice telling him what to do. He reached for Logan's shirt and started undressing him. Once the shirt was over Logan's head, they made eye contact again. Logan's eyes stayed locked on his as Clay opened his shorts and pushed them off. And Clay was unable to look away. He was caught by that sharp gaze. The look in them was intense, making his pulse race, his chest rising and falling with his rapid breaths. He could see how much Logan wanted him, but he knew that even at this point, Logan would let him walk away if he wanted. But he didn't want to. He might not be ready to accept Logan's collar, but he wanted nothing more than to be with him again. To serve him, to please him, to do whatever Logan wanted him to do. He needed it more than anything. To show it, he pushed Logan's boxers off and then waited there quietly, hands at his sides, for Logan's next command.

Logan sat back on the bed. "You know what I want."

Clay nodded, his eyes drifting down to look at Logan's big erection.

"Then get on your knees and do it."

Clay slowly dropped to his knees. Logan spread his legs and Clay moved between them. His hand closed around Logan's shaft, but he hesitated, kneeling there with his head bowed.

Logan spoke again, his voice hard. "Don't keep me waiting, Clay."

Arousal rushed through Clay at Logan's harsh voice. He leaned forward and sucked him into his mouth. And as he moved his mouth up and down on that thick shaft, that wonderful sense of pleasure washed over him. But it wasn't just physical pleasure. Yes, Logan tasted good and he loved the way his lips were stretched wide as he sucked, loved the way Logan felt in his mouth. But it was the knowledge that he was making Logan feel good that had his belly doing that crazy yet familiar tingling lift. It was Logan's groans of satisfaction that had shivers chasing up and down his spine. *He* was the one responsible for bringing Logan so much pleasure.

Clay continued to hold Logan's cock steady so he could suck faster and faster, his only thought to please him. He rubbed his free hand up and down the hard muscles of Logan's thigh, feeling them clench every time he tongued his slit or the sensitive underside of his cockhead. Logan's fingers brushed his. Clay maintained the contact and Logan laced their fingers together. Clay held on tight. He looked up at Logan and saw him watching with that fiercely possessive look that Clay hadn't seen in so long. That he hadn't even realized he'd missed until now. As he watched Logan watching him, he tried to convey what he was feeling in his eyes. Tried to let Logan know that he was happy to be kneeling at his feet, serving him like that. When Logan tightened his fingers on his even more, Clay understood that Logan knew everything he was feeling.

Clay lowered his eyes again, concentrating on bringing Logan to climax. But Logan put a finger under his chin and lifted his head. Clay immediately stopped sucking. Letting his shaft drop from his mouth, he licked his lips and knelt there, waiting to see what Logan wanted.

"On the bed. Lie down on your back."

Clay was on his feet before he even realized it. The want, the *need,* to follow Logan's every order was strong in him once more. As soon as he was settled on his back, Logan laid on top of him, his heavy frame pressing him into the mattress. Clay loved that feeling, loved knowing that he was under Logan's control. He could give in to Logan's strength, let him take over.

He spread his legs to make room for Logan, gasping as their naked cocks rubbed together. Logan's lips trailed up his neck to his earlobe and even though Clay knew he would bite him, when it came, his hips still jerked in reaction. Logan moved down his body, touching him everywhere. Hard sucking tugs at his nipples. Fingers softly trailing down his sides. Sharp nips of teeth on his stomach. Long licks of his tongue along the crease where his hip and thigh met. Finally, *finally* Logan grasped his cock and pumped him slowly. Clay moved his hips in rhythm with Logan's strokes, but he knew better than to try and rush Logan's pace. He felt Logan's hot breath on his balls just before he sucked one into his mouth. Clay gasped sharply, his hips thrusting up hard as Logan swirled his tongue around his sac, sucking him lightly. Clay brought his knees up, planting his feet on the bed. His hands drifted down to rest on Logan's shoulders. "Logan, that feels so good."

Clay trembled as Logan licked his way down to his entrance. At the first push of that hot tongue inside him, his legs fell open wide. He lay there, open for Logan as he fucked his tongue in and out of Clay. Logan's big hands squeezed and caressed his thighs, pushing them open even further. Clay writhed on the bed, moaning as he circled his hips up to Logan's touch again and again. Everything Logan was doing to him felt amazing, but his cock was aching for attention. He asked Logan to touch him there. His response was quick.

"No. I want my hands here." He squeezed his thigh. "And here," he said, pushing a finger deep inside him.

Clay cried out as that thick digit entered him. It felt good, but he was greedy. He wanted more. Wanted to feel Logan's cock fucking into him, stretching him and hitting against his spot. And he wanted to have his shaft stroked. Since Logan wouldn't do it, maybe he could do it himself. He stroked his hands down his belly, stopping just short of his cockhead. "Logan, can I touch myself?"

Logan looked up at him from between his legs, his eyes hot with lust as he pushed another finger inside him. Clay waited breathlessly for his answer, but it was slow in coming. Logan twisted his fingers, pumping them in and out before he spread them apart. Logan's warm breath washed over his skin as he whispered, "No." Then he speared his tongue inside him. Clay yanked his hands away from where they'd been so close to grasping his cock, slapping them onto the bed. His shaft throbbed, pre-cum leaking onto his belly as Logan's tongue slid into him deeper than before with his fingers holding him open. It felt good, so fucking good, but it made him want Logan inside him even more.

Logan looked up Clay's body. He was trembling, breathing swift and hard as he balled up the comforter in his clenched fists. He spoke, his voice shaky and desperate.

"Logan, I need you inside me."

Logan pulled his tongue from his lover's body. "You want me? Want me inside you?"

Clay nodded jerkily, his hips thrusting up.

"Then beg me."

Clay did, begging him to fuck him, telling him how much he wanted him, and saying please over and over. But it wasn't what he wanted to hear. So Logan kept going, thrusting his tongue inside his channel again and again, licking at his heavy sac, and giving him quick little bites on the insides of his thighs. Logan was pushing Clay hard, taking him right to the edge, but not giving him enough to send him over. He wouldn't. Not until he got what he wanted from his lover.

Clay was shaking, legs restlessly shifting on the bed as Logan teased and touched and caressed him. He begged, but still Logan tormented him, keeping him just shy of release and denying him what he wanted. He tried again. "Logan, please. I need you, please come inside me." Logan stopped what he was doing and slid up his body. His bright hazel eyes stared down, so focused on him that Clay felt like he was the only thing Logan saw, the only thing he cared about.

"Beg me, Clay."

And suddenly Clay knew what he wanted. One little word was all it would take. "Please … Sir." He didn't say anything else. He didn't have to. Because Logan started pushing inside him, slowly, every inch increasing the pleasure until his whole body was tingling.

Logan groaned as he sank into the welcoming heat of his lover's body. He knew it was the right time for them. He wasn't going to hold back. Clay was ready, more than ready to submit to him once more. Once Logan was all the way inside, he stilled for a moment and looked down at Clay. His eyes were closed; head tilted slightly back, his lip sucked into his mouth. Logan started to move, watching as Clay's face tightened with tension. He pushed in hard and deep, keeping their bodies pressed together so that his stomach rubbed against Clay's straining shaft with each of his thrusts. "Is this what you wanted, Clay?" Clay moaned a yes and Logan licked at the sweat on his neck. "Mmm … Can you take a little more, baby? Take it a little harder?"

Clay moaned again, his answer coming in between choppy breaths. "Yes … more. I want more."

Logan increased his speed, driving into Clay faster and faster. Clay grabbed onto Logan's forearms to hold himself steady as Logan fucked him hard, the bed rocking from his movements. He changed the angle of his thrusts, reaching for and hitting that sweet spot deep inside his lover. Clay's mouth fell open with a gasp, his blunt nails digging into his arms.

Clay kept his feet braced on the bed, his legs open for his lover. The feeling of Logan thrusting inside him, stretching him, and taking him how he wanted had his cock so hard he thought he was going to burst at any moment. Clay pushed his hips up, increasing the friction and pressure of Logan's hard abs rubbing against his shaft. But still he wanted more. He stroked his hands down Logan's sweaty back until he grasped his ass. He felt the muscles there clenching and flexing as he tried to pull Logan into him even harder. "More! I need more." Logan doubled the strength and the intensity of his thrusts until Clay felt completely dominated by the big man slamming his cock into him … hard, tight, fast.

Logan growled deep in his throat "I'll give you more. Give you all this tight little ass can take."

Clay cried out as he felt his orgasm rising, his stomach clenching, his balls drawing up tight and hard. He choked out a warning to Logan. "I'm about to come!"

Logan denied him, his voice harsh from his heavy breathing. "No, you're not. You'll wait until I give you permission."

Logan roughly grasped his arms, planting his hands on either side of his head and holding on tightly to his wrists. Clay moaned at how right it felt to have those big hands holding him down. Yet as the pleasure started to increase to almost unbearable levels, he fought it. He tried to get his arms free, but Logan only tightened his grip, squeezing his wrists hard enough to leave bruises. Clay shook his head back and forth. He couldn't hold his orgasm back any longer. He needed release. "I can't … I can't take it. Need to come!" Logan leaned down and crushed his lips with his, kissing Clay and cutting off anything else he was going to say. But Logan's tongue in his mouth only made it worse. He tore his face away. "Please! No more. Just let me come." Logan sank his teeth into Clay's bottom lip and dragged him back. He kissed him again and Clay screamed into his mouth. Finally, Logan released him but he didn't stop moving. He kept pounding into him again and again as he spoke.

"You want this, baby. Want me. Stop fighting it." Logan's voice changed to a silky whisper. "Remember what it felt like to submit to me, Clay? What it felt like to let me control you … let me own you." Suddenly Logan changed his movement too. His strokes were still as hard as ever, but now they were longer, slower, Logan pumping into him with a smooth roll of his hips. "Don't you want that again? That beautiful sweet peace of submitting to your Dom?"

Clay arched his head back into the pillows as he sobbed out a yes. Logan kissed him again, softly this time.

"Just let go, baby. Take me inside you and give yourself up to me. That's all you have to do. Just let go."

Clay looked up at Logan. He watched his firm lips telling him to let go, met the sharp eyes that were able to command him with just a look. And gradually it became easier. His orgasm was still there, pulsing in his cock, his body still trembling. But his head was calm. Clay let go like he said and stopped fighting what he was feeling. His body was Logan's to do with as he wanted and he would get his release when Logan … when his Dom gave it to him.

Logan leaned down, his tongue softly lapping at his neck before Clay heard his husky whisper in his ear. "Wrap your legs around me." Clay followed the order immediately, squeezing his thighs against Logan's waist. A protesting "no" escaped him as Logan let go of one of his wrists, but it changed quickly to a moan as Logan grasped his shaft. He pushed his hips up, the feeling of his cock sliding so wetly in Logan's rough fist taking him closer and closer to the edge. But he didn't fight it this time and he didn't ask for permission to come. He still trembled. Still gasped. But he let Logan do what he wanted. Then finally came the command he was waiting for.

"Come for me, Clay."

Logan squeezed his fist tight around his cock, pumping him swiftly, and Clay came hard. He threw his head back with a shout, tightening his legs even further around Logan, thrusting up so their hips slammed together. As Clay's cum poured onto his stomach in a hot rush, Logan increased his speed again. He repeatedly brushed across that sensitive place inside him, pushing his climax to another level. Clay couldn't help it. He turned his head and bit Logan's arm, needing another outlet for the intense pleasure coursing through him. Clay rode out the waves of ecstasy as Logan continued to ride him. Eventually, his body calmed and his muscles relaxed as all the tension drained out of him. Clay looked up at Logan. His

Dom's jaw was clenched tight and his eyes were heavy lidded with passion.

"Thank me like a good boy."

Clay was still feeling the aftershocks of his orgasm, but he managed to whisper, "Thank you. Thank you, Sir."

Logan smiled at him, a lazy triumphant smile before he leaned down and kissed him. This time, Clay didn't try to break their kiss. He wrapped his arms around Logan as he thrust hard several more times, the heat of his release flooding into him and filling him up.

77

Clay rested against Logan, just enjoying the feeling of being held by his lover. Logan kissed him softly, stroking his rough hands down his sweaty back to calm him. As he laid there, he was relaxed and peaceful. He let Logan take care of him, the feeling that he belonged to Logan reinforced with every caress. But soon the heat of Logan's big body, his light touches, and gentle kisses did more than calm him. He was becoming aroused, his shaft hardening. He pressed against Logan, grinding his cock against his hip. Clay rubbed Logan's chest, smoothing his hands over the hard muscles. His lover looked at him with a knowing glint in his eyes. Clay shifted, pressing his cock against Logan's flat stomach. "Logan, I'm sorry. But I need…"

Logan rolled Clay onto his back and leaned over him. "Don't apologize. I need you just as much." Logan kissed his sub, stroking his tongue in slow and deep as he reached down Clay's body. He slid a finger inside him, softly pumping it in and out. "I can feel my cum inside you," he whispered. "Wet. Marking you as mine." Clay moaned and rubbed his leg against him. His ass clenched on the finger he had inside him and he groaned. "Does that excite you, Clay?" Clay nodded at him slowly, his eyes dark with passion, his face still flushed. Logan slid back on top of his lover. "Maybe I should fill you up again. Would you like that?" Again Clay nodded, but as always, Logan wanted to hear him say it. "I asked you a question, Clay."

"Yes, Sir. I want to feel you come inside me."

Logan reached down and grasped his shaft, lining himself up to Clay's entrance. Then he pushed all the way inside him with one thrust, making him gasp. Logan set a steady pace, withdrawing slowly before plunging back in. "What does it mean to you, Clay, to have my cum inside you? Tell me."

Clay licked his lips but he didn't hesitate to answer. "I feel like you're a part of me. Like I belong to you and I want to keep you inside me." Clay's breath was coming faster, his words coming in between moans. "Want to walk around like that in front of everyone, but only you know that you've claimed me that way." Clay paused for a moment with his eyes closed before he looked back at him. "That you're the only one who has ever claimed me that way."

A hot streak of love and possessiveness rushed through Logan. "I'll give you that and more. Show you in every way I can that you're mine. Because you do belong to me." Logan kept thrusting inside that tight heat, his earlier release giving his cock a smooth glide. "I want to spend every day with you. I want you underneath me every night. Want my collar back around your neck." Clay nodded and wrapped his arms around his shoulders. Logan let him pull him down until they were pressed chest to chest. Their lips met in a soft kiss, Clay's lips parting beneath his. Logan stroked his tongue inside, sucking at Clay's, gently mastering his mouth. Logan broke their kiss and trailed his lips up that long, elegant neck. He whispered all the things he wanted to do to Clay in his ear. He told him how much he loved him, how much he loved his submission. He pushed Clay's leg up, hooking it over his shoulder. "I love how open you are for me." He fisted Clay's cock, stroking it as he pushed into him harder. "I love everything about you, Clay. Even your crazy temper." That startled a laugh from his lover before he told him back, "I love you, too." Logan's heart thumped to hear that from his lover while he was inside him. He stroked Clay faster, thrusting into him just as quickly until he was arching off the bed and moaning. And at the first rhythmic squeezing of Clay's ass on his cock, Logan commanded him to come, following with his own orgasm immediately after.

****

For the second time that night, Clay lay wrapped in Logan's arms. When he was calm again, he asked a question, his voice tinged with guilt. "Did I just use you?"

Logan brushed a soft kiss over Clay's shorn hair. He missed his silky curls but he didn't bring it up. He understood why Clay had cut them off. "Why would you say that?"

"Because I needed this from you tonight and you gave it to me. And I feel like maybe you shouldn't have since we're not completely a couple again."

Logan lightly grasped Clay's chin, forcing him to meet his eyes. "Clay, it's been a long time since you got what you needed from me. But that's why I'm here. It's my responsibility and my pleasure to take care of you, however you need." Logan brushed a thumb across his cheek. "And you have to realize I needed that too. It hasn't been easy for me to be around you, wanting to dominate you, knowing that you wanted it just as much but weren't ready to admit it to yourself."

Clay changed the subject slightly. "I still don't want this part of us to be public. I'm just not comfortable with that."

"That's okay, Clay. No one needs to know. Just like we discussed before, we'll both work to make sure we keep that part of our relationship private." Logan gave him a searching look. "I just hope you aren't ashamed of how you feel."

Clay's eyes slid away from his. "I don't know. I kinda think I am."

But Logan wouldn't let him hide. His hand still gentle on his jaw, Logan turned Clay's face back to his. "I wish you wouldn't think like that. To accept that you want to be at someone else's feet and to acknowledge their dominance over you is not an easy thing to do. It takes a lot of strength to just let go and accept that part of yourself while trusting that they will take care of you the way you need them to. And I promise there's nothing weird or wrong with the way our love for each other and the pleasure we take from one another is all tied up in my need to control you and your need to submit to me. It's not wrong. Just different than most people."

"I know. I'm starting to understand a little better. I've been reading the book you gave me."

Logan's brow creased in confusion. "What bo—"

"What the fuck?!"

Logan looked over his shoulder and saw Quan standing there, his eyes wide with shock. They'd been so into their conversation, he hadn't heard the door open. They were on top of the covers so Logan rolled on top of Clay to cover him. He looked back over his shoulder again. "Quan, can you wait outside for a minute?"

Quan didn't say a word, he just backed out of the room with his eyes directed to the ceiling.

Logan looked back down at Clay. "I'm sorry about that."

Clay shrugged. He was blushing but his eyes sparkled with humor. "I'm sure Quan is more embarrassed than either of us."

Logan laughed softly and kissed him. "You're probably right. Clay, let me stay with you tonight. I don't want you alone after all of this." Clay looked like he wanted to say yes, but he started to shake his head. Logan took control of the situation because there was no way he was allowing Clay to be alone in his head after the way he'd let go and submitted to him tonight. "No. I *am* staying with you. The only choice you have is whether it's in this room or mine."

Clay looked at him for a moment before he lowered his eyes and whispered, "Okay. Here. But let me tell Quan."

Logan shook his head and got up from the bed. He pulled on his pants. "I'll talk to Quan. And when I get back, I expect to find you in this bed and under the covers." He waited for Clay's quiet "Yes, Sir." before he stepped outside to talk to Quan.

"Hey, man. I apologize for what you saw when you walked in. I know that's probably not how you want to picture your best friend."

Quan had a pained expression on his face. "Getting an eyeful of your naked ass was definitely not on my bucket list, Sarge."

Logan cleared his throat and reached in his back pocket for his wallet. "Look, Clay has agreed to stay with me tonight. So why don't you take my room? You can order whatever you want and put it on my charge."

"Clay agreed to stay with you, or did you order him to?"

Logan was surprised to hear the note of hostility in Quan's voice. "It's not like that, Quan."

"Then why don't you tell me how it is? Sarge, I respect you as my team leader, but I don't want my friend mixed up with somebody who's going to be ordering him around."

Logan was taken aback until he remembered Clay's remark that he should have listened to Quan's warnings. "Quan, maybe you and I should talk. I'd like to set your mind at ease about my relationship with Clay."

Quan studied him for a moment before he answered. "Fine. We can talk. But for tonight, I want my own room, not yours."

Logan handed over his credit card. He'd pay for the room gladly if that's what it took to get Quan on his side. Clay was all that mattered. He watched Quan walk off down the hall. He was glad that his doubts about their relationship were out in the open. Now he could talk to him about it. That would probably help Clay be more at ease with their relationship too.

Logan went back into Clay's room. Clay was there in bed, waiting for him under the covers, just like he'd instructed.

78

Logan and Clay hadn't talked any further. Clay had finally crashed and Logan let him sleep. And of course there wasn't any privacy on the ride home. But when the HPD bus dropped them off at their cars that evening, Logan pulled Clay aside.

"Clay, I think we both know that you want to be with me again."

Clay looked back at Logan, slightly confused. "Yeah. I do."

"Then there's no reason you shouldn't be wearing these." Logan pulled the dog tags he had made for him out of his pocket.

Clay started to reach for them but he hesitated. "Logan, I want to be yours again. But I just ... I need ... I don't know. More time or something to make sure that you won't go behind my back again."

Logan had never regretted the decisions he'd made with Alison and Clay's promotion more than he did at that moment. Watching Clay so conflicted hurt him so much. It was his fault that Clay felt this way. He was supposed to take care of his sub, not cause him pain. Logan started to tell Clay to take his time but then he thought maybe he was going about this wrong. Maybe he shouldn't let Clay work through this on his own, but should guide him like a submissive needed their Dominant to guide them. There were still people in the parking lot so he didn't pull Clay to him like he wanted to. But he stepped closer.

"Clay, look at me." Logan waited until those blue eyes, stormy with confusion, met his. "Baby, I'm sorry that you're hurting over this. But it's time to let it go. No more waiting to see if you trust me. The way you see that I'm trustworthy is to *be* with me, Clay. So no more waiting. Either you want my collar or you don't."

Clay's mouth turned down in a frown. "Are you giving me an ultimatum?"

Logan shook his head. "I'm not. But you clearly want to be mine again. The way you submitted to me last night proves it. You're just stuck in your head, waiting for a signal that everything is perfect before you give in. Well, you can't wait for that. Our relationship will be great, but it won't be perfect. I'm going to piss you off sometimes and sometimes you're going to piss me off. But we stay together through it all. That's how relationships work." Logan reached out for Clay's hand and pressed the dog tags, along with his house key, into his palm. "Take tonight and tomorrow to think over what I've said. And if you want to be with me, if you want to wear my collar again, you'll be at my house tomorrow night after our shift."

Clay's fingers closed over the tangle of metal in his hand. "What if I'm not ready for that?"

"You are if you let yourself be. You're fighting against what you want, Clay. But like I told you in bed last night, stop fighting and just let go."

****

Clay paced around the locker room. His shift was nearly over which meant it was almost time to tell Logan his decision. Logan said he wasn't giving Clay an ultimatum, but that's exactly what it felt like. He wanted him to make up his mind and decide whether or not he wanted his collar tonight. But he needed more time! He needed to be sure. He didn't want to say yes and then back out later if he wasn't ready. He loved wearing Logan's collar, he knew that. But it was a bigger relationship commitment than any he'd ever made before. He dived in head first with Logan before and he couldn't help but think he needed to take more time before doing it again. A familiar voice calling his name interrupted his thoughts. He stopped and turned around to see Carlos standing there.

"Hey, Carlos. What's up?"

Carlos slid his hands in his pockets as he came forward. "What's up with you, Clay? You look like something is seriously bothering you right now."

Clay blew out a harsh breath and rubbed his hand over his shaved head. "Logan wants me to make a decision tonight. One I don't know if I'm ready to make."

"Talk to me."

Clay looked at Carlos. They were friends and he was always glad to have the big man at his back. But they weren't particularly close. Still, he might be the right person to talk to as he was well aware of what it was like to be in a BDSM relationship.

"Logan wants me to make up my mind tonight. To decide whether or not I want to be with him as his submissive." Carlos nodded so he continued on. "But you know what he did before. What if he pulls some shit like that again? If I put that collar on, it's on. I don't want to remove it because he pisses me off. But, at the same time, I don't want to wear it if I don't trust that we won't have those problems again."

Carlos looked at him for a long moment with his discerning gaze before he spoke. "Clay, Logan hurt you once. But that doesn't mean he'll do it again. He broke your trust. And I understand it's hard to come back from that, especially as a submissive. But he made a mistake. He's admitted to it and saw how it hurt you. Do you really think he would do that to you again? Logan isn't one to purposely hurt anyone, especially those on his team and definitely not you. He's wanted you for a long time and probably loved you even earlier than he realizes."

Clay thought about what Carlos had said. Logan was a good man. And he did believe that Logan wouldn't hurt him if he could avoid it. He opened his mouth to respond but before he could say anything, Carlos asked him a question that surprised the shit out of him.

"Did you get the book I left you?"

"*You* left that book?"

Carlos laughed. "Don't sound so shocked."

"When I realized it wasn't Logan, I just assumed it was Tiffany."

"Hey, I can be helpful and insightful too. I saw how conflicted you both were and I wanted my friends to be happy. I figured a little information might help."

Clay grinned. "Awww. Thanks, Los." His voice was teasing, but he really was touched by Carlos's words.

"You're welcome. Now before we start braiding each other's hair…"

Clay rolled his eyes. Carlos had even less hair than he did.

"What did you think of the book?"

Clay told the honest truth. "I think it fucking made sense. It's crazy. With everything else in my life, I have to be in control, but when it comes to Logan… I just want to let him take over. And it feels right to let him do it."

"Clay, it sounds to me like you want to accept Logan's collar. You're just afraid of the what ifs. But I've never known you to avoid something because you were afraid. So why are you doing so now?"

****

Logan sat at his desk. He sighed and scrubbed his palms over his face. He hoped he made the right decision in telling Clay that he needed to make a decision tonight. He didn't want to rush him or make him feel like it was now or never. He was gambling that the feeling he had about Clay needing to be guided was right. Logan sighed. All he could do was wait and see.

In the meantime, he needed to get through his talk with Q. He checked his phone and realized Quan would probably be back in the locker room by now, getting ready to go if he wasn't gone already.

The musty air of the locker room hit him in the face as he walked in. He was right. Quan was there putting his things into his bag. Logan headed over to him. "Hey, Quan, is now a good time to talk?" Quan looked up at him. Before Logan could say anything else, Q started talking.

"I thought about things last night and on the way home. What goes on between you and Clay behind closed doors is none of my business. But Clay has looked out for me since I joined this team so I can't help but do the same for him. That's why I spoke up when I saw him changing after getting with you. I didn't understand it and I was worried."

Logan finally spoke up. "We both made mistakes at the beginning of our relationship. I lost my head for awhile there and overstepped my bounds."

Quan laughed. "I can understand that. When I first started dating my wife, I went a little crazy myself. Finally, she told me to either get out of her space or get lost for good. I learned real quick to back up." He shook his head with a smile on his face, obviously thinking of his wife. "I guess what I'm saying is, I can understand you losing your head as you say, as long as you rein that shit in. Interfering in his career wasn't cool. But I know Clay wants to be with you. I see him watching you. His eyes follow you wherever you go. And when you walk into a room, he gets this look on his face and he's totally focused on you, like nothing else going on around him matters." Quan laughed and shook his head. "It's complete tunnel vision."

Logan's pulse quickened. Hearing someone else acknowledge Clay's feelings for him somehow made it more real. Made him realize that if others could see it so obviously, then Clay wasn't as ashamed of their type of relationship as he thought. Logan gave his attention back to Quan as he finished talking.

"I want my friend to be happy and as long as you keep him that way, then I don't care about anything else that goes on between you two. But if you hurt him or step out of line again, just remember … I know how to make it look like an accident."

Logan grinned and stuck out his hand for Quan to shake. "I promise I'll take care of him. And I won't step out of line again." They shook as though they were sealing a deal. Quan picked up his bag to leave and Logan watched him go. He was surprised as hell at how that conversation had gone. He expected to have to explain how their Dom/sub relationship worked and assure Quan that he didn't want to control Clay outside the bedroom before Quan would accept them as a couple. Logan rolled his shoulders, feeling the tension he'd been carrying slowly draining away. It was a good night for clearing up old business. He couldn't help but hope that he would walk into his house and find Clay naked and kneeling on his bedroom floor, his head bowed in perfect submission. Logan couldn't stop the huge smile that broke across his face at the thought.

79

Logan drove down his street filled with anticipation, praying that Clay would be there. But when he pulled in his driveway, his heart sank. His was the only car in the driveway. And the house was dark. He went inside, just in case Clay was in there in the dark. But he wasn't. He flipped on the light and stood there in shock. His chest was so tight that he could barely draw a breath. Clay wasn't there. He'd been so sure that Clay just needed a little push to get him to fully come back to him, but clearly that had backfired because *Clay wasn't there.*

Logan dropped his bags and slowly walked over to the couch. He started to sink down in defeat, but before his butt hit the cushion, he sprang back up. He wasn't letting Clay go that easily. He would have to tell him why he'd chosen not to come to him before Logan would accept that Clay didn't want his collar.

He strode across the living room, determined to find Clay and find out what was going on in his head. But when he threw open the door to leave, Clay was standing there, his hand raised and clasping the house key as though he'd been about to slide it into the lock.

"I'm sorry I'm late."

Relief washed over him in a wave so strong it nearly crushed him. Nearly drove him to the ground so that he would be the one kneeling at Clay's feet. He reached out and grasped the back of Clay's neck, yanking him into a wild and frantic kiss. He backed up into the house, pulling Clay with him and closing the door. He finally broke their kiss so that they could breathe, but he buried his face in Clay's neck and wrapped his arms around him tight. "Don't ever scare me like that again, goddamnit."

Clay pressed his body close against Logan's, feeling a shudder run through his big frame. "I'm sorry, I didn't mean to. I went for a run to think things over and lost track of time. I was rushing when I got back to shower and left my phone in my desk like a dumb ass. I couldn't call you to tell you I was running late so I just did my best to get here as quick as I could." Logan's chest expanded against his as he took a deep breath. His hold finally loosened.

"And you're here because…"

Clay expected that. He knew Logan would want a straight forward answer from him. He stepped from between Logan and the door, circling around until he was behind him. Logan followed, pivoting on his heel so they were facing each other again. Clay took a deep breath and then slowly sank to his knees. His talk with Carlos had cleared his head and opened his eyes. He wanted to be with Logan and the only reason he was holding back was because of fear. But he'd never lived his life in fear before and he wasn't about to start now. Not with something as important as his relationship with this man on the line.

"I'm here because I need you, Logan. Need you to be my Dom again. Need you to control me. All I want is to submit to you. I'll probably never fully understand why I feel like that but, honestly, I don't fucking care anymore. All I know is that I've felt like I really haven't been able to breathe since we've been apart. But when I'm with you and you're in control or when I'm under you and I hear your voice, everything is easy. Everything with you makes sense and I can breathe freely. Anything happening outside of us is bullshit and it doesn't matter." Clay paused and took another deep breath. "I don't care about anything else. We'll figure it out like you said. I just want to be yours again."

Logan looked down at his sub kneeling before him. Clay's face was at ease, peaceful, that beautiful look of submission clear in his eyes. He had to swallow hard so he could speak past the lump in his throat. "Clay … I … Shit. I think I need a minute." Clay touched his thigh lightly.

"Please, Sir. Don't say anything." His other hand rose to his throat. "Just … my collar."

Logan smiled softly at his sub before he held out his hand. "Come upstairs with me." They went up to his bedroom. Logan left him standing by the bed as he dug through the dresser drawer until his fingers touched the smooth metal of Clay's collar. Walking back over to Clay, he ordered him to take his clothes off. Clay followed the order without any hesitation and when he stood naked before him, Logan clasped the collar back around his neck. The first time he collared Clay he'd been bursting with so many emotions. But this time, all he could think about was how lucky he was, and how much he loved the man standing still before him. Clay closed his eyes as Logan traced his finger over the letters engraved in steel. "Clay, look at me." Clay obeyed and Logan looked into those blue eyes that he loved. He lightly clasped his hand around Clay's throat, rubbing his thumb over his pulse. "You're mine," he whispered.

Clay nodded slowly. "I'm yours." But then his lips curled up in a slight smile. "I'm yours. But you're mine too."

Logan's lips twitched in a smile as he nodded in agreement. He kissed his lover, walking him backwards to the bed. When they bumped up against the mattress, Logan gently pushed Clay down until he lay on the bed. He stripped himself of his clothes and shoes and lay down on top of his sub. He was still amazed by what Clay had said, his heart beating hard with the knowledge that Clay was finally, totally his. He pressed his lips to Clay's lightly. "I love you."

"I love you too."

Logan smiled and kissed him again before he moved down his body, trailing the lightest, softest kisses all along his smooth skin. When he reached his lover's shaft, he lapped at the precum spilling from his slit. "You taste so good to me, Clay." He pressed his face against Clay's soft belly and inhaled deeply. "And you smell even better."

Clay groaned and pushed his hips up. "Sir, please…"

Logan knew exactly what Clay was asking. His lover didn't want to wait tonight and neither did he. He wanted to be inside his lover … his *submissive*, now. But although he was throbbing to push inside of Clay's tight channel, he took care to prepare him first. He licked his way down to his entrance and pushed his tongue in. He looked up Clay's body, watching as his hips rose and fell and his eyes shut tight with pleasure as Logan fucked his tongue in and out of him. He was still watching as he pulled his tongue away and slid one finger then two inside his lover, stretching him wide before pressing in deep to tap against that sensitive bundle of nerves. He saw when Clay's eyes sprang open, his lips parting on a sweet gasp.

"I'm ready, Sir!"

Logan smiled. "Are you rushing me, little sub?"

Clay shook his head back and forth on the pillow. "No, Sir. Not rushing. But maybe begging. *Please*. I need you."

Logan kept his fingers deep inside his lover and licked a long, slow path up Clay's cock. He sucked him slowly, watching as Clay writhed on the bed, whispering, "Please," over and over. Logan smiled again as he let his sub's shaft drop from his mouth. He rolled off Clay and got up to get the lube from the nightstand. But Clay's hand on his arm stopped him.

"Let me do it. Let me get you ready, Sir."

Logan agreed, thinking Clay was going to get the lube himself. But once he sat back down, Clay leaned over him and sucked his cock into his mouth. Logan inhaled sharply at the sudden pleasure Clay's mouth brought him. It wasn't what he'd expected, but he wasn't going to stop it. He leaned back on his forearms, giving his sub room to get as close as he wanted. Clay sucked him slowly, his tongue stroking up and down his shaft, getting him wet. Logan brought his hand to the back of Clay's head, pushing down as he thrust his hips up. His cockhead bumped the back of Clay's throat, but his lover didn't gag or stop. No, he just moaned and sucked faster, trying to take even more of his cock. Logan groaned at how good it felt, at his sub's eagerness, at how fucking sexy Clay looked curled over his lap with his lips stretched wide around his cock and his collar around his neck. He kept thrusting up and Clay took all of him, his moans sending tingles up and down his shaft. But soon, the pleasure was too much. He had to stop him because more than anything, he wanted to be inside his sub when he found his release.

Logan pulled Clay off him. He scooted up until his back was against the headboard and pulled Clay with him so he was straddling his lap. "You got me wet. Now show me that you want to make your Dom feel even better. Ride me."

Clay licked his swollen and reddened lips and nodded. He raised his hips and reached back to grasp his cock. Logan groaned at the feel of Clay's hand on him, but when those sweet walls started to slide down his shaft, he had to press back against the headboard to keep himself from thrusting up hard into his lover. He let Clay ease himself down at his own pace, wanting him to be comfortable as they came together as Dom and sub for the first time in a long while.

When he was seated all the way inside, Logan smoothed his hands down Clay's warm back until he cupped his ass. Squeezing lightly, he pushed him up. "Ride me, baby." Clay nodded and started moving, his breath already coming faster, soft moans coming from his lips. Logan relaxed against the headboard. He watched his sub working to bring both of them pleasure, still helping him to move with his hands on his ass. As that pleasure increased, he planted his feet on the bed and raised his knees so he could thrust up, driving his shaft deep into his lover each time Clay sank down. Clay looked at him with his face flushed, his lips parted as though he wanted to say something. "Talk to me, baby." His voice came out in a whisper husky with desire. After only a second's hesitation, Clay obeyed and spoke up.

"I love you, Master."

Logan froze. Just went absolutely fucking still, unable to believe what he'd heard. "What did you say?"

Clay stopped moving too. "I said I love you, Master."

Logan shook his head. "Baby, you don't have to call me that. I don't want you to—"

Clay leaned forward and kissed him, cutting off his protest. "I want to. I meant it when I said I wanted to submit to you. No holding back this time. When I'm with you and we're alone, you are my Master. I may not always call you that, but that's the way I feel."

Logan tucked his fingers beneath Clay's collar, pulling him forward again until their lips met in a whisper of a kiss. He rested his forehead against Clay's, so overcome with emotion he could hardly stand it. "Clay, I love you too. Love you more than anything that has ever passed through my life." He gave Clay another soft kiss. His sub's lips parted and Logan stroked inside, softly curling his tongue around his lover's. But soon, his sub was squirming against him and the kiss turned heated and passionate. Logan pulled back and stroked his hands up and down Clay's smooth thighs. "Keep going, Clay. Make us both come." Clay started moving again, rising quickly up and down on his cock. Clay gasped as he came down hard while Logan thrust up.

"Oh god, that feels …"

Logan smiled and pushed his hips up again. "Feels what, baby? Tell me."

Clay moaned with pleasure before he spoke. "Feels so good. You're so deep inside me."

Logan continued the movement of his hips, pulling Clay down so he kept striking that sensitive spot inside him. "You feel good too, baby. You're so tight. So hot around my cock. You fit me like you were made for me." Clay cried out and his hips jerked forward. He started to lose his rhythm as he moved, his orgasm obviously approaching. Clay tightened his legs around his hips and buried his face in his neck.

"Master, I need…"

Logan didn't even let his sub finish his sentence before he slipped his hand between their bodies to grasp his throbbing shaft. He pumped him slow but hard, squeezing his fist around that hard, slick flesh. As his own orgasm pulled his belly in tight and rose up his shaft, he turned his lips to Clay's ear, softly telling him to let go. To come for him. Clay gave a choked cry before he lifted his head and kissed him again. The second their lips met, Logan thrust up and released deep inside his lover, Clay's release spilling down into his hand at the same time. They were both shaking as they came together, moaning into each other's mouths as the pleasure swept over them both.

Finally their bodies eased, but Clay still moved on him slightly. And Logan stayed inside him, enjoying the soft squeezing of Clay's inner muscles on his still throbbing cock. He wrapped his arms around his sub tightly, holding him so close that he felt Clay's heart beating against his chest. Their lips had stayed together through their climax and they were still that way now. They kissed again and again with all the love and passion they felt, only breaking for whispered exchanges of I love you.

80

The next morning, sunlight streamed into Logan's bedroom. Clay lay against Logan's chest. He was breathing hard, his body still tingling with delicious aftershocks of pleasure. "Logan…" He licked his lips, took a deep breath and tried again. "Logan, that was …" He trailed off, both because he still couldn't catch his breath and because he couldn't think of a word to describe how good it had just been between them. Logan laughed, a low, sexy rumble that had him pressing to get even closer to his Dom.

"What can I say? I missed you." He swept a hand down his back to cup his ass. "Missed dominating this beautiful body."

"Maybe I should leave more often if that's what will be waiting on me when I get back."

Logan's arms came around him in a sudden, tight hug. "You may not run away from me again."

Clay heard both the command and worry in Logan's voice and responded immediately. "I was only joking." Logan pulled him up so he was sprawled over his big body and looking down into his eyes.

"Clay, we are going to argue, going to fight. With our natures, there's no way to avoid that. And truthfully, I don't want you to roll over for me on anything. But you cannot cut out on me when you're angry. I won't allow it. You're mine and you will stay with me. We'll fight it out together."

A shiver chased down Clay's spine at Logan's possessive tone and words. Who would have ever thought he would want to be with someone who topped him so completely? Maybe that's why he'd bounced from relationship to relationship. He hadn't been satisfied before like he was now. But he did need to make something clear to Logan. "I won't run away from you again, Logan. I promise. But sometimes, I'm going to need some space. I just need to get out and run or swim to clear my head."

"That's fine. As long as you come back to me."

Clay smiled before he leaned down and kissed those full lips. "I'll always come back to you, Logan. I don't want to be anywhere else." Logan's eyes filled with both love and heat at his declaration so Clay wasn't surprised when that big hand palmed the back of his head and pulled him down into deep, slow kiss.

****

"And this here is Senior Corporal Clay Foster. He thinks he's hot shit because he's a scout."

Clay looked up. Brady stood in front of his desk with a young, pretty blonde woman standing next to him. He stood up. "Who is this, Brady?"

"This is Andy. My little sister."

Andy swung her hair over her shoulder and held her hand out. "It's Andrea, actually. And I can see why Brady called you hot stuff."

Clay's eyebrows shot up. He wouldn't have expected someone related to Brady to be so direct.

Brady coughed. "I said hot shit, Andy. Not hot stuff."

Andrea smiled at Clay flirtatiously. "You say potato…"

Clay didn't know what to say to that. He caught movement from the corner of his eye. Logan was approaching.

"Hey, Sarge. This is my sister, Andy."

Clay noticed she didn't flirt with Logan as she shook his hand and said hello. After the two moved on, Clay turned to Logan.

"Look at you, no more outrageous outbursts. I'm so proud."

Logan laughed. "No need. You know who you belong to."

Clay smiled at him from beneath his lashes. "I do. I'm yours."

Logan growled low. "You're damn right you are."

To Clay's amazement, Logan reached out and pulled him into a fierce kiss. His eyes widened, but then he relaxed and kissed Logan back. They were definitely out of the closet now. And he was glad. Glad that he didn't have to hide who he was anymore and glad he could proudly claim such a good man as his own.

Logan heard more than one person exclaim, "Holy shit!" But he didn't care. They weren't going to hide anymore. He kept kissing his sub, practically bending him backwards and staking his claim in front of everyone there. When he released Clay, he looked at him in a daze.

"Jesus, Logan…"

Logan just smiled.

Clay shook his head. They both noticed the dead silence in the room, and Clay turned to look at the crowd openly staring at them. He glared at everybody there. "That's right, motherfuckers! Sarge and I are a couple. A big, *gay,* man-lovin' couple! Any of you got a problem with that?" Logan looked around and saw a bunch of slack jaws, but no one said anything to Clay's challenge. Tiffany was leaning against Carlos, both of them shaking with quiet laughter. Clay continued his righteous tirade. "And you can spread the word that if anybody is thinking about coming between us, they might as well fold up those plans and move on to the next territory. Logan and I are bonded in a way most of you can never comprehend." He started to reach under his shirt for his tags. "He's my do—" Logan slapped a hand over Clay's mouth, shutting him up before he could go any further.

"You all will have to excuse, Senior Corporal Foster. You know how he likes to run off at the mouth." He paused to look at his co-workers. "But we *are* together and I hope all of you are alright with that." The group was still quiet. Finally, Hector spoke up.

"Well, Sarge. We sort of already knew."

A chorus of *yeahs* and *no shits* went around the room. Clay bit his palm and he let him go. "How?"

Hector laughed. "Give us some credit. For the last couple of months, your moods have been a direct reflection of each other's. When one of you is happy or pissed, so is the other. Not to mention all the sexified eye contact you two had going on. We're not dumb, we knew something was up. Well, maybe except for Brady. He thought you two were working on a secret project every time we saw Clay sneaking into your office."

Brady protested loudly. "Hey! I thought that one time!"

Everybody laughed, including Logan and Clay.

"So, yeah, we know and we're all cool with it. And if there's anybody here who does have a problem with it, we've got your back."

****

Logan knocked before entering Captain Hayden's office. The first thing he noticed was Clay sitting before his desk. He looked angry. Logan's hackles immediately went up.

"What's going on here? I'm Senior Corporal Foster's immediate superior and I should have been informed of any meetings that concern him."

"Have a seat, Sergeant Pierce. This actually concerns you both. I just wanted to get a little information from Senior Corporal Foster first."

Logan sat looking at Clay to make sure he was alright.

Hayden rested his elbows on his desk and steepled his fingers together. "It has reached my attention that the two of you are involved. In a relationship of a … sexual nature."

Logan didn't bother to deny it. "Yes, we are." He left it at that.

"I see."

"Don't waste our time, Captain. We aren't breaking any regulations by being together. So why are we in your office?"

"Haven't you? You promoted someone on your team in exchange for sexual favors."

Clay made a choked sound of rage and started to rise out of his chair. Logan put his hand out to stop him and Clay sat back down. "That's a very ugly accusation to make and one you have no evidence to back up. I followed all protocols in my recommendations for promotion. I selected the top three candidates from my team based on test scores, seniority, work performance, training, and attendance. I sent them upstairs and *they* made the decision on who to promote. I didn't in any way influence them and I never told Clay his promotion was based on anything he did for me."

"That may all be true, but it still looks bad."

"It doesn't look bad to anyone but you and maybe a few other narrow-minded people."

"Fine, but I'm considering having Senior Corporal Foster reassigned to another team."

"Why?"

"With your … personal involvement, I'm concerned that your judgment will be compromised out in the field. Especially if one of you is hurt."

"That's bullshit and you know it. First of all, we've already made it through that hurdle. Or did you forget that I was shot recently? Senior Corporal Foster did exactly what he was supposed to do in that situation. And we already have one couple on our team. They've never had any problems and I don't see you trying to reassign them. Is it because they're a hetero couple, Captain Hayden? Because if you try to move Clay without any reason, believe me when I say I will let the brass know it's because you're discriminating against a gay couple. How do you think *that* will look, Captain?"

Hayden leaned back in his chair. "Fine. But just know I'll have my eye on you both and your team, Sergeant Pierce. If there are any problems due to this relationship, they will be dealt with."

He looked at them but Logan only glared right back.

"You're dismissed."

Out in the hall, Logan touched Clay on the arm. "Are you okay?"

Clay looked at him, anger still in his expression before it slowly bled away. "I'm fine. I knew that prick would try to cause trouble. But you handled it well."

"And you let me."

Clay smiled. "Maybe sometimes I can let you be in control at work too. Especially when it comes to dealing with that asshole. If I would have spoken up, we'd probably both be fired."

Logan laughed as they walked down the hall. "One day you're going to have to tell me what the deal is with you two."

Clay's smile widened. "That's easy. He hit on me once and I turned him down. I don't date married men."

Logan stopped and looked at Clay in shock. "Are you telling me…"

"Yep. He's so far in the closet, it's a wonder he doesn't smell like mothballs."

81

"Your birthday is Friday. What do you want?"

They were securing their weapons after some time in the gun range. Clay took off his eye wear. "Ugh. Are you gonna be one of those lazy boyfriends that can't choose a gift on their own?"

"No. In fact, I already have your gift. But that doesn't mean I can't also get you something that you especially want."

"Well, in that case..." Clay pursed his lips and pretended to think. "What do I want ... let's see..." He tapped his finger on his chin then sat straightened as though suddenly inspired. "I know! I want to spend the next few days at your house. Just you and me alone until we're back on rotation."

Logan smiled. "Is this a birthday gift for you or for me?"

"Mostly for me. *Maybe* a little bit for you. But that's only one thing I want. I'll tell you the other later."

Logan shook his head and grinned. "I can definitely make that happen. We'll just swing by your place after work to get your stuff."

Clay grinned wickedly. "My bag is already packed and in the car."

****

Their first day of their mini-vacation they were relaxing in Logan's bed. They hadn't gotten up to eat yet but Logan decided he didn't want to wait to give Clay his gift. He reached into his nightstand and pulled out Clay's present. Clay's face was equal parts curious and excited as Logan handed him the small box wrapped in red paper. "I know your birthday isn't until Friday, but I want you to have the chance to enjoy your gift while we're here."

Clay took the box and ripped the paper off with all the enthusiasm of a hyper eight-year-old. But when he opened the box, he looked confused. "A key? Is this like the key to your heart? Because that's pretty damn corny."

Logan laughed and pulled the key out of the box, showing him the paper beneath it. It was a title. "It's the key to my, well, I guess I should say *your* Mustang Boss."

Clay's eyes widened almost comically. "You're giving me your car? But you love that fucking car!"

Logan leaned over and kissed him lightly. "I love you more. And every time I walk past it, I think of you. The way you gave yourself to me on that car was amazing. But when we were apart, I really believed that times like that were what caused you to leave me. Until you came to take care of me and I asked you to think of something that aroused you. You could have thought of anything, but that was the first thing that popped into your head. That eased my mind. Made me realize that you do love what we have together. So, to me, that car represents so much of us. And I want you to have it so you know how much I love you."

Clay looked at him for a long moment before he leaned over and rested his forehead against his. "Logan, I love you more than a rookie cop loves his nightstick."

Logan hugged Clay to him tight and laughed. "Not the most romantic of sentiments and that sounded sort of dirty, but I love you too."

Clay rolled his eyes. "Funny. Fine. I never thought I would love anyone, not like this. But I love you and I'm so glad my prissy refusal to run in the rain led to us making out in your car."

Clay pressed his lips to Logan's in a slow kiss, whispering thank you before he pulled away. He looked down at the key in his hand, a huge grin breaking across his face.

"This is the raddest gift ever." He clenched the key in his fist and threw the covers back. "Let's go get breakfast. I'm driving."

****

Logan smiled to himself as he gently rubbed Clay down with a big, fluffy bath towel. His sub was so happy and satisfied, he reminded Logan of a lazy cat purring in the sun on a windowsill. All he needed were canary feathers sticking out of his mouth to make the image complete. For three days, they'd done nothing but laze around, watch TV, and eat cookies and cream ice cream. And they made love, of course. He'd taken Clay with the tender touch of a lover, the commanding strength of a Dom and everything in between. This time, he'd been careful not to indulge himself too much in the wonderful gripping heat of his sub, determined to keep his promise to himself to never again hurt Clay like he had when he first visited. But there were plenty of other ways to make them both feel good as he'd just demonstrated in the shower.

Finished toweling Clay off, he threw the towel on the hook and put his collar back around his throat. Once the lock clicked closed, Clay gave a deep sigh. Logan nuzzled Clay's neck, kissing the soft skin just above his collar. "You have no idea what it does to me, knowing how much you love wearing my collar."

Clay turned and faced him. "Probably exactly what it does to me every time I see you look at me wearing it with that possessive look on your face."

Logan brushed his fingers across the metal, warm from the steamy heat in the room. "Probably." He pulled Clay into the bedroom to dress. They'd each just thrown on fresh tees and shorts when Logan's phone rang. "It's Hayden." He tossed the phone on the bed, prepared to ignore the call.

"Go ahead and take it. Just don't let him talk you into coming in."

"As if he could," Logan said with a snort. He sat down on the bed to take the call. He went to pull Clay into his lap but Clay shook his head and resisted. He had a slightly nervous expression on his face before he took a deep breath and left the room. Logan frowned as he watched Clay leave. *What was that about?* He rushed through his conversation with the captain. He wasn't calling with anything pressing.

Logan disconnected the call and went to find his lover. He didn't have to go far. He stepped out into the hall and there Clay was. He was kneeling on the floor. Naked. In front of the playroom door.

"I want to try again, Logan."

82

Logan's breath slammed out of his chest. He definitely hadn't been expecting that. He hadn't even planned to bring up the playroom for a long time. He'd wanted to wait to make sure that Clay was fully comfortable as his submissive before they went there again. "We don't have to do this now, baby. I don't want you to feel rushed into anything."

"I know you're worried that I'll freak out again. But I promise you I won't." Clay held up the key to the room. "Please, Sir. It's the other thing I wanted for my birthday."

Logan knew Clay was manipulating him. But he didn't mind. If Clay cared enough about it to bring it up like that, then it must be important to him. He stalked forward already in Dom mode. He put his hand on Clay's head pushing it back and forcing eye contact. "If we do this, you will tell me immediately if anything is wrong. And if I say we stop, we stop. Do you understand?"

Clay licked his lips and nodded, an eager light shining in his eyes. "Yes, Sir."

"Good. Now get up and open the door."

Clay fit the key into the lock with shaking fingers and pushed the door open. Logan followed him into the room, so close behind him the soft cotton of his t-shirt and shorts brushed Clay's naked skin. Logan flicked on the lights and Clay got his third look at their playroom. The first time he'd been in awe of what Logan had built for them. The second time, when he peeped in on his own, he'd wondered if he'd ever come into that room again. This time, it felt like he was entering his space. His and Logan's. He came to a stop in the center of the room and Logan circled around in front of him.

"Hmm… what should I do to you tonight?"

Clay stood there quietly. Patiently. He knew however Logan chose to play would only bring them both pleasure.

Logan stroked his thumb over Clay's nipple rings. He gave him a slow, lazy smile. "I know one thing I want to do." Logan went to the cabinet that held his toys.

Clay wasn't surprised to see the flash of silver that was the chain to his nipple rings. But that wasn't all Logan pulled out. He selected a cock ring. Lube. A thick dildo. Clay's breath came a little faster, his shaft hardening. Logan walked over to the wall that held his whips and paddles. He chose a whip with a long, thin tail. Logan came back to him and told him to put his arms out, palms up. He obeyed and Logan began laying his toys in his hands one by one. He started to get a closer look at them but a sharp command from Logan stopped him.

"Eyes on me! You will keep your eyes on me at all times. Is that clear, sub?"

Arousal streaked through him, his cock coming fully erect in a rush. "Yes, Sir." He kept his eyes on Logan's. He didn't look down when the whip was draped across his arms. And he didn't look down when Logan attached the Y-shaped chain to his nipple rings, giving them a firm tug. Logan smiled at him, his eyes smoldering as he pulled Clay across the room by his chain. He followed, of course, still holding the items Logan gave him, going just slow enough that there was sweet, painful tension in the chain.

When they reached a table that came up to about the top of Logan's thighs, they stopped. Logan took all the toys out of his hands and ordered Clay to lie down. Once he was settled on his back, his head on the leather pad on one end of the table, Logan went around to his feet. He grabbed his calves, pulling him down until his ass was at the end of the table then pushed Clay's legs up until his knees were bent. Leather shackles closed around ankles. Clay took a deep breath, waiting. He expected Logan to shackle his wrists as well and he did. He laid there with his arms and legs bound to the table, gooseflesh rising on his skin as Logan's palms skimmed along his body.

"I love seeing you like this, Clay. Naked. Restrained." He stroked a single finger up his shaft. "Aroused. Just for me."

Clay swallowed hard and nodded with his eyes wide and still locked on Logan's. He watched as Logan bent and licked down his thigh with slow, teasing laps of his tongue. When he reached his groin, he swiped his tongue once across his cock and Clay's hips jerked up. Logan's hand firmly gripped his thigh.

"Stay still. Don't move unless I say you can."

Clay nodded again, forcing himself to stay still as Logan went to work on him. His Dom sucked his shaft into his mouth, so softly and slowly it was almost as if he couldn't feel it. But he did. The silky glide of Logan's lips along his shaft stole the breath from his body as he gasped with pleasure. Too soon though, Logan released him. Before the whine of protest could cross his lips, Logan's tongue, hot and wet, dipped inside him. His fingers twitched but he didn't move in any other way as Logan fucked his tongue in and out of Clay. But he was breathing hard, his chest pumping, as moan after moan slipped up his throat. Logan groaned, the sound vibrating against his skin.

"You're so hot, baby."

Restrained as he was, Clay couldn't do anything but lay there as Logan took his tongue from him and replaced it with a finger, then two, pumping and scissoring them inside him. Logan brought the dildo to Clay's mouth, and without being asked, he opened up and sucked it, laving his tongue along it to get it wet. When Logan was satisfied, he pulled the toy from between his lips, trailing it down Clay's body, and pushing it inside him slowly. The toy wasn't as big as Logan, but Clay still felt stretched and full.

Logan straightened. He left the toy inside him, picked up his chain, and took the whip off his belly. "You loved the flogger. Let's see how this makes you feel."

Logan flicked the whip and the tail landed with a sting on his thigh. Clay gasped at that initial pain, but the hot sensation it left behind felt fucking amazing. His eyes were locked on Logan's as he flicked the whip again and again. He strained to keep his body still, though he was desperate to rise up and meet each of those sharp strikes. Every time he heard it swish through the air, his cock pulsed with anticipation. Every where it landed on his body burned white-hot. Logan kept the chain taut so his nipples were constantly stimulated. Every so often, he would yank on it, sparking pleasure-pain in that sensitive flesh. And he kept flicking the whip against him. Still, he watched Logan. Saw his Dom's jaw clench tight with tension. Saw his eyes darken with passion. Saw his nostrils flare as though he were trying to take in the scent of arousal in the room.

Suddenly, Logan stopped. He laid the whip back across Clay's stomach and dropped the chain. He undressed slowly and deliberately, making Clay feel as though he were watching a show just for him as Logan pulled his shirt over his head and pushed his shorts and boxers down his strong thighs. Logan stroked a hand across his belly.

"Such pretty marks."

He bent and sucked a stinging patch of reddened skin into his mouth. Clay didn't mean to move but he couldn't help it. Logan's mouth sucking so hard on that sensitive spot hurt in such a delicious way that he gasped and thrust his hips up.

Logan jerked his head up and looked at him. "I thought I told you not to move?"

Clay closed his eyes. "I'm sorry. I couldn't help it."

Logan's voice was hard. "Just like you can't help taking your eyes off me without my permission?"

Clay's eyes snapped open. *Fuck.*

His Dom's fingers brushed against his ass. There was a buzzing sound. Apparently, the toy inside him was also a vibrator. Clay groaned but this time he didn't move. A thick drop of pre-cum slipped from his cockhead but he didn't need to worry about coming without permission. Logan slid a cock ring down his shaft. And it vibrated too.

"Oh god. Please, Sir."

Logan picked up the whip again and walked around the table until he was standing behind his head.

"Please what?"

But Clay didn't answer. He didn't know what he was begging for. And even if he did, he wouldn't have been able to get the words out. His mind was completely filled with the pleasure the two vibrating toys sent coursing through him and keeping his body still in the midst of all of it.

"That's what I thought. You just lay there like a good little sub." Logan's hand brushed his jaw. "Open up, baby. You have permission to move."

Clay parted his lips and Logan's hot shaft slid between them. He started to suck immediately, moving his head back and forth to take all of Logan into his mouth. He was grateful that Logan had given him permission to move because that whip sang through the air again and struck his thigh. He jerked in reflex. He moaned, trying to let Logan know he wanted more by pushing his hips up. And Logan understood. The whip landed on him everywhere; his chest, his thighs, his cock. It burned his skin where it touched until his entire body was one mass of shaking, aroused heat. He screamed in sweet pain around Logan's shaft as the whip landed on the tender flesh of his sac. His head jerked back so that even more of Logan's cock slipped down his throat. Logan groaned and flicked him there again. Clay trembled in ecstasy. He writhed and jerked on the table as the sting of the whip and the vibration of his Master's toys sent every cell in his body into pleasure overload. His hands twitched in his shackles, wanting to touch Logan or fuck, touch himself, touch *anything* to anchor himself. To keep from shattering into a billion pieces. But he couldn't. He just had to lay there as the sensations grew more and more powerful until he thought he would explode. Yet, somehow, he managed to keep pleasuring his Dom, sucking him hard, dragging his tongue along the thick vein running along his shaft.

But with a deep groan, Logan pulled himself out of his mouth, the whip falling still at his side. He was breathing just as hard as Clay was, his chest visibly rising and falling. There was a metallic clink as Logan picked up the neglected chain that lay on his chest and went back to the foot of the table. The vibrator in his ass stopped just before Logan pulled it out of him and dropped it on the floor. Logan picked up the bottle of lube, pouring it onto his shaft and pumping until he was slick all the way to the base of his cock.

"I have to be inside you, baby. Right now." He pushed his cock deep inside Clay with one stroke.

Clay cried out, biting his lip as he fought to keep his eyes from drifting shut.

Logan wrapped the chain around his fist, tugging slightly as he watched his sub. Sweat dampened his skin. His lips were parted as he dragged in fast heaving breaths, his eyes sparkling with passion

Logan started moving inside his sub, pushing in slow and deep. He held the tension tight on the chain so that every time Clay moved, he would feel a sharp tug in his nipples. Logan kept stroking into his sub as he leaned down and brushed their lips together. "Breathe slowly, baby. Slowly." Clay shook his head quickly.

"I ca- I can't."

Logan jerked the chain once to get Clay's attention before he let it drop on the table. "You can." He lightly wrapped his hand around Clay's throat, stroking his thumb across his rapid pulse. "Eyes on me, baby." Clay's eyes met his, the blue almost entirely taken over by the black of his pupils. "Breathe with me, Clay." He pressed his lips gently to Clay's, resting his thumb with the smallest bit of pressure against his pulse. "Breathe with me. In … out…" Clay focused on him and took a deep breath, releasing it when Logan told him to. "That's good, baby. Stay with me. Breathe in …" Logan lay on top of Clay so that he could feel his chest expand against his. "Out …" His hips met Clay's again and again as he thrust inside him, the sweet gripping heat of his walls almost making him lose his concentration. But he stayed slow and steady, telling Clay how good he felt, how much he loved him, and over and over telling him when to breathe so that eventually they were breathing almost as one.

Clay's head calmed as he breathed with his Dom. The pleasure was still intense. But now, instead of feeling like it was going to shake him apart, it washed over him. Washed through him until all he was aware of was Logan's voice telling him when to breathe. In … Out … He was only aware of Logan's lips against his. Logan's skin against his own. Logan pushing deep inside him. He felt Logan reach down and take his cock ring off. His orgasm rushed up his shaft, but he didn't have to fight to hold it back. Because he was floating in such peaceful bliss that he didn't want it to end. Didn't want that orgasm to come and take away the connection he felt to his Dom. He just breathed, everything else fading. He didn't feel the hard table against his back or the shackles on his limbs. He just felt Logan. He sighed softly, his gaze locked on Logan's hazel eyes. In … out… He knew he was flying and he embraced it. It felt good. So good. And the heat of Logan's big body let him know he was safe. Logan's voice was soft and low. Clay didn't know if it was because he was whispering or if he was hearing it through the thick fog of pleasure in his head. But he heard him. Breathe … In … Out…

Logan pushed deeper and harder inside him. His big hand wrapped around Clay's cock, stroking and pumping him closer and closer to orgasm. Clay forced out a whisper. "No … don't make me come. Please, Master. Let me stay…"

Logan shushed him. "It's okay, baby. Trust me. Just let go. I promise you'll go even higher." He squeezed his hand around him. "Come for me, Clay."

Clay obeyed his Dom's command, pushing his hips up, letting go, releasing into Logan's hand. He tilted his head back against the leather pad. His orgasm coursed through his body, tightening his muscles as he strained against his shackles. Clay gasped, hovering there in a moment of pleasure so strong it took his breath away. And when he felt his Dom coming inside him, he spiraled higher into another orgasm, calling out his Master's name, accepting his kiss when his lips pressed to his. Finally, he collapsed back against the table, every muscle in his body completely sated.

Clay jerked against his cuffs. He barely knew what he was doing but he knew he wanted to touch Logan. To feel his Master. Logan released him from the restraints and he wrapped his limbs around Logan's big body, holding on tight.

Logan let Clay hold him so he knew he was there and he was safe. With a slight grunt from Clay's weight, he picked him up and carried him over to the bed in the room. He wasn't sure if Clay was aware enough to walk. Besides, he wanted to feel his slender body pressed up against his. He got them in the big bed and under the covers, Clay still wrapped around him, his face tucked into his neck. Logan rubbed Clay's back gently, easing him down. He felt more than heard Clay's whisper against his skin.

"Take care of me, Logan."

Logan pressed his lips to Clay's in a soft kiss. "Always."

THE END

Other Books by Christa Tomlinson

Martini Seduction

ChristaTomlinson.blogspot.com
Twitter: @christa_writes
FaceBook & Goodreads: Christa Tomlinson
tumblr: mschris314

6235028R10342

Printed in Great Britain
by Amazon.co.uk, Ltd.,
Marston Gate.